LINDSAY McKENNA

& JOAN JOHNSTON

CHASE THE CLOUDS
&
HAWK'S WAY: COLT

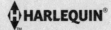

ISBN-13: 978-1-335-03997-2

Chase the Clouds & Hawk's Way: Colt

Copyright © 2019 by Harlequin Books S.A.

The publisher acknowledges the copyright holders of the individual works as follows:

Chase the Clouds
Copyright © 1983 by Lindsay McKenna

Hawk's Way: Colt
Originally published as Hawk's Way: The Substitute Groom
Copyright © 1998 by Joan Mertens Johnston, Inc.

Recycling programs for this product may not exist in your area.

HARLEQUIN®

Printed in U.S.A.

™www.Harlequin.com

CONTENTS

Lindsay McKenna is proud to have served her country in the US Navy as an aerographer's mate third class—also known as a weather forecaster. She was a pioneer in the military romance subgenre and loves to combine heart-pounding action with soulful and poignant romance. True to her military roots, she is the originator of the long-running and reader-favorite Morgan's Mercenaries series. She does extensive hands-on research, including flying in aircraft such as a P3-B Orion sub-hunter and a B-52 bomber. She was the first romance writer to sign her books in the Pentagon bookstore. Visit her online at lindsaymckenna.com.

Books by Lindsay McKenna

Shadow Warriors

Running Fire
Taking Fire
Never Surrender
Breaking Point
Degree of Risk

Jackson Hole, Wyoming

Out Rider
Night Hawk
Wolf Haven
High Country Rebel
The Loner

Visit the Author Profile page
at Harlequin.com for more titles.

CHASE THE CLOUDS

Lindsay McKenna

To Nancy Csonka and Joan Schwartz,
fellow horsewomen who share my love of a good horse,
the outdoors and our friendship.

Chapter 1

"Mrs. Daguerre, I can assure you I'm not used to having people fall short of their obligations to me. Especially ones where a legal contract is signed and services are promised."

Danielle stiffened in her chair and stared across the small office that was located within the main stabling barn. She was tall for a horse trainer, almost five foot nine, but she felt diminutive against the man who stood in the doorway blocking the afternoon April sun that slanted across his broad shoulders. Easing out of the black leather desk chair, she folded her arms against her small breasts, feeling positively threatened by his detached coolness. His eyes, the shade of pewter gray, assessed her with mild interest.

"Mr. Reese," she began, taking a firm tone that she would normally use with misbehaving horses, "my ex-husband signed that document over a year ago to ride your three-day-event thoroughbred, I didn't."

He gave her a thin, cutting smile, one corner of his generous mouth pulling upward. Removing the Stetson from his rich, dark hair, he let the hat dangle in his right hand. "Right now I don't care who signed it. I'm sorry that your marriage was broken up, but an agreement is an agreement."

"Your stallion, Altair, has a nasty name on the show circuit," she reminded him stubbornly. As much as she hated to use her ex-husband's name, she went on, "Jean's notes tell me that he's shy of water jumps, headstrong and impulsive and won't listen to his rider."

His cool, twisted smile remained as he studied her across the distance. "Yes, I'm afraid he's a bit like me in some respects—hard to handle."

Dany's nostrils flared with a show of contempt. Pointing at the fact sheets compiled on the jumper, she said, "You can't take a range horse and make him a Grand Prix jumper, Mr. Reese. It just can't be done. Your stallion has been mishandled too long, and I don't have the time or inclination to try and retrain him for you, contract or no contract."

His gray eyes glittered with an unnamed emotion. "Altair was out of the finest thoroughbred stock money can buy, Mrs. Daguerre. The fact that his dam was stolen and then abandoned in the middle of the Nevada desert with Altair at her side has no bearing on his abilities. It's true he was raised in the wild with a herd of mustangs. He was caught as a four-year-old by wranglers who busted him for use as a cow horse." He shrugged his broad shoulders. "I saw him by accident when I was looking over a herd of Charolais, and bought him immediately."

Dany tried to quell her frustration. "It's a very touching story, Mr. Reese, but—"

"You haven't heard all of it," he ground out softly.

Something in the tone of his voice warned her to remain motionless. "All right," she capitulated, "tell me the rest of it. But it won't change my mind."

"The more facts you have, the better you'll be able to weigh your decision," he parried.

"I'm waiting...."

"The wrangler who owned him tried to beat the spirit out of Altair. Consequently, he's pretty scarred up from it, both physically and emotionally. I knew he was thoroughbred by his conformation. When the owner showed me the mare, her tattoo number was stamped on the inside of her upper lip. All I had to do was call the registry and confirm Altair's breeding. He can't be registered, but in Grand Prix, papers don't mean a thing. Ability does."

"I suppose it doesn't mean a thing that he's a range horse?"

Sam Reese gave her an odd smile. "You can come from the wrong side of the tracks and still make it. I'm sure you're familiar with Nautilus, the palomino gelding they found at some riding stable?"

Dany nodded. "Yes, a rags-to-riches story of a Heinz-variety gelding who made it big in the Olympics as a jumper. That's a one-in-a-million shot."

"Altair's unique."

"He's trouble with a capital 'T,' Mr. Reese." She pulled up the file, frowning. "Jean didn't make these notes for nothing. He has excellent ability to size up a Grand Prix candidate for the jumping circuit."

"Then why did he agree to show Altair if he thought the stallion was such a loss?"

It was Dany's turn to give him a withering smile. "Because Jean thought he could ride anything and make it win."

"He has—so far. But," he hesitated, tilting his head, watching her with a more gentle expression. "I've been following his career the last four years, and it seems to me he had one hell of a trainer behind the scenes working the kinks out of these animals before they ever showed." He pointed at her. "You're the real reason why he's skyrocketed to fame and has winner after winner on his hands."

She couldn't stand still a moment longer, unable to bear remembering the last four miserable years of her life. "Please—"

He reached out, capturing her arm and turning her toward him. Dany was wildly aware of his masculine aura and she pulled her arm away. "I made a mistake by hiring three different male trainers to coach Altair. He needs a woman's touch."

She took a step away. "Doesn't every male," she noted with sarcasm. "I have no wish to get mangled by that sorrel stallion. I've heard rumors that Altair has injured all his trainers to some degree."

"And in every instance it was their fault," he growled. "He's an intelligent horse who won't be beaten or cajoled into doing something. He has to be reasoned with psychologically and respected."

"I have no wish to end up with a broken neck or fractured skull because of that red devil!"

"You're reacting to rumors, that's all."

Danielle's eyes widened, their blueness becoming clouded with cobalt flecks. How could this—this "cowboy" from California suddenly walk in unannounced and demand that she fulfill this agreement made so long ago? The only business that she wanted to conduct today was to turn over control of the Virginia training and stable business to her new partner. Had it only been nine months since the divorce from Jean Baptiste Daguerre? Her heart wrenched in anger and pain over the shock of his sudden departure. Jean was the brilliant, flamboyant part of their duo, and she was only the trainer who stayed behind the scenes doing the groundwork and strenuous training of thoroughbreds for their blue-blooded owners of the East Coast. Jean had ridden nearly every one of the horses she had lovingly trained to the very heights of equine stardom. He would show them in stadium jumping, dressage and the dangerous, spectacular three-day cross-country eventing. The more dangerous, the more closely timed the event, the better his electric performance on the horse. Choking down a lump forming in her throat, she was unable to meet Sam Reese's inquiring gaze. It was too bad Jean's performance in their marriage had gotten such poor marks. She sighed. It was just as much her fault; she spent too much time training the young horses and too little time with Jean.

"My attorneys have made inquiries as to Mr. Daguerre's whereabouts, and they've informed me he has left for a series of commitments in France. I have a Grand Prix hopeful standing in my barn, Mrs. Daguerre, and when your ex-husband saw Altair last year, he said he'd campaign him." He gave a slight shrug of his shoulders. "Fortunately, you haven't left the States and your credentials are well respected in this country. I don't care who fulfills the commitment." His voice, husky and low, hardened. "But one of you will. I haven't spent thousands of dollars on this stallion to see him wasted in the hands of some second-class amateur."

Dany shook her head. "I'm a trainer, Mr. Reese, not a show rider. There's a big difference."

His face was darkly tanned, chiseled as if sculpted by the sun and wind. He looked as though he would be at ease with any element that nature could conjure up. There was a faint look of surprise in his challenging gaze. "You can double as both."

Dany uncrossed her arms, holding them stiffly at her sides. She wasn't going to honor any commitment signed by Jean! "I'm too tall, Mr. Reese! Most of your riders are five-five to five-seven. Even the male riders are usually around a hundred and forty pounds. I'm one forty and my weight will cause the horse to tire on a long and demanding cross-country course. And my height would interfere with the horse's movement, especially if he's sixteen hands or less. You can't mix and match something like this, you know."

He relaxed against the doorjamb, oddly out of place in his Western attire. "I wouldn't change one inch or pound on you," he murmured appreciatively, making a thorough appraisal of her body.

Dany colored fiercely, getting ready to unleash a blast of anger at the lazily smiling Westerner. "How—"

"Now calm down," he defended. "I meant it as a compliment. You Eastern women all seem to be a little uptight. Anyway, Altair is seventeen hands high and can easily carry you. Even with your height, you have that grace and flexibility which can only contribute to some of the more intricate jumps that have to be scaled. So you see, there's no problem there."

She stood rooted to the spot, her body drawn into a stiff posture. She didn't realize that it made her look elegantly classical in her black knee-high English riding boots, white long-sleeved blouse and canary yellow riding breeches. The blouse set off the rich, shining blackness of her hair and accented the natural ruddiness of her complexion. Her thin brows knitted in displeasure. "Your horse could be eighteen hands tall, and I still wouldn't ride him!" she hurled back, her voice quivering with anger. "And you can keep your low opinion of Easterners to yourself, Mr. Reese. Now, if you'll excuse me, I'm handing over the reins of this place to my new partner, who's due to arrive any minute now." She walked determinedly up to him, angrily holding his amused gaze.

"I don't think he'll mind waiting," he drawled, remaining between her and the door.

She planted her hands on her hips, glaring up at his ruggedly handsome face. If they had met under other circumstances, she would have found him devastatingly intriguing. She had still not gotten over her anger at Jean's impulsive departure, and her life had no place for a man. In fact, she found herself agitated at men in general since the divorce. She wanted to slap his rugged face for the open expression of enjoyment that she saw there.

"If you don't move, I'll—"

"You're worse than a female mountain lion that's been woke up too early in the morning and is starving for a fresh kill," he drawled. "And before you cock that fist at me I think I'd better inform you that I'm your new partner, Mrs. Daguerre."

Danielle's lips parted, and she took a step back, staring up at him in shock. "What? But...the contract was signed by Mr. Jack Ferguson. I don't understand. I thought he bought..."

Sam Reese straightened up and slipped his large hand around her upper arm, gently guiding her back to the desk chair and sat her down. "I own the Sierra Corporation," he explained, resting his bulk on the edge of the desk, watching her closely.

Touching her brow in confusion, she gave him a guarded look of distrust. The man sitting before her was both powerful and rich to own a corporation the size of Sierra. Even though the selling price on half interest of the stable had been more than fair, she found that most of the money would immediately be sent to bill collectors on past due notices. That was another item that Jean had forgotten to mention: He hadn't handled the finances very well, and she found out by accident that the magnitude of the mismanagement totaled near a hundred thousand dollars. It had been the last factor to split their foundering marriage. And it meant selling the controlling interest of her dream: Richland Stables. Something she had slaved and toiled for all her twenty-nine years of life. Richland sat nestled between the rolling, gentle hills of Virginia, two hundred acres of luxurious slopes that were ideal for training young jumpers. Sighing, Danielle forced her thoughts back to the present and to this man who seemed to shadow her like a hound straight from hell.

She buried her face in her hands for a moment, trying to collect her broken, fragmented thoughts. He must have taken her gesture as one of utter defeat.

"Look," he murmured. "I apologize for dropping it on you like this. I can see you're tired and you've had quite a rough month. My half brother Jack Ferguson signed the sales agreement on your stable. He sent photos of your facility to my ranch out in California six months ago because he knew I was looking for a base of operation back East for Altair. I bought it sight unseen."

She felt the sting of tears prickling at the back of her eyes, and she shut them tightly, fighting back the deluge of emotion that threatened to engulf her. Why couldn't he be flip or arrogant like Jean? That always brought out her anger, and she was able to withstand any barrage. But this man—he was throwing her completely off base. His work-roughened fingers slipped around her wrist, pulling her hand gently away from her face.

"Here," he growled, "you might need this," and placed a white handkerchief in her palm.

A new, more disturbing sensation coursed electrically through her. Danielle looked up, her lashes thickly matted with tears. His face seemed open and undisguised of intrigue or game playing. He was so diametrically opposite of Jean that it was crumbling her defenses more quickly than she could replace them. This perfect stranger was leaning across the desk, his features sympathetic, offering her solace. She blinked twice and then murmured, "Thank you." She dabbed at her eyes, clenching the linen cloth tightly within her long, artistic fingers.

"Look, Danielle—may I call you that? Westerners hate formality." He gave her a frank smile. "We're mostly homesteader folk and would rather sit down over a whiskey and discuss our troubles. I'll take you to lunch, and we can discuss this problem over some good food. Besides, you look a little shook up."

She shivered inwardly as he spoke her name. It rolled off his tongue like a soft growl of that mountain lion he had mentioned. Her heart was aching, and at the moment, she was aware of only pain and loss.

"Come on," he urged, pulling her to her feet. "You're getting paler by the second. Don't worry. Everything will turn out all right."

Danielle sat quietly in the darkened restaurant, a glass of wine in front of her. She stared down at the salad, her appetite nonexistent.

"You know, if you don't eat, you aren't going to be any good for me," Sam murmured, setting the fork down and wiping his mouth with the cloth napkin.

Her eyes widened. "What?"

"I have a proposal for you," he began. "And one that I think might do you a lot of good." He rested his elbows on the table, leaning forward. "Fly back to my ranch that sits above Placerville and work Altair for me throughout the late spring. Then, if he comes along under your hand, I'll put him on any show circuit you want. I can even have you both flown back East here for the Devon show. What do you say?"

She took a drink of the wine, trying to shore up her broken defenses. "Your ranch?" she echoed.

Sam sipped the whiskey, the shadows playing across his face reminding her of a medieval knight who had just stepped out of the past into the present and into her life.

"The Cross Bar-U sits in the High Sierra mountains eight thousand feet above Placerville and close to the Truckee River. It's God's unaltered handiwork up there. The Truckee is one of the most violent rivers in the West, and the mountains are some of the finest in the world. I have thousands of acres of rich grassland, steep hills and rolling meadows perfect for training Altair. It's a vast, virgin country, Danielle. Far different than your tame hills here in Virginia." He allowed himself a small smile, his voice vibrating with a low-key excitement. "You would have a suite of rooms at the main house."

She found herself being pulled along by the fervor in his voice. She colored as he picked up one of her hands, pressing it between his own.

"Danielle, you're one of the best trainers in the U.S. when it comes to polishing off an event horse."

Her pulse accelerated unevenly, and she was acutely aware of the strong, callused fingers capturing her hand. His voice was a husky balm to her shredded heart, and his touch soothed her frantic, worried mind. Hesitantly, she withdrew her hand, tucking it in her lap, unable to meet his warm, inviting eyes that seemed to be dappled with silver flecks of excitement.

"My ex-husband was the rider, Mr.—"

"Call me Sam. And frankly, Danielle, I've had a thorough check made into both your backgrounds. Your ex-husband took chances with the horses under his tutelage. The sprained ligaments, the bowed tendons...no, you were the one who brought those animals along and gave them their distance to go that extra mile when it was asked of them. Look, I wouldn't trust anyone else with Altair. He's an athletic, daring stallion who can go all the way. But he's a sensitively calibrated instrument also. He needs your touch. He can't be mishandled at this stage by a whip or a club in some man's hands. You're the only one who can do it."

She touched her hair in confusion, pushing a strand behind her ear that had escaped from the severe chignon she wore while training and riding. Her hair was nearly long enough to reach her slender waist and had to be tightly knotted at the nape of her neck so that she could get her protective hard hat on her head. "Sam—" Her voice quavered and she gave a slight shrug of her shoulders. "Please—so much is happening—I can't think straight. Give me time…."

"I can't do that. Not under the circumstances. Look, you'll love the Sierras. I believe the change of location and environment might do you a world of good. Might bring back that sparkle to your blue eyes and put a dash of color on those pale cheeks." He stared at her intently for a moment. "It may make you smile again. You have a beautiful mouth."

Danielle shivered at the husky inference in his tone. There was a veiled, hungry look in his gray eyes, and she stared wordlessly across the table at him, feeling her body respond of its own volition to the invitation. "I just can't pack up and leave Richland! I have several coming five-year-olds here that need daily training and—"

"You have two capable assistants," he countered. "Surely they can manage the three animals that are here."

She sighed heavily. Since Jean had left, the bulk of their numerous clientele had left Richland. She wished that their clients had known that it was her ability that had made those horses winners. But she couldn't ride—at least that's what Jean had always impressed upon her—and clients didn't want just a good trainer, they wanted a brilliant rider to make their horse a winner. And she was anything but a brilliant show rider.

"I'd be willing to invest fifty thousand in Richland for renovation purposes plus an advertising campaign that will bring you in some of the biggest clients in the world. You give me four months of your time and I'll make sure Richland becomes a center for Grand Prix hopefuls on both sides of the Atlantic."

She stared in shock at him. Fifty thousand...what she could do with that money! It would enable her to buy another hot-walker to cool out her charges after their demanding morning runs, another groom to help in the more mundane duties around the barn and—it was too good to turn down.

"Look," she began unevenly, "the offer is wonderful, and to tell you the truth, it would help Richland." She lifted her lashes, meeting his steady gaze, her heart beating painfully in her breast. "Sam, I'm *not* a show rider. Oh, sure, I can ride. But I'm not a Grand Prix rider. I have no experience...no—"

"Who told you that?" he demanded quietly. "You train world-class hunters and jumpers and you stand here and tell me with such incredible humbleness that you can't ride them?" Disbelief flared in his gray eyes.

Dany chewed on her lower lip, evading his extraordinary eyes. She could lose herself in their pewter color. "I'd rather not discuss it."

He sat back, a quizzical expression written on his features. The seconds strung tautly between them. He watched her silently for a moment. "You ever seen Altair?"

She shook her head. "No."

"Hell, I'll change the deal. You fly back with me and take a look at him. If he doesn't sell you on staying at the Cross Bar-U and riding him in shows, then I'll let you come back East. Deal?" He held out his large hand toward her.

Danielle's lips parted, and she stared down at his hand. She could come back to Virginia if she didn't like the horse. "You'd release me from the contract if I'm not impressed with Altair?" she hedged carefully. "And still put the fifty thousand into the stable?"

Sam nodded his head. "That's right, Danielle. Now, we got a deal?"

She slipped her hand into the warmth of his. "Deal," she murmured.

Sam reluctantly released his hold and leaned back, smiling boyishly. "Welcome to the Sierras, Danielle. You're going to love it there."

Chapter 2

"Martha," Sam thundered as he walked into the main foyer of the ranch house, "we're home."

Dany stole a look around at his so-called ranch house. It was a magnificent two-story castle, reminding her of the grand haciendas of the Spanish dons in California during the eighteenth century. The red tile floor gleamed dully beneath their feet, and the halls were made of dark rough wood, accentuating the definite masculinity of the interior. She followed Sam down the hall, and he led her into a sitting room. Everywhere she looked she noticed oil paintings of family members. It was obvious from the rich furnishings and age of the ranch that it had all been handed down for at least a century, coming finally to the man who now stood before her.

"She must be in the kitchen, Danielle. Sit down and rest. I'll be right back."

"I think I'll stand, Sam. I need some exercise to shake off the tiredness."

He nodded, putting down two of her suitcases. "We'll remedy that very shortly. I hope you're ready to see the best eventing hunter in the U.S."

She had to smile at his unabashed enthusiasm. "Whenever you are," she assured him. She wanted to add that it didn't matter, having made up her mind to decline training Altair. Tomorrow morning she would leave for Virginia. As lovely and rugged as the drive to the ranch was, it contrasted startlingly with the gentleness inherent in Virginia woodland. Even though tall redwoods and spruce towered over the small, winding highway leading up to the Cross Bar-U and the fragrance of pine refreshed her senses, the snowcapped mountains looked like giant predators surrounding her. Where could she possibly ride a horse in those jagged peaks?

Martha came flying around the corner, her skirt rustling, a wooden spoon in one hand and a ball of bread dough in the other. She was a short plump woman, reminiscent of a pigeon. She stared across the room at Dany. "Oh, lordy!" she exclaimed, her applelike cheeks glowing pink from the heat of the kitchen. "Where's Sam! Oh, you must be Mrs. Daguerre. I didn't expect you for another hour!" She frowned, turning on her heel. "Sam! Where are you? I swear, you're worse than a little boy. Spring'n surprises on me like this. Wait till I—"

Dany put her hand over her mouth to suppress a smile as Sam wandered back into the room. Martha couldn't be more than five feet tall, and Sam towered over her like a redwood in comparison. The housekeeper waved her wooden spoon threateningly up at him. "Sam Reese, if you were twenty-five years younger, I'd take you across my knee, boy! The very idea of coming an hour early!" she scolded.

Sam took off his hat, grinning contentedly, a twinkle in his eyes as he glanced over at Dany. "This is Martha. She's been with our family all of her life. She more or less runs the household, and me," he added drolly. "I think the last time I got hit with her wooden spoon was when I was ten years old."

Martha belligerently placed her hand on her hip. "And it isn't like you didn't have it coming, Sam Reese."

Dany laughed heartily, wiping the tears from her eyes, watching the two of them stand there self-consciously. "I had no idea Sam was such a rambunctious youngster."

Martha glared back up at her full-grown charge. "He still is. He still is. Listen, Sam, you take Mrs.—"

"Please, call me Dany," she offered.

Sam raised one eyebrow speculatively. "Dany? Nice nickname," he complimented her huskily.

"Most of my friends know me as Dany," she explained. "Or, you can call me Danielle, Martha. Whichever is easiest. I'll answer to just about anything."

Martha dipped her head. "Just don't answer late for dinner, Dany. I only ring that bell once!"

"Believe me," she assured the feisty housekeeper, barely able to contain a smile, "I won't. I don't want to get whacked with a spoon."

Martha blushed furiously. "Oh, I'd never do that!" She waved it up in Sam's general direction. "He knows I'm just like an old hunting dog with no teeth left. All bark and no bite."

"Most of the time," Sam kidded. He held out his hand toward Dany. "Martha will make sure the boys bring in your gear. Come on, I'll show you where you'll be staying."

When Sam Reese said a suite of rooms, he meant exactly that. The ranch house was large, but because of the homey atmosphere and earthiness of colors throughout it, it seemed smaller and more intimate to her. Sam opened a door on the second floor, urging her in. She stood inside the room, her eyes widening in appreciation. He halted at her shoulder, watching her expression with a look of pleasure in his eyes.

"Well, do you think this will do? Over here you have a full bath including a whirlpool." He looked down at her. "That's for times when you bite the dust and you're sore."

She laughed. "Are you trying to tell me that Altair is accustomed to throwing his riders?"

"He's a handful," he remarked cryptically. "And the next room, which incidentally joins my suite, is a living room." He opened another door. There was a set of large windows with the beige drapes pulled back to allow a cascade of sunshine to spill into the pale green room. Dany stood there, admiring it silently.

"It's lovely, Sam." She tilted her head, catching his pleased expression. "And flowers!" A delicate blue vase in the center of the pecan table seemed to overflow with blossoms. She walked over to the table, caressing one of the petals.

"Those come from the property here. With the snow leaving and the temperature starting to rise, they're popping up all over the place. Martha picked them especially for you. She said ladies from the East would appreciate flowers."

Leaning over them, she cupped them within her hands and inhaled their fragrance. She closed her eyes, murmuring, "I never expected such a warm welcome."

"Part of the Western tradition," he assured her. "You're like one of the family now, you know. Martha will treat you like a daughter and dote on you, if you let her." He hesitated at the other door leading to his suite. "Listen, you rest for a while, and later, when you come down, I'll take you out to see Altair."

Dany straightened up, her eyes giving away the excitement she felt. "I would like to rest. But I'm dying to see Altair...."

"He can wait two more hours. Now get changed into something more comfortable and take a nap."

"Is that an order?"

"No, just a strong suggestion."

Dany tossed her head, laughing. "It's good advice. I'll see you later, Sam."

He dipped his head and opened the door. "Look, if you need anything, just come on in. I'm going to be slaving over some paperwork that's built up over the last week."

Dany unpacked one suitcase, leaving the others sitting where the ranch hands had placed them. She hung up her black silk robe and tucked her toiletry articles in the bathroom. Changing into a pair of russet-colored jodhpurs and a yellow blouse, she loosened her ebony hair, allowing it to flow freely across her shoulders. The queen-size bed looked inviting, and against her

better judgment, she lay down on it, intent on resting about twenty minutes before viewing the stallion.

New sounds, sounds of cattle lowing plaintively and
of horses whickering in friendly fashion, lulled her
into a restful state. She had not meant to sleep, but the
sun was warm against her back as she curled up on the
huge expanse of the bed, and weeks of emotional exhaustion were placed into limbo.

Danielle moaned, hearing herself cry out. "No!"
she screamed. The voice, her voice, reverberated into
her restless, sleeping state, and she choked off another
cry. In the dream, she saw herself transformed into a
horse who was being whipped cruelly by the handler.
The horse struggled, trying to escape the biting flick
of the whip that Jean had in his hand. Pain seared her
heart and she moaned. Jean was yelling, driving her
back into a corner. She was trying to escape the whip
and the pain.

"Dany?" a new voice called. The husky, warm voice
sliced again into the anguish of the nightmare. She
whimpered, feeling the caress of a man's hand against
her arm, moving up across her shoulder in a caring
fashion. "Dany, wake up. You're having a bad dream."

She gasped, blinking open her eyes. Sam Reese sat
on the edge of the bed leaning across, his hand resting on her shoulder. Tearstains glistened against her
cheeks, and he reached over, touching her skin with
his fingers, making an awkward attempt to remove
the wetness.

"You're all right, lady," he soothed. "You were crying out and I heard you next door. Just take it easy. Everything is going to be fine."

The rough caress of his fingers against her face sent a new, aching sensation through her tense body. The musky scent of his masculine body invaded her nostrils, and her heart pounded without restraint. She was captured by the tenderness of his expression, his eyes broadcasting genuine concern. Dany shivered, confused by his care and affection. She pushed his hand away, struggling to sit up and get away from his powerful male body.

"I'm all right," she gulped, rubbing her face. Her hair fell in blue black sheets about her pale features.

Sam nodded, watching her in silence for long moments. He caressed the crown of her head, his hand barely skimming the surface of her hair. "I was right," he murmured softly, "you have lovely hair, Dany. You ought to wear it down more often. Makes you look like a princess." A bashful smile pulled one corner of his mouth, and he hesitantly drew his hand away, resting it against his thigh.

It took a few moments to retrieve her senses. The sun was no longer shining and darkness had claimed the day. She was excruciatingly aware of Sam Reese as he sat quietly beside her, making no further attempt to touch her. Finally, she raised her head, meeting his gaze.

"I'm sorry," she apologized in a thick voice.

"What for? We all have bad dreams every once in a while. I've put you through a great deal in just a few days time, Dany, and it's caught up with you."

She shook her head. "No, it wasn't you," she whispered. "Oh, I'll admit it's been hectic and surprising, but that wasn't it." She gave a broken, helpless shrug. "Just the past coming back to haunt me again. As usual."

He pursed his lips, nodding sagely. "You know there's one sure cure for the past."

"What's that?"

"Get involved in the present. Let the past go. It's dead and gone. You did what you had to do and gave it your best shot." He forced a weak smile. "Take my word for it, I've been there, too."

Dany chewed on her lower lip, glancing at him. His face was so strong, and yet, an innate gentleness burned in the depth of his slate gray eyes. There was inbred harshness in the lines of his thirty-five-year-old face. The lines which gave his face character had obviously been earned. The furrowed, broad forehead had seen worry, and the creases that fanned from the corner of each eye and the lines around his mouth spoke of laughter, laughter that she wished she could share with him. She gasped at the sudden, unexpected thought, and he must have mistaken her reaction.

"Getting divorced isn't the end of the world," he said. "I had my turn at it, too. Tried to put a thoroughbred in a plow horse's harness, and it just didn't work."

Dany smiled tentatively at the expression, watching his eyes cloud with unspoken memories. "I like the way you Westerners talk, Sam. You seem to put everything into such simple perspective."

It was his turn to share a smile, and he clasped her hand, giving it a squeeze. "Simple but effective," he agreed, sliding off the bed and standing. "Why don't you take a bath and gradually get yourself back together? Dinner won't be for another hour."

"But what about Altair?"

Sam looked out the window and walked over to the drapes, drawing them closed. "Tomorrow morning is the earliest you're doing anything. If you'd like, I'll have Martha send up a tray and you can eat here."

"That sounds wonderful, Sam. I hope I didn't ruin any plans you had for dinner…."

"No. I always eat alone anyway. Besides, your comfort comes first."

"I appreciate your thoughtfulness. What time can we go see Altair tomorrow?"

"Whenever you get up. He's in the stud barn that sits across from the bunkhouse. Chances are, you'll sleep in tomorrow."

"I've got news for you. Trainers are up around four-thirty with the dawn. If I sleep past six, I'll be surprised."

He nodded. "Well, I'll leave you be for now. Good night, Dany."

She heard the tenor in his voice, and it made her want to ask him to stay. The loneliness was evident in the look he gave her, and yet, he wasn't going to force his will upon her. How vastly different from Jean!

After a delicious meal of beef rump roast, potatoes and peas that Martha brought up, Dany took a long, fragrant bath and then slipped back into bed for the night. This time there were no bad dreams. Only an aching remembrance of Sam's hand on her cheek wiping her tears away.

Chapter 3

She awoke exactly at four-thirty. Dawn was barely breaking its hold on the night as Dany tiptoed downstairs to the kitchen. To her surprise, the coffee had already been made. She poured herself a cup, putting cream and sugar in it, and then walked quietly out the back door. A thin blanket of fog hovered a few feet off the ground throughout the valley. The ranch sat on the southern end of the valley, surrounded on all sides by a thick forest of pines. The restless snort of horses waiting for their feeding hour was a welcome sound. Pulling her coat around her more tightly, Dany grasped the handle of the mug and meandered in the direction of the paddocks and the stable.

Her hair swung with the natural rhythm of her body, the shorter tendrils framing her face from the dampness of the early morning humidity created by the ground fog. She turned the corner of the bunkhouse, catching sight of Sam leaning up against the fence. Dany stopped, her breath catching in her breast as she drank in his unmoving form. The brim of the hat was drawn down across his eyes, the denim jacket molded against the broad expanse of his shoulders and back. One leg was cocked lazily on the last rung of the fence, and he held a steaming mug of coffee in both hands as he seemed to be watching something in the distance. Her gaze traveled the meadow that disappeared out into the white blanket.

There, not much more than a mile away, she could barely make out an outline of a horse standing alertly. She watched as Sam put his fingers to his mouth. A shrill whistle broke the morning stillness. She heard the answering call; the unmistakable bugling scream of a stallion. Sam set the coffee mug on the post and climbed into the paddock, walking toward the horse who appeared magically out of the fog.

Dany shivered as she watched the man and the stallion come together. Sam walked unconcernedly as the giant red stallion strained forward like a huge unstoppable freight train that had no brakes. She stifled a cry of warning, watching the sorrel suddenly veer off to the right and playfully scramble in a circle about the man. It had to be Altair! She released her held breath, awed by the sight of the magnificent thoroughbred. Altair reared, pawing his front legs through the air, and then came down only a few feet from Sam, snorting vehemently. It was as if the two males were squaring off at one another, each king of his own special domain. Danielle stood transfixed by the beauty and rugged handsomeness of the spectacle. Sam spoke in a quiet, firm tone to the stallion, holding out his hand. Altair's small ears twitched, and he turned his intelligent eyes upon the man, snorting again. Pawing restlessly, the stallion flicked his thick flaxen tail, and bent his head to take the treat.

She walked toward them as Altair nibbled the offering from Sam's hand. By the time she got to the fence, they had both seen her. Sam put his arm across the stallion's neck and led him over to the fence.

"Good morning. I see you caught us at our favorite game."

"For a moment I thought he was going to run you over," she admitted.

"He's been known to do that to people he didn't like. Come here, Altair. I want to introduce your new rider and trainer." He pulled the horse by the mane, and the stallion docilely complied.

Dany flinched inwardly at the word "rider." She did not share Sam's belief that she could be one. Her eyes widened in appreciation, noting the thoroughbred's impeccable conformation. Altair nuzzled her arm, his nostrils flaring as he caught her scent. She watched him carefully; she never really trusted any stallion. They were male animals ruled by an instinctive sexual drive and not capable of thinking, only reacting.

Sam stood back, admiring both of them, his hands on his hips. "He certainly seems to take to you. Of course, he'd be stupid not to."

Dany smiled distantly, keenly assessing the stallion's personality, watching his ears and the look in his large brown eyes. "He's far from stupid, Sam. And I can see he allows very few people to tell him what to do."

Sam laughed, joining her at the fence. "No one *tells* Altair a thing. They have to *ask*." And then he frowned, picking up his coffee mug and taking a sip from it. "Which is where I've run into a lot of trouble with his riders lately. They treat him like an unthinking animal with only four legs and the power of a runaway truck. They don't realize he's thinking in his own terms and his forte is correctly judging complicated jumps. He's a dynamic hunter who will challenge everything except a water obstacle."

Dany ran her fingers down the stallion's sleek, silky neck, enjoying the play of muscles beneath his skin. She noted with a sinking feeling that long thin scars marred his beautiful copper coat. "My God, who did this to him?" she whispered, running her fingers along one scar that ran the length of his left shoulder. Her heart turned over in compassion as she noted several more scars around his mouth and across the top of his nose.

Sam came around, affectionately scratching Altair's ears. "Remember me telling you that the wrangler who captured him tried to break his spirit?" he asked huskily.

Dany looked up, aware of the simmering anger hidden in his voice and reflected in his eyes. "This is outright cruelty!" she protested, her voice strangled with emotion. Gently, she reached up, caressing Altair's scarred muzzle. The stallion moved away from her hand, the white of his eye showing as he took another step backward. She shook her head. "I don't blame him for jerking away," she said tightly. "What did they do, use wire to try and keep his head and nose down?"

"Yes. It didn't work, but it made him head shy with

everyone except me." Sam gave her a smile of encouragement. "And I think he'll eventually let you touch his mouth without going crazy. I can see he's already responding to you in a way he's never done before with anyone else."

"Typical male."

"Yes, and thank God you're the one to help him over some of his worst faults," Sam said fervently. "Altair may not appreciate your beauty, but I do." He grinned and playfully put his arm across the stallion's neck and leaned against him.

"How do you get the bit into his mouth if he's head shy?"

Sam pursed his mouth, casting a troubled glance in her direction. "Very carefully. We use the snaffle only when he shows in the dressage portion of the show."

Dany gave him an incredulous look. "What on earth do you use, then?" It was beyond comprehension in her mind to ride an eventing horse without a bit in his mouth! Riding over a thousand pounds of horseflesh at twenty-five to thirty miles an hour over a grueling, dangerous course without the control of a bit was impossible to comprehend. No wonder Altair has injured his previous riders, she thought, experiencing a sinking feeling in the pit of her stomach.

"We use an aluminum hackamore, Dany."

She searched her memory for the use of the training device. Hackamores were invented for the horse that wouldn't carry a bit in its mouth. The rawhide or aluminum loop fit around the muzzle and when it was pulled on, it exerted pressure against sensitive nerve endings that lay on either cheek of the horse's jaw. She gave Sam a distrustful look. "Is that why the riders have been injured?"

"No. Do you think I'd ask you to ride and train him if he wasn't manageable?" he demanded.

She bristled. "At this moment, I think anything is possible! You bind me with a contract that was signed by my ex-husband and practically blackmail me to fly me out here to retrain this horse." She was aware of the effort he was making to control his temper as his gray eyes darkened like ominous thunderclouds.

"I'm not in the habit of risking people's lives, particularly a woman who I think can salvage my stallion and bring him into his own. I need you alive, not dead, Dany. Sure, he can be dangerous because of his past. But he's responsive. Altair is not deliberately cruel or vicious. God knows, he ought to be, for what he's suffered. But look at him. Does he look unsafe?"

As if listening to the heated conversation between them, Altair walked between them, head down, standing quietly while they glared across his back at one another. Dany put her hands on her hips in defiance.

"I won't ride him unless he's got a bit in his mouth, that's final."

"Fine. You find a way to do it, and we'll both be happy. He's extremely responsive to the hackamore, though."

She shook her head. "Sam Reese, either you're the most eccentric man I've ever met with an even more eccentric horse or—"

"We're both unique," he interrupted. His gaze lingered on her. "And so are you. You're one of a kind, lady. Just the gal to help Altair to become the best Grand Prix jumper in the world."

She didn't know how to react to his backhanded compliments, and was continually uncomfortable beneath his warming, caressing gaze. "Tell me what else he has problems with," she muttered. "The fly in the ointment, no doubt."

"He doesn't like water. He'll damn near do anything to avoid it. Including dumping his rider into an oxer or earth bank."

Dany looked over at him. "Did your riders quit, or were they killed?"

Sam managed a sour grin. "None killed. One got hurt pretty seriously, and he was out of action for two months. It was after Tony's fall that I decided I wasn't going to risk anyone's life until I could get Richland Stables to honor its commitment."

Dany frowned, allowing Altair to nuzzle her hair with his velvety nose. "Are you going to let me help you, big boy?" she asked the stallion, giving him a playful pat on the forehead. Altair backed away, snorting. A mare from another pasture whickered a greeting, and the sorrel thoroughbred raised his magnificent head, standing like a marble statue. He bugled out an answering call, the sound raucous and harsh to their ears. Sam smiled and slipped between the railings.

"That's his way of making sweet talk to them."

"He's a nice-looking horse, Sam. So I can't blame the mares for wanting to entice him over to their paddocks," she grudgingly admitted.

He took her arm and led her down toward the stable. "We've got his yearling crop in here. I bred him to five of my best broodmares. Let's see what you think of the results." Dany reviewed the thoroughbred yearlings and stood in the passage between the large, roomy box stalls with Sam. "That's simply amazing," she admitted. "There's a uniformity in conformation I've rarely seen. Each one looks like a stamp of Altair."

"Exactly. He's prepotent as hell. I bred him to five different bloodlines to see how his genes would affect the mare's breeding line. In every case, his stamp came out," Sam said, sounding somewhat incredulous. "The legs on every yearling are absolutely straight. They're bred to withstand the strain of jumping."

Dany smiled. "And you can hardly wait for them to mature enough to put them on the circuit, right?"

He walked her out of the barn, and they ambled at a slow pace toward the house. The sun was barely edging the tip of the Sierras, sending streamers of light through the fog as the thickened mist began to evaporate. The cobalt blue sky turned a shade paler as the sun ascended across the peaks, promising another cool spring day. She was aware of his body only inches from her own, and once again, her skin prickled with a pleasurable tingle as his arm occasionally brushed against her.

Halting at the back porch, he pushed the hat off his forehead, watching her closely. "Well, what do you think? Is he reason enough to stay on?"

She avoided his gray eyes. Instead, she turned her back to him, drawing in a deep, steadying breath. "Please don't think my decision has anything to do with Altair's conformation or potential, Sam." She girded herself inwardly, closing her eyes tightly for a moment. "But I can't stay. This is too strange an environment for me to stay here. I'm used to the eastern circuit, and I'm familiar with the people and the land."

"You're the only woman capable of bringing Altair around," he growled.

Dany gritted her teeth. The man was stubborn! Irritation stirred to life within her, and she compressed her lips and turned, meeting his fiery gaze. Part of her resolve disappeared immediately. Sam Reese was no longer pleasant-looking in any sense of the word. He was towering over her, his eyes an angry silver hue. She took a step back, feeling the masculine aura of strength so sharply that it made her dizzy.

"It's not the training aspect that bothers me," she managed, her voice strident.

"Then what the hell is it?"

She opened her mouth and then closed it, her sapphire eyes glittering with golden fire. Why did she want to escape? Was she running from Sam? Or her fear of having to ride in shows? She sensed her body's own hungry needs that had lain dormant for over nine months. She didn't want a careless affair with him. He was able to manipulate her as no other man ever had, and it frightened her thoroughly. "I'm turning your offer down, it's as simple as that."

Sam smiled savagely. "Nothing's as simple as that, Mrs. Daguerre. Remember, there's been a contract signed, and I'll hold you to it if I have to."

Her nostrils flared with contempt. "You wouldn't dare!"

"What are you running from?" he asked, his voice suddenly lined with impatience. He reached out, grabbing her arm and drawing her near. "Sorry," he breathed thickly, "but you're too good a trainer and I need you for that horse out there. I don't care what you're running from, but you aren't leaving this commitment. You'll fulfill the obligations."

Dany muffled a curse, jerking her arm away from his branding fingers of fire on her skin. "You—you bastard," she hissed. "All right," she blurted out in reckless abandon, "I'll stay! But keep away from me while I'm training that horse. Do you hear me? I don't want a thing to do with you!"

She rubbed her arm, taking two more steps away from him. God, how she hated that composed, implacable look on his stony face. How had she led herself to think it was as simple as flying out to his ranch? His tenderness and care from the night before had thrown her off guard. Well, his true personality was now surfacing. He was just as arrogant and imperious as that stallion of his. Her lips curled away from her teeth. "I despise you for thinking you can run my life for me, Mr. Reese. You're so used to molding everything to the way you want it. It's obvious you come from generations of men who are used to getting their way. Well, you may get your way for a while, but as soon as I'm done with Altair, I'm leaving. And I don't care if I have to run away in the dead of night to do it!"

Sam smiled lazily, beginning to relax. He pulled the brim of the cowboy hat down across his eyes. "If you leave, you'll find yourself in high country full of cougar, bear and bobcat. And at this time of year, they're coming out of a hard winter and they're hungry. So forget that idea."

Chapter 4

The next morning Dany woke up, determined to get to work on Altair. She threw on her hunt breeches, knee-high black riding boots, and grabbed her protective hard hat and leather gloves. Stopping in the kitchen, she borrowed a jar of molasses from Martha and headed determinedly out to the stud barn.

Cowboys dressed in blue chambray shirts, dusty, dirty jeans or well-worn chaps looked with mild interest as she walked briskly into dark passages between the box stalls. Dany halted for a moment, allowing her eyes to adjust to the dimness. She found Altair in his stall and placed the jump saddle and other riding equipment down beside the ties. She still felt testy and belligerent from her confrontation with Sam yesterday, and she sent a warning glance at one cowboy who started to say something and then, apparently, thought better of it.

Altair whickered gently as she approached. "Just like him, aren't you?" she whispered. "All sweet talk on the outside and mean on the inside. Come on, it's time for us to get acquainted."

The big red stallion stood quietly in the ties in the middle of the aisle as she brushed him down vigorously until his copper coat shone like a newly minted penny. Two ranch hands sitting down at the end of the stable watched her in silence, each chewing on a wad of tobacco lodged in his weather-hardened cheek. Dany was positive that they had never seen someone in English riding clothes, and that irritated her even more. Damn Sam Reese! The breeze was slight, stirring through the barn, as she rummaged around until she located the tack room. In there, she found Altair's hackamore hanging and a snaffle bit beside it. Fashioning a double bridle composed of the snaffle along with the hackamore, Dany brought out the bridle and opened the jar of thick, sweet molasses, spreading the brown syrup onto the snaffle.

"You're going to like this," she muttered. Approaching the curious stallion, Dany placed her right arm between his ears, holding the headstall. With her left hand, she held the snaffle close to the stallion's mouth. His large nostrils flared as he picked up the sweet scent.

"That's right," she crooned, putting the snaffle in the palm of her hand and resting it on his lips. "Easy… easy…" she whispered as he opened his mouth and began licking the molasses off the bit.

Dany gave a sigh of relief as she deftly slid the snaffle into the stallion's mouth, placing the hackamore over his nose and then sliding the headstall behind his small ears. Altair stood there, chomping in an exaggerated fashion as he mouthed the snaffle. Dany remained near, crooning softly to him and patting him. She followed the same procedures ten more times until Altair docilely accepted the bit. The next stage of the plan would be more dangerous; she would not only have to get used to the horse but also balance control through the hackamore and snaffle. Would he rear or flip over backward on her if she pulled too hard on the reins that were attached to the snaffle? Chances of injury on a horse "sunfishing" on her were great. It would mean leaping off his back at exactly the right moment or getting crushed under a thousand pounds of flailing horse. She slipped the snaffle bit into Altair's mouth one more time and the bridle over his large, broad head and snapped the throatlatch closed. She decided to use a strap attached from the cinch to the noseband known as a standing martingale. It would stop Altair from jerking his head up and hitting her.

Taking a riding crop, Dany slipped it over her wrist and drew on the thin riding gloves. She recalled times when the palms of her hands had been cut open by horses who had pulled the leather reins sharply through her grip. Wearing the gloves protected her hands, plus it gave her more grip with the sometimes slippery reins. Fixing the hard hat firmly on her head, she buckled it tightly, the chin strap snug against her jaw. Looking up at Altair, she muttered, "Okay, big boy, let's find out what you're made of. If it's anything like that owner of yours, this ought to be one heck of an experience for both of us."

Altair brushed her shoulder affectionately, beginning to prance airily as she led him out into the bright afternoon sunshine. He tossed his head, sensing the ex-

citement of his rider. Dany looked around and decided
to ride him in a pasture that seemed free of fences at the
other end. If she did get in trouble with him, then there
was open area to deal with the situation. She placed the
toe of her boot in the stirrup, leaping easily upon the
stallion's broad back. Altair sidled, tucking his head
and humping his rear playfully. Dany monitored the
pressure on the hackamore, forcing him to stop the
small, harmless bucks. All cross-country horses were
bred hot, and few could stand still for more than one
second if they were asked. Altair was no different.

The stallion felt good between her tightly clenched
thighs, and she carefully moved her calves against his
well-sprung barrel, gently putting pressure against him,
asking him to move out at a slow trot. A small smile
of appreciation smoothed the frown on her features
as he moved out in a fluid, unbroken stride. His nostrils flared, drinking in great draughts of wind, as she
moved him in large, lazy circles, checking his sense of
balance, of motion and flexibility, against the hackamore. He responded beautifully.

For twenty minutes, Dany tested Altair's weaknesses and strengths, finding him an utter delight to
ride. Although tall for a rider, she looked like a minia-
ture jockey astride the giant copper stallion, his flaxen
mane and tail flowing like white silk behind him. Dany
spotted several oxer jumps a good two miles away.
Sitting deeply in the seat of the saddle, she pushed
downward with her spine, giving him the signal to gallop. Altair surged forward in an unbroken, pounding
rhythm. His length of reach was phenomenal, because
his legs were long in proportion to his extreme height.
The ground began to blur into a ribbon of green, and

the wind created by the thoroughbred's speed sheared against Dany's face, causing her eyes to water.

Dany began to pull Altair in, applying just a slight pressure against the snaffle and more against the hackamore as the oxers came up quickly. She reached down, touching his sleek neck and shoulder, checking for sweat; there was none. She was pleased that he was in such good condition and began to croon to the stallion, asking him to slow his pace even more. Rising up off the saddle, knees pushed inward against the small patch of leather, Dany leaned forward on his withers to check his speed even more, her face inches from his arched neck. A small puddle of water appeared over the next small rise, and Altair was suddenly airborne, popping over the puddle as if it were a jump. Dany's neck snapped back and she felt her body being pulled back by the mighty thrust of power from the unexpected leap. Her thighs tightened like a steel trap against the saddle. Altair landed heavily, startled by the sudden shift of his rider's weight. She slammed forward, her face smacking into the crest of the stallion's neck. For a moment, blackness threatened to engulf her, but she hung on, gripping his mane.

"Whoa," she croaked, sitting up and pulling him to a stop. Her nose ached abominably, and she shook her head, trying to escape the pain that radiated outward from it. She reached up with her gloved hand. "Oh, damn," she muttered, staring at the blood on her fingers.

"Problems?" a cool voice inquired.

Dany jerked around in the saddle, startled.

Sam's eyes narrowed and he lost that infuriating smile when he saw the blood. He kicked the gelding forward, coming abreast of her and grabbing Altair's reins. She blushed angrily, pinching her nose shut to try and halt the bleeding, and jerked the reins out of his hand. "I told you to leave me alone!" she said.

"You're hurt," he said, his voice losing its coolness and reflecting genuine care.

"Well, it won't be the first or last time."

Sam swore softly, glaring at her. "You're a hellion just like that horse when you want to be. Why don't you climb down off there and let me see how badly hurt—"

Keeping her hand over her nose, Dany kneed Altair, and the stallion made a quick turn. "No thanks! Just stay out of my way. Do you understand me?"

He sat there on his black gelding, his gray eyes sparks of fury. "You two deserve each other," was all he growled, and yanked his horse around, galloping back toward the group of cows and men waiting for him about a mile away.

Tears ran down her cheeks, and she spit out the distasteful metallic taste of blood from her mouth. That would serve her right.

She should have checked over the terrain first. It was clear that she would have to begin work in earnest with Altair on all sorts of water situations. She gave him a pat. "Come on, big boy, get me home so I can get a cold cloth on this nose. I hope it's not broken. God, it hurts."

She had managed to remove the bit from Altair's mouth and was trying to unsaddle him when Sam appeared out of nowhere. He lifted the saddle off in one smooth motion and gripped her arm firmly with the other. Dany muffled her protest as he dragged her down the aisle toward the house.

"You might as well quit struggling," he declared

grimly, handing the saddle to one of his hands. He stopped long enough to say, "Jake, cool Altair down and then put him back in his paddock."

Dany tried to pull away. Blood was still trickling from her nose, and she put her other hand up to try to halt it. "Let me go!" she cried.

"Stop it," he ordered, pulling her along.

They passed Martha, whose eyes widened with surprise as he guided her through the kitchen. Sam took her to his suite, forcing her to sit down on a stool in the huge bathroom. He threw his hat down and took a washrag, running it under a faucet. Dany sat there, tears streaming down her face, infuriated and embarrassed.

Martha came on the run, panting as she waddled around the bedroom door to the bathroom. "Sam, what's happened to her?"

His fingers slid along Dany's jaw, and she tried to jerk away. "If you don't sit still," he threatened softly, the moistness of his breath fanning across her face, "I'm going to take you over my knee."

Martha crowded in, her keen brown eyes assessing Dany's nose. "I'll go call Dr. Hart right away."

"Do that."

"No!" Dany protested, acutely aware of his strong fingers against her chin and jaw.

"Yes!" Sam thundered to the departing Martha. He glared back down at her. "You're certainly hardheaded." She winced as he gently placed the cloth against her nose. "You may have broken it," he growled, carefully blotting away the blood.

"Oh, shut up!" she mumbled, grabbing the cloth out of his hands. She stood up, examining her nose in the mirror. It was swelling on one side, and she touched it tentatively.

"Why don't you sit down before you fall down and get a damn concussion," he ordered tightly, his eyes broadcasting his concern.

She wasn't going to do one blasted thing he ordered. She might have to live here for a month or two, but that was all! Stubbornly, she remained on her feet, the pain increasing and making her eyes narrow. The cold cloth against her hot skin felt good, and she rinsed out the cloth and put it back against her nose. "You might as well be talking to a wall," she muttered, glaring up at him. "I'm not doing a thing you tell me!"

He leaned forward, his face a mask of tightly controlled fury. "I don't need my rider fainting on me and striking her head against the tile floor of this bathroom. Now sit down before you fall down!"

She wanted to stick her tongue out at him in sheer frustration. He was treating her like a twelve-year-old child. "Don't be ridiculous," she said haughtily. "I'm not going to faint! I've been hurt a lot worse than this and had to take care of myself without anybody's help. So just let me be!"

"That's part of your trouble. You're so self-sufficient that you don't know how to handle someone's offer to help. You've got to be part Irish with stubbornness like that."

His verbal tirade sounded hollow, the words seeming to blur together, and Dany blinked, dropping the cloth from her hands. Lights danced in front of her eyes, and she felt waves of pain shooting up into her forehead. She moaned, and her knees suddenly buckled beneath her.

"Dany," Sam whispered, barely catching her as she collapsed into his strong arms. The last thing she remembered was his arms encircling her and the warmth of his sun-hardened body pressed against hers.

Dany awoke, groggy, immediately aware of a heavy adhesive bandage across her nose. It was dark except for a small light on the nightstand beside her bed. She sensed movement rather than heard it and gasped as a bulky shadow moved from the darkness to the light.

"It's just me," Sam growled, coming over and standing above her.

Dany let out a sigh of relief, her fingers resting at the base of her throat. She felt the bed sag beneath his weight. Her eyes flew open, and she stared up at his harshly lined face. Assorted impressions hit her at once. Someone had dressed her in her black silk nightgown, and she was comfortably ensconced in her own bed. Dark smudges hovered around Sam's eyes, fatigue showing in their darkened depths. Guilt at her outburst earlier caused her to be contrite.

"How long have I been out?"

"About four hours. You went from a faint into sleep. Doc Hart said you were exhausted. He just called me about an hour ago and said you're also anemic. So that means you cool your heels for a while and take it easy and rest."

"Wonderful," she retorted, her voice thick.

"How do you feel?" he asked, managing to soften his tone.

"I'm hungry."

A slow grin appeared on his generous mouth. "Hungry?"

She glared over at him, pulling up the blanket across her breasts. "Yes, hungry. Is it a crime to be hungry after getting punched in the nose?"

His hand came forward and caressed her cheek. "Okay, okay, don't get excited. I'll go see what Martha saved from tonight's meal."

"No, I'll go down and eat. I can get up and walk."

His hand rested firmly on her naked shoulder, his fingers a burning brand to her flesh. She was all too aware of the thin spaghetti strap that held the nightgown up over her body. A blush rushed across her face, and she gave in, just to get him to leave. "Okay, I'll eat here," she muttered.

Sam smiled benignly. "That's better. You know, lady, you're worse than a flighty two-year-old filly that needs breaking." He slid his hand upward, lightly caressing her arm.

Her lips parted and she stared at him, his touch communicating much more than words possibly could. His fingers came to rest on her shoulder, his eyes a dark, turbulent gray. Her heart hammered at the base of her throat as she read the intent of his gaze. His fingers tightening against her shoulder, Sam leaned down. "Women and horses ought to be broken with love," he whispered, his breath warm against her face. "All you need is a gentle hand, Dany."

His mouth grazed her lips lightly. A deep, keening ache began within her body, and she tilted her head up hungry for further contact with his teasing, tantalizing male mouth. The fresh scent of pine intermingled with horses filled her flared nostrils. To her, it was one of the most natural scents in the world, and she relaxed as he cradled her face between his work-roughened hands. His mouth moved insistently against her lips, tasting them with delicious slowness. Instinctively she curved her arm around his neck, desiring more of what he offered.

A low groan emitted from him. "God, Dany, I need you," he murmured thickly against her ear.

She pulled away from him, reluctant to end the contact. "You're right," she admitted unsteadily. "A gentle hand and a kind word are all anyone needs." She had not meant for it to sound bitter, but it came out that way.

Sam slowly rose, an unreadable expression dropping over his face. "You need it, too, Dany," he reminded her darkly.

Desperate at the turn of the conversation, Dany cast about for anything to break the last of the heady spell. "Who put me in my nightgown?" she demanded peevishly.

He studied her for long seconds before answering. "Don't look so worried. Martha shooed us out of the room. She said it wouldn't be proper to have a bunch of gaping fools around when she dressed you. I'll be back in a few minutes with your dinner."

Dany scrunched down between the covers, groaning to herself. She shut her eyes tightly, embarrassed by the entire incident. Unconsciously, she touched her lips, aware that the strength of Sam's mouth had acted like a brand upon her. It shouldn't have happened. Not now. Unable to vent her fear and anxiety at Sam, she turned it upon Altair. "Damn you," she breathed softly. It was going to be the last time the stallion injured her, she promised. Tomorrow morning, Altair was going to start to like water...or else.

* * *

She ate ravenously, occasionally flinging a distrustful look in Sam's direction as he sat opposite her on a chair in the corner of the room. He got up, pouring himself more coffee and refilling her china cup.

"You know, you need fresh air, sunshine and some good ranch food in that body of yours to help get you back on your feet. I want you to take a week off and just rest, Dany. I can ride Altair enough to keep him in condition. I need you at your best. Not your worst."

She put the cup down, her eyes narrowing with frustration. "I run my own life, Sam Reese. How many times do I have to repeat that sentence? Tomorrow morning I'm going to begin to retrain Altair."

"You will not. Dr. Hart said you're this close to folding." He held up two fingers that were barely a quarter of an inch apart. "Quit pushing yourself. You have a roof over your head, money coming in and a job."

"Yes, and a tyrant for a boss. No thanks. I'll fulfill my bargain and leave your wonderful services as soon as possible."

He shook his head, sipping the coffee slowly. "Your compliments aren't going to get you anywhere, so quit throwing the barbs. I've been stung by a lot worse, believe me. You're exhausted, very close to a broken nose and you need to relax."

Dany bowed her head, her black hair providing a curtain between them. Deep inside she knew that he was right. There was no way that she could ride for at least a week; the jarring effect would do nothing but aggravate her nose. "You're right," she admitted quietly.

She heard him rise and looked up in his direction. His face showed his own tiredness and worry as he leaned over, taking the tray from her lap. "You got some sense after all," he murmured. "I'll look in on you tomorrow sometime. Take one of those pills the doctor left for you before you go to sleep."

She frowned, watching him walk slowly toward the door. "Don't do me any favors, Sam. You don't have to keep a check on me each day. I won't run away."

His eyes flared briefly with anger. "If I want to see how you're feeling tomorrow, I'll come. It has nothing to do with our business agreement. Understand?"

Dany opened her mouth and then shut it, glaring at him until he closed the door after him. Taking the glass of water, she placed the pill in her mouth. Shutting off the lamp, she snuggled back into bed. If it was a sleeping pill, it wasn't working. She lay there in darkness staring up at the ceiling, thinking of Sam and how he affected her.

Chapter 5

It was well past noon, and Dany waited nervously for Sam to come and visit her as he had promised. Martha had come up earlier, bearing a bowl of rich chicken soup and a slice of thickly crusted homemade bread. She nibbled at it, occasionally glancing up at the oak door, waiting for him to appear. Sighing deeply, she reprimanded herself and listened to music from the stereo, curling up on the sofa to read a novel. The nourishing hot soup and bread lulled her to sleep, and the book dropped from her hand, her head lolling against the overstuffed pillows on the sofa arm.

The scent of pine entered her nostrils, and she stirred slowly, her black hair in disarray about her shoulders. Sam finished tucking a blanket in around her body and was rising as she barely opened her eyes. "Oh," she murmured groggily, "I must have fallen asleep...."

"Keep on sleeping, lady. I just came in to check on

you," he whispered, picking up his jacket and throwing it over his broad shoulder.

She was warm, drowsy and content. The husky concern in his voice was a healing balm, and she closed her eyes once again.

It was near evening when Sam gently shook her awake. A flicker of genuine concern crossed his rugged face as he sat down opposite her, folding his hands across his knees. Dany sat up, stiff from being in one position for so many hours.

"Do you realize you have two black eyes?" Sam asked, a grin beginning to appear on his mouth.

Her eyes widened and she gazed across the distance at him. "I do?"

"You look like a raccoon with a mask."

She frowned, slowly got to her feet, and put the blanket on the arm of the sofa. "What time is it?"

"Nearly six. Martha was getting worried about you sleeping so long, so I told her I'd come up and—"

"Check on me," she finished.

"Do you mind?"

"I'm not used to being looked after." She ran her fingers through her rich dark hair and caught a wistful look on his upturned face. Right now the room was comfortable with his presence, and it made her feel at home. It struck her that it seemed so natural—as if they always sat down at the end of each day to discuss little things together. She frowned, noting that he still wore a chambray shirt that was splattered with mud.

"What did you do today to get so dirty?"

"Put up fence posts on the western range. That herd of cattle we brought down from there yesterday had broke through it. Guess they thought the grass was greener on the other side."

"They're worse than horses," she muttered.

"Look, I won't stay," he said, rising. "Do you feel up to joining me downstairs for dinner tonight?"

"Of course," she said readily.

"I'll see you downstairs in half an hour, then. Wear something comfortable. We don't get dressed up like you Easterners do."

After dinner, he guided her into the library where a fire was roaring in the adobe brick fireplace. He handed her a snifter of apricot brandy, and she thanked him, lounging on the sofa in front of the fire. The room was filled with trophy racks of elk, whitetail, bighorn and bear. "Shot by my father and grandfather," he offered in way of explanation.

She looked at him down the length of the couch where he sat, freshly showered in a long-sleeve white shirt and blue jeans. She studied him curiously as the dancing shadows contrasted against the weathered planes of his face. She swirled the contents of brandy, inhaling its sweet fragrance.

"You're not a hunter?" she inquired.

"No. I'm environmentally inclined, Dany. We have bald eagles and condors up here on our ranch, and I'd like to keep them around."

"Condors?"

"Yes, largest birds on earth. They're from the vulture family. Maybe when you're feeling better, we'll take a two-day pack trip into the high country and I'll show you a pair of them. They should be nesting by now."

"I'm glad you didn't kill these poor stuffed animals," she confessed.

It was his turn to study her. "Oh?"

"I would have thought less of you," she admitted softly. "I don't believe in killing for killing's sake. To eat, yes. But look at that lovely elk. Wouldn't he look majestic traversing your land? I'd love to catch a look at him on some early morning ride with his cows." She gave him a shy glance. "Don't mind me, I get carried away with my idealism."

"Who said it was idealism?"

Dany sipped the brandy. "Jean always accused me of being a dreamer of sorts." She gave an embarrassed laugh. "My idea of entertainment was to go to a movie and escape the real world for an hour or two. Silly, isn't it?"

"Not at all. We all have our escapes. I find mine by riding a horse and packing for three or four days into the interior."

The silence grew between them, the fire popping and crackling enjoyably in the background. "I thought I had responsibility," she said quietly. "But from the looks of things, you have a ranch and several other businesses to run."

Sam shrugged, finishing the contents of his snifter and getting up. He lounged his body against the mantel, watching her. "I grew up in it, Dany. By the time my father died, I had learned to run the entire operation."

"Did you want to?"

"What? Run the family business?" He allowed a partial smile to touch his mouth. "You've got an interesting insight into people. Probably why you're such a good horse trainer," he complimented. "Yes and no, to answer your question. At heart, I'm just an ordinary cowpoke who loves the land and the animals. I'd trade the other three companies away and just keep the ranch if I could. Money doesn't mean that much to me in one sense. I'm happier with the earth in my hands and special people to fill the rest of my life."

She colored in a pretty blush, catching the inference of his last huskily spoken words. She wanted to change the subject and remove the emphasis of his gaze upon her. Once again, she felt impelled to open up to him, but she remembered yesterday's encounter and tried to deflect the conversation.

"Did you notice that I had a snaffle in Altair's mouth?" she asked.

"Yes, I did. I suppose you used your beautiful feminine wiles to persuade him to carry it."

"First time I've heard of molasses being used to get a man to do something for you," she taunted dryly, grinning.

Sam returned the smile. "Touché. Did he give you much of a problem?"

"No. He mouthed it at first, and after I got on him, I diverted his attention by doing some figure eights and some simple dressage maneuvers."

"You also used a standing martingale on him. Any trouble with that?"

"Not really. I purposely left it long so he wouldn't feel hindered. I think if I'd made it shorter, he would have thrown a royal fit."

"He's done that already. You're the first trainer he's had that saw his need to be able to raise and lower his neck as he wanted," he said, congratulating her.

Dany warmed beneath his praise. How different

Sam was from Jean. She shuddered inwardly when she recalled how Jean would sharply criticize her continuing efforts to polish off the jumpers for him. Jean wanted a "push-button horse" to ride so that all he had to do was not fall off. She had worked longer hours as a consequence to please her critical ex-husband. Stealing a look up at Sam, Dany tried to suppress the fragile happiness that Sam seemed to be planting inside her. "Do you always give your trainers such support?" she asked.

He tipped his head, watching her lazily. "When they deserve it. Frankly, you've surprised me with the speed of your training methods. Usually it takes weeks to get a horse to adjust to new equipment being used on him. Altair was carrying that snaffle and martingale like it had always been a part of him. Sometimes, lady, I think you're a beautiful witch who has cast a spell over me and my horse."

She managed a smile. "If I were a powerful witch that could cast spells, then I wouldn't have ended up with a fractured nose," she laughed.

He frowned. "You scared me out there yesterday afternoon," he growled.

"What? Falling on my nose? This isn't the first time, you know. I've broken it twice in the last eight years." She grimaced. "But I have to admit this was the most embarrassing."

"Why?"

"The other two were at least in the line of duty," she complained good-naturedly. "Once my hunter went headfirst down a steep bank, and the second time, I got thrown into a stone wall."

Sam grimaced. "You could have fooled me."

"Luck," she promised, "pure, unadulterated good luck. But—" she carefully touched her nose "—I don't know about this time."

"Relax. The doc said it was badly bruised but not broken. Your luck's still holding. Give yourself a week's rest in the meantime. I gave him a ten-mile trot and canter this morning, and I'll gradually have the distance lengthened each day."

"He's in wonderful shape, Sam. You've done an excellent job of conditioning him for the circuit," she said, standing up and giving him the glass. He seemed pleased with her compliment and took her arm, leading her out of the cozy room.

"I'll make a deal with you, Dany," he said, walking her upstairs.

She was acutely aware of his fingers around her arm. It sent a tingling shiver up her limb, making her heart beat faster. "What?" she asked, looking up at him as he stopped and turned her around at her door.

"I've got one of my oldest broodmares foaling in the next five days. If you can babysit her, I'd feel a lot better. That way, you can get the rest you need and still get some physical exercise without overdoing it. The boys that work for me are range men and not grooms. It would take a big worry off my shoulders if you could check in on her while I'm gone."

Her brows moved downward. "Gone?"

Sam slid his hands across her shoulders, his thumb gently tracing the outline of her jaw and neck. "Yes," he answered absently, studying her upturned face intently. "Business down in San Francisco. Board meetings and all that. I'll be back next Friday." He brushed her temple. "Maybe your black eyes will have disappeared by then."

His fingers, rough and callused, caressed her burning skin, a brand trailing fire across her cheek and throat. Her pulse leaped crazily, her heart thudding in response as his fingers tightened against her shoulders, drawing her toward him. "I'll miss you, Dany," he whispered, and his mouth touched her lips in a brief caress. His breath was warm and he smelled of pine and the outdoors. She was losing her grip on reality, his nearness creating a new, more frightening chaos within her yearning body. She made an effort to push away. "No, don't fight," he ordered huskily, and then his mouth claimed her lips, parting them, asking entrance into their moist depths.

Danielle moaned, closing her eyes, crushed against his rock-hard body, vibrantly aware of his maleness pushing insistently against her captured hips. An aching need began to uncoil deep within her lower body, and she felt the hunger for physical contact explode violently within her, leaving her legs weak.

Her lips throbbed with the intensity of his kiss, and she shakily touched them, staring wide-eyed up into Sam's face. She leaned weakly against the door, unable to speak. He reached out, his fingers sliding through her thick tresses.

"A parting gift," he offered huskily, "so you won't forget me over the next five days."

Dany leaned against the boxstall, wistfully content to watch the new bay foal rise unsteadily to her feet. The filly had been born without complications two hours earlier. During the half-hour delivery, Dany had

held the mare's head and offered her pats of encouragement. Everyone seemed delighted with the new baby.
It was Friday afternoon, and no matter what she did,
her thoughts always returned to Sam. His one devastating kiss had shattered her soul and resurrected
an aching awareness of her needs. Each night she lay
awake, making comparisons between Jean and Sam.
How could Sam's one kiss make up for all that she had
been missing in four years of marriage? Jean had never
taken time to explore, tease or arouse. But Sam…she
closed her eyes, resting her head against the gate. He
had deliberately aroused her in a way that had caught
her completely off guard. But it had not caught her
body off guard at all. She sighed, shaking her head and
sinking her hands deeply into the pockets of her jacket.

She walked over to the stud barn, finding Altair
outside eating contentedly in his paddock. As soon as
he saw her, he whinnied and trotted over to the fence
where she stood. Dany patted him affectionately. "You
miss him, too, don't you? Who would have thought
I would miss him this much, Altair? All we do is
fight—" she smiled secretly "—and make up. I guess
that isn't all bad, is it, big boy?"

This morning had been her first ride since bumping
her nose. It had turned out to be an outstanding gallop,
and they had explored about six miles of hilly terrain,
jumping fallen logs and brush thickets along the way.
They had returned by mid-morning, dirty, spattered
with mud and scraped by brambles or low-hanging
twigs, but happy nonetheless. Altair nuzzled her gently,
looking for the sugar cubes she inevitably carried in
her pocket. She smiled, allowing him one cube.

Rain was forecast for early Saturday morning, and

she waited with anticipation, having already put the plastic covering over her hard hat. Giving him one last fond pat, she ambled to the main ranch house. Tomorrow, Altair would begin his water training in earnest—no matter how many spills it took to get him to canter disinterestedly through any puddle. She had chosen a particularly low area where water was sure to collect, and felt that it wouldn't be too slippery for him to pull a tendon or ligament. Grimacing, Dany knew tomorrow would be hell on them both. Going inside, she poured herself a cup of coffee and sat at the kitchen table.

Martha looked up, her face locked in concentration as she furiously mixed a batch of bread dough. "Well, Miss Dany, how is our red horse out there?"

"He doesn't know what he's in for tomorrow morning," she answered.

Martha frowned dramatically. "Well, you just be careful, young lady! I never seen Sam so upset as when you fainted on him in the bathroom. The man was positively beside himself!"

"What?"

"Missy, that man was plumb scared out of his wits when you keeled over last week. Didn't you know that, girl?"

"Why—uh—no," she stammered, blushing fiercely.

"Well," Martha grumbled, "you'd best be extra careful on that stallion. Sam must think an awful lot of you to be that worried. He didn't leave your side from the time you fainted until you woke up some four hours later. Tried to get him to go downstairs and eat. I told him I'd stay with you…but he said no." She shook her gray head. "You're lucky to have a man like that, missy. I hope you appreciate him for it."

Dany got up, shocked by her admissions. Sam Reese never left her side? She set the cup down, even more disturbed, and decided to walk into the quiet living room. Her heart ached with loneliness. She didn't want to admit that she missed him during the last five days. Another part of her injured heart trembled with fear. She had just left a marriage where she thought she had been in love. It was her idealism, she surmised, getting in her way again. Jean always accused her of being a romantic who saw the world through rose-colored glasses. Worriedly, she trudged upstairs to her suite, unsure of which feeling to believe and anxious to hear Sam's voice booming throughout the house, announcing his return.

It was near ten o'clock when Danielle felt tiredness creeping up on her again. Dr. Hart had come over on Thursday and taken the bandage off her nose, warning her that she could still continue to go to bed early and sleep late, since she had borderline anemia. Her nose looked as good as new, and the bruised shadows beneath her eyes had disappeared. She pressed her fingers gently against the bridge of her nose, feeling tenderness but very little pain. As she climbed into bed around ten-thirty she heard the first thunderstorms of the evening rumbling toward the silent ranch house. Snuggling down beneath the goose-down covers, a knife of loneliness twisted in her heart. She had looked forward to seeing Sam, and she was worried about him traveling through the turbulent weather. Gratefully, her tired body gave out on her fretting mind, and she slept deeply as lightning forked across the black, roiling sky.

It was raining heavily when she got up at six o'clock the next morning and made her way down to the stud barn. She looked toward the parking area, disappointed at not seeing Sam's pickup there. He was already half a day late returning from San Francisco. The rain was biting and the wind surprisingly cold, sweeping down from Canada and dropping temperatures below normal for this time of year. It didn't matter. Altair was going to get his baptism in water today. Or fire, depending upon how he looked at it, she thought wryly.

Mounting up, she urged the red stallion out of the barn, asking him to move into a slow trot. Snorting, the thoroughbred bowed his head against the slashing rain. Dany brought down a pair of plastic goggles, protecting her eyes, but drastically limiting her vision. The cooler weather made him more energetic than usual. Altair moved out briskly under the sensitive monitoring of her hands and legs.

After a mile, she pushed him into a slow canter, his long legs eating up the distance easily. The stallion turned a dark sienna from being thoroughly wetted by the rain. They were both getting soaked to the skin, and twin jets of spray and mist shot from his flared nostrils as he continued to splash through the water that surrounded him on all sides. Dany felt moisture trickling down between her slicker and neck, realizing she would be thoroughly soaked within another half hour. His body moved fluidly beneath her, and she shouted praise into his ear, reaching forward and patting the crest of his neck.

The real test began at the end of the gray, mist-filled valley. By now, there were big puddles, and Dany felt the sorrel begin to lag and try to avoid them. She deliberately shifted her full weight, throwing the animal to the right or left so that his hooves sank into the two inches of water. They both worked hard and with total concentration for at least an hour before Dany pulled him down to a slow trot. Altair blew and snorted, his massive chest gleaming with sweat, mud and rainwater.

She shivered in the saddle, suddenly realizing that the rain had turned into huge, wet flakes of snow. To her the month of April meant spring weather. But to her dismay, the visibility deteriorated rapidly, and in just a few minutes she had trouble seeing. Altair whinnied worriedly, prancing to the left toward the towering mountains that were suddenly obscured by a thick curtain of snow pushed along with gusting winds. The flakes were partly made up of ice, and they stung Dany's face. Bowing her head, she tried to protect herself as she urged Altair into a canter.

Another horrifying thought occurred to her: They were at eight thousand feet in the Sierras. Gradually, old stories of freak snowstorms in the Rockies came to life in her memory. The wind was howling around them, and snow was collecting in inches. Altair was frantic, tossing his head skyward and lunging against the confines of the bit, wanting to get home to the safety of his barn. Grimly, she decided that she had no choice; to allow a risky gallop in the blinding snow would invite a fall and he could break a leg. She had to fight him every inch of the way and pray to God that they didn't get lost.

Only one thought comforted her—this horse knew the way home. She allowed Altair just enough slack on the reins to sense his way toward the ranch. Her hands lost all feeling, and ice collected on Altair's muzzle and eyelashes. A series of small hills rose like gray shadows in front of them, and Dany slowed the stallion even more; the snow was now four inches deep and continuing to accumulate at a frightening rate. Luckily, the thoroughbred was a trained hunter and knew the consistency of the ground beneath his hooves. At one point, they slid sideways, but gingerly Altair collected himself and made a half leap, landing in a bank of drifting snow. Dany called encouragement to the stallion, continually patting his neck and crooning to him. She was frightened but believed in the intelligence of the horse to find the ranch.

Suddenly, Altair pitched forward and Dany was flung over his head, landing with solid impact in a mound of snow. The stallion scrambled shakily to his feet, blowing hard, his head hanging from the exertion of the trek. Dany shook her head, thankful for her hard hat, feeling a depression that had been made in the side of it. She must have struck a rock. Crawling to her knees, she reached out, picking up Altair's slippery reins. She reeled against him momentarily, blackness closing in on her, clutching at the saddle, until it passed. Oh, God, she thought dazedly, what if I don't get him home? What if he breaks a leg out here because of my stupidity? Those thoughts forced her back into the saddle. She leaned forward, trying to shield herself from the screaming storm. Altair hung his head, more content to continue at a plodding walk through the knee-deep snow.

Dany gave a cry of relief as she saw the shadow of the stud barn suddenly appear before them. Slipping off Altair, she collapsed against the door, pounding on it weakly with her fist. Altair whinnied loudly, his bugling cry soaked up by the blizzard.

She felt the door give and struggled to stand as several men rushed forward.

"Dany!" Sam thundered, lifting her upward.

"Thank God," she whispered, pulling Altair within the warm barn. "Sam, Sam, you've got to look at Altair's leg. We fell…maybe a mile from here." Her voice was weak, trembling, and she clung to him in order to remain standing.

"I'm not worried about the damn horse," he growled, forcing her around to face him. "I was worried sick about you! Are you all right?"

"Just a headache." Her teeth were chattering.

Sam handed the reins over to Jake. "Get him rubbed down. I'll come out later and check his legs."

"Right, boss."

"Can you walk?" he demanded.

Dany removed the goggles and hard hat, her fingers nerveless. They dropped to the floor, and she bent to pick them up. "Give me a moment," she whispered thickly. "My hands, Sam. I can't feel a thing."

"Leave that gear. Jake will bring it in later. Come on, let's get you inside and get these wet clothes off you."

Her black hair had become unknotted during the fall and hung in thick, wet ropes about her shoulders. Martha brought blankets up to her room and peppermint tea laced with hundred proof whiskey. Dany shook so badly that she could barely undress herself. Her fingers seemed frostbittten, and she sat on the bed as Sam unbuttoned the rain slicker and then her blouse, pulling them impatiently off her cool skin. "I'm sorry," she murmured, her teeth chattering every few seconds.

He gave her a dark, angry look, pulling off her riding boots, sending them flying across the floor. "Why didn't you tell Martha where you had gone?"

She gave him a blank stare. "I did—"

"God, Dany, we looked everywhere for you. The moment I got home this morning I knew the weather was going to turn sour. Martha said you went out to get Altair used to the water. How far did you go?"

She shivered convulsively as he jerked a heavy woolen blanket around her skimpily clad form and then helped her to the bathroom. "I—I think you call it the Bluff."

He groaned, shaking his head. "That's nearly thirteen miles away. Are you telling me you came all the way back through that?" he asked disbelievingly, making her sit on a stool while he turned on the faucets to the bathtub.

Dany closed her eyes, trembling uncontrollably now. "Y-yes. Sam… I'm so—so cold," she whispered.

He straightened up and put his hands on his hips. "I'll get Martha to help you," he said gruffly.

As the feeling started coming back to her fingers, she felt like crying. Martha's tough exterior melted as she continued to dip Dany's blue fingers back into the water. "This is the only way, Dany. I'm sorry it hurts so much. We caught it just in time. Why, if you'd gone fifteen or twenty minutes longer, you might have lost them. You'll feel better soon. Here, have another drink of this tea. That'll warm your innards up."

Dany peeked warily up at Sam as he reentered the room after she had managed to dry off with Martha's help. She had found a long flannel nightgown and gotten it over her head, wanting nothing more than the warmth that the bed offered. Martha hurried down to the kitchen to warm up some beef broth.

"How's Altair?" she squeaked, her throat still feeling constricted.

"He'll be fine. He came out of this mess a lot better than you did." Sam shook his head, pulling a chair up to the bed. "Lady, you get in more trouble than a yearling colt does, you know that?"

"Ever since I came west, Sam, I've been nothing more than a liability. Maybe you ought to let me go back home—back East where—"

He growled, "This is your home for now."

She looked at him sharply. "You mean you're still going to force me to show Altair?"

"Do I have a choice?" he asked dryly. "I have to get my money back from all the medical bills you're incurring." He stared at her. "Are you always so accident-prone, Dany?"

"Normally, no."

"It wasn't your fault, really. How could you know that at this time of year we get freak blizzards?" He reached out, capturing her hand. "I went crazy trying to find you, Dany. I had seven men out on horseback searching for you until the snow started. And we had to come in. I couldn't afford to lose someone else to this damn storm."

"I need an Easterner's survival guide to the West, Sam," she muttered, completely shaken by his gesture.

"Starting tomorrow, I intend to give you a short course in it, believe me," he answered grimly. "How's your head and nose feel?"

"I've got a slight headache is all. My nose survived fine," she admitted, feeling the warmth of his presence freeing her at last from the fear that had shadowed her trek home to the barn. "I just wonder if my stay here is going to continue to be so eventful."

Sam groaned, getting to his feet. "I hope not."

"Sam, you should have seen Altair," she began. "He went through all kinds of water situations! He balked a little at first, but gradually he was going through them like a champ. He trusted me enough to let me guide him through them. And you should have seen him on the way home! He's so sure-footed. I'll tell you, I'm not going to worry about riding that horse in a muddy eventing field. He's the kind that will fall on his nose or hindquarters to get up and push on. He's simply magnificent."

Sam rested his hands loosely on his hips, enjoying her enthusiasm. "Dany, you damn near got killed out there less than two hours ago and now you're bubbling about that stallion." He sighed. "Well, I guess I should have known better. But it proves me out—you are a rider as well as a trainer."

Chapter 6

"You didn't hear what I asked you at the kitchen table downstairs earlier. I wanted to take you into Placerville at first opportunity and get you some Western boots, a hat and wrangling jeans. Since the doc has put your work duties on a thirty-day suspension, I thought you might let me introduce you to how a rancher makes a living."

There was a hint of excitement in Sam's voice, and Dany smiled. She had been resting up for two days now, and Sam's enthusiasm was catching. "You mean you're going to make a cowgirl out of me?"

Sam laughed. "Hardly. With your past accident record, I think it best you sit astride a good quarter horse and just watch. We'll be taking the main herd up to high pasture very shortly. It's an eight-day trek into the heart of the Sierras. Juan will be bringing the chuck wagon along, and we'll be eating and sleeping out under the stars. How about it?"

A tremor of excitement coursed through her, and she sat up a little straighter. "But what about Altair? Who will exercise him?"

"He'll be my personal riding horse on the trip."

The shock was apparent in her expression, and Sam provided an explanation.

"Dany, long before he ever became an eventing horse, he was a cow horse. Remember?"

She laughed. "I don't know of another eventer who has such a background except for Nautilus."

Sam rose, smiling. "Wait till you see him work. I might even let you climb aboard and cut a cow or two on him. It's an experience you'll never forget."

Dany stood, walking at his shoulder until they came to the door separating the suites. "It sounds wonderful, Sam. I don't know how good I am at camping because I've never done it before."

"No Girl Scout training?" he teased warmly, looking down at her.

She grinned. "None. I think I'll be a liability."

"Never," he whispered, reaching out and caressing her pale cheek.

Dany felt the roughness of his fingers against her skin, and a tingle shivered through her body. He was so close. So dizzyingly masculine. She was mesmerized by the silvered fire deep within his darkening eyes as he hungrily studied her. Her lips parted and her breathing became shallow. Unconsciously, she leaned her cheek toward his hand, feeling its very fiber.

Reluctantly, he dropped his hand. "You get some rest, Dany," he ordered thickly. "We'll talk more of this tonight at dinner."

She stood there awkwardly, feeling as if the sun

had suddenly left the sky. She closed the door quietly, walking thoughtfully back to the couch. He could have kissed her then, just as he had outside her door before he had left for San Francisco. Touching her lips, she found herself wanting him to take her into his arms again. The admission startled her. Looking at her watch, she realized that it would be five hours before she saw him again. And somehow, that was an excruciatingly long time to wait for his return. It was well past eight that evening when Sam entered through the kitchen, carefully placing his muddy boots outside the door. Dany had shared dinner with Martha much earlier and was helping her clean up the dishes. She noted the tiredness in Sam's eyes; there were smudges of gray shadowing beneath each one.

"Go get cleaned up, Sam, we'll warm up your dinner."

Sam managed a small smile of gratefulness as he leaned over, placing a kiss on Martha's hair. "Thanks. I'm sorry I'm late."

Dany dried her hands on the towel, leaning against the draining board. "Did you have problems, Sam?"

"Yes. But I'll tell you more about it later." He glanced over his shoulder at the small table. "Will you join me while I eat dinner?" he asked.

Dany colored. Martha raised one eyebrow, watching her expectantly. "Well—yes, if you want...."

Martha had gone off to bed, and Dany had just finished setting the table when Sam appeared silently at the door.

"Smells delicious," he said, sitting down.

"I'll bet you're starved," she said, placing the steaming portion of lamb's ribs on the blue and white porcelain plate.

"Beyond starvation," he promised fervently. "Sit down," he coaxed. "I can wait on myself."

"Let me," she protested. "Martha says you fend too well for yourself. So sit there and I'll bring over the mashed potatoes and peas."

A lulling warmth settled pleasantly over the kitchen as she served the vegetables. There was something elemental and relaxing in sharing dinner. Without another word, Sam dug hungrily into the food. For the next fifteen minutes, very few words were traded, while Dany fussed over the dishes and made a new pot of coffee. Standing at the sink, she stole a glance over at him. His hair was dark and gleamed wetly from the recent shower. He had traded the dirty chambray shirt and jeans for a clean pair of jeans and a long-sleeved white shirt. She marveled at the contrast between the dark hair on the back of his hands and the cotton material. He glanced up, wiping his mouth with the napkin.

"Delicious," he murmured.

Dany filled his ceramic mug with coffee. "Thank Martha. All I did was volunteer to peel the potatoes."

"Food cooked with love always tastes better," he persisted. "Let's have our coffee in the study."

She trailed behind, a cup balanced between her hands. Sam motioned for her to sit on the couch facing the blazing fireplace. Curling up comfortably on it, Dany acknowledged that the intimacy of the atmosphere was inducing her to relax. Sam leaned his tall body up against the mantel, sipping his coffee.

"You looked right at home in the kitchen," he commented, a hint of mirth in his low-pitched voice.

"I love to cook," she confided. "And I haven't had a chance to do much of it in the last few years." She gave an embarrassed shrug. "In my case, cooking helps me relax after a long day of fighting with headstrong young colts who think they know more than I do."

"I guess that for you, kitchen work isn't a drudgery that some women feel it is."

Dany laughed fully. "After shoveling and mucking out stalls for three-quarters of my life, Sam Reese, you *know* kitchen work is preferable!"

He laughed. "Come on, you have to agree that there's something therapeutic about cleaning out stalls. Admit it."

"Oh, you'll get no argument there. I like stretching my muscles and working up a sweat." She wrinkled her nose. "Not very feminine, huh?"

He shrugged. "I don't like women who are lazy. I enjoy someone who relishes hard physical labor as much as I do. I like sharing the beauty of this place with someone who can stand and watch the sun rise over the Sierras or sit on a rainy afternoon and listen to the rain fall." He smiled self-consciously, his voice vibrant with conviction and his eyes darkened with the passion behind his words.

Dany was moved by his sudden admission. She was secretly thrilled at being allowed to share some of his innermost thoughts about himself and what made him happy. And incredibly, she felt herself agreeing with his personal philosophy completely. The crystalline moment shimmered between them as they looked at one another.

Sam finished off the coffee and went to the liquor cabinet, pouring two brandies. He came over, handed her a snifter and sat down near her on the couch. Leaning back, he placed his booted feet up on the ponderosa pine coffee table in front of them and exhaled softly. "This is heaven," he murmured appreciatively.

Dany watched him, noticing the lines of tension melting from around his eyes and mouth. Did it take so little to make him tranquil? She was surprised to realize that she was just as relaxed. A fireplace, a study built of dark pine and padded with a thick orange carpet, plus a man contributed to her contentment. But it wasn't just any man. It was Sam Reese. It was an exquisite torment, she admitted hesitantly to herself; and when he was away on business, she missed him acutely. Yet, when he was near, her emotions became inexplicably confused.

Sam rolled his head to the left, barely opening his eyes, drinking in her features. "This is my favorite time of night," he confided huskily. "Good food, good drink and a good woman. What else is there?"

Her fingers followed the delicate curve of the crystal snifter, and she choked upon an unnamed emotion that his low voice had coaxed suddenly to life. He was a scant eight inches from her body and it would be so easy to reach out and touch his arm or to rest her head against his broad, incredibly strong-looking shoulder. She sighed deeply, marshaling her scattered, tumultuous feelings. "I thought you wanted to talk to me further about Placerville."

His brows drew momentarily downward in unspoken displeasure for the disruption of the fragile truce between them. With a slow motion, he roused himself back into a sitting position. Placing the snifter on the coffee table, he murmured, "So I did. Have you decided to go with us on the drive?"

"Why not? If you can put up with a tenderfoot, I may as well try it."

"That's one thing I like about you, Dany. You don't let a new experience frighten you."

She managed a weak smile. "Oh, yes, I do. I find the past and experiences from it still stop me in some ways. Your initial proposal to come out here did, believe me."

He grinned ruefully. "A little friendly persuasion changed your mind, though."

"If that's your idea of friendly persuasion, I'd hate to meet you as an adversary in one of your other business ventures."

Sam nodded thoughtfully. "You're right about that. Although, I'm not unfair, I do enjoy the challenge. Those corporate businesses are a bore compared to running a ranch. Well, would you like to drive down to Placerville tomorrow morning with me? Martha wants me to pick up some dry goods for her. Maybe you can help me with that. I'm always terrible at getting the right brand or the best bargain."

Dany smiled. "A man with your prestige and finances and you're worried Martha will swat you with that wooden spoon," she teased gently.

"Not really, Dany. I learned a long time ago that money is not the key to personal happiness. I could be dirt-farmer poor and still enjoy life."

"Until the last six years, I was dirt-farmer poor," she commented.

His disturbing gray gaze met her eyes. "And were you happy?"

Dany's heart began to beat more strongly. She licked

her lips. "Yes. Yes, I was very happy. Of course, when my hunters began making strong showings on the major Grand Prix circuit, that was great, too."

"And then what happened?" he inquired huskily. "When I look in your blue eyes I see a terrible anguish, Dany. You aren't happy now. What will it take to erase that pain?"

Her throat constricted with tears, and she tore her gaze from him. His concern was evident by the compassionate glint in his eyes. How much harder this was to handle than Jean's acid retorts. Sam's way did not allow her to flippantly disregard his curiosity. Compressing her lips, she forced the words out, hoping to hide the strain of feeling behind them. "As I said before, the divorce is still too fresh."

Sam shook his head and reached out, gently guiding her chin toward him until their eyes met. "No, lady. There's more than that. You're so incredibly transparent. I watch the color of your eyes change. I see a shadow in there. It goes deeper than a divorce, Dany. There's a hurt…" He groped to find the correct words.

His fingers were like a branding iron to her flesh, and she sought to escape his touch. Dany fled off the couch, setting the snifter down more loudly than she intended on the table. Walking to the fireplace, she stopped, defensively folding her arms against her breasts. Why was he able to get beyond her walls that were meant to keep people out of her private anguish? An impulsive urge to confide in him burgeoned, but she checked the desire out of long habit. She'd been injured once by her innate honesty in a relationship. She had always been truthful with Jean, and where did it get her? *Nowhere,* a bitter voice shrilled warningly inside her head. The trust that she used to have had been utterly destroyed, and it made it that much harder to trust again.

"Just because you've forced me to honor a contract signed by my ex-husband doesn't give you the right to question me personally," she flung back heatedly.

Sam rose, his eyes narrowing. "No, it doesn't," he agreed. He hooked his thumbs in his belt, standing there like a bulwark of undeniable strength. "Why won't you allow anyone close to you, Dany? Are you afraid to give even a small piece of yourself to another human being? Is the cost that great to you?"

Her azure eyes widened. "Stop it!" she cried harshly. "You have no right—"

In one fluid, unbroken motion, Sam was there at her side. She tried to back away, but his hands upon her shoulders gently imprisoned her. A small cry broke from her lips as she tried to shake off his hold. His fingers tightened until she stood trembling within his grasp. His face was inches away from her own, and she felt the moistness of his breath against her hair and cheek.

"I want the right to know you, Dany," he whispered huskily. "Look at me! Why are you so afraid to meet someone's eyes?" His fingers captured her chin, forcing her to look up into his pewter gray gaze.

Her heart pounded without respite in her chest, and she gasped for breath. He was too close! She had to escape the virile masculinity that threatened to overwhelm her senses. The color of his eyes darkened to slate, and he released her chin, his fingers featherlight, caressing the length of her clean jaw and slender throat.

"There," he whispered, "that's better. My wild, injured filly. So afraid of a man's hands. You flinch every time I touch you. I won't hurt you, Dany. I only want to make you happy," he murmured thickly.

Her lips parted as his mouth descended gently upon her own. He tasted, touched and outlined her lips with quivering tenderness, asking entrance, but not demanding it. A soft moan vibrated within her throat, and she tried to pull away, deluged by a tidal wave of desire. Sam's hand pressed insistently against her back, pulling her firmly against his hard body. Her heart cried for the protection and gentleness he offered. His tongue traced her lips once again, teasing, enticing. Her senses reeled, plunging headlong down an endless corridor. The pressure of his mouth increased and instinctively she melted against him, a supple willow, within his masterful embrace. A hundred careening sensations exploded within her as his tongue entwined with hers. She was aware of the roughness of his skin against her cheek, the heady masculine smell, the kneading, gentling stroke of his fingers against the length of her spine. Slowly, ever so slowly, he drew away from her wet, throbbing lips. His eyes were a fiery silver gray, a hungry shadow within them that momentarily frightened her. Gradually, he helped her regain her balance, holding her as if she were a fragile crystal ornament within his arms.

Dany could not tear her gaze from his rugged face. Her nostrils flared as she experienced an overwhelming sensation of attraction to him. She was trembling outwardly, and she could feel him tightly controlling his own quivering need for her. Tears welled up into her eyes, quickly streaking her flushed cheeks. Sam frowned, taking his fingers and caressing her skin.

"Don't…" she protested weakly, "don't, Sam. I—I can't take this," she croaked. "Not yet…"

His eyes grew troubled and he frowned, carefully cradling her chin. "Honey, I would never do anything to hurt you. I wanted to show you that sharing something didn't mean it had to be painful."

Dany took a long, unsteady breath, feeling safe within his arms. She made an effort to disengage herself, but her legs wouldn't move. She felt pleasantly immobilized by his strength and the aura of magnetism that swirled around him. "Sam," she begged, her voice scratchy, "I don't think I could take that type of pain again." She touched her throat, swallowing hard against a forming lump.

He caressed her hair, his fingers trailing through the silken tresses. "But don't you see," he coaxed thickly. "You must start to trust in something again. It's healing, Dany."

She slowly looked up, her eyes wide and dazed with emotional exhaustion that the last few minutes of traumatic events had produced. "Don't you see?" she cried with anguish in her voice. "I don't know how to act. I'm confused. I—I thought I knew who I was…what I wanted. And it's all changed now, Sam. I feel so hopelessly adrift…a cork in some endless ocean. If I don't know myself, or trust my own perceptions of people around me yet, how can I reach out and trust another man?"

His expression was still concerned, but his arms slipped free of her body and his voice sounded discouraged when he said, "How much of your soul did he strip from you, Dany? How could anyone do that much damage?"

Her heart felt serrated by his blunt questions. She shut her eyes tightly. "I'm sorry I don't meet your expectations. I can't overcome this distrust the way you expect me to."

"Dany," Sam began, speaking softly, "you are a woman with an incredible training record handling some of the mightiest and most powerful horseflesh in the U.S., and I guess that I've expected the same kind of toughness and resiliency in you emotionally. You are hurt far more deeply than I ever was from my marriage." He gave a slight shrug of his broad shoulders. "If I ever meet that ex of yours, I'm liable to wring his damn neck for what he's done to you, Dany."

She colored fiercely, her eyes widening at the growl in his voice. Throughout her life she had fought for every inch of ground that she had won and without help—except from her riding master. In Terrence she had found a friend, a mentor and someone she could lean on when she got tired. Sam's face held a tenderness that she had never seen before as he watched her through his half-closed eyes. A shiver of long-forgotten care enveloped her. In Sam she saw the beginning of a friendship...of trust and perhaps most importantly, honesty.

"Oh, Sam..." she whispered painfully. "I'm sorry, too... I just feel so torn inside and unsure of myself. You're strong and you seem to know exactly who you are and where you're going." She spread her hands out before her in a gesture of futility. "I don't know where I am."

He caught her right hand, capturing it firmly within his grasp. "You're here with me, honey. That's all that matters and all that counts," he urged.

Tears slid down her cheeks and she sniffed. "I know...and I'm glad. Really, I am. It's just that I'm— scared." Somehow his gesture of gentleness had allowed her the courage to confront her worst fear. She felt Sam's fingers tighten momentarily on her hand.

"Scared of what?" he coaxed softly. "I can see a shadow in your eyes, haunting you when you're alone. It can't be so bad as all that."

She reclaimed her hand, trying to dry her cheeks of the tears, and gave a helpless laugh. "Yes, it is. At least it is to me."

"Tell me," he said, setting down the snifter on the coffee table.

The silence grew in the study until there was only the crackling and popping of the fire. Dany took in a breath and exhaled slowly. "It's about riding in shows, Sam," she forced out, her voice strained. "I can't ride for you. I can train, yes...but, please, don't ask me to ride Altair in a show." Her voice trembled and she stole a glance up at him. "Four years ago, right after I met Jean, I rode a thoroughbred called Crusader's Prince." She watched his face change when she mentioned the jumper's name and froze.

"Don't tell me—" he began.

Dany chewed on her lower lip. "Yes, I was the one." She clasped her hands in a nervous gesture in her lap. "Now do you see why I'm afraid to ride, Sam? I killed a horse, a very valuable, expensive horse, because of my own inexperience. Crusader was the top money-making jumper in the U.S., and I took him over a wall too fast. He had to be shot because of a broken leg. I miscounted the strides between jumps." She held back a sob, misery in her voice. "Oh, Sam, I can't ride Altair...it wouldn't be fair to you or to him. He's too magnificent to be killed. Don't you see?" she begged, her voice scratchy with tears.

Sam leaned forward, pulling her hands apart and holding them. "I do remember Crusader having to be destroyed, Dany. But if my memory serves me correctly the course had received record amounts of rain the night before and the ground was a muddy hell. And you weren't the only one who had problems. If I recall, one other animal had to be destroyed and two riders went to the hospital."

She was reliving the horror of the entire sequence in her mind as she had done thousands of times before. "Jean warned me not to ride the horse. He said I didn't have the experience," she said softly. "He was right, you know. I had no business doing it."

Sam snorted. "I'll just bet your ex never let you forget it, too."

"I just don't have what it takes. I don't have that fine edge of timing in critical jumps."

"The hell you don't. Look, Dany, let's treat this problem as if we were training a young horse."

"What?"

"What is the basis of training a horse to jump?"

She gave him a perplexed look. "Patience and schooling a horse over low, tightly spaced jumps at first and then working up gradually in height to larger jumps. Why?"

"If we are going to get you over your fear of riding Altair at a show, don't you think we ought to do the same thing for you? We could design some courses and gradually make them higher and more intricate until you feel confident on Altair. By that time, Santa

Barbara will be around the corner and you'll both be ready to take that show by storm. What do you think about the plan?"

The roughness of his hand upon her fingers gave her a comfort she had never experienced before. Her heart ached with fear and unsureness. "Sam, I just couldn't live with myself if I destroyed another horse because of my—"

"Dammit, you listen to me! Crusader would have died out there with another seasoned jumper because of lousy footing. The judges should have canceled the run and rescheduled it for another day, but they didn't. If you can train jumpers to become aware of their strides and realize their takeoff point to scale a jump, you can ride in any show successfully." His voice gathered conviction. "Honey, Altair is one of the most sure-footed horses you've ever had the pleasure of meeting. That's where his questionable background as a cow horse comes in. He's used to scrambling up and down rocky ravines chasing wild cows or negotiating steep hills and jumping over logs hidden by underbrush. In the years I've owned him, he's never fallen once." His voice quivered with encouragement. "Honey, you *can* do it. In a way, both you and Altair are scarred by the past. But your weaknesses aren't in the same area. Together, you're complementary and strong. The stallion trusts you and that's nine-tenths of the battle right there. You know a horse will go the distance if he trusts you."

She could only stare, mesmerized by his confidence in her abilities. "Both of you trust me and I don't even trust myself," she admitted. "I can't promise you anything, Sam. This fear is so big in me that I break out in a sweat every time I think about it. That's why I fought so hard to stay in Virginia. I didn't want out of the contract because of Altair's problems. I just didn't have the courage to ride him because of the past."

"That was four years ago, Dany, and you've accumulated that much more experience under your belt." He reluctantly released her hand. "Get to bed, you're looking tired," he urged softly. "We'll get you suited up in boots and jeans tomorrow and then we'll set out for the pastures in a couple days."

Chapter 7

The morning of the ride was crisp, cold and clear. The sun was still behind the craggy crown of the mountains as they moved their mounts down the meadow toward the milling herd in the far distance. Dany sat happily in the Western saddle, snug in the beautiful sheepskin coat Sam had given her that morning. She glanced down at the new cowhide chaps that would protect her legs from bushes and brambles on the long ride, and just shook her head. She felt indescribably happy as she glanced around at the ten hands who rode in front of her. It was as if she had stepped into a time machine and had been transported magically back to the days of the Chisholm Trail. Her gaze lingered on the man heading up the group: Sam Reese. He was a tall and broad-shouldered man sitting with a born ease in the saddle. Altair, his copper coat shining like red fire, sidled and pranced beneath him. Her breath caught in her throat as she watched them move with a primal grace and beauty she had never imagined. Dany wanted to join him but she checked the childish desire. She elected to remain with Juan, instead.

Juan, the cook for the drive, sat happily ensconced on the seat of the chuck wagon. He clucked in Spanish to his team of bays and then winked over at Dany. "Your first drive, *señora?*" he shouted above all the noise.

Dany smiled. "The first! It's so exciting."

"*Sí,* it is. But also, hard work. The boss going to make you work like the rest of his hands?"

"I don't know. I told him I wanted to help and not just watch."

Juan grinned, showing the gap between his front teeth. His dark brown eyes danced with merriment. "You ride one of the best cutting horses on the ranch, *señora,* do you know that?"

Dany looked down at Bomarc in surprise. "No. You mean if a cow bolts from the herd, he'll go after it?"

"*Sí, sí.* Aye! He's a cutting devil. Only one other horse can match him and that's Altair." Juan waved his finger at Dany in good humor. "You must be a very good rider or the boss would never let you ride the gray. *Sí,* I think he wants you to work."

Dany laughed fully, feeling so many weights and shadows from the past slipping off her shoulders. It must be the beauty of the morning, the excitement-charged air and her sense of adventure that was doing it. "Looks like I have to earn my keep, doesn't it?"

Juan grinned and nodded his head emphatically. "*Sí, sí.* The gray, he likes to work drag," he explained. "It will be up to you and these other hands to establish a good speed for the herd. If a cow breaks, you must hang on and point him. He'll know what to do."

They arrived at the main holding pen almost an hour later, and Dany sensed Bomarc's anticipation, the gelding's ears twitching as the plaintive mooing of the cows, calves and steers heightened. The main gates were dragged open, and the first few Herefords drifted through to the freedom of the lush green pastures carpeted with white patches of snow. Horses snorted and pawed. Cowboys remained slouched in the saddles, the hats drawn down across their eyes. At one point, Sam swung by to check on her. She marveled at the glint in his gray eyes that gave away his excitement. He smiled, touching the brim of his hat as he cantered Altair past where she stood. Dany smiled shyly, basking in the light of his obvious care. Two border collies barked and snapped at the heels of several anxious cows, keeping them in line. Mud and slush were flung in all directions as a few Herefords broke from the main group. Dany watched in admiration as the chunky quarter horses spurted out after their rebellious charges, quickly bringing them back into line.

Finally, over two thousand head of cattle were loose and ambling across the floor of the valley under the careful guidance of the ranch hands. Bomarc had broken out in a light sweat, columns of steam flowing out of his flared nostrils as he airily pranced along. Dany leaned down, crooning softly to the horse, understanding his excitement because it was affecting her just as much. As the herd stretched out over half a mile, Dany lost sight of Sam. He remained near the head of the herd with several other wranglers. Juan brought up the rear with the chuck wagon, its wheels sinking deeply into the freshly plowed mud that had been churned up by the cattle. She was grateful for the sheepskin coat, because, even though the sun had risen above the peaks, the morning was still chilly.

A cow broke from the herd close to where she rode. A ranch hand gave a shout, pointing at Dany. Without any warning, Bomarc swung deftly to the right, galloping hard to thwart the escape. Dany clung to the gelding, her heart rate soaring with adrenaline. The reins remained loose in her hands to give the horse the freedom of his head as she leaned into the next move that Bomarc made. The gelding neatly sealed off the Hereford's escape by coming alongside and forcing it to return to the bulk of the herd. Dany laughed gaily, patting her horse as the gelding pranced back to his original station, blowing and snorting. "You love it!" she accused the horse.

A cowpoke cantered over, grinning. "That was some pretty fancy riding, Mrs. Daguerre," he complimented.

Dany thanked him, aware that she had been splattered by mud during the escapade.

"Looks like the boss was right. You can ride. Want to take this side of the herd?"

"Sure. Why not?"

"Good enough. If you or the gray get tired, we'll change you off for a quieter spot."

"Will this be busy?" she asked, wiping a fleck of mud off her face.

"Shortly, ma'am." He pointed toward the foothills looming in the distance. "The herd will want to turn back the minute we reach the hills. It's our job to make sure they go up there. Take that lasso on the right side of your saddle and keep it in your hand. You can use it to haze some of them back by slapping it against your chaps. The sound scares them into thinking twice before trying to break."

Dany nodded. "Got it."

"Okay, it's all yours, ma'am." He tipped the brim of his hat to her and spun his quarter horse around. Dany shook her head, elated. She suddenly caught sight of Sam as he skirted the herd, unable to tear her gaze from his form. Dany was barely able to contain her excitement as he pulled to a stop in front of her. He was smiling broadly.

"I see you got your first taste of chasing a stray."

"Yes. Mud from head to toe. But I loved it! Why didn't you tell me Bomarc was good at this?"

He turned Altair around, riding next to her. "A good rider deserves a good horse," he answered.

"I thought you wanted me safe where I couldn't hurt myself."

His gaze was warming, their legs touching briefly. Dany felt the pleasant shock of contact with his body. He squinted up toward the head of the herd, briefly watching another Hereford trying to make an unsuccessful break.

"Look, I don't want you to think I expect you to put in a twelve-hour day, Dany. It means changing mounts at least three times. Just put Bomarc back in with the others in the remuda and ask Pete for another horse." He reached over, his leather glove rough against the smoothness of her cheek. Gently, he rubbed a smudge of mud away. "You look beautiful even when you're dirty," he teased.

Her breath caught in her throat at the simple gesture.

His hand was so large. Powerful. Yet, he had been gentle. She met his smiling eyes. "Dress me up and can't take me anywhere," she agreed, laughing.

"Listen, I'll see you when we break for chow at noontime. In the meantime, let Bomarc take care of you," he ordered.

Dany watched him ride off down the line, deciding that Sam was a centaur; half man, half horse. And what a magnificent team he and Altair made. She sighed, painfully aware of how happy he made he feel. Frowning momentarily, she returned to her duties, unable to probe too closely the joy simmering within her heart. She would take each day one at a time.

The sun was high by the time they broke for lunch. Now in the foothills, Dany found the chaps invaluable. The brush was knee high and occasionally thorny. Already, several wide scratches had marred the flawless surface of her chaps. She dismounted from a black quarter horse who was panting and wet with sweat. Tiredly, she leaned against the mare, her legs feeling rubbery. How many cows had they cut? God, she had lost count! Sam was right; it was hard, never-ending work. Stupid cows, she thought, lifting the hat off her head and wiping the perspiration from her brow.

Tying the black on a hastily erected rope that stretched between two towering pines, she loosened the saddle cinch to make the horse more comfortable. The snow was deeper in the shade beneath the pines, and she slogged her way through it out into the sunlight to where Juan was dishing out the chow at the chuck wagon. Picking up an aluminum plate, she waited in line. Discreetly, she looked around for Sam. Why should she be looking for him anyway? Juan filled her plate with a fragrant concoction of steaming chili and hot corn bread, handing her a cup of thick, black coffee. Dany found an old unoccupied log and sat down, decidedly starved.

"Mind if I join you?" came Sam's voice across her shoulder.

Dany lifted her chin, looking to her right. "Oh…no, of course not. Where were you?"

He straddled the log, facing her, and set the mug of coffee down by his foot. "Looking for me? That's a good sign," he teased genially. "I was making one last tour of the line before I came in. Trail bosses are the first up in the morning and the last to go to bed at night."

Dany returned to eating the spicy chili. It brought tears to her eyes. "You sound more like a babysitter. Are you pleased with the progress of the herd?" she asked.

"So far, so good," he agreed. "How are you? You look a little flushed."

She warmed at his concern. "It's the chili," she laughed. "You mean you can actually see me behind my mask of mud?"

"Nothing could hide your beauty, Dany," he returned fervently.

"Thanks! And I suppose you're going to tell me there's no shower or hot tub available tonight?"

"We'll be camping near a lake tonight. You can get a washcloth and towel from Juan and get cleaned up." He smiled recklessly. "Think you'll make it?"

"Why not? I love this. All of it," she confided.

Sam frowned momentarily, saying nothing. "You really like it?" he probed darkly.

Dany was thrown off by his sudden seriousness. "Yes, of course. How could I lie about something like this," she said gesturing around the makeshift camp.

He gave her a hesitant smile. "Let me hear you say that by the third day, lady. By tomorrow morning, you're going to be so sore I'll probably have to lift you into the saddle."

"Probably," she answered, finishing off the last of the chili. She wiped her watering eyes, giggling. "I'm not crying because I'm unhappy. This chili is something else!"

Sam nodded. "Juan's a hell of a cook. The boys would mutiny on me if he wasn't along. And you know what? I think you're more of a Westerner than you realize. There aren't too many Eastern women I know who could gobble down that spicy chili without complaining."

"It's called being starved," she answered, sipping the coffee. The silence lengthened pleasantly between them, with sunlight lacing like fragile fingers of light between the evergreens. Dany relaxed within his aura of strength, suddenly content. Sam was drinking his coffee, his head turned, watching the herd of cattle in the distance. His profile was clean and rugged, reminding her of the scope of the Sierras in which they sat. Her heart mushroomed with a silent joy as she studied him. Dany found herself being mesmerized, and she tried to ignore the feelings it conjured up. Darn her romantic, blind heart. She was sitting with an incredibly handsome, masculine man in a wild, primeval country, and her imagination had run away with her once again. Grimly, she got up, fighting back the fantasies that were created by the moment and the place and the man. Sam looked back at her.

"Where you going?"

"To check on the black," she lied, feeling guilty as she saw the momentary bafflement in his eyes.

"She'll be fine," he drawled, watching her closely. "Why don't you rest for a while, Dany? We're going to be covering a lot of rugged territory this afternoon and you should sit a spell."

She shrugged unsurely. "I feel like walking a bit, Sam."

"Okay. Just watch out for rattlers. They start coming out this time of year to get a patch of sun to warm their cold bodies."

"What?" she blurted.

"Poisonous snakes," he added. "Just watch where you're stepping, Dany. Don't go wandering outside the camp."

"Sure. Of course," she murmured, shaken. Snakes. She hated snakes. Taking the plate back to Juan, she washed her utensils and dried them off. On her way to the horses, she kept her head down, watching for anything that might resemble a snake.

By eight that evening, Dany wasn't sure she could extricate herself from the saddle. She was used to riding, but not this type where she was jerked from side to side at a moment's notice. Her third horse of the day, a chestnut, appeared tired, and she spent extra time rubbing her charge down as the men began to come in and wait in line for their supper. Resting momentarily against the gelding, Dany closed her eyes, aware of the strong scent of sweat surrounding them. A hand slid across her shoulder and she gave a small gasp.

Sam's worried face hovered above her in the fading light. "You all right?" he asked.

Dany inhaled deeply, resting against the chestnut once again. "You scared me to death," she whispered.

He removed his hand somewhat reluctantly. "Sorry. I thought you were feeling faint or something. Come on over by the campfire, I think it's time you sat down and rested awhile," he urged gently.

Dany made no move to step away as his arm encircled her waist. Gratefully, she leaned against his seemingly tireless body. He had been raised in this country and toughened by it. She was a newcomer and felt inexplicably humbled by the majesty and power of the Sierras and the incredible demands of the drive. Cattle lowed in the distance, many of them grazing contentedly on the newly sprouted grass.

"We made good time today," Sam was saying as he guided her over to a log that sat near the fire. "Pete said you did a hell of a job."

Dany managed a tired smile, sinking to the beckoning length of the log. "Oh," she groaned, "it feels so good to sit down on something that doesn't move!"

Sam's hand rested reassuringly on her shoulder. "Stay here," he murmured. "I'll get us something to eat and then we'll sit here by the fire."

Dany was too exhausted to dispute the wisdom of his decision. The mouthwatering odor of grilled steak hung in the air, adding a bluish haze over the camp area. He joined her five minutes later on the log, and Dany forced herself to eat. Other cowboys sat around the blazing fire, murmuring, sharing stories of the day's ride and stretching out to relax. Darkness fell rapidly and the stars glimmered like dew droplets against the velvet expanse of the sky. Dany rested her arms against her thighs, cradling her chin. She had eaten heavily and now felt drowsy.

"Where does a tired cowpoke bed down around here, Sam?" she asked.

"Over there. Come on, I'll help you get settled. You look like you're going to keel over any moment."

Dany rose stiffly, excruciatingly aware of the crying ache of certain muscles. She grimaced up at Sam, who stood patiently waiting. "Are you still good for your word?" she asked.

Sam moved toward the circle of pines up on a small rise. "Sure. What do you want?"

"I think I'll need a boost into the saddle tomorrow," she confided, grinning sheepishly. "I thought I was in good shape for riding, but I guess I'm not. How many hours did we spend in the saddle today?"

"About ten. Tomorrow will be the same. We have even rougher country to get across tomorrow." He halted, taking one of the sleeping bags and unraveling it. Scooping up large handfuls of dried pine needles beneath it to make it soft, he unzipped it. "If you're too tired to wash up, just climb in. I'd advise you to sleep in your clothes until it gets warmer."

Dany looked longingly at the bed and touched her cheek, aware of how gritty it felt. "I should wash...."

"Okay. Come on, I'll take you down to the lake."

She followed numbly, sometimes stumbling and tripping on the rutted trail to the lake. Sam's form seemed to melt into the darkness in front of her. At the lake, he sat on a large boulder as she dipped the cloth into the icy waters and began washing her hands, arms and face.

"Beautiful night," he said huskily. "You ever seen a night like this back in Virginia?"

The coldness of the water revived her drowsy senses, and she blinked, looking up into the night. "No. The stars seem so close."

"Almost close enough to reach out and pick one. Like a Christmas tree ornament," he mused.

Dany slowly stood, awed by the tone of reverence in his voice. His flesh and blood were one with this land, and he was as much a part of it as it was of him. She smiled tiredly. "I think your ex-wife had to be crazy not to love this place, Sam. It's so beautiful and untamed. Like you," she murmured.

His eyes met hers in a searching stare. "Cynthia never developed an appreciation of nature." He half laughed as he rose. "Only certain things that nature made, like diamonds, gold and furs." His voice was heavy with irony.

"Everyone has their concept of what's important, Sam."

He stood quietly by her side, watching her in silence. "So, what is important to you, lady from the East Coast?" he murmured, his voice a husky, stroking quality.

Dany shivered, wildly aware of his quiet masculinity. "People. Feelings. Honesty," she admitted. "More than anything, honesty," she repeated half to herself.

"And you're ex-husband was not honest?"

Dany exhaled softly, feeling her heart wrench. "No. He—" She halted, unsure of what to say next. Her heart was hammering now at his closeness, at the longing that cried out for him from her soul.

He caressed her cheek with the back of his fingers, sending tremors of pleasure through her body. "I've studied his progress on the Grand Prix circuit, Dany. And he didn't start making it big until he married you. You were the reason for his international stardom, you know."

Dany stepped back, biting her lower lip. She hung her head, hearing the truth, aching inwardly because of it. "I was such a blind, romantic fool," she whispered rawly. Lifting her chin, she met his warming gray eyes. "Jean accused me of being an idealistic fool. And I was. I believed he loved me…." Hot tears scalded her eyes, and she turned her back to him, dashing them quickly away. Dany felt his hands settle on her arms, as he pulled her body back against his hard, unyielding body. She wanted to simply sink into his arms, to be held and protected for just a few blissful, unguarded moments.

"That's what I find so refreshing about you, Dany. Your lovely blue eyes tell me everything," he whispered against her ear, his breath warm and moist against her cheek. "Don't ever stop looking at the world through them. I watched you out here today. I saw the joy in them." He sighed heavily, his fingers tightening against her sensitized flesh. "I heard you laughing and saw the flush of pink in your cheeks when you were working with Pete. You loved what you were doing. And your laughter has affected everyone here in a positive way." He gave her a small shake as if to reinforce the point. "Don't throw such a magnificent part of yourself away, Dany, because some man lied and used you to his own calculating end. All men aren't like him."

Dany half turned, her lips parted, as she gazed up into his features. A slight smile pulled at one corner of his mouth, and he released her from his grip. Her pulse pounded achingly at the base of her throat; she was at a loss for any reply. Instead, she could only stare wordlessly up at Sam like a child. He reached out, taming a strand of her captured hair, and tucked it behind her right ear. "Let's get back," he said thickly, "or I won't be held accountable." The moment her head hit the pillow of pine needles beneath the sleeping bag, she sank into a healing slumber. She dreamed of Sam and his words of encouragement. And his steadying hands upon her body. She longed to feel the quivering touch of his mouth against her lips. Someone gave her a quick shake on the shoulder, and she groggily let the dreams evaporate, tucked back into a secret chamber of her heart.

"Time to wake up, *señora,*" Juan called cheerfully, slipping by her and going to wake the next cowhand.

Dany moved and then let out a groan. Her body felt like one huge bruise. Birds were chirping gaily around the awakening camp as if to urge the sun to hurry up its rise. The fresh scent of pine mixed with the mouth-watering smell of bacon frying over an open fire. The odor of coffee perking was strong, and Dany looked around, searching for Sam. She heard the snort of a horse and turned to see him riding up from the herd at a lazy trot. He pulled up, calling to some of the men and giving orders. Dismounting, Sam tied Altair to the tether rope and walked over to where she stood.

"Good morning," he said, taking off his hat.

Touching her hair, which she knew must be in terrible disarray, she murmured, "Good morning."

"I think the outdoors is good for you," he commented. "You look even more beautiful this morning."

She felt the heat of a blush stealing across her throat and managed a soft laugh. "Sam Reese, you must have gotten an A in school for blarney. Look at my hair! There're pine needles in it."

He came forward, helping her sort the needles out of her hair. "You look like the earth goddess, Ceres. No, on second thought, her lovely daughter, Persephone."

Dany made a face, suppressing a giggle. She noticed that he was freshly shaven and looked equally breathtaking to her. "Just don't let the god Pluto come up with his chariot drawn by black horses and carry me down to the depths of hell," she teased in return. The last pine needle was dislodged, and she shook loose her bound hair until it spilled like sheets of water across her shoulders. Sam's normally unreadable features softened, his eyes becoming narrowed shadows of pewter gray.

"God," he breathed softly, "you ought to wear your hair down all the time, Dany."

That simple compliment began her second day of the drive. Breakfast was over by five, and they were all in the saddle by five-thirty, pushing the lazy, sluggish herd even higher into the brush-laden hills. Sam's expression was one of forlorn wistfulness as he rode off, leaving her. Dany gloried in those few parting seconds. It was as if he had reached out, invisibly kissing her lips in farewell. Sighing, she gloried in the beauty of the Sierras, the call of the mating birds and the lullaby of lowing provided by the herd.

Bomarc moved easily beneath her as she and five other cowhands continued to push, cajole and drive the end of the herd up a particularly steep, rocky incline.

The temperature had risen steadily, and at first opportunity, Dany pulled the gelding to a halt and strapped the coat behind her saddle. Rolling up her sleeves she put on a pair of deerskin gloves and took up the lasso in her right hand. Bomarc scrambled nimbly over a series of small hills, easily catching up with the reluctant herd.

The sun was nearly overhead when a Hereford with long, bent horns broke from the herd. Dany pressed her leg against Bomarc, and they scrambled down into a V-shaped ravine after the sullen Hereford. The cow, having made the trek for many years, was determined to make good her escape. Instead of dodging back toward the herd, she clawed up and over the lip of the ravine, scrambling for the heavy brush and forest three hundred yards ahead.

Dany yelled encouragement to the gelding, leaning forward as the horse lunged over the top, sending a spray of rocks and dirt flying in all directions. Wind tore past her face as she guided the horse to the right side of the cow. Giving a loud yell, Dany slapped the lasso against her chaps. The sound echoed like pistol shot. The cow doggedly ran on, desperately moving for the cover of the brush.

"Damn!" she breathed angrily. She saw the low-hanging branches looming closer as Bomarc ran hard, his hooves pounding deeply into the slushy mud and snow. She squeezed him hard, asking for one last spurt of power. The gray dove ahead of the old cow and, at the last second, leaned to the left, colliding heavily with the animal.

Dany heard someone yelling far behind her and disregarded the cry. The forest was close and they were

going too fast, the cow stubbornly resisting the gelding's nudge. Leaning over, she drove the gray into the
cow, taking the rope and slashing it down across the
Hereford's eyes. Both horse and cow collided heavily
as they jointly made a swing to the left, back toward
the herd. Dany threw her weight to the right, suddenly
feeling Bomarc falter, slipping in the mud and the carpet of slick pine needles. She was going down! Throwing the reins forward, Dany let go of the rope, bringing
her arms up to protect her head. The ground came
rushing up in a thunderous crash. She felt Bomarc's
weight on her leg and heard the horse grunt heavily.
Blackness rimmed her vision, but she lay perfectly still
as the gelding rested momentarily against her left leg.
The gray got shakily to his feet, mud dripping off his
sweaty body. She didn't move, waiting for the blackness to disappear before she tried to get up.

"Dany! Dany!"

She turned groggily toward Sam's voice, watching
Altair slide to a stop. Sam dismounted, running over
to where she lay. "Dany..." he breathed heavily, leaning over her. "Are you—"

She gave him a silly grin. "I'm okay," she muttered.

His eyes broadcast his undisguised concern as he
cradled her head and shoulders against his body. She
glanced down at her muddy arms and legs and shook
with silent laughter. Sam looked down at her strangely,
undecided as to her condition.

"I'm okay," she managed between giggles. "Oh,
God, I must look like the original mud pie!"

Sam managed an unsteady smile as he gently
squeezed her arms and legs to make sure nothing
was broken. Dany rested against his shoulder, her ear

pressed against his chest. His heart was pounding thunderously, matching the cadence of her own.

"You scared the hell out of me," he growled. "Didn't you hear me calling you back?"

She slowly sat up. "No. That cow really wanted to escape."

"You should have let her go, Dany," he remonstrated, getting to his feet. "You could have hurt yourself badly in those woods. Look at those low-hanging branches," he ordered, his voice taking on a sterner note.

Properly chastised, Dany said, "I'm sorry. I didn't think."

Handling her as if she were fragile cargo, he helped her stand, seemingly afraid to release his protective hold. Reluctantly, Sam withdrew his support and rested his hands against her hips. "Better get back to the wagon and get a change of clothes," he suggested.

She nodded, moving over to where her horse stood. Running her hands down each of Bomarc's legs, she checked for injuries. Finding none, she finally stood up. Sam had mounted, scowling. Flipping the reins over the gray's head, Dany swung back into the saddle, joining him. "What's the matter?" she asked.

"You take too many chances," he growled.

"Me?" And then she smiled impishly. "Isn't that what you're trying to get me to do?"

He grinned hesitantly. "Lady, if this kind of ground doesn't faze you, then we won't have much of a problem getting you confident to ride."

"I don't know which is worse: taking a chance riding in a show or taking a chance on men," she muttered.

Sam laughed. "Sometimes one isn't much safer than the other," he commented.

"Oh, yes, it is. I can always mend a broken bone or a torn muscle. You never heal a wound to the heart," Dany murmured.

He regarded her darkly. "You can," he said, "with time."

Chapter 8

By the end of the second day, the first plateau of hills had been scaled. Dany stood by a stream, admiring the setting sun as it spread its reddish rays over the warming land. The temperature had risen all day, and by nightfall there wasn't a cowhand who hadn't rolled up his long-sleeved shirt. Men and horses had sweated heavily all afternoon with water being consumed at a phenomenal rate. Juan had just set up the camp and a fire crackled pleasantly in the background. Someone had taken out a harmonica, and the forlorn tune wafted like a ghostly melody between the large conifers, adding to the magic of the moment.

She had discovered a stream and washed her hair less than an hour ago. It hung in dark, thick sheets about her shoulders. Taking a washcloth, she scrubbed herself free of grime. Bomarc stood patiently while she put him in the stream, washing the dried mud from his shoulder and flank. One of the cowhands shook his head as he rode by, and she returned the grin. She hadn't seen any of them giving their horse a bath.

Softly humming a tune, Dany had enough energy left to help Juan in preparations for the dinner. The Mexican bobbed his head, thanking her profusely. Soon, small chunks of onion, potato and carrots simmered in beef broth within the huge blackened kettle sitting over the fire. The hands were unsaddling their tired mounts and wearily waiting for their mug of steaming hot coffee.

Juan finished kneading the biscuit dough, asking Dany to roll it out on the uneven surface of the back of the chuck wagon gate. "I hear you gave old Lizzie a run for her money, *señora*."

Dany lifted the rolling pin, sprinkling more white flour on it. "Lizzie?" she laughed.

"That old boss cow. Pete said she tried to make for the brush, but you stopped her. You fell?"

She scratched her nose, unknowingly leaving a patch of flour on the tip of it. "Yes. Bomarc and I took a small spill. We got her turned back, though."

"Bravo! They said you were magnificent!" His almond eyes fairly gleamed with pride.

"Sam said I was stupid," she muttered, flattening out the dough more. "There," she murmured. Taking a plastic glass, she dipped it in flour and began to cut out the biscuits, quickly putting them on the baking sheets Juan provided.

"Who said you were stupid?" Sam rumbled from behind her.

Dany gave a start, whirling around. "Oh!" she gasped.

Sam looked down at her, unable to contain a grin. He reached over, rubbing the flour off her nose. "Are you always this messy in a kitchen?" he teased warmly.

Dany blushed scarlet and looked down, groaning. White splotches of flour decorated her arms and her jeans. "I should have worn a tablecloth like Juan," she muttered, returning his grin.

"Something, anyway. Now, getting back to your earlier comment, who said you were stupid?"

She returned to her duties. "My words, not yours," she corrected. "About chasing Lizzie back to the herd."

Sam leaned lazily against the wagon, watching her. "I didn't say that. You're new at this, Dany, and I just don't want you taking chances, that's all."

"I know. And you think you have worries now. Wait till we get to Santa Barbara."

"Are you always that reckless?" he wanted to know.

Dany shrugged her shoulders. "There's a difference between being reckless and taking a calculated risk."

"That's why Altair loves you. He's the same damn way. By the way, do you want to ride him tomorrow?"

Her eyebrows moved up. "Me?"

"Sure. Why not? You've handled Bomarc well. I don't think it's wise that I ride Altair for eight solid days. I want him to remember your touch and your cues."

She nodded, wiping her nose with the back of her hand. Why did it always itch when her fingers had something on them? "What kind of country will we be in tomorrow?"

"Rolling hills. Like the state of Virginia."

"Good! I was getting tired of all this brush," she

admitted. "Have you seen my chaps? They look like they've gone through World War III already!"

He grinned, taking off his hat and running his fingers through his dark hair. "Makes you a veteran now, Dany. After dinner, I'd like to take you for a walk. How about it?"

She stopped making the biscuits, gazing up into his strong face. Perhaps it was being outdoors for two days. Or maybe it was the infectious magic of the Sierras. But she wanted to be with Sam. "Yes," she whispered, "I'd like that, Sam."

"Good." He touched her nose again. "If I didn't know better, I'd think you were born with flour on your nose," he teased as he was leaving.

The night remained warm, with a slight breeze drifting through the shadowed mountains from the west. The stars hung like sparkling crystals in the sky as they walked slowly up an unseen trail. The fragrant pine scent wafted up from the carpet of needles beneath their feet, and Dany inhaled deeply. She was acutely conscious of Sam's body only inches from her own. A silent unspoken strength exuded from him as surely as warmth did from the sun. On a purely feminine whim, she had tied a red ribbon around her thick ponytail. She felt his hand grip her elbow and steady her as they climbed to a rock outcropping.

"Sore?" he asked as they halted at the rim.

Dany nodded, scanning the darkness. "I was lucky I didn't break a leg or ankle today when Bomarc fell," she admitted.

"We both know that. You laid there and started laughing like a ten-year-old kid," he muttered.

She laughed softly, continuing up the narrowed trail ahead of him. She gingerly tested the earth before placing all her weight on each foot as they progressed. "Well, I can imagine how funny I looked drenched from head to foot in mud and pine needles!"

"That you did and I'm glad you came up laughing. Most women wouldn't."

"Most women aren't Grand Prix level trainers, either," she reminded him tartly.

His hands slid about her waist, pulling her to a stop. Dany held her breath, feeling the warmth of his leanly muscled body against her back. He pointed to the right. "And riders," he reminded her gently. "We're about ten miles across the valley from where a pair of condors make their home."

She remained still within his arms, his male scent a special, inviting fragrance to her senses. "Didn't you say they were rare?"

Sam leaned against the rock, drawing her against him. "Yes. They're on the endangered species list. We have a pair that mates and has one or two young ones every year. I've had officials from the Sierra Club come up and watch them for a month so a scientific record can be compiled on them." He sighed. "We really don't know that much about them. They're loners who stay as far away from civilization as possible."

Dany twisted her head, drinking in his troubled face. "Like you?"

He smiled absently, gazing down at her. "A loner, or staying as far away from civilization as I can?"

"Both."

"What do you think of loners?" he breathed, rubbing his cheek gently against the side of her head.

Her pulse pounded at the base of her throat. "That—" she stammered, losing her sense of equilibrium in the face of his overpowering presence, "that they are either very self-assured people or they are afraid to get involved emotionally."

"Then you're a loner by your own definition," he whispered, sliding his hand up the expanse of her arm and resting it on her shoulder.

Dany compressed her lips. "Are you accusing me of being afraid to get involved again?" she flared.

"Yes, I am, honey. I was that way for a long time after my divorce, too."

Dany stiffened, moving out of his arms. She wished for her coat now, suddenly chilled as she turned and met his shadowed gaze. "No one heals in nine months, Sam! Not if they really loved the person they left."

"You loved him, but he didn't love you?"

Pain wrung in her chest. "If you must know, yes! Please, can't we get on another subject?" she whispered in anguish. Why must he keep bringing up her dead marriage? Her mistake?

"I'm sorry, honey," he murmured.

She rubbed her arms in displeasure. "My personal life is my business, not yours."

"When I care about someone, I make it my business," he replied, his voice hardening. "Plus, I've stumbled onto some information that might upset you a great deal."

"Meaning what? You're talking in riddles."

"Did you know that your ex-husband is going to be showing at Santa Barbara, Dany?"

She heard herself inhale sharply. "What?"

Sam remained against the rock, watching the play

of emotions across her face. "The show brochure came a day before we left on the drive. He's riding the favorite French candidate, named Falcon. You're going to be riding against him, Dany. I don't know how you feel toward him. I worry that you might be a little more emotional than normal, and I don't want to see you injured. It's as simple as that."

Tears pricked her eyes and she swallowed convulsively. A collision of feelings exploded within her. Jean was back! And in all of his international glory. Well, he had finally gotten what he wanted: the best Grand Prix horse in Europe to ride. And Sam...all his courting and courtesy were nothing more than to test the waters of her emotional stability to make sure his horse had a chance to win!

"How do you feel about riding against him?" Sam prodded coolly.

Gritting her teeth she snarled, "Like I feel toward you!"

"Anger isn't going to make it, Dany. Why are you upset with me?"

She tried to brush past him, but he reached out, easily capturing her shoulder. Turning her around, he pulled her close. "I asked you why," he demanded.

"All—all this care you've given me is nothing more than a show! You just wanted to make sure I was in good enough shape mentally and emotionally to ride that damn horse for you! I should have known better. Now let me go!" She tried to twist out of his grip. His fingers tightened, biting deeply into her flesh.

"Stop it!" he growled. "Dany...stop struggling!"

She found herself helplessly trapped against his rigid body. "I can't figure you out, woman," he breathed angrily, his face scant inches from her own. "One moment you're fighting me because I show you some affection. The next second you're angry because I'm concerned for your safety. What in the hell do you want from me?" he ground out.

Pinned completely against him, Dany felt his heart pounding thunderously. She made one more effort to escape from his grip. The ribbon that she had tied in her hair loosened as she twisted her head, the rich cascades falling around her shoulders, glinting like blue cobalt in the thin wash of moonlight. She felt his hand cupping her chin, drawing her face upward. Her lips parted in response as she heard him groan her name, his arms capturing her totally.

His mouth fell upon her lips in a plundering, breath-stealing kiss. This time, there was no tenderness, no gentleness. Fire erupted from her as his tongue invaded the moist recesses of her mouth, plunging her into a spiraling vortex of utter sensation. His mouth moved insistently against her lips, and suddenly, she felt his steel grip easing. Her legs would not hold her, and she leaned heavily against him.

"Dany... Dany..." he whispered roughly. His fingers moved through her hair, capturing the tresses, pulling her head back. She melted into his arms, helpless to stop him from assailing her again. Her hand had moved upward against his chest, weakly pushing him away. But this time, this time his mouth brushed her throbbing lips. He kissed away the pain, his tongue grazing the outline of her lips, tasting the sweetness of her mouth, coaxing her gently to become a partner. His hands moved caressingly up her rib cage, lingering against the fullness of her breast, making her shiver with need. The roughness of his face against her cheek, the warmth of his breath, the male hardness insistent against her hips, threw her into a cascading waterfall of flaring desire.

Gradually Dany floated back to earth, still in Sam's arms. At first she thought she was trembling. But it wasn't she. It was he. His breath was coming in gulps, and she sensed his need for her in that raw moment. She could barely stand after that shattering kiss. Touching her lips, she gazed up in wonder at him. His eyes were hooded, watching her with silvered fire deep in their recesses. Dany shivered, never more fully aware of her ability to arouse a man. She had never been kissed like this…. A small moan echoed in her throat as she began to understand for the first time how much she had missed in her hollow, one-sided marriage.

A white-hot streak of panic made her suddenly stiffen. Was she in love with Sam Reese? Could love make her feel like this? Conflicting emotions raged across her widening azure eyes.

"Dany?" he asked unsteadily. His eyes spoke of a man who also could not endure an unbalanced relationship. He caressed her cheek, tenderly touching her lips. "I'm sorry, honey. I didn't mean to upset you. I damn near couldn't stop myself…. You drive a man to the edge of desire…."

Chapter 9

For the next two days, although Dany was avoiding Sam, she felt that they were on a collision course, and it had forced her to reevaluate her life. For the first time in four years, there was a feeling of order in her life, despite the explosive chemistry between her and Sam.

On the morning of the third day, Sam gently shook her awake. "Wake up, sleepyhead. We've got a special project ahead of us today. Come on, the coffee's on," he urged softly.

Perplexed and half-asleep, Dany obeyed, stumbling out of the sleeping bag. Dawn was barely edging the darkened horizon, a pastel ribbon of pink dimly outlined the craggy cliffs that surrounded them. A bird cawed somewhere in the rugged mountains, the echo continuing down the long, narrow valley. Dany tucked stray strands of hair behind her ears, shoved on her boots and joined Sam at the small fire.

"Why are we up so early?" she mumbled, accepting a mug of coffee from him.

Sam pushed the hat back on his head and pointed toward two large peaks that sat east of the camp. "We're going to scout ahead today. There's a narrow pass about half a day's ride from here that needs to be checked. Sometimes, because of blizzards and heavy snowfall, the river is too high for the cattle to swim. If that has happened, we have to use the alternative route up to the high pastures." He looked at her. "Want to go along?"

She pursed her lips, noting the twinkle in his gray eyes. A grin tugged at her mouth. "Sure. Why not?"

He sobered. "It will give us some time to talk, Dany. I think we owe it to one another." He came over, standing very close to her, stroking her blue black hair. "If you don't feel ready for this, you can back out. I'll understand."

There was uncertainty in his voice and it amazed her. Sam Reese had always seemed so sure of himself, but now she saw the vulnerability in his eyes. Her heart throbbed in her chest. "No…no, I want to go," she whispered.

The camp was barely stirring to life as they rode out at a slow trot toward the last threshold before the pastures. The snow had melted completely, and the ground had dried up, making the footing excellent. Dany stole a glance over at Sam as they rode in silence. What was on his mind? The last two days, he seemed to be brooding about something. Her instincts told her it was about their budding relationship. She no longer tried to deny her own feelings for him: She loved him. And it was a kind of love that she had never experienced. He made her happy by just being there. It wasn't just a physical desire or attraction. It was a blending of his masculinity and her femininity on so many complementary levels.

The sun was peeking over the rim of the mountains when they set out, covering mile after mile at an easy pace. At one point, they halted and Dany tied her coat behind the saddle. She smiled over at Sam, and he nodded, his eyes smiling in return.

At noon, they stopped and unpacked the lunch Juan had made the night before. The chicken sandwich and crisp apples tasted delicious, washed down afterward by cold spring water. Sam had gotten up and loosened the cinches on both horses and then sat down on a rock beside her. He stretched his frame against the sun-heated boulder and touched her hair in silence, running the silken strands thoughtfully through his fingers. "You have the most beautiful hair," he murmured. "When I first met you, I thought you were a prim, strict schoolteacher type."

She turned her eyes gravely to him. "And now, Sam?"

He smiled distantly, leaning his head back and closing his eyes. "You're like a multifaceted diamond. So many different, interesting sides," he teased.

Dany laughed softly. "If that's a compliment, I'll take it."

His hand rested on her golden-tanned forearm. "What did Jean think you were, honey?"

Her stomach knotted, her heart twisting in pain. "A trainer for his horses," she admitted finally.

"A wife? Lover? Housekeeper? What else?" he pressed.

Dany leaned back against the rock, closing her eyes. She was content with his nearness. "Sometimes housekeeper, always the teacher and, occasionally, his wife."

"Did you really love him?"

Dany cleared her throat. "At the time I thought I did. But distance has taken care of that perspective, Sam. What can I say? He was dashing, elegant and handsome. Hundreds of women were green with jealousy when we got engaged. I thought he loved me...."

Sam's fingers tightened momentarily on her arm, as if to take away the pain reflected in her voice. "In his own selfish way, he probably did."

She managed a cutting grimace. "It was his international playboy image and his knack at spending our hard-earned money that caused our divorce."

"So you put Richland on the market to pay the debts?"

The lump grew in her throat, and she barely rasped out, "Yes."

"So a homestead means a great deal to you, despite the amount of traveling you did on the East Coast?"

Dany pushed off the rock, standing above him. The wind playfully lifted strands of her hair around her shoulders. "Home means a great deal to everyone, Sam."

He barely opened his eyes, watching her. "I'm just interested in what it means to you, Dany. Not many people would sell off half their dream."

Her face contorted. "I didn't have a choice! And it has been ground into me that dreams don't come true. Or, if they do, they evaporate very quickly." She turned her back on him, walking back over to the horses. Dreams, Jean had said, were the paradise of fools. The only thing that counted was the here and now. One couldn't dream of being a Grand Prix winner. It had to be proved each time they rode. Dany pulled on the cinch, tightening it. The shadow of Sam's tall figure blocked out the sun, and he took the leather strap from her trembling fingers and finished looping it through, bringing the stirrup down. Resting his arm on the saddle, he looked down at her.

"There's nothing wrong with dreaming, Dany," he began huskily. "Ever since I was a young kid, I had dreams. Most of them have come true. Some of them have been shattered. But that doesn't stop me from trying again."

Her eyes were wide, filled with anguish as she met his gaze. "Dreams are for people who can afford them."

He smiled lazily. "Come on, let's mount up. We'll talk more on this as we ride," he urged.

They rode at a steady trot, their legs occasionally touching as they continued up the incline toward the pass. Dany finally broke the silence. "Which one of your dreams was destroyed, Sam?"

"My marriage," he admitted.

"What happened?"

"I had it in my head that one marriage in a lifetime was plenty." He grinned. "Of course, in today's market, more people are getting divorced than staying married. Cynthia and I are one of those statistics."

"Why did it happen?" Dany asked, surprised at her own need to know. Ordinarily she would never be so bold or brash to ask such a personal question. But Sam seemed to be inviting her to explore other nuances of himself.

"It was a merger of two large corporations," he admitted. "Looking back on it, I should have known better. But then, at twenty-three, I was still wet behind the

ears. Especially to the ways and wiles of women. I saw
Cyn at a party in San Francisco and fell hopelessly and
romantically in love with her. She was a dream come
true for me, so I thought. She had beauty, flawless el-
egance and sophistication." A twinkle remained in his
eyes. "She also had an appetite for rich men who could
give her the baubles that went along with the territory."

"So, you married her?"

"Yes. You see, that's where I discovered the difference between romantic love and real love. After about
a year, the passion began to fade and she grew tired
of me and the ranch. She wanted to stay in San Francisco and I wanted to live in the Sierras. Neither of us
made much of an effort to compromise our positions.
We ended up being married five years and living apart
three of them. Finally, she met another very rich gentleman and asked for a divorce. I gave it to her. Now
she's remarried and is happily basking in the light of
San Francisco society."

"You sound so flip about the whole episode," Dany
accused.

"At the time, I was anything but flip. I was hurting
just like you are. I did a lot of soul-searching and asked
myself a lot of questions, although I never allowed Cyn
to destroy a part of me—like Jean has destroyed your
confidence in your abilities as a rider. You either let
that hurt, anger and distrust go or carry Jean and the
past around with you every day."

She grimaced. "Ouch. Easier said than done," she
returned dejectedly.

He pulled Altair down to a walk, giving the horses
a deserved rest. "I think you were lonely, Dany, when
you met Jean. People marry for that reason. And, it's

not wrong to do it. But I think you've spent most of your adult life around animals and not people. He knew you were naive and manipulated the circumstances to his own best advantage. After all, marrying the best Grand Prix trainer in the U.S. was a shrewd move on his part. The loser in the game was you."

She could barely hold his gaze. "You're so damn perceptive," she rasped. "Why weren't you around when I needed a sounding board to try and figure that out myself? You're right: I spent too much time around horses and let the rest of the world slip through my fingers."

Sam wrapped the reins around the horn and rolled up the sleeves on his shirt. The wind had picked up significantly as they entered the rocky terrain of the pass, but the sun was hot. "Horses don't divorce you," he said wryly.

She laughed. It was true. Animals had never tried to trick or deceive her. Not like their human counterparts. "Somehow, I don't think a horse can give me the emotional support I'm looking for," she said.

Sam raised his eyes upward. "Thank God," he murmured.

Dany joined his rich laughter. Suddenly, she felt more at ease than ever before. The walls of the rocky pass rose on either side of them as they moved down the dusty trail. The clip-clop of hooves striking the hardened earth echoed through the expanse. The sky was a bright, cerulean blue, and the sun struck the planes of yellow ochre stone, lending it a golden radiance. The silent camaraderie between them grew, and Dany traded a smile with him from time to time.

They rode another two miles before she picked

up the sound of water in the distance. As they came around another curve the sparkling expanse of a wide river met her curious gaze. Dany dismounted, marveling at the wild, inherent beauty of the river. A waterfall roared a half a mile away, water spilling over the lip of the gorge above them. The river frothed and foamed, indicating strong currents at work beneath its sparkling surface. Sam dismounted, hanging his hat on the saddle horn. He hobbled both horses and unsaddled them. Dany slipped the bridles off their heads so that they could eat a well-earned lunch on the lush grass.

"This is incredibly beautiful," she said, awe in her tone.

"I love coming here," he murmured. He walked upstream, gauging the river with narrowed eyes.

Dany knelt down, splashing water on her face, the coolness refreshing to her hot, perspiring body. She glanced up at him, a grin on her mouth. "What I'd give for a bath! This is perfect. Look at that sandbar. There's a small inlet that's sure to be warmer than the river."

Sam turned. "Go ahead. Take one."

She got to her feet, wiping her hands on her jeans. "You mean it?"

"Sure. I'm going to walk about half a mile downstream on foot and check the crossing point. We'll give the horses a breather and let them eat while I'm gone." He grinned recklessly. "Although, it would be far more enjoyable to stay and scrub your back."

Dany colored, pulling the sleeping bag off the saddle and hunting for her towel and soap. "I'll make a point of hurrying then," she retorted.

Sam picked up his hat. "Take your time, honey. I'll

be back in about forty minutes. Just watch for snakes. There's water moccasins up here, you know."

Dany groaned, distressed. "Sam! You just ruined my enthusiasm."

"Sorry. But you always have to be careful out in the wilds, Dany. I'll be back in a while."

By the time she had finished searching for snakes, Sam had disappeared around the curve of the river bank. Dany smiled eagerly as she undressed and placed the clothes on a nearby rock. The sun struck her skin, warming her deliciously. Sitting on the bank, she slid her toe into the inviting inlet. It was cool, but not icy. Well, she decided firmly, a few minutes of discomfort are better than staying dirty. She gasped as the blue green water closed about her as she dog-paddled to the sand beach until she stood in knee deep water. Soaping her body quickly, Dany scrubbed her skin until it glowed a healthy pink. Taking a quick dip, she rinsed off. Then, holding her breath, she dove under, wetting her black hair. Again, she scrubbed furiously. The breeze on her wet skin made goose pimples rise on her flesh. She rinsed her hair and took one last dip, swimming for the shore.

Scrambling out, she struggled back into the clothes. Almost immediately, she felt better. Looking down toward the curve, she didn't see Sam returning yet. Taking advantage of the time, she lay on the fragrant grass, closing her eyes and allowing the heat of the sun to lull her to sleep.

She was startled awake by Altair's challenging scream. The red stallion reared high into the air, his hooves pawing the air directly above her. His nostrils were flared, and the whites of his eyes could be seen.

A cry lodged in her throat, and Dany threw up her arm to protect her face as the stallion came down. The earth shook heavily where he landed. The stallion pawed the ground squealing savagely. She rolled away, shakily getting to her feet.

"Dany!" Sam thundered, running toward her.

Dany twisted around, confused. His face was contorted with concern as he reached out for her. His fingers bit deeply into her flesh as he nearly jerked her off her feet. She fell heavily against him as he dragged her away from the angry stallion.

Black hair swirled around her face, and she shakily pushed it away in order to see. "What happened?" she cried.

"It must be a snake," he rasped. He thrust her aside. "Stay here," he ordered.

Dany watched wide-eyed as Sam went forward. Altair had stopped pawing and stood quivering. Sam crooned to him, moving up to where the stallion remained frozen. He took him by the halter, releasing the hobbles and leading him away from the area. After tying him to a low-hanging tree limb, Sam returned to her side.

"Want to see what got him so upset?"

She nodded, suddenly grateful for his arm about her waist. The area where she had fallen asleep was completely harrowed. The grass had been torn up in clumps by Altair's striking hooves. And there, in the middle of the furrowed area lay the remains of a snake. Dany took a step back, gasping.

"Oh, God, Sam," she whispered tightly. "I fell asleep. He—" She glanced over at the red stallion. "Altair must have seen the snake coming toward me...."

She shivered, burying herself within his arms. "I could have been killed," she breathed.

Sam caressed her head, holding her tightly. "Yes. If the snake hadn't bit you, Altair might have struck you by mistake. He has a long history of hating snakes and will go to any length to kill one," he muttered grimly. "You all right, honey? God, you're shaking like a leaf. Here, let me take a look at you."

She stood trembling within the shelter of his arms as the full impact of what might have happened crashed down on her. "W-was it a poisonous snake?" she chattered.

"Yes, looks like a copperhead. Probably came down to the river looking for rodents taking a drink of water this time of day. Well, you look okay. A few grass stains on your elbow here, but otherwise, all right. How do you feel? You look pale."

Her legs were suddenly turning to jelly, and she reached out, gripping Sam's arm. "I—I don't feel very well, Sam...."

In the next instant, he had scooped her up into his arms as if she were a mere feather. Gratefully, she rested her head against his shoulder, shutting her eyes tightly. His arms were protective and strong around her body as she slid her hands around his neck, seeking his closeness. The enormity of the events shook her deeply. She could have been bitten. She could have died! Oh, God, she didn't want to die! Not now. Not realizing how much she loved Sam! A sob tore from her lips, and she clung tightly to Sam.

"Shhhh," he whispered, gently depositing her beneath a pine tree. "Everything is all right, Dany." He placed a kiss on her head, awkwardly brushing away the tears rolling down her cheeks. He knelt at her side, bringing her against his sun-warmed body and crooning wordless endearments. Dany sighed softly, feeling his heart thundering against her breasts. It seemed natural as he raised her chin, his mouth claiming her wet, salty lips with quivering tenderness, tasting them. The pressure increased as she parted her lips, allowing his exploring tongue deep into the moist depths of her mouth. A soft moan of need vibrated in her throat, and she pressed her body against him instinctively. Sam groaned, gripping her shoulder. He pulled her away, his eyes blazing with barely constrained desire.

"I want you," he whispered thickly. "God, how I need you, Dany...."

The brush with death had torn any remnants of her uncertainty and distrust away. Shyly, she reached up, caressing his weather-hardened cheek. "Love me," she sighed, "please... Sam, love me..." He kissed her tear-wet lashes, cheeks and lips in answer. With maddening slowness, he stripped the clothes from his powerfully built body. Dany reveled in the broad planes of his muscular chest, the chiseled flatness of his stomach and his long, athletic thighs. His skin was a soft golden color, his muscles rippling with breathtaking movement as he slid down beside her, his mouth capturing her lips, pulling her fiercely against him. His fingers expertly worked the buttons free, slipping the blouse off her shoulders. She trembled as he trailed a series of fiery kisses the length of her neck to the valley between her breasts. Each touch quickened her awakening desires. Her skin tightened beneath each grazing caress of his featherlight touch. His mouth teased the flesh of her taut breasts, and she gasped, arching beneath him.

She was no longer thinking, only reacting. She was a musical instrument within the hands of a master, and for the first time in years, she wanted to be an active participant in the sharing of love. His hand cupped the small of her back, lifting her upward to meet him. Her fingers dug deeply into his thickly corded shoulder muscles, breath suspended in anticipation. His entry was swift, penetrating and fiery, and a small cry broke from her lips. She buried her head momentarily against his neck, sweat grazing her cheek. Gently, ever so gently, he brought her back into rhythm with himself. The seconds of pain fled, replaced with a delicious sense of delectable euphoria. She was mindless, simply swirling into a layer of intensified pleasure never before experienced. Sam groaned, gripping her tightly, and she gloried in those moments of mutual climax. Clinging silently to his quivering body afterward, Dany rested her spent, damp form against him. Her hair spilled across his shoulder and chest like an ebony blanket as she nuzzled against his cheek. Moments, precious, delicious moments were spilled by her satiated senses.

Sam cradled her tenderly within his arms. He leaned over, smoothing away small tendrils that clung damply to her cheek. His eyes were dark with consumed passion as he stroked her hair.

"I knew it would be good," he murmured huskily, "but I never realized…"

Dany saw the face of a man fulfilled. No longer did the partial mask remain to hide his incredible range of emotions. There was a boyish vulnerability in his eyes as he drank in her form, and it delighted her. She ran her fingers through the silken mat of hair on his broad, powerful chest, a tremulous smile on her lips. "Oh, Sam," she whispered and then tears caught in her throat and she was unable to continue. He laughed throatily, pulling her near, burying his face within the shining mass of hair.

"You're mine," he growled fiercely. Then he sealed this promise with a long and delicious kiss.

Chapter 10

It was dusk by the time they got back to the herd. Cowboys on horseback walked their mounts slowly around the huge circle of cattle, singing softly to settle them down for the night hours. Somewhere out on the open stretch of the oblong valley floor, the mournful tune of the harmonica brought back nostalgic moments to Dany. She rode in silence beside Sam, content to be close to him, their legs brushing often against the other. Her body remained bathed with the glow of his lovemaking earlier. She could only stare at him like a child who had been given the precious gift of love. The comparison between Jean's loving and Sam's was jolting. Sam had loved her as a sharing partner in a beautiful experience. Jean had never shared anything; it had always been take—take and never give. With that knowledge, Dany began to put the pieces of her marriage into

perspective. She glanced to the left, realizing that she
owed it all to the man who rode at her side. Occasionally Sam would catch her wide-eyed gaze and smile,
as if sharing that intimate secret with her.

Juan welcomed them back in a mixture of Spanish
and English. Dany sat near the chuck wagon, ravenously consuming her meal as she watched Sam talk to
his men about the day's progress on the drive. Later,
as darkness fell, she noticed the horizon seeming to
blaze with flashes of light. Juan muttered something in
Spanish as he finished washing the rest of the tin plates.
Dany got up, handing the plate to him. She tugged at
the dish towel stuffed in his back pocket and began
drying the stack of dishes for him.

"Is that lightning?" she asked.

"*Sí, sí.* Not good, *señora.* These cattle…" And he
shook his head, keeping the rest of his thoughts to
himself.

"I would think they're used to lightning," she commented, placing the dried utensils on one corner of the
wagon tailgate.

"*Sí,* you would think that. But these Herefords will
get restless. I think the boss will keep everyone up tonight to ride around the herd and keep them calm."

Dany noticed that more than one ranch hand was
watching the horizon apprehensively where the line
of thunderstorms were building. There was an unspoken tenseness building in the camp, and she hurriedly
finished the drying chores and sought out Sam. She
found him with his head drovers near a stand of pine.
He slid his hand around her shoulder, making her feel
welcome to the small knot of men.

"Juan said the thunderstorms might scare the herd, Sam."

"There's a good possibility of that," he agreed quietly. He looked up at his men. "Pete, you take five of the boys for night duty and keep those cows content. If they start to spook, send a runner back and we'll get everyone in the saddle."

"Right, Boss."

Sam steered her out of the grove and onto the open plain. The cattle looked like shadowy black shapes moving sluggishly beneath the increasing light of the moon. Dany sensed his concern and turned, looking up into his worried features. "Did you expect storms on the drive?"

"Yes and no," he muttered, stroking her cheek tenderly. "Sometimes we get bad ones at this time of year, but I was hoping that we would get lucky and miss them."

"No Irish blood in you for luck," she teased fondly.

Sam smiled absently. "None," he agreed, his eyes soft with tenderness as he gazed down at her.

"If it rains, that means that the river in the pass will rise."

He leaned down kissing her forehead gently. "See, you're more of a cowgirl than you realized. Yes, if it rises any more, we won't be able to swim the herd across. But I'm more worried about them spooking and then running across this meadow into the foothills." He sighed heavily. "God, that will be a mess if that happens. It means spending days re-collecting the scattered herd, and we'll have to destroy those with broken legs."

Dany lunged upward, tangled in her sleeping bag. The crash of thunder was deafening. Nearby, she heard the men shouting, the horses whinnying nervously and the cattle bellowing. A bolt of lightning ripped the belly of the sky open and thunder growled savagely. Dany rose shakily to her feet, throwing on her boots. Juan ran around the end of the chuck wagon, his eyes wide.

"*Señora!* Quick! Get on Altair. The herd is going to break!" he shouted.

Large drops of rain plopped on the dry earth. Dany blinked, running jerkily toward the line of tied horses. Sam had given orders that they remain saddled. All she had to do was slip Altair's hackamore on him and she could leave. Her heart was pumping strongly now. Sam, where was Sam? She yelled out for him, cupping her hands to her mouth. Again, she called for him. Indecision tore at her, and she grabbed the bridle, soothing Altair. Fingers shaking, she managed to get it over the horse's head. A cacophony of harsh sounds broke simultaneously around her. She mounted, her leg barely across the stallion's back when the herd panicked. Altair plunged forward, snorting loudly.

Three blinding, brilliant bolts hit the valley floor simultaneously. A tree exploded, the sound rupturing like an artillery shell. As a dark, willful mass, the herd veered and broke blindly into the blackness and sudden downpour. A scream lodged at the back of her throat as Dany saw a wall of Herefords bearing down directly on where she stood on the frightened, rearing stallion. She froze for only a second, leaning far forward on Altair, asking him to leap into the unknown darkness beyond the wagon. She saw Juan on another horse, swallowed up almost immediately by the engulfing inkiness.

Rain fell like slashing, cutting knives. Dany threw

her hand across her eyes, totally disoriented. She heard the roar of the herd behind her, the shouts of the cowboys and the earthshaking tremors caused by the lightning, thunder and the hooves of the crazed cattle. The earth quickly changed into mud, and Altair lengthened his giant stride, flying through the pandemonium. Dany tried to gather her scattered, shocked senses. She had to get out from in front of the stampede! If she fell—the thought of being trampled made her stomach tighten, and desperately she tried to recall the layout of the valley. Guiding Altair to the right on a slight angle, she would cut diagonally in front of the herd, and keep the distance between them!

The entire experience was foreign to her. Diving headlong into darkness and rain at full speed was sheer stupidity. It invited disaster, but she had no choice. Where was Sam? Was he safe? And Altair. Oh, God, she couldn't allow Altair to be injured. Dany increased the angle of the turn, hoping desperately to meet the safety of the tree line. She was soaked to the skin, her shirt clinging to her, water running in rivulets across her drawn face. The charging herd was much closer. Gripping the rain-slick reins tightly, Dany called out to the horse, asking him for a final effort. The stallion lunged strongly, his nostrils wide, drinking in great draughts of wind to sustain his effort.

Suddenly, they were surrounded by trees. Dany pulled Altair to a skidding stop, pine branches whipping back and cutting at her unprotected body. Her breath came in great ragged sobs as she leaned weakly against the stallion's wet mane. Herefords careened so close that she guided Altair further into the tree line for protection. As she sat huddled in the saddle, the temperature began dropping and the wind picked up in gusts. Dany shivered, her hair in long ropes about her face and shoulders. Finally, the lightning eased and the thick, inky blackness descended once more. The bulk of the herd had passed, and the shouts of the men and the bawling of cattle seemed like a distant nightmare.

The dawn crawled cautiously onto the horizon, forcing the night back inches at a time from its tenacious hold on the earth. Dany had remained mounted throughout the long night, searching for Sam. It was an impossible task. Part of the herd had been gathered at the far end of the valley, and she saw both cattle and riders wearily coming back in this direction. Dany saw Juan's dejected features brighten as she came within shouting distance. He seemed relieved, and animatedly gestured, running out to meet her.

"Señora! Señora, pronto!" he shouted.

Dany swallowed hard, kicking Altair into a gallop. She finally slid him to a stop, shakily dismounting. "What is it?" she demanded breathlessly.

"The boss, he's over on the eastern edge of the meadow. He's worried about you."

Dany touched her breast, closing her eyes. "Thank God he's safe!" she whispered fiercely.

Juan grinned broadly. *"Sí,* he's tough. He said as soon as I saw you to get you over to him."

Remounting, she tossed the cook a broad smile. "Thanks, Juan."

Some of her initial joy faded as she rode along the edge of the flatland. Cowboys were putting animals who had broken their legs during the night out of their misery. Seeing Sam made her heartbeat rise. He caught sight of her, pulling Bomarc away from the herd and meeting her halfway. Dany pulled Altair to a stop, reaching out and touching his extended hand.

"You all right?" he asked, gripping her hand tightly.

"Yes. A little tired, that's all," she answered breathlessly. "And you?" She searched his worn face, the exhaustion from the search for the herd evident on his features.

A crooked smile crossed his mouth. "I'll live now that I know you're safe. Look, you go back and help Juan get some breakfast on. We're going to be waylaid here a day just getting the herd back together and repairing the chuck wagon."

Dany nodded, reluctant to break the touch of their fingers. "Be careful," she whispered.

Sam grinned carelessly. "Now that I got someone who cares whether or not I break my neck, I will," he responded, turning Bomarc away and heading back to the main herd.

They arrived back at the Cross Bar-U on the ninth day, tired, dirty and worn. There wasn't a horse whose head wasn't hanging from exhaustion or a cowpoke whose face didn't speak of the trouble on the trail. Dany slid off Altair, resting her head against the horse for a moment. Sam came up, sliding his arm around her shoulders.

"Honey, you get inside and take a long, hot bath," he ordered.

Dany met his gaze, forcing a small smile. "It sounds like heaven," she agreed.

"I'll see you at dinner tonight. Get some rest."

Martha welcomed her back with open arms, giving

her a long hug. Shooing her upstairs, the old woman insisted upon drawing the bath water herself, clucking sympathetically over the events of the drive as Dany related them.

"Missy, you just lay there and soak," she said sternly, shaking her finger at her. "I'll bring you up a healthy lunch in about an hour."

She dozed off in the bath much to her own surprise. Martha had slipped in and out of the suite without awakening her, depositing a tray with thick beef sandwiches, potato chips and a tall, cool glass of iced lemonade on it. Still in her robe, Dany hungrily consumed the food and didn't fight the need to simply fall on the bed and sleep.

It was dark when she awoke. The warm late-spring breeze stirred in the room as Dany slowly sat up, pushing her dark hair off her face. Looking at her watch on the dresser, she saw that it was nearly eight o'clock. With a groan, she pushed off the bed and slowly dressed in a pair of burgundy slacks and a pale pink blouse.

There was a reassuring familiarity to the ranch house as she padded downstairs. She heard Sam's voice in the kitchen and walked into the well-lit room. Martha had just finished dishes and clucked at her sympathetically.

"Miss Dany, you look positively exhausted!"

Dany shrugged, peering over her shoulder at the food to be placed into the refrigerator. "I feel a lot better," she murmured.

"Come and sit down," Sam said. "Martha can get that."

Martha's mouth thinned stubbornly. "You hear Sam? Go sit down before I take a wooden paddle to you."

Dany smiled, exchanging a warm glance with Sam

as she sat opposite him. He looked at her carefully, missing nothing. "You do look better," he agreed, sipping his coffee.

"I don't think my rear is ever going to be the same. Do you realize I've got saddle sores?" she said, laughing good-naturedly.

"You earned them," Sam said, suppressing a grin.

"Humph, is that all I get for my trouble?"

"Yup. That and the knowledge that you can do a hell of a good job at ranch work."

Martha placed the fragrant meal before her. "You children enjoy yourselves. I'm going to bed. This has been too much of a busy day for my eighty-year-old body."

Sam murmured good-night to her, and the silence settled like a warm cloak over the kitchen. Dany ate the barbecued chicken with relish, polishing off the mashed potatoes, corn and a salad. Sam leaned back, a pleased expression in his eyes.

"At least you're eating," he murmured. "Looks like the Sierras are good for you after all."

She wanted to say, "you're good for me," but didn't. Instead, a blush stained her cheeks in response. Even in her sleep she had dreamed of Sam loving her. Each magical touch of his fingers upon her body lingered in her mind. She stared at his work-roughened hands, amazed at the innate gentleness in them when he had loved her.

"Tomorrow morning, Dany, I'm going to have a small jump course set up for you and Altair. We've got about two weeks before the Santa Barbara show, and we might as well start building your confidence."

Her head snapped up and she met his gaze. "I suppose you're right," she whispered. Getting up, she washed off the plate and silverware, placing them in the dishwasher. Dany leaned against the draining board, her arms across her chest in a defensive gesture.

"Scared?" he inquired gently.

"Very."

"I'll be with you every step of the way, Dany."

"I know. But..."

Sam tilted his head. "What?"

She gave a shrug of defeat. "No matter how much you want to help me, Sam, in the end, I have to do it myself."

"I know that, honey. I don't expect you to win at Santa Barbara, Dany. You know that, don't you?"

"But if I do it, I'm planning on placing," she said.

Sam shook his head. "It's too soon to be that competitive, although you certainly have that quality in you. No, the main thing is to get you to feel comfortable about riding in major shows again."

Dany took a long, uneven breath. "God, I don't know, Sam. Jean is going to be there and—"

Sam walked over, standing above her. "One step at a time, Dany. I'll make damn sure he isn't around to try to wreck your confidence before you ride."

Dany waited until Sam came up to join her at the beginning of the small jump course he had erected earlier. It was nearly ten o'clock and already she could feel the coolness of the morning evaporating.

"Ready?" he asked, his voice low and soothing.

"I suppose. First, let's count the strides between jumps."

Sam remained silent as she walked the distance between each jump, mentally calculating how many strides it would take. At a certain point, the jumper had to lift off in order to make it a clean leap and not touch the rails. It was a timed event. Whoever had the least amount of faults and finished with the fastest time would be the winner. If a horse touched the jump, then he accumulated faults against his final score.

Dany was familiar with the odd names given the different and various jumps. There was the oxer, the brush and the in-and-out. Each posed a different problem for the horse and rider. The in-and-out asked the horse to be collected and well in hand because a half-stride too much would throw both the horse and rider into the second jump. The brush consisted of still bristles at the top of it, and no horse wanted it to brush its sensitive back legs. On the Grand Prix circuit, Dany had to count strides along the two or three mile course and keep those figures in her head. One stride too many could result in disaster, and Dany was all too aware of the possibility. Because of her burgeoning feelings toward Sam and her love of the scarred red stallion, she didn't want to disappoint them. Chewing on her lip, she finished pacing the course, giving Sam a curt nod.

With Sam's help, she mounted the frisky Altair. The sorrel pawed eagerly at the ground, wanting to be released. Dany carefully wove the reins of the hackamore and snaffle between her leather-gloved fingers. Sam's hand rested reassuringly on her thigh as he looked up at her.

"Are you going to try and work with the snaffle more today?"

"A little. Right now all I want to do is remember the count," she answered, her voice taut and more brisk than she meant it to be.

"You'll do fine, honey," he soothed, stepping away.

Hard hat in place, Dany compressed her lips, then squeezed Altair. The stallion moved out easily, making large, lazy circles while she warmed him up. No hot-blooded horse, particularly an animal in peak physical condition, was ever asked to jump without properly warming up. More than one horse had been injured and pulled a ligament because he was "cold." After fifteen minutes of figure eights, circles and some light dressage movements, Dany felt the stallion become more supple and responsive.

There were eight jumps facing her when she brought Altair around and out of a final circle. Sam stood off to the right, a stopwatch in his hand. Nudging him into a controlled gallop, she mentally counted each stride to the first oxer, which was two and a half feet high. On cue from her leg, Altair lifted his front legs, his mighty hindquarters coiling like a spring and thrusting them up and over the small jump.

Each jump became a small victory for her. Finally after sailing over the eighth one without a fault she broke into a grin. Leaning down, she patted Altair enthusiastically, praising the stallion. She trotted him back to where Sam stood.

"Well?" she gasped, pulling him to a stop and dismounting.

Sam smiled. "Not a bad time and no faults. You did damn well. Both of you," he said, placing his arm around her and drawing her against his body.

Dany laughed freely, automatically slipping her arms around his waist, resting her head against his shoulder. It seemed so natural until the importance of the gesture dawned upon her. She extricated herself from his arms, and he gave her a questioning glance, but said nothing.

"Let's do it again," Sam suggested. "Each time it will get easier. How did Altair handle for you?"

"Great. He's a doll about cuing for takeoffs, and when I wanted him to slow slightly, I used the snaffle and he responded right away."

Sam took off his hat, pushing his hair back with his fingers as he eyed the stallion. "I wonder if it would be wise to show him in just the snaffle if he continues to progress at Santa Barbara."

"Don't throw too many new things my way, Sam. He's used to the pressure of the hackamore, and I think he's going to be a handful at a show. I'll probably use the hackamore on the cross-country and the snaffle for the dressage test."

"Keeping the snaffle in his mouth for the cross-country would be a wise idea."

"Yes. Tell me, how does he behave at a show?"

Sam grinned mischievously. "He talks to all the ladies."

Dany laughed. "This horse is so much like you it isn't even funny," she commented wryly.

"Oh? In what way?"

"You're all male and you're both incredibly confident. A gentle hand and a soft voice will get more out of you than a crop or spurs."

His eyes darkened. "Maybe I am a little like the stallion," he agreed. "But not just any woman's touch would do," he murmured huskily. "Just yours." He reached over, patting Altair. "See? He's responding beautifully to your voice and hands. You're an unbeatable combination."

Dany colored beneath his loving gaze and gathered up the reins, remounting. She got positively weak in the knees every time he spoke to her in that tone of voice. Sam Reese could get to be an intoxicating habit.

By noon they halted. Sam helped her cool out Altair and then wash him in the shower at the end of the barn. It was sharing the little things with Sam that made her heart sing with newfound joy. It brought back painful memories of times when Jean would idly sit back while she worked, talking about his latest win or who he was going to be competing against at the next show. He never offered to help bathe her charges, walk them out or wrap their slender, valuable legs after a grueling training session.

They stood in the stall, both of them kneeling down by Altair's front legs. Sam passed her the thick cotton matting beneath Altair's belly, and Dany carefully wrapped Altair's foreleg. Sam covered her fingers, and she gently disengaged them while he held the cotton in place. Picking up the elastic bandage, Dany expertly wrapped it around the cotton. She caught Sam watching her with a tender flame of interest in his gray eyes.

"You make everything fun," she admitted, beginning to wrap the second leg.

"Must be the company I've been keeping lately."

She laughed softly. "I feel like I've got an unbeatable team working beside me and I can do nothing but win."

He captured her fingers for a moment against the horse's leg. "You're already a winner, Dany. You just don't realize it yet."

She moved to Altair's hind legs, unable to meet his gaze, swallowing the tears lodged in her throat. Sam got up and leaned against the boxstall as she began wrapping the fourth leg.

"You have any family, Dany?" he asked softly.

Altair snorted, pulling a mouthful of hay from the net suspended in the corner of the stall. Dany changed position and completed the wrap. She got to her feet, dusting the fresh straw off from her breeches. "Yes, my mother."

"She lives back East?"

"Yes." Dany brushed strands of hair away from her temple, gathering up the accessories and placing them into a small tack box.

"What about your father?"

Dany remained silent, and she nervously moved from the stall, letting him slide the door shut. He finally cornered her in the tack room. Grasping her arm, he forced her to turn and face him. "I'm stepping on a sore spot with you, Dany. Tell me it's none of my business and I won't ask you any more questions," he murmured.

His closeness always brought out the strength that she needed to break through yet another old barrier. "No, Sam, I'll tell you." She tossed the cloth down on the saddle that she was going to clean. "My mother really doesn't care for the occupation I'm in, to tell you the truth. My dad—well, he was an alcoholic and left us to fend for ourselves when I was eleven years old." She gave a small shrug. "Actually, we were both glad to see him go. He used to beat up on Mom…"

"Did he hurt you?"

"No. Not physically."

"Just emotionally and mentally," Sam growled.

"A lot of people have had it rougher than me," she

reminded him. She picked up the saddle soap, turning it slowly in her hands. "Maybe that's why I didn't marry until I was twenty-four, Sam. I didn't want the unhappiness I saw in my mother's marriage. She always said she got married too young and I should wait.… Well, I did and I still made a lousy choice."

"Not really," Sam answered softly, catching her unhappy gaze. "You didn't marry an alcoholic. A lot of children coming out of a family situation like that usually end up the same way. You didn't."

She got up, tossing the soap back upon the cloth. "I don't know why I'm still punishing myself for having made a mistake in marrying Jean. When I was a child I swore I'd never marry the wrong man like my mom did." Her voice took on a wistful note and she faced Sam. "I had it all figured out. My husband would be loving, giving and sharing. The exact opposite of my dad. Instead I fell for a guy that was interested in using me as a stepping stone to get to the top and I lay right down and let him do it." Her voice quivered. "I'm so angry at myself!"

Sam got up and came over, pulling her into his arms. She didn't resist, resting her head against his chin. "You have a lot of stored-up anger to release, honey. And until you do that, you'll never be free of him or forgive yourself for the mistakes you made." He gave her a small shake. "Dany, don't berate yourself for making errors. The trick is never to repeat the same one twice." He held her at arm's length and offered her a smile. "Just make new ones."

Tears swelled in her eyes and she gave a little laugh. "You're crazy, Sam Reese!"

He leaned down, brushing her lips in a featherlight

kiss. "Maybe," he agreed throatily. He raised his head, a lambent gray flame deep in the recesses of his eyes as he studied her for several heartrending seconds. "You're a very special woman, Dany," he whispered, "and I want the chance to know more about you...your past, your present and what you dream for the future. Just keep trusting me and let's keep talking and both our dreams might get answered if we work at it, honey. Come on, we've got to make some plans for transporting Altair to Santa Barbara." He grinned and pulled her close, giving her a quick hug.

Chapter 11

Dany made a last-minute check on Altair's thickly padded stall that had been specially built within the cargo hold of the airplane. She busied herself with a myriad of details, trying to fight back the fear that shadowed every minute of her day. Where had the two weeks gone in preparation for Santa Barbara? Sam had been with her at least two hours each morning as she took Altair over more complex and demanding jump sequences. She had gained more respect for Sam and his knowledge of the Grand Prix circuit—he was not just an owner of a potential champion, but a man who had valued insight into the demanding world of international jumping events.

Dany made sure the leather cap that Altair wore between his ears was snugly fastened; in case the stallion jerked his head up unexpectedly, the cap could prevent a concussion. Sam had helped her wrap his legs earlier, and she double-checked to make sure that they were holding.

"About ready?" Sam asked, walking up the ramp.

She turned. "Yes."

He smiled, giving the order to remove the ramp. Dany remained at Altair's side as Sam and his ranch hand Pete, came aboard. Speaking soothingly to the nervous stallion as the door to the aircraft was closed, Dany continued to rub his neck in a reassuring motion. Sam came over, resting against the stall, putting one arm across her shoulders and the other on Altair's shoulder.

"Who's more nervous?" he asked softly. "You or the horse?"

She shook her head. "It's a toss-up," she admitted.

"You'll both do fine, honey."

They landed at Los Angeles International Airport without incident. From there, a horse trailer and truck were waiting to whisk them to the grounds where the Grand Prix event would be held. The temperature was in the nineties, and Dany was thankful for the air-conditioning in the truck as they reached their final destination. Her nervousness increased as they received their pass from the gate guard and got directions to the stabling area.

Everywhere she looked she saw sleek thoroughbreds and Hanoverians prancing lightly, eager for workouts. Her pulse picked up more strongly, and a new sense of anticipation spread throughout her. She was proud of Altair and wanted to note the expressions on other riders' faces when she took him out to acclimate him to the grounds. Sam glanced over at her as they pulled into the stabling area.

"You're excited," was all he said, a slight grin shadowing his mouth.

"I shouldn't be. I ought to be scared to death."

He shut off the engine and slid out. "You'll experience both extremes," he warned lightly. "Come on, let's help Pete get this big red horse out of that stuffy trailer before he decides to throw a temper tantrum."

"You want to get him bedded down with Pete and I'll go over to the show office and make sure we're registered with the show secretary?"

"Go ahead," Sam agreed.

People in English riding habits were all about. Their snorting, prancing mounts cantered over the lush grass expanse throughout the complex. As she reached for the screen door, a darkly tanned hand closed over her own.

"*Chérie,* I never expected to see you here."

Dany froze, jerking her hand away. "Jean!" she breathed sharply.

Jean grinned boyishly, taking his riding cap off and bowing gallantly. "The same. Ahh, you look as lovely as ever. And," he murmured, eyeing her critically, "I would say you are thinner." He grinned broadly, his green eyes dancing with mirth. "You tempt me, Danielle. As always."

Dany's eyes narrowed, and she stepped away from him. "Lying as usual, I see. Save your pretty words to use on someone who cares, Jean." She pulled open the screen, moving quickly inside to the show secretary's desk. Her heart was beating erratically, and anguish coursed through her. Jean had followed her in, and now he stood near the wall, one leg propped lazily over his other booted foot, watching her with amused curiosity.

Her business completed, Dany turned, wanting to run out the door to escape the presence of her ex-husband. She felt his hand on her arm, slowing her down once she was outside.

"Where are you going in such a hurry?"

Dany wrenched her arm away from him, coming to a halt. Her nostrils flared with anger. "Leave me alone, Jean! You've used me and gotten what you've wanted. So quit rubbing salt into the wounds!" she cried.

"Used you?" he echoed, raising his eyebrows. His narrow face became less readable. "Ahh, you think I used you as a stepping-stone for success."

"You bet I do."

He shrugged his shoulders eloquently. "But Danielle, it has worked out for you, also. You see, you're riding a Grand Prix candidate yourself. You also benefited from our—liaison. *Oui?*"

Blood was pounding through her skull and she barely held her temper in check. "I'm riding a horse *you* contracted to show! I don't want the limelight, Jean. I never did. Now—" her voice wobbled "—now it's caused so many problems because I have to fulfill the terms of the contract."

Jean frowned. "*Chérie,* you're out of your mind riding that red cow horse. He's got a name on the circuit, you know."

"Which is why you probably left the country," she growled. "This is the first time I've seen you turn tail and be a coward, Jean."

Jean colored fiercely, his dark jade eyes glittering like cold diamonds. "That horse is a killer."

"No more than you are," she hurled back.

He managed a sour grin. "Well, if he doesn't kill

you, you'll kill him, *chérie*. Which will it be, eh? Last time it was Crusader's Prince. Who will end up in the hospital this time, I wonder?"

Dany stood frozen, her face devoid of emotion, her heart plummeting to her stomach. Jean had often been short and abrupt during their marriage, but never outwardly cruel. Not like now. Why had he hurled all that old guilt back into her face? She glared at him. "Neither of us," she rasped.

"You're a trainer, not a rider, Danielle." He gave a small bow. "I must be off. I wonder, should I tell the press that two losers are trying to win here, eh?"

She clenched her fist. "You cold-blooded—"

"Listen, when it comes down to my winning this title and anyone threatening my position, I'll make sure I'm not the loser. *Au revoir.*"

Dany purposely walked back to the barn at a slow pace, trying to harness the clashing, roiling emotions that must have been evident on her face. Tears of anger slashed down her cheeks, and she stopped, wiping them away before entering the cool barn complex. Down at the end of the hall in the breezy passageway she could see Sam and Pete saddling up Altair. Compressing her lips into a set line, she took a firmer step, stopping at the tack trunk to grab her hard hat and leather gloves.

Sam smiled down at her as she came around the rear of Altair. Then he frowned, his gaze traveling up and down her rigid body. "Dany?"

"It's nothing," she snapped, taking the reins and leading the stallion out into the paddock. Just as she was about to mount, she felt Sam's restraining hand on her arm.

"Nothing is something," he returned, making it obvious he wanted an explanation.

"Not now, Sam! Give me a boost up on Altair. I need some time to think." She gave him a begging look and he relented. She settled firmly in the Stübben jump saddle, allowing the short stirrups to slide onto her black, booted feet. His hand rested on her knee.

"Warm him up slow, honey," was all he said.

Sam's quiet, reassuring voice assuaged some of the roaring anger, and Dany managed to give a nod of her head. "I will," she promised, her voice thick with tears.

The actual three-mile Grand Prix cross-country course was off-limits to the competitors, but a lovely area of two miles of rolling hills with test jumps had been arranged to keep the finely honed athletes in top condition for the performance. It had been nine months since Altair had attended a show, and Dany wanted to check his reactions. The stallion arched his neck, his head perpendicular to the ground as she signaled him to remain on the bit.

Dany worked him in wide circles and figure eights, asking him to switch leads from right to left or vice versa as warm-up. The fields were crowded with some of the finest Grand Prix jumpers in the world, and she purposely shut out their existence, concentrating one hundred percent on Altair's actions and responsiveness. The moment that she took the jump position, her knees and calves firmly against his barrel, body lifted off and slightly forward from the saddle, Altair tensed. The first series of jumps were three-and-a-half to four-and-a-half feet in height, and he scaled them effortlessly.

She worked nearly an hour, finally bringing him down to a slow trot as she came to the gate where Sam had been standing and watching them. Dropping the reins, Dany slid off the saddle.

"Well?" she asked.

"Honey, you two look like champions out there." Sam pulled the cowboy hat down over his forehead. "Matter of fact, you should have seen every rider on that course watching you at one time or another. They know they have some competition from you two." He grinned and slipped his arm around her shoulders, giving her a hug. "You look good, Dany," he whispered.

Her confidence rose slightly beneath his compliment. She matched his stride, taking off the hard hat and tucking it beneath her arm. As if reading her thoughts, Sam glanced down at her.

"Something's bothering you."

She gave a slight shrug of her shoulders. "I had the misfortune of running into Jean over at the secretary's office," she explained timidly, worried at his reaction. Dany saw his gray eyes turn brittle and probing.

"That's why you were snapping when you mounted up Altair."

"Yes, I'm sorry." They halted at the pickup, and she turned to him. "Oh, Sam, do you really think I have any business showing Altair?"

He gripped her, giving her a small shake. "Every right," he whispered fiercely. "Do you have any idea of how beautiful you and Altair look together as a team? My God, Dany, there wasn't a rider or a trainer who wasn't watching both of you out there earlier. You're championship material." His mouth pulled into an understanding smile. "Come on, let's get over to the motel and get cleaned up. We deserve some rest before tomorrow morning."

She grimaced, climbing into the pickup. "Don't remind me, although the dressage test will be the easiest of the three."

"You'll make them all look easy," he promised, throwing the truck into gear.

Once at the motel, which was a few miles from the show grounds, Sam escorted her to a room which adjoined his own. As if sensing her need to be alone, he left telling her that if she needed anything, to knock on the inner door. In some respects, it was almost like being at home. Dany caught herself wistfully thinking of the ranch as "home," sharply reminding herself that it was only temporary. Pulling off the boots, and stepping out of the breeches and blouse, she took a cooling shower. Wrapped in a towel, she lay down on the bed, falling asleep immediately.

She awoke from the sound sleep near six o'clock that night. Refreshed, Dany slipped into a sleeveless summer dress of pale pink. Funny, she mused while tying the dainty white sash around her waist, I've never wanted to wear dresses before. Sam seemed so appreciative when she did appear in a dress or skirt that his silent admiration coaxed her into rediscovering her femininity.

Knocking softly on the door, she waited patiently until Sam pulled it open. His face mirrored his reaction. "You look lovely," was all he said, but it was enough.

Dany couldn't meet his burning, intense gaze. Each time she was near him, it was agony to stop herself from gliding effortlessly back into his arms. She wanted to rest against the solidness of his body and to be loved openly, without reserve. Memory of that afternoon in the canyon seared her thoughts daily. They had worked so hard in the last two weeks in preparation for Santa Barbara that a stolen kiss or a long embrace was all that had been shared between them.

"With you looking that nice, I'd say we'll have to go someplace special to eat. Hungry?"

"Starved," she admitted.

Sam picked up his Western suit coat, catching her hand and leading her through his room. "Feel better now that you've slept?" he asked.

"Much."

"How's the confidence level holding?"

"It's fragile."

"Mmm, you look incredibly fragile, vulnerable and lovely," he said, turning and gently brushing her cheek with a kiss. He halted at the door and pulled her against him, nuzzling her earlobe with delicious slowness.

Dany moaned softly, falling against the hard oak of his body, hungry for the smell, feel and taste of him once again. He gave her confidence, solace and affection that she was starved for. Turning her head, she felt the molding of his mouth against her parting, yielding lips. It was a searching, hungry kiss, and Sam pulled away, studying her darkly.

"God, how I've missed holding and touching you," he breathed huskily, his breath moist and warm against her face. "Do you know how hard it was not to ask you to stay with me?"

Dany swallowed. "Time, Sam. I needed the time alone," she breathed softly.

His eyes warmed and he smiled, fingers trailing down the length of her clean jawline. "And now, honey?" he asked lazily, already knowing her answer.

She was afraid to say it. His thumb circled the sensitive skin beneath her earlobe, creating a wild, tingling sensation throughout her whole body. He leaned down, capturing her parted lips in a breath-stealing kiss.

"Say it," he murmured against her lips, brushing them softly. "Say that you want to stay with me tonight, Dany."

Her body quivered beneath his taming fingers, and she sighed languorously, helpless to do anything but surrender. "Yes," she whispered, "I—"

Sam kissed her again, effectively hushing her. He raised his head, cupping her face between his large callused hands. "*Yes* is all I ever need to hear, honey. I need you like I've never needed another woman." His gray eyes darkened with desire as he searched each nuance of her face. "I see the fear in your eyes, Dany. Fear from the past. I won't ask anything more of you until you're ready to give it. Tonight, let me love you like I've dreamed of loving you."

Time eddied and swirled like a slow-moving stream for the rest of the evening. A quiet Chinese restaurant provided the needed tranquility and sense of isolation Dany had sought. She was constantly amazed by Sam's insight into her unspoken requirements, falling more deeply in love with him with each thoughtful gesture he bestowed upon her. As they sat drinking their tea she reflected upon his ability to accurately assess her needs; there was a hidden sensitivity to Sam Reese. Most men with the power of corporations and millions of dollars behind them tended to be shrewd, cold and sometimes even ruthless toward others. She had watched Sam deal courteously with a waiter, the maitre d' and the young man who had parked their vehicle. Yet, when Jean had taken her to dinner, which hadn't been often, he walked with his chin thrust outward, a smugness surrounding him that managed to insult anyone who had to deal with him.

She set her cup down, meeting Sam's melting gray gaze. "You know," she began quietly, "the more I'm around you, the more I wonder what I saw in Jean."

Sam cocked his head attentively, resting his jaw against his folded hands. "Oh? In what way?"

"Little things." She gave a shy smile, embarrassed. "You're so…" She groped for the right words, unused to expressing her emotions or insights. "Why are you so kind to everyone? Jean would embarrass me with his swaggering attitude whenever we went out. You treat everyone as if they were your friend."

He shared a smile with her. "Martha beat it into me when I was real young to observe the Golden Rule."

Dany laughed with him. "I would think all the money and corporations you own would make you callous."

"In a lot of owners it does," he conceded, toying with the small teacup. "I learned a long time ago to use brute force or power only when necessary. You get more bees with honey than vinegar, you know."

Mesmerized by the mellow huskiness in his voice, Dany felt her heart swelling with undeniable love for him. There was a natural agreement of emotions between them, a common ground where both could find solace and protection from the world. The thought of holding him when he felt the need to be cradled against her body sent a new, exhilarating rush throughout her body. She wasn't the only one who needed to be held.

On the way back, Dany persuaded him to make one more check on Altair. Pete met them at the stallion's boxstall. He had arranged a small cot outside the stall door, since no Grand Prix jumper was ever left unattended. Sometimes because of the stress of traveling, time changes or weather conditions, the international athletes would come down with colic. It took the watchful eye of a groom who knew the horse's temperament to be able to spot the first telltale signs of colic, which could kill a horse if the complications were severe enough.

Sam sent Pete on an errand to pick up a few more bales of straw from the main barn, leaving them in the darkness with Altair. Dany allowed the stallion to rest his head against her shoulder as she gently scratched his forelock. Sam remained at her side, his arm around her waist. The night was broken by the softened snort of horses, voices of other grooms further down the dimly lit corridor and the jingle of bits, bridles and saddles being lovingly cleaned one last time before the dawn of the grueling three-day test.

Dany was content to be in the cradle of Sam's arms with Altair nibbling playfully with her fingers, when suddenly the stallion lifted his massive head. Dany looked down the passageway, frowning. A lean figure seemed to melt out of the graying depths, materializing before them like a ghost. She gasped, her eyes widening.

"Jean!"

Her ex-husband stood there, hands languidly resting on his hips.

"Giving your horse a last-minute pep talk?"

Her heart hammered as she heard the steeliness in

his softened voice. Simultaneously she felt Sam's arm tighten, bringing her protectively against him. Jean hadn't missed the symbolic and instinctive gesture, and a slow smile tugged at his thin-lipped mouth as he met Sam's hooded gaze.

"I'd think you would be over giving your horse a talk, Daguerre," he returned coolly.

She froze, aware of the brittle truce drawn between the two men who faced one another in the dimness of the passageway. There was no mistaking Sam's warning in his baritone voice, and she saw Jean's eyes flicker with a second of fear. It was such a fleeting re-action that Dany blinked, thinking she had been making it up in her active imagination.

The Frenchman shrugged eloquently, regaining his flamboyant smile. "Monsieur Reese, I can assure you my horse is ready to win handily in every event. I let him sleep."

"Then I suggest you do the same thing."

Dany inhaled softly, her eyes widening. There was nothing compromising about Sam in any way. For the first time she was seeing the dangerous side of his personality. And Jean was fully aware of it, too.

Jean lost his smile, considering the Westerner for what seemed an eternity. His eyes flashed with anger, and he swung his gaze to Dany. "Just remember," he breathed angrily, "you'll be alone out there for the next three days. He won't be there. It will be you and me. Remember that."

Sam gently disengaged his arm from Dany, giving her a push toward the truck. "Dany, I'll see you in a few moments."

"But—"

Sam turned his head. "Now," he ordered.

Dany looked at each of them, suddenly shaky with adrenaline. "No, I won't have you fighting—"

Jean laughed. "I only have one question for you, Danielle. Just one."

Sam glared over at him and then back at her as she stood poised like a startled gazelle ready for flight. "Daguerre, I'm warning you—"

She was shaken by the ugly turn of events. Anger soared through her, clearing her confused, muddled thoughts. "What?" she challenged, her voice echoing oddly through the corridor.

Jean pointed to Sam. "Are you allowing yourself to be used again? You're developing a habit of falling in love with men who, shall we say, use your impressive talents with horses."

His scathing comment sliced into her heart; a knife twisting painfully in her chest. Tears sprang to her eyes, and she covered her mouth with her hands. She heard Sam mutter a curse as he stepped forward, gripping Jean by the collar, slamming him up against the boxstall.

"You son of a—"

"No!" Dany cried.

Sam's grip tightened on the Frenchman until the color drained from his face. Jean struggled, but was no match in size or bulk. Sam growled, "That's the last filthy thing to come out of your mouth. You hear me?" His nostrils flared as he glared down at the rider. "No more insults, Daguerre, or you won't be able to climb up on that horse of yours tomorrow morning. You got that?"

Tears blurred her vision as she stood there watching the two men glare at one another. Finally, Jean gave the barest nod of his head, and Sam released his grip. "Now get out of here and stay away from Dany," he snarled.

He adjusted his shirt, hastily disappearing back into the shadows, his footfalls disappearing quickly, fading into the night. Sam turned, his gray eyes chips of glacial anger as he perused her. His expression changed swiftly as he saw her standing there in tears. "Dany?"

She took a step away from him, her eyes large and stricken. Was it the truth? Had she fallen in love with Sam just like she had with Jean? Was she making the same mistake again? Oh, God! "No," she cried softly, avoiding his outstretched hand.

"Don't listen to him!" Sam growled. He gripped her arm, halting her flight toward the door of the complex. "Dany, stand still, dammit!"

She whirled around, throwing her hands out, meeting the wall of his chest. "No!" she sobbed, "leave me alone!" All she wanted to do was escape, to have time to think over Jean's horrifying accusation. Was it only a game to Sam? Had he wooed and enticed her all this time just to ride Altair? Her heart shrank in agony against the possibility. But she had done it once, and could do it again. How many times had she heard of women getting a divorce and within a year "bouncing" into another similar situation?

"Honey," he begged roughly, capturing her within his arms and holding her against his body, "it isn't true." He brushed her hair in a kiss, sighing raggedly. "Believe me, Dany, believe…"

"I don't know what to believe," she sobbed helplessly, burying her face in her hands.

"Come on," he urged, "we've got some sorting out and talking to do."

It was useless to try and fight him, and she gave in, blinded by her tears, being led like a sobbing child to the truck. By the time they had reached the motel, the tears had ceased. She sat woodenly in a chair within his room as he closed the door. One small lamp chased away the darkness, and his face was shadowed and unreadable as he tossed the cowboy hat and his suit coat to an empty chair. Pulling up another one, he sat opposite her, his face serious and at the same time, probing.

"Let's start from the beginning, Dany," he urged.

"Which one?" she wanted to know, her voice thick and hoarse.

"The one with me. It's the only one that counts now," he countered patiently. "Sure, I wanted you to train and ride Altair. But I would never use your trust or—" His voice softened and there was an unsureness evident in his gray gaze. He stared at her hard for a long moment and finally released a sigh. "This is a hell of a way and time to tell you that I love you," he growled. "I damn near admitted it the day we made love up in the canyon, Dany. But I thought I'd scare you off. I didn't think you were ready for the kind of commitment that I felt toward you." He captured her hands, squeezing them gently. "I wanted to give you the time to work through the anger and hurt of your first marriage, Dany. I was willing to keep our relationship free of any serious commitment until you wanted to take another step."

She stared at him, lips parting, stunned. "You—love me?"

He managed a sour grin. "I suppose it didn't cross

your mind that a man from the West might fall in love with a woman from the East?"

Dany gave a shaky laugh. "You really do?" She was like a breathless child in that instant, and Sam groaned softly, getting to his feet, pulling her within the circle of his arms.

"More than life itself, Dany," he whispered roughly, capturing her body solidly against his own, his mouth finding her wet, salty lips.

Time stood on the threshold of eternity in that exquisite moment. A small cry echoed in her throat as she allowed him to deepen the kiss, his tongue finding each sensitive point within her mouth, a molten fire spreading wildly throughout her responding body. He captured her hips against him, and she was aware of his maleness. Entwining her fingers around his thickly corded neck, Dany returned the passion fully, wanting to drown herself completely within him in every possible way.

Dragging his mouth from her bruised lips, he whispered hoarsely, "We belong to each other, Dany. I want to love you so much. These past two weeks have been hell on both of us. Come to bed with me."

She was breathless from his branding kiss, eyes wide and lustrous with invitation. "I didn't know... Oh, Sam, I love you, too. So much that I—"

He bent down, smothering her lips in a soul-searching kiss. "Shh, honey, just show me. That's all I'll ever need...."

If time had halted on the edge of eternity, then infinity was composed of a cocoon of unequaled, shared love. He led her to the bed and with painstaking slowness, unbuttoned her pale pink dress. She was hyp-

notized by the tender flame in his gray eyes as he
hungrily devoured her upturned face. Slipping his fingers inside the dress, his work-roughened fingers sent
thrilling shocks through her body as he slipped it over
her shoulders.

Leaning down, he placed light, teasing kisses from
her shoulder to her collarbone to the cleavage of her
breasts. Dany drew in a tiny gasp as she felt the bra
slipping away from her flesh, being replaced by Sam's
tormenting hands. Pushing her gently back against
the pillows, he lay down beside her, running his hand
across the expanse of her body. Her hair was like a blue
black sheet framing her head and shoulders, and Sam
smiled, running his fingers through the silken strands.

"You're so beautiful," he whispered against her ear,
nibbling at the lobe. Her breathing became shallow and
fast as he continued to taunt and tease her until she was
arching against him. She waited in a warm, molten
haze as he unbuttoned his shirt and undressed fully.
Each muscle led cleanly into another, and she stared
at him in silent admiration. Welcoming him back to
her open arms, Dany sighed softly, closing her eyes,
vibrantly aware of his lean maleness.

His mouth closed over her nipple, coaxing it to hardness, and she arched upward, moaning his name over
and over again breathlessly, fingers digging deeply
into his back. "Please," she cried, "now...please..."
Caressing her heated flesh, he stroked the sensitive
skin of her thighs, asking entrance to the moist dampness of her yielding body. A fiery hunger seemed to
consume her, and she arched to meet him, fusing with
him in a primal explosion of volcanic need. Now they
were molded into one, the throbbing rhythm sending

them to higher and higher levels of exquisite pleasure. Reaching the pinnacle, she froze in ecstasy within his strong embrace, then pressed against his damp body as she felt him tense and shudder, their hearts beating wildly in unison.

A smothering joy enveloped her as she reached out, the flat of her palm against the stubbled roughness of his face. Sam caressed her, taking a deep breath of air. "God, how I love you," he said thickly.

Chapter 12

They awoke at exactly six, still clasped in each other's arms. As Dany slowly awoke through the process of bathing and toweling off, it dawned upon her that today was the first of the three tests: dressage. Wrapping the yellow towel around her body, she walked back into the bedroom where Sam was still dozing and began to dress for the event. Climbing into her white breeches and blouse, she felt that she was still wrapped in a blanket of happiness. She was back in the bathroom coaxing her hair into its neat chignon when she saw Sam enter. His hair was tousled and his eyes still filled with sleep as he slid his arms around her waist, drawing her back against him. Dany smiled, closing her eyes, loving his closeness.

"I don't sleep well when you aren't beside me," he breathed against her ear, giving her a kiss on the cheek.

"I could come back to bed, but who will get Altair

ready for the dressage test at eight?" she teased, relishing his hard-muscled arms around her.

He raised one eyebrow, lifting his head and staring at her in the mirror. "Good question. Still, I vote for the bed."

Dany turned in his arms, facing him. "You're serious, aren't you?"

Sam rocked her gently back and forth in his arms. "Sure am. It's all your fault, you know. I was going to wait until this show was over to propose to you, lady. I had it all planned. We'd take a couple of days off and go back into the interior. I wanted to woo you with the beauty of the land at its best and then catch you in a mellow moment so that you would be forced to say yes."

She basked in the tenderness of his gaze, reaching up and taming the unruly strands of hair. "Yes to what? I willingly went to bed with you."

He leaned back against the doorframe, cradling her against him. "Is that all you thought I wanted from you? Bed?" he questioned.

Dany caught the seriousness in his eyes and the inflection in his voice. She had been happy and teased him instead of responding to that pensive look dwelling in his pewter gray eyes. A blush swept up her neck and across her face. "Well—I—"

"I told you last night I loved you, Dany. Bed's only a small part of it." He looked around the bathroom, a smile edging his mouth. "This is a hell of a place to propose, you know that?"

She didn't know whether to laugh or cry and stood there resting against his naked body. His smile deepened.

"Well? Will you be my friend, my lover and my wife?"

Tears sprang to her eyes and she opened her mouth and then closed it. He was so right for her; he had been her friend in every sense of the word since their first meeting and it was an ingredient she had sought in her first marriage and found sadly lacking. Sam caressed her cheek, cupping her chin, forcing her to meet his eyes.

"Just nod yes or no," he coaxed.

Dany nodded and Sam picked her up, nearly crushing her in his impulsive embrace. Finally, she gave a half sob and half laugh as he set her back on her feet. He led her from the bathroom and in one deft motion picked her up, carrying her back to his room, depositing her on the bed. She snuggled into his awaiting arms, burying her head against his shoulder, yearning simply to be held, feeling his heart beat like a solid drum against her breast.

"You give me so much happiness," she whispered brokenly.

"Mmm," he growled close to her ear, "it's mutual, honey, believe me."

"I never dreamed..." she choked out.

Sam rested above her, absently stroking her bound hair. "What?" he urged.

Dany wiped the tears away. "Oh, my riding master, Terrence," she blurted out softly. She sniffed again. "He always told me to chase the clouds, to go after what I wanted and never be afraid to try it."

"Sounds like a wise old man."

Dany met his warming gaze, melting inwardly. "I loved you from the moment I saw you, Sam, and I was afraid to admit it. Thank God I had the courage to come out West with you."

Sam smiled patiently. "And here we've been fighting like cats and dogs all this time. The instant I saw you it was as if I'd been struck by a bolt of lightning. I was desperate to know you better." He raised his head, frowning. "I think I would have moved heaven and hell to have that privilege, Dany. I knew you were frightened and you were still carrying too many fresh scars from your marriage." He gazed down at her fondly. "Dany, you made my blood run like no woman ever has. Maybe it was your vulnerability, I don't know. You have so much strength of character and I saw it every time you handled Altair, and at the same time, you had the capacity to know when to lean and give in when you were feeling weak."

She gave a small laugh. "I learned a long time ago that pride is the first of my emotions that is expendable. Don't worry, darling, I'll be the first to fall into your arms when I feel like it."

"That's another nice thing about us I like," he murmured, kissing her brow. "We both can say we were wrong and make up. Compromise is so much a part of a successful marriage and I think with one another we have that very rare ingredient."

She nodded, glancing at her watch. "Sam, do you realize in an hour I have to be in the ring?"

He sighed, a quizzical smile pulling at the corner of his mouth. "Spoken like a true horsewoman. You want to leave me for that stallion, is that it?"

She laughed, sitting up on the edge of the bed, straightening out her white blouse. "Give the choice, I'll pick you."

He got up, turning on the shower. "That does my ego a world of good. Give me ten minutes and then we'll get over to the barn area. Pete ought to have him ready to go by the time we get there."

The dressage arena had a solid sand base, making footing for the demanding performance of the three-day eventers excellent. Dany sat quietly on Altair waiting for her number to be called next. A large crowd was watching as horses and riders put themselves through the strenuous, demanding test, politely clapping after each performance. Altair chewed on the snaffle bit, white flecks of foam appearing at the corners of his mouth. Pete patiently wiped his muzzle clean with a damp cloth, patting the horse.

Sam stood at her knee, his hand resting on her thigh. "You're going to knock 'em dead," he said, looking up at her, his mood serious.

She gave a nod. Of the three tests, this was the easiest. The one she dreaded the most was tomorrow morning. "He's ready," she agreed, rubbing the stallion's neck fondly.

"He'll do fine in that snaffle for you," Sam noted. "Tomorrow you'll probably want to switch to the hackamore."

"For the cross-country and the in-stadium jumping," she agreed. It was nearly impossible to have contact with the horse's sensitive mouth without a bit in the dressage portion. Dany said a silent prayer that Altair would continue to bend and flex to her invisible hand movements and do as she asked. Her number, twenty-two, was called and she gathered up the reins. Altair immediately tensed, standing alertly, waiting for the next order.

"Good luck, honey," Sam called, stepping away. He

gave her a warm, intimate smile that sent her confidence soaring.

Dressage was the epitome of balance and teamwork between horse and human. At the Grand Prix level it was an art; the horse and rider moved together through the intricate steps in a fluid motion. Stopping at the judges' stand, Dany nodded curtly to the three and then swung Altair to one end of the immaculate arena. There was a hushed silence over the crowd. Every fifty to sixty feet a letter was placed along the rail around the oval arena. The rider had to memorize in advance the dressage pattern and at the exact moment the horse paralleled the black-and-white letter, he was asked to change gait or execute a different delicate, demanding pattern.

Altair flexed beautifully; he was fully on the snaffle, his large nostrils flared, ears back toward his rider and attentive for the signals to come. His copper coat shone like red brass in the early morning sunlight as he broke into a brilliantly extended trot, his long legs thrusting out to their maximum length. It was rare that the dressage crowd would ever whisper or make any noise to break the concentration of horse to rider, but a small ripple of awe passed through the multitude as the stallion's beautifully controlled movements flowed like molten copper into each demanding step.

With the test completed, Dany kept her face straight and serious, bringing Altair back to the center of the arena and once again nodded to the judges, before leaving the ring. She fastened her gaze on Sam in the distance as she rode out at a slow trot, unanimous applause breaking wildly in back of them. Once clear of the crowd, Dany slipped off Altair, giving him an enthusiastic hug. Sam came over, grinning broadly.

"Look at that." He pointed at the scoreboard. "A 72! That's the best score here today. Congratulations." He swept her into his arms, kissing her soundly.

She laughed, returning his hug, stunned by Altair's near-perfect performance. Pete clapped her on the back and, smiling happily, led Altair back to the boxstall while Dany and Sam followed behind at a leisurely pace.

"You don't want to stick around and watch the competition?" Sam asked.

She shook her head. "No, I couldn't stand the tension." She gave him a brilliant smile. "He was wonderful, Sam! What a perfect gentleman!"

He rested his arm across her shoulders drawing her near. "Altair has always come through for me when I really needed him at his best. He's giving you the same now, honey. I think tomorrow will make all the difference in the world. You're going to feel safe on him, Dany."

Her ebullient mood ebbed a bit at the horrifying thought of the cross-country. She resisted the fear that was eating a hole in her confidence, remembering how Altair had saved her life the night of the cattle stampede during the storm. Between Sam's love and Altair's sure-footedness, she had little to worry about. Stealing a glance up at Sam's handsome face, she murmured, "Terrence would skin me alive if I didn't ride that wonderful stallion tomorrow. He'd shake his finger, scowl and give me the dickens."

"Well," Sam murmured gruffly, leaning down and

kissing her hair, "I think good loving will do the same thing. What do you think?"

She rested against his strong body. "I think you're right, darling."

It was the first day of the rest of her life and Dany knew it. She sat astride the prancing red stallion who snorted with charged vitality as they waited their turn to begin the three-mile cross-country course. Sam had been right: By holding her and loving her all night long he had chased back the fear and put it into proper perspective. She had awakened earlier glorying in the joyous feelings of being loved and loving in return. And it was as if the stallion had sensed her newly found confidence, his flaxen tail lifting and flowing like white silk in the early morning breeze that caressed the demanding course. Today she wore her hard hat, a pair of canary yellow breeches, her black knee-high boots and a white T-shirt with the number twenty-two attached to the front and back of it.

Her mind was zeroed in on the eighteen jumps that would stress and challenge even the most seasoned eventer. Altair hadn't jumped in nine months, and she was aware that he was rusty. She would have to make up the difference. Altair was allowing her to take charge, and he was responsive—something Sam had said he had never done with any of his other riders. She leaned down, rubbing his neck in a soothing circular motion, feeling him relax beneath her gloved hand.

Out of the corner of her eye she saw Jean coming up on his beautiful French thoroughbred. The animal shone like fine steel in the sunlight, moving well beneath Jean's skillful hands.

"Congratulations on your dressage score, *ma ché-rie*," he greeted, pulling the gelding he rode to a halt.

Dany's eyes narrowed distrustfully. "Not bad for a 'cow horse,' is that it?"

Jean grinned mirthlessly, eyeing the sorrel stallion with a measuring stare. "No, being number two in the standings is not bad at all," he agreed. "Still, that is only one-third of the entire score." His voice dropped, lined with a threat. "You'll be lucky if you don't end up on the ground somewhere on this course today. Did you see that earthen wall? Jump number fourteen? The horses will be tired by the time they reach that devil. I'll bet that half of them won't make the steep angle of it and fall backward."

"Fourteen is negotiable if you get the proper takeoff point," she said, angry over his suggestion that Altair would not finish the course.

Jean shrugged. "*Oui*. After scaling that monster it is an eight-foot vertical drop on the other side to the water below it. I understand your cow horse hates water. I wonder what he'll do once he sees it? Balk at the top? Rear and sunfish over backward taking you with him?"

She compressed her lips, gathering up the reins to the hackamore. "You aren't scaring me any more, Jean," she warned, her voice cold with fury. "This horse is more sure-footed than any other animal here. I'll bet my life on it."

He smiled thinly. "You may just do that. Anyway, good luck. It's the least I can do for my lovely ex-wife under the circumstances."

"There's no luck involved, Jean, you ought to know that," she flung back, urging Altair as far away from him as she could get. Anger wove with her confidence, and suddenly, all the butterfly feelings in her stomach ceased. She heard their number being called and trotted Altair up to the chute.

The timer glanced down at his stopwatch, holding a white flag up. Dany swallowed hard, lips flattened, narrowing her perception to the course. The stallion was restive, his small, fine ears flicking back and forth nervously. She glanced to her left, meeting, catching Sam's gaze. In that instant the last of her uncertainty disappeared, and she squeezed the horse's barrel hard with her calves and knees as the buzzer sounded.

Altair lunged forward and the wind sheared at her face making her eyes water from the terrific speed built up within seconds by the thoroughbred. She allowed Altair to stretch to full stride, then she checked him with the hackamore, feeling him immediately slow down his approach to the first fence. She cued him at the exact moment that she wanted him to lift off. The stallion raised his front legs, tucking them high and close to his belly, sailing effortlessly across the four-and-a-half-foot wall which consisted of rough-cut logs. Dany shouted praise in his ear, and she felt a new, strange elation pushing off all of her fears. Just the steadiness of Altair's ground-eating stride was soothing, and her world narrowed to counting off strides, and sizing up the dangerous jumps as they flew along at a dizzying pace.

The first six jumps were warm-ups compared to the next series, and Dany sat deep in the saddle forcing the horse to stretch to his maximum length as the next jump, a triple combination, loomed ahead. Unlike stadium jumps, the cross-country jumps were composed of natural elements for the most part. Logs did not move, stone was solid and earth did not yield. If an eventer hit log, stone or earth, it could end up in a split-second catastrophe.

She heard Altair exhaling great jets of air through his flared nostrils and felt the incredible strength and suppleness of his body moving solidly beneath her as she rose up in the saddle, leaning forward, releasing some of the pressure against the hackamore. The triple combination was composed of earth, logs and brush jammed in between the logs. The stallion launched, his powerful hindquarters propelling them up the slanting combination, forcing him to stretch the full length of his tremendous body. The brush slapped at his legs and belly, and Altair tucked his hind legs deep beneath him as they cleared the obstacle, landing heavily into a pool of muddied water. Snorting loudly, Altair's ears pinned against his neck as he lunged up onto dry land at Dany's coaxing.

Shouts of spectators roared into her consciousness as she swung him sharply up into the thickly wooded hills toward the most challenging jumps. She wasn't going to push Altair at a wild, uncontrolled gallop just to get the time. He was in magnificent condition and moving easily beneath her urging. His life wasn't worth a few seconds on the clock. All she wanted to do was finish the course in one piece with the horse.

They negotiated twelve and thirteen handily, the footing becoming slippery because of the morning's heavy dew. There were spectators all along the course, and as she rounded a steeply inclined hill, Dany saw television cameras poised near the fourteenth jump. The seconds seemed like a lifetime as she called to Altair and the stallion attacked the hill. The earthen bank was four feet above the ground with two logs and a small space on the top of it. It meant an all-out effort to make that leap to the bank and then in the next half-stride, they would have to sail off into space over the jump that dropped vertically for eight feet into yet another water hole.

Her hands tightened on the slippery reins. Altair's breathing came in huge enginelike chugs as he threw himself upward toward the bank. Dany rose in the saddle, signaling Altair. Clamping her knees like steel against his barrel, Dany rose perpendicular as the stallion lifted his front end. She literally stood at an angle in the stirrups, body straining over his neck, reins loose so that he could use his neck as a balancing lever. Everything became a blur as the horse sprang like a coiled spring. In a second, they were on top of the bank, clawing at the slippery conditions. Dany felt Altair wobble and threw her weight the opposite direction, giving him his head to rebalance himself. The stallion righted himself and in the same instant was leaping over the poles off the shelf of the bank, airborne, plunging down, his front legs extended like long shock absorbers as they hit the water. The water was belly deep, and Dany fell against Altair's neck, off balance, muddy water surrounding them. Blindly, she gripped his mane, calling him, asking him to go beyond the limits of even his endurance and climb out of the precarious conditions.

Altair lunged out of the water, shaking his head, blowing great jets of moisture from his fully distended nostrils, eyes wide and rolling. He listened to her soothing voice, allowing himself to be directed down the series of small hills toward the flat where the last series of jumps sat.

They came out of the woods, a streak of dark copper flowing against the landscape of greenery. The worst was over and Dany took him safely across the last jumps. Now, only three hundred yards remained to the finish, and she crouched low, like a jockey, pushing him with each flowing stride he took with her hands, legs and body, asking one more second out of his magnificent machine of a body. She was dully aware of the screams, applause and shouts as they raced across the finish line. Dany released the reins, asking him to slow to a canter, to a trot and finally to an exhausted walk. Quickly she slipped off his back, feeling the stallion trembling with the exertion. Worriedly she ran her hands expertly down his legs, concerned that he might have strained a ligament. It was only when Sam placed his hand on her shoulder that she stood up. Both he and Pete were grinning.

"You were magnificent!" Sam said, embracing her.

"Sam, you have the fastest time!" Pete bubbled, taking the stallion and quickly unsaddling him, putting a cooler over his hot, sweaty body.

She collapsed against Sam, so weak that her knees were giving away. He held her against him for a long moment. "You were great out there," he whispered huskily. "Both of you were fantastic. Do you realize the people love you and that red horse of ours?"

Shakily, Sam removed the hard hat, wiping the mud and water from her own face. "We made it, that's all I care about. Oh, Sam, it was a lot harder than I thought," she whispered, closing her eyes and allowing him to support her totally. "Fourteen was the worst jump I've ever encountered. My God, there will be horses killed out there today on that one, Sam. It isn't right," she cried bitterly. "What's the matter with these damn course designers? Can't they tell the difference between a jump that challenges the horse and one that could injure or kill him?"

"Easy, honey, you're coming down out of that adrenaline surge," he soothed softly, guiding her toward the truck that sat in the distance.

Dany wouldn't be consoled. For a long time three-day eventing had been treading a dangerous area: designers were creating jumps that did more than challenge. They were hurting some of the finest jumpers in the world and she wondered when they were going to come to their senses. And fourteen was a murderer. Tears rolled down her cheeks, making white tracks in the grime of her face. Several reporters and photographers ran up to them, begging for a story, and Sam adroitly held them at bay, promising them an interview later after the results were in.

Dany spent half the day rubbing down Altair thoroughly with liniment. There was a camaraderie between Pete and Sam as they worked to make the stallion's tight, tense muscles relax so that he could be rested enough for the in-stadium jumping which would take place tomorrow afternoon. Worriedly, Dany watched as Altair nibbled disinterestedly at his hay. She leaned against the boxstall, just watching him. Sam came over, placing his arm around her waist.

"He's exhausted," he explained. "His appetite will increase by this evening."

"It was a grueling course," she muttered. Looking up into his strong, serene face Dany felt some of her own tension dissipating.

"I don't think either of you were prepared for it,

honey. Let's face it, he's been off the circuit for nine months, and this is your first show in four years. Don't be too hard on yourself. You both gave an incredible effort out there this morning. Come on," Sam urged, "let's get you back over to the motel. I think a hot bath and bed are in order for you."

It was dark when she awoke in Sam's room. Dany felt groggy, acutely aware of how many sore muscles were screaming in protest when she moved, sliding her feet across the bed and sitting up. Rubbing her face tiredly, she felt incredibly exhausted. Was Altair feeling the same? He must be, she thought. By the third day, all eventers were incredibly fatigued. They would be no exception to that rule. In-stadium jumping was hard, but not nearly as dangerous as the cross-country portion. She sighed, her dark hair flowing across her shoulders as she bowed her head forward.

"Dany?"

She looked up to see Sam walking quietly from the door of his room to where she sat. "How are you feeling?" he asked, coming and sitting down beside her on the bed.

"Like I've been in an auto accident. Poor Altair, he must be feeling three times as bad as I do."

"Actually I just got done saying good-night to him and he's got his appetite back and eating his way through four quarts of grain right now."

She turned, her eyes widening. "And his legs?"

"Slight puffiness in his rear fetlocks, but nothing more. It's to be expected under the circumstances. Pete's rubbing them down with a good gracing solution right now. He'll be ready to go by noon tomorrow, don't worry."

She shared a warming smile with him, and leaned over to kiss his strong mouth. Sam groaned softly, slipping his arms around her, laying her back on the bed. His mouth molded tenderly to her lips, parting them, seeking entrance. Finally, he broke contact, his face inches above her own.

"You're beautiful in your sleep, do you know that? I came in to check on you a couple of times and I had to fight the urge to simply lay down beside you and hold you." He traced the outline of her eyebrow. "I'm so proud of you, Dany. You looked like some sort of goddess this morning on Altair, so much a part of him, yet controlling his incredible energy with just a slight, guiding touch of your hand." His voice shook with emotion as he drank in every element of her upturned face. "You are a champion, honey. Never doubt that again. And if you never want to ride again at a show, I'll understand that, too."

She frowned. "What do you mean?" she asked softly.

"I'm not marrying you so that you can ride Altair. I just want you to know that if you decide to quit right now, it would be all right with me."

A broken smile fled across her lips as she stared up at him. How understanding and sensitive he was! Caressing his jaw, she said, "Sam, as long as I feel capable of doing it, I'm going to continue."

"Why?"

"For the challenge. What else?"

"For me."

She shrugged lightly. "We have a winner. Why

shouldn't he be shown to his full potential? You can't help it if your future wife is going to be his rider."

"You're sure about that, Dany?"

She nodded. "Positive."

He pursed his lips, watching her closely. "Well, if he continues to do this well on the circuit, maybe in another year we can retire him to stud and you won't have to show any longer."

Dany smiled provocatively. "Are you going to put me out to pasture, too?" she teased.

"Your choice, lady."

She responded to his hand sliding up the silken material of the dark blue nightgown. Children had been a missing and important ingredient in her life. How many times had she wished for a child? The idea of having children with Sam smothered her with an indefinable joy. Laughing throatily, she pulled him down upon her, kissing him passionately. "I like the idea of children, but I never want to be treated like a broodmare."

He laughed with her. "Somehow, honey, I could never see you having a child once a year for the next twenty or so like a mare does."

"We'll let Altair do his duties and keep the mares happy," she answered, smiling.

Sam turned over on his back, pulling her on top of him. Her black hair fell across her shoulders, framing her oval face as she leaned down, brushing his mouth with a tender kiss. He ran his fingers through the silken mass, his eyes burning with simmering passion. "I'll keep you happy," he growled.

Dany closed her eyes, responding as his hand brushed the fullness of her breast, sighing languidly.

"You're one of a kind," she agreed breathlessly. "Just like that red horse of yours."

The day was cloudy and humid with pollution making the sun appear like a dull orange globe in the sky. Dany sat astride Altair, warming him up for the last leg of the three-day event show. Sam had told her that they stood in fourth place among thirty other international competitors last night. At first, she didn't believe him. But then, after a late dinner, he took her over to the secretary's office and gave her a copy of the standings. Altair was showing strongly and to her surprise, had outmatched Jean and his French charge.

Now, the stadium was filled to overflowing with people who loved to watch the very best jumpers in the world compete in a fourteen-fence test of their endurance and strength. By the third day, most eventers were close to exhaustion and only the ones that had been carefully tuned for the grueling pace would be able to make the demanding course with few or little faults. Each time a pole was knocked down, it was considered a fault. If the horse brushed the pole with his front or back feet, it was considered a "tic" but was not counted off as long as the pole remained in its couplings.

The course had to be completed within one hundred fifteen seconds, a little less than two minutes. If the eventer was taken around too slowly, time penalties were given in equivalency of faults. The more faults incurred, the less chance for placing in the top ten for money and trophies. As Dany tested Altair over the warm-up jumps, she saw Jean astride his gray eventer. His time had been two seconds slower than Altair's over the cross-country portion, and she leaned down, stroking her stallion's neck, crooning to him. Altair had courage and heart; it was an unbeatable combination. She was beginning to appreciate his unique upbringing in the Nevada desert, because his footing had been extraordinary under the circumstances yesterday. She knew by listening to several other riders that one horse had to be destroyed because of jump fourteen and that two riders had been sent to the hospital. Altair might be a "cow" horse, but she trusted her life to the magnificent scarred stallion without reserve. He had proven his mettle yesterday to her satisfaction.

Jean rode over, his face set and scowling. "You surprised me, Danielle."

"Oh, in what way?"

"I'd have thought that red devil would be laid up from yesterday's course."

Dany smiled, rubbing Altair's forelock affectionately. "He did well under the circumstances."

"Beginner's luck," Jean drawled.

Anger flared in her eyes. "Luck has nothing to do with it! We've worked long and hard up in the Sierras and it's paying off. What's the matter, haven't you got someone to condition your horse for you now?"

Jean's eyes narrowed. "He'll fall apart on you in there," he warned, ignoring her barb.

"Just make sure your priceless horse doesn't do the same thing. Looks like he's favoring his left front."

He shrugged. "I get paid regardless," was his flippant reply.

Dany glared at him. "Just stay out of our way, Jean, and keep your comments to yourself."

A slow smile pulled at his thin lips. "Yes, you are finally growing into a world-class rider. It looks as though Reese has helped you as much as you have helped his horse."

"Yes, and for once it was done for the right reasons, Jean."

"He loves you?"

"Yes, he does. But not because I will or won't ride his horse. It's not like our arrangement used to be, Jean." Her voice trembled with a backlog of repressed anger and emotion.

He tipped his hard hat in her direction. "My lovely rose is growing thorns. Don't let your standings go to your head, *ma petite*. It's not over yet."

Dany heard their number called, and she gathered up the single reins of the hackamore. She had found that the media had seized upon Altair's background and the fact that he was the only stallion in the competition. Normally eventing was dominated by geldings, a few mares and fewer stallions. The press was also curious to find out why Altair only wore a hackamore, and Dany had twice avoided interviews with reporters, asking Sam to explain the reasons. Many jumpers wore a tie-down or standing martingale so that they could not escape the snaffle bit. Altair wore none, again making him an exception to the rule, creating even more interest.

As she entered the grassy arena, she noted that the jumps were between four feet nine inches and five feet six inches in height. The triple combination, a series of three jumps placed closely together, forced the horse to spread himself across the six feet of the jump. It was not going to be an easy course in any sense of the word. The buzzer sounded and Dany positioned Altair. The moment he leaped over the first jump the timing would begin. She placed him at an angle on the first jump, saving seconds of time that might have been wasted in making a turn to get to the second one. Altair seemed to catch her excitement, his ears laid back, nostrils flared as he thundered down toward a series of three jumps in a row. Dany rated him, asking him to slow up slightly. If he approached the triple jump too quickly, he would miss the all-important midstrides between the second and third jump and would crash into the third one. He sailed cleanly over all three, his legs tucked deeply beneath him on each one.

They scaled two five-foot-three-inch walls composed of poles and painted boards. The water jump was next and Dany urged him up and over that. She glanced back briefly to make sure that he landed well outside the water because if one hoof had landed in the water, it would have been counted as a fault.

Now a series of demanding jumps faced them. She took the double and in an unprecedented move to save time, she pivoted Altair at a gallop on his hind legs on what could only be described as a "roll back" in Western lingo. A roar went up from the crowd as the stallion leaned into the turn pivoting ninety degrees and galloping toward a wall looming eight feet in front of them. Sam shouted encouragement, and she was out of the saddle, leaning over his neck as he pulled out of the jump. They bore down on the two final jumps, taking them handily, and cantered out of the stadium to the wild applause of the cheering spectators. It was a clean round, and Dany grinned, patting Altair on the neck.

Sam and Pete met her near the entrance of the warm-up area, all smiles. Pete simply shook his head. "Mrs. Daguerre, you are one fine rider."

Sam laughed deeply, gripping her hand momentarily. "I don't think any of those English people in there are ever going to recover from the fact that Altair did a roll back in there. That was fantastic, honey!"

She colored beneath his praise. "Thank Altair. If it hadn't been for all his cow-cutting training, I could never have asked it of him."

Sam winked. "Let's cool the old guy out, he deserves it. You have the best time so far."

Pete walked out Altair in the area while they found seats to sit and watch the other contestants. Dany took congratulations from the people around her and anxiously watched as Jean took his French jumper through the course. The horse was obviously favoring his one leg by the end of it, having collected eight faults as a result. Sam kept tabs on the times and faults of the other riders. When the last rider had completed the jumping he turned to her.

"Congratulations, honey. You and Altair took second place. Not bad for a range pony and a beautiful woman who didn't think she had what it took to be the best."

Dany smothered a cry, hand against her lips as she gave him a startled look. She had not entered the competition to win; she had only wanted to come out alive and uninjured. Sam stood, pulling her to her feet.

"Come on, you've got a trophy, ribbon and a sizable check to pick up. Let's get you down to Altair and into the saddle."

As she rode Altair in to receive his rewards the crowd exploded into enthusiastic applause and shouts of encouragement. Tears glittered in her eyes as she accepted the silver bowl and the check. It wasn't a bad day's work for a scarred, abused stallion who had suffered at the hands of more than one rider; but more important she had regained her confidence in her own abilities. Dany leaned down with her head against Altair's arched neck, hugging him without reserve. She sat back up, and waved to the crowd as she took a victory canter around the arena. As they rode out of the arches she saw Sam waiting for them in the distance. She and Altair were both riding toward a future that was paved with happiness and a shared commitment. If it hadn't been for Sam, she might have never restored her confidence.

Halting Altair, Dany dismounted, handing the trophy and reins of the stallion to Pete. She didn't care if the eyes of the entire world were watching them as she walked up to him. A lump wedged in her throat, effectively silencing her.

"Come here," Sam commanded softly, opening his arms to her.

With a tearful smile she stepped inside the circle of his arms. He embraced her tightly, for a long time, his head resting against her own. Sam made it easy for her to lean on him when she wanted. The thought flooded her heart with love, and Dany embraced him fiercely in return.

He pulled scant inches away, his eyes strangely moist. Dany reached up and caressed his leathery cheek. "We can't stand out here like a couple of children crying," she muttered, dashing her tears on her own cheek away with the back of her hand.

He smiled tenderly, leaning over and brushing her waiting lips in a kiss. "Why not?" he demanded gruffly, pulling her close. "They're tears of joy."

Dany closed her eyes, content to remain against his incredibly strong body. "I don't mind crying for happiness," she admitted.

"Then we'll be crying often, honey."

Dany smiled blissfully. "We owe you so much, Sam...."

"Shh," he commanded, placing a kiss on her hair. "There is no scorekeeping where we're concerned, Dany. Never." He tucked her beneath his arm, leading her away from the stadium.

Dany stole a look up at him as they walked toward the quieter area of the stables. There was an unspoken aura of happiness lingering in his lightened gray eyes. He walked like a man who was on top of the clouds. She was there, too, she realized. "You've helped me chase the clouds, Sam," she said, catching his gaze.

His hand tightened momentarily against her waist. "Your riding master taught you that, didn't he?"

"Yes. But thanks to you, I was able to scale a few hurdles of my own to reach those heights."

Sam tried to appear nonchalant about his part in the healing of her fears. "I don't know, honey," he drawled, "when you've got a hammerhead of a stallion and a stubborn cowboy from California to help, how can you lose?"

Dany laughed fully, reaching up impulsively, curving her arms around his neck. Sam drew to a halt, a careless smile edging his mouth. "More than that," she whispered, "I've fallen in love. And that means more than scaling the heights of any career." Her voice shook with emotion. "More than anything," she promised fiercely.

He lost his smile, studying her in the intervening

silence. "We've all found love in one another, honey. And when you've got love like we do, everything else around us automatically turns to success."

"I'll never care about the trappings of success, Sam. All I'll ever need is your love and understanding," she admitted softly.

He groaned, sweeping her against him. "And you've had my love since the day we met," he murmured thickly. "You're mine, now and forever."

* * * * *

Joan Johnston is the *New York Times* and *USA TODAY* bestselling author of more than fifty novels with more than fifteen million copies of her books in print. She has been a director of theater, drama critic, newspaper editor, college professor and attorney on her way to becoming a full-time writer. You can find out more about Joan at joanjohnston.com or on Facebook at Joan Johnston Author.

Books by Joan Johnston

Hawk's Way: Jesse
Hawk's Way: Adam
Hawk's Way: Faron
Hawk's Way: Garth
Hawk's Way: Carter
Hawk's Way: Falcon
Hawk's Way: Zach
Hawk's Way: Billy
Hawk's Way: Mac
Hawk's Way: Colt

Visit the Author Profile page
at Harlequin.com for more titles.

HAWK'S WAY: COLT

Joan Johnston

Chapter 1

"Watch your wingtip! You're too close. We're going to— Bail out, Huck! God, no, Huck!"

Colt Whitelaw sat bolt upright in bed, his eyes wild with remembered terror. His heart was racing, his hands were clenched, and his sheet-draped body was drenched in sweat. It took him a moment to realize where he was. Home, at Hawk's Pride, his parents' ranch in northwest Texas. He'd been jet-lagged when he'd arrived late last night. That was the excuse he'd used, anyway, to go right to bed. To avoid doing what had to be done.

I have to see Jenny. I have to tell her there won't be any wedding next month, that Huck was killed six days ago in a midair collision over the Egyptian desert.

Colt felt the sting in his nose, the tickle at the back of his throat. He wasn't going to cry anymore. His best friend was gone, and nothing could bring him back.

"Colt, I heard some noise. Are you all right?"

"I'm fine, Mom," Colt said, blinking against the afternoon sun. He had locked the bedroom door, or he knew his mother would already have been inside. He was thirty-two, but he was her baby, the youngest of eight adopted kids and the only one who'd been an infant when Zach and Rebecca Whitelaw had made him a part of their family.

"Are you ready to get up?" his mother asked through the door. "Can I make you something to eat? Or do you need more sleep?"

He couldn't eat. He couldn't sleep anymore. He couldn't do anything until he'd spoken to Jenny. "I'm fine, Mom," he said. "I think I'll take a shower."

"Everything you need is in the bathroom. Make yourself at home."

Make yourself at home. He supposed he deserved that. Three of his sisters were married and lived nearby, while the rest of his siblings worked on the family ranch. He hadn't been back to Hawk's Pride except for a brief visit at Labor Day or Christmas for ten years. It wasn't his home anymore, although at one time his father had expected him to manage the ranch. Colt had wanted to fly jets.

His brother Jake had become ramrod instead. His brother Louis—who was calling himself Rabb these days, short for Rabbit, a nickname he'd acquired as a result of eating a lot of carrots as a kid—worked the cattle, while his sister Frannie trained cutting horses. His brother Avery did the bookkeeping and legal work.

There was no place for him at Hawk's Pride now.

Colt made himself get out of bed. He groaned as his bruised right knee protested, along with his left shoulder. He'd survived the crash between his and Huck's training jets with minor injuries. The Air Force had exonerated him of blame in the incident, but he was on leave until he was fully recuperated.

He walked gingerly across the hall to the bathroom wearing only a pair of Jockey shorts and caught his mother peeking around the corner at the end of the hall. She jumped back out of sight, and he felt himself grinning as he closed the bathroom door behind him. Even if he didn't plan to stay, it was good to be home.

A half hour later Colt looked himself over in the mirror above the dresser in his former bedroom. The doctor had said the six stitches across his chin wouldn't leave much of scar, but he'd decided not to try to shave around them. The day's growth of beard made him look disreputable but was countered by a military haircut that had left his black hair just long enough to part.

He rubbed his hands over the thighs of a pair of butter-soft jeans he'd found in a drawer and curled his toes in the scuffed leather cowboy boots he'd found in the closet. He wore a tucked-in white T-shirt but didn't have a Western belt, so the jeans rode low on his hips. He settled a battered Stetson on his head, completing his transformation into the Texas cowboy he once had been.

"Colt?"

Colt turned and found his mother standing in his open bedroom doorway, her heart in her eyes. There had always been a chance he'd be killed flying jets. This time he'd come damned close. He reached out and pulled her into his arms.

His birth mother had been a teenager, alone and in trouble, when she'd given him up to the Whitelaws for adoption. He often wondered about her, but he didn't miss her. In Rebecca Whitelaw he had the best mother any kid could want.

"Are you all right?" she asked, leaning back to look into his eyes. "How about some breakfast? Is there anything I can do for you?"

"I'm fine, Mom. Really. I don't think I could eat anything. I need to see Jenny, to tell her about Huck."

His mother leaned back, her eyes wide with disbelief. "You mean the Air Force hasn't contacted her?"

Colt shook his head. "Huck named his father as next of kin for notification purposes. The way things are between her and the senator, you can bet Huck's dad hasn't said a word to her, and I didn't want to tell her over the phone."

"I can't believe what's happened. Jenny's been waiting years for her brothers to grow up, so she'd be free to marry. And now, with the youngest graduating in June and her wedding day set, Huck is killed. It's just not fair!"

Colt rocked his mother in his arms. "I know, Mom." Colt felt his throat swelling closed. *Oh, God, Jenny. I'm so sorry. For your sake, I wish it had been me.*

He let go of his mother and took a step back. "I may be gone awhile. If Jenny needs anything, I want to be there for her."

"I understand," his mother said. She brushed her fingertips across his chin, coming as near as she dared without touching his stitches. "I know how close the three of you were."

Inseparable, Colt thought. *We were inseparable.*

"I'm sure Jenny will appreciate having you there,"

his mother continued. "Tell her to call if there's anything we can do."

"I will, Mom."

Colt decided to ride horseback to Jenny's ranch, mostly because it postponed the moment when he would have to tell her about Huck's death. It also gave him a chance to see the changes that had been wrought in the eight months since he'd last been home. Hawk's Pride looked more successful than ever. Which, by contrast, made the poverty on Jenny's ranch, the Double D, even more evident.

Fields that should have been planted in hay lay barren, a windmill wobbled and squeaked, fence posts needed to be repaired or replaced, the stock needed fattening, and a sun-scorched barn needed paint. Nevertheless, with its deep canyons and myriad arroyos, the land possessed a certain rugged charm.

His first sight of the ranch house, which looked as though it belonged in a Depression-era movie, confirmed his growing suspicion. If Jenny wasn't flat broke, he'd eat his hat.

Colt was surprised when he rode around the side of the barn to find himself staring at another rider on horseback. "Jenny. Hi."

The instantaneous smile made her bluer-than-blue eyes crinkle at the corners. His gut clenched.

I thought with Huck dead I'd feel different. But, heaven help me, I'm still in love with my best friend's girl.

"Colt! What a wonderful surprise!" Jenny cried. "Where's Huck? Did he come home on leave with you?"

"I'm alone," he managed to say.

She wore frayed jeans and a faded Western plaid shirt and sat on a rawboned nag that looked like it was a week from the glue factory. She nudged the animal, and it took the few steps that put them knee to knee. He could see the spattering of freckles on her nose and the corn silk blond wisps at her temples that had escaped her ponytail.

"I'm so glad to see you!" she said, reaching out to lay a hand on his thigh. "How long has it been?"

His flesh felt seared where she touched him. He reined his horse sideways to break the contact between them. "Since Labor Day."

"It seems like yesterday."

It seemed like forever. "How are you?" he asked.

Her smile broadened, creating an enchanting dimple in her left cheek. "Great! Counting down. After ten long years, just forty-two more days till I'm Mrs. Huckleberry Duncan."

Huck should have married her ten years ago, Colt thought. But Huck had followed where Colt led, and Colt had taken him off to fly jets. Jenny had stayed behind to raise her four younger brothers.

She was thirty-two now, Colt knew, because they were the same age. The freckles and the ponytail gave her a youthful appearance, but she wasn't a girl any longer. He loved the laugh crinkles that age had put at the corners of her eyes, but he hated the worry lines in her forehead, because he was at least partly responsible for putting them there.

Colt knew life hadn't been easy for Jenny. She'd been a nurse for her mother, who'd died of breast cancer when Jenny turned fifteen, and then mother to her four brothers. It was finally time for her chance at happily ever after. Only Huck was dead. "Jenny—"

"Come inside," she said, turning her horse toward the house. He kneed his horse and followed her.

There was no lush green lawn, no purple morning glories trailing up the porch rail, nothing to lessen the starkness of the faded, single-story, wood-frame ranch house that sat in the middle of the northwest Texas prairie. Jenny rode around back to the kitchen door, dismounted and tied the reins to a hitching post.

As she stepped up onto the sagging covered porch she said, "Let me get you something to drink. You must be thirsty after such a long, hot ride."

"A glass of iced tea would be nice," he said as he dismounted. "Are any of your brothers around?"

"I don't see much of Tyler or James or Sam, now that they're out on their own. Randy won't be home from school for another hour."

"Good," Colt said as he followed her into the kitchen. "That'll give us some time alone to talk. How are things going?"

She shot him a mischievous grin as the screen door slammed behind him, then crossed to an old, round-cornered Coldspot refrigerator and pulled out a jar of iced tea. "It's a good thing Huck and I are finally getting hitched. If it weren't for the money he'll get from his trust fund when he marries, I'd have to turn the Double D over to the bank."

He hadn't expected her to be so honest. Maybe if she'd known about Huck, she wouldn't have been. "You're about to lose the Double D?"

"Not that I'd miss all the hard work, you understand,

but this ranch has been in my family for so many generations, it'd be a shame to let it go."

"I didn't realize things had gotten so bad," he said.

"In forty-two days, all my troubles will be over. But enough about me. How'd you cut your chin? Fooling around with Huck, I'll bet. His last letter was full of—"

"Jenny, Huck is…" *Dead. Gone forever. Never coming back.* He swallowed hard.

"Huck is what?" she asked, her back to him as she reached for a glass from the cupboard above the sink.

"Huck died six days ago."

As she turned, her eyes wide, her mouth open in shocked surprise, the glass slipped from her hand and crashed to the floor. "No!" She pressed a clenched fist against her heart. "How?"

"I killed him."

All the blood left Jenny's head in a *whoosh,* and she swayed. She heard broken glass crunch under Colt's boots as he stepped close enough to catch her before her knees gave way and lifted her into his arms. She clung to his neck in a daze as he carried her into the bedroom and sat her on her four-poster bed.

He tried to stand up, to move away, but she clutched at him and wouldn't let go. "Stay here," she rasped past a throat that had swollen closed. "Explain."

She felt the tension in his shoulders. Felt the shudder that racked his frame as he settled down beside her. It took a long time for him to speak. She noticed the dust motes in the sunlight streaming through her bedroom window, the country tune about "friends in low places" on the radio that always played in the kitchen, the screech of a windmill that needed repair.

Everything was just as it had been a moment before. And nothing was the same.

Colt cleared his throat. "I knew Huck had been sick with some kind of flu bug the night before we were scheduled for a training flight. He said he was fine, but I should have known better and grounded him. Whatever illness he had affected his equilibrium."

She felt the slight shrug in Colt's shoulders before he said, "His wingtip brushed mine and…" He swallowed hard. "I bailed out. Huck didn't."

This isn't real. I'm dreaming. Colt isn't really sitting here beside me. He's with Huck, training jet pilots in Egypt.

She brushed a hand across the short dark hair at Colt's nape. *So soft.* She laid her cheek against his and felt the night's growth of beard. *So prickly.*

I can feel. So this must be real, she thought. As real as the tight band of pain that bound her chest and made it so hard to breathe.

Colt leaned back and looked into her face. She had never seen such agony in a human being's eyes. "I'm so sorry, Jenny. So very sorry. I should have done something. I should have—"

"I doubt you could've kept him on the ground," she said in a shaky voice. "Huck was as crazy about flying as you are."

"I outranked him. I could've made it an order."

"You loved him too much to deny him anything he wanted," Jenny said simply. *Even me.*

Jenny didn't know where that last thought had come from, but she pushed it back into whatever dark hole it lived in. When they were kids, she'd known Colt Whitelaw had a crush on her. She'd even thought she might like to go out with him, if he asked. But Huck had liked her, too, and once Colt found out his best friend wanted her, he'd kept his distance. She had become—would always be—Huck's girl.

Only, now Huck was dead.

"Oh, God, Colt. I don't think I can bear it!" Jenny cried. "I don't think I can live without him!"

Many times over the past ten years she'd wondered what she would do if something happened to Huck, and he didn't come back to her. But he always did. Lately, like a combat veteran who counts the days until he can leave the battlefield, she'd counted the days until Huck would come home at last, and they'd be married and live happily ever after.

"It's not fair, Colt. It's not fair!" she wailed.

"I know," he said, rubbing her back soothingly. "I know."

The tears came then, spilling over in hot tracks down her face. And excruciating grief. She let out a howl of rage and pain. Throughout it all she clung to Colt, held tight to him, as though the mere presence of another human could keep her from hurting so much.

Jenny cried until her throat was raw, until she was too weak to lift a hand to wipe away the tears. It didn't take long for exhaustion to claim her. She was already worn-out from overwork and from too many sleepless nights spent worrying about how she was going to keep the ranch afloat on a sea of debt.

Jenny had pinned all her hopes for saving the ranch on the trust fund Huck would receive when they married. Now there would be no wedding. She hadn't merely lost the man she loved. She had also lost her home.

"What am I going to do, Colt?" she whispered. "How can I go on now?"

"I'm here, Jenny. I'll always be here for you," Colt murmured in her ear. "I love you, Jenny."

Jenny knew Colt hadn't meant it the way it sounded. Colt loved her the same way he loved Huck. He'd been a good friend to her, always willing to pitch in to help with her brothers, something Huck never seemed to have the time to do. It had been easy to lean on Colt, to lay her troubles on his strong shoulders whenever Huck was too busy to lend a hand.

Jenny was suddenly aware of how tightly her arms were wrapped around Colt's neck. And in turn, how his hands were tangled in her hair.

"Colt, let go. Let me go!" She struggled to free herself from his embrace, from the illusion of safety, the awful, welcome comfort he offered.

He stared at her in confusion. "What's wrong, Jenny? Tell me what I can do to help."

"Nothing!" She took a deep, shuddering breath. "Get out, Colt. Go away. I don't want you here."

"Because I killed him?"

She should have let him believe that was why she wanted him gone. One look at his face, and she couldn't do it. "Oh, Colt, don't you see? It would be so easy to turn to you, to depend on you. That wouldn't be fair to you. No one can take Huck's place."

The color faded from his face, until there were only two blotches of red on his cheeks. "I feel responsible for what happened. The least I can do is make sure you don't lose the Double D. I've got money. Let me help you, Jenny."

"You've always been there for me, and I love you for

it. But money can't give me what I need most. Money can't bring Huck back."

She saw him wince before he said, "I miss him, too. He's going to leave a big hole in both our lives. But that doesn't change the fact this place needs a lot of work."

The words stung. "I've done the best I can."

"I know that! But admit it, Jenny. You're going to need help holding on to this place."

"I'm not admitting anything," she said stubbornly.

"You know Huck would want me to help you. Let me do this for him."

She shook her head. "I couldn't take your money, Colt. And I know how committed you are to flying jets. You'll be long gone before—"

"I've got up to sixty days' leave for recuperation. That's enough time to get some work done around here. I want to be here for you. Let me help you, Jenny. Please."

She lifted her chin. "I won't take charity, Colt. Even from you."

"Don't be ridiculous. We're friends."

"Friends. Not relations," Jenny said. "You have no obligation to help me, Colt."

His expression made it plain she'd offended him, but the only thing she had left was her pride. It was humiliating enough to be left at the altar—even if unwillingly—by Huck, without having to go begging for help to bail the Double D out of debt.

"You would have taken Huck's money," he said.

"He would have been my husband."

"Then marry me, Jenny, if that's what it takes. But damn it, let me help!"

The silence that followed his statement hung between them like temptation in the Garden of Eden. Jenny threaded her hands together to hide the fact they were trembling. "I know you must be hurting as badly as I am right now. But I won't take advantage of your grief—"

"Marry me, Jenny," he said, reaching out to separate her hands and hold them tightly in his. "On the day you would've married Huck. You should have a June wedding. You've waited long enough for it. You should walk down the aisle looking beautiful and knowing there's someone waiting who's willing to shoulder half the burden the rest of your life. We both know it's been your dream for a very long time. Let me make it come true. I owe you that much."

She stared at Colt, unable to look away. He understood about lost dreams. He almost hadn't made good on his dream of becoming a jet pilot. She was the one who'd urged him to confront his parents and tell them he didn't want to be a rancher, that he wanted to fly jets. She'd also been the one who shared his joy when he realized his parents were happy for him, not disappointed as he'd expected them to be.

Colt knew better than anyone what it had meant to her to sacrifice her own dreams for the sake of her brothers. She looked down at Colt's hands—large and strong and capable—then up into his blue eyes, as red-rimmed as her own, and focused on her with such earnest entreaty that she found it hard to look away.

"Suppose we did marry, Colt. Then what? I can't follow you around the world the way Huck did. My home is here on the Double D. Are you willing to give up flying?"

She watched his Adam's apple bob as he swallowed. "I can't."

"Then I can't marry you."

"Why not?"

"I won't trade one absentee partner for another," she said flatly. "I deserve better."

"Then take the damned money!"

"I don't need your charity."

"You sure as hell do!"

She yanked her hands free and said, "Get out, Colt. Leave. Go."

Colt stood his ground. "I owe Huck for not protecting him better. *I* stole your dream of happily ever after. Let me do this for you. For Huck. Marry me, Jenny."

Her chin quivered. She wanted so much to accept. It was the easy way out. But it was all wrong. "It wouldn't work, Colt."

"Why not?"

"For one thing, I don't love you."

"That doesn't matter."

She shook her head. "I can't believe you'd want to marry someone who—"

"Say yes, Jenny."

"What would people think—"

"To hell with what people think! At least you'd keep the Double D."

She stared at him, wanting to accept, but knowing such a marriage would be disastrous for both of them. "What happens when you fall in love with some other woman?"

"That isn't going to happen."

"How do you know?" she insisted.

He looked away, then turned back. "I gave my heart

to someone a long time ago. There won't be anyone else."

"Oh." She was surprised by the jolt of jealousy she felt at his admission. Colt had often dated, but all the relationships had been brief. She'd never imagined him in love with some other woman. It had always been— only been—the three of them.

He reached for her hands again and held them tight. "If we don't get married, you're going to lose the only home you've ever known."

"Don't threaten me, Colt."

"It's the situation that's threatening."

"What about sex?" She lifted her eyes to his and saw the glint of humor there, despite everything. They'd always spoken freely to each other. She wasn't going to pull her punches now. "Or were you planning on a celibate marriage?"

"I wouldn't expect you to come to bed with me right away," he said, answering with as much care as the subject deserved. "But I'd expect our marriage to include physical relations eventually."

"I see." There had been a time—one time—about six years ago when his hand had accidentally brushed against her breast, and she'd felt her insides draw up tight. They'd both been horribly embarrassed, and it had never happened again. But she'd been aware of him ever since in a way she hadn't been before that day.

Still, it was unsettling to think of Colt having the right to touch her as a man touched a woman. It had always been forbidden, because she was Huck's girl.

Huck is dead. Huck is never coming back.

"Say yes, Jenny."

She looked into Colt's eyes, searching for the right

answer. He looked so sure of himself. So certain he was doing the right thing. She shuddered to think what people would say if she showed up at church on the day she'd planned to marry Huck with a substitute groom.

Then she imagined what it would be like if she lost the ranch and had to go to work in town. Or had to live as a maiden aunt in the home of one of her brothers. And there were other considerations, things Colt didn't know about and which she could never tell him, that made her want to cling to the only home she had ever known.

She needed time, but there wasn't much. Her wedding date, June 20, was forty-two days away. Ten days after that, another mortgage payment would come due. And she had no money to pay.

It was selfish to marry Colt under the circumstances. She was crazy even to consider the possibility. But it was the only solution she could see—at the moment—for her desperate situation.

"All right," she said at last. "I'll consider your proposal."

"When will I know your answer?"

Jenny managed a crooked smile. "As soon as I do."

Chapter 2

"Hey, Jenny, wake up!"

Jenny rolled over in bed and stared, bleary-eyed, at her eighteen-year-old brother, Randy. She'd spent most of the night crying and had only gotten to sleep as the sun was coming up. She groaned, rolled back over and mumbled, "Let me sleep."

"Colt's in the kitchen. He wants to know where he should start to work."

"Tell him…" She snuggled deeper into the covers, already drifting back to sleep.

"I've got to get moving, or I'm going to miss the bus," Randy said. He gave her shoulder a shove and asked, "What do you want me to tell Colt?"

"Tell him to go away," she said, covering her head with a pillow.

"Are you sure?"

"I'm sure."

A persistent knock on her bedroom door drew her back to consciousness. She decided to ignore it. With any luck, Colt would take the hint and go away. She didn't want to see him. She didn't want to see anyone, looking and feeling like she did.

The door opened a crack and Colt said, "Jenny? Are you awake?"

"How can I sleep with all these interruptions?" she muttered irritably.

He took that as an invitation to come in, and a moment later she felt his presence by the bed. Which was when she realized she was wearing one of Randy's old football jersey, and from what she could feel of the breeze from the open window on her bare thighs, it wasn't covering much.

She rolled onto her back, reaching for the sheet and blanket she must have kicked off and dragging them up to cover her. "What do you want, Colt?"

"I brought you a cup of coffee."

She squinted one eye open. "You expect me to drink that?"

"Why not?"

"It's likely to wake me up."

She saw the smile tilt his lips and the appearance of devastating twin dimples in his cheeks. "That's the general idea," he said. He seated himself beside her on the mattress and tousled her hair. "Come on, sleepyhead. Rise and shine."

She brushed his hand away. "I don't want to get up."

"Too bad," he said, sliding an arm under her shoulders to lift her up and sticking the coffee cup against her lips. "I need some marching orders, and you're the only one here to give them to me."

Against her better judgment, she took a sip of the scalding liquid. "Oh, Lord. That's strong enough that it might even work."

"I hope so," he said. "Because I'm planning to spend the day with you. I'll be glad to join you in bed, if that's what you'd prefer—"

She pushed the coffee away and scooted across the bed and out of it, tugging on the hem of the football jersey as she stood. "Give me a minute to get showered and dressed." She headed for her chest of drawers to retrieve clean underwear and socks.

"I'll leave the coffee here, in case you need another jolt," he said, setting the heavy ceramic mug on the end table beside her bed. "Oh, and Jenny…"

She turned to look at him over her shoulder.

"If you're wearing Saturday on Wednesday, what happens when you get to the weekend?"

Jenny stared at him uncomprehendingly until she realized she was wearing panties her brother Randy had given her for Christmas that were labeled with the days of the week. "So you'll only have to do laundry once every seven days," Randy had quipped.

She flushed with embarrassment at the thought of Colt glimpsing her underwear and snapped, "Well, you could always barge into my bedroom again on Saturday to find out."

"Touché," he said with a mock salute. "I'll be waiting for you in the kitchen."

The shower didn't help. Jenny's eyelids felt like they weighed a pound each, and they scratched her eyeballs every time she blinked. Her mouth was dry, her throat was sore, and her whole body ached. She was angry at being forced out of bed, but she didn't have the energy to fight.

"Your breakfast is on the table," Colt said when she arrived in the kitchen doorway.

She stared at the trestle table, where he'd put out a wrinkled cloth place mat and napkin—who had time to iron?—with a set of mix-matched silverware. He'd made scrambled eggs and toast and provided a cup of orange juice beside another cup of steaming coffee. She felt both grateful and resentful. "I could have made something for myself."

He pulled out the ladder-back chair at the head of the table and shoved her into it. "Sure you could. If you weren't dead on your feet. Eat."

"Are you going to join me?"

"I ate before I came over."

"Are you going to hover like that, watching every bite that goes into my mouth?"

He sat down in the chair to her right, then bounced up again. "Ouch!"

"Oh. Watch out for the nail in that chair."

"You've got nails sticking out of the kitchen chairs?"

She nodded, since her mouth was full of toast, then swallowed and answered, "My brothers' football buddies did a lot of leaning back in those chairs. Afraid they couldn't take the strain. Had to nail them back together."

"Why don't you fix them right?"

She shrugged. "No time. No money. No need." She gave him a beatific smile. "We know where the nails are."

"Any other sharp points I need to avoid—besides your barbed tongue?" he said. "If Huck were here—"

Colt caught himself too late. The words were out, invoking Huck's presence.

Jenny felt the beginning of tears and blinked to fight them back. The fork fell from her hand and clattered onto her plate. She covered her face with her hands as an awful wave of grief rolled over her. "Why did this have to happen?"

She felt herself being lifted into Colt's arms, then felt him settling into the ladder-back chair in her stead. Her arms slid around his neck, and she hid her face against his throat. "I can't pretend this is just another day, Colt. Please, let me go back to bed. I want to sleep."

"When you wake up, he'll still be gone," Colt said soberly. "I know. I've had a week longer than you to deal with Huck's death. The only thing that helps is work."

"I'm so tired. I didn't sleep last night."

"If I let you sleep now, you'll be awake all night tonight," Colt said. "Then you'll be tired again tomorrow. Work now. Sleep later. Can you eat any more?"

She shook her head.

He forced her off his lap and onto her feet. "Where do you suggest we start?" he asked as he led her toward the back door.

"The cattle and horses need to be fed. I've got a few chickens that have probably laid eggs. The barn needs to be scraped and painted, the windmill in the west pasture isn't working, the back porch needs some new posts before it falls down, there's a leak in the roof that should be patched, I've got supplies to pick up in town—"

"Whoa!" Colt said. "We'll start with feeding the

stock, then go pick up the supplies in town. Everything else can wait till we've both had a good night's sleep."

Jenny looked at Colt—really looked at him. Judging by the dark circles under his eyes, he hadn't slept much, either. Perhaps he was right. Perhaps work was the best way to keep the demons at bay. But they both needed to rest, as well, and she'd just come up with a solution for the problem.

"The stock tank in the south pasture needs to be checked before the day is over," she said. There happened to be a sprawling live oak near that tank. Once they got there, she'd tell Colt she needed to lie down for a little while in the shade and take a nap, and that she needed him to keep her company.

Even though Jenny was clearly exhausted, Colt had trouble keeping up with her throughout the day. The worst moments came when friends in town offered their condolences, along with memories of Huck that were so poignant they were painful.

At the feed store Mr. Brubaker said to Jenny, "Remember the time you and Huck and Colt climbed up and painted J.W. + H.D. = True Love on the town's water tower? If I ain't mistaken, it's still there."

Tom Tuttle at Tuttle's Hardware said to Colt, "Always knew one of you boys would get hisself killed flying them jets. Glad it weren't you, Colt. Sorry about Huck, Miss Jenny."

At the Stanton Hotel Café, Ida Mae Cooper said, "I recall the first time the three of you came in here together for a cherry soda. You were skinny as a beanpole in those days, Colt, and couldn't take your eyes off Huck's girl."

Colt shot a look at Jenny to see if she'd made anything of Ida Mae's announcement, but she merely looked forlorn. She settled onto the red plastic seat of one of the several stools along the 1950s-era soda fountain and said, "No cherry soda for me, Ida Mae. Just strong black coffee."

Colt slid onto the stool next to her. "I'd like that cherry soda, Ida Mae."

Jenny glared at him as though he'd betrayed some trust, as though they couldn't have cherry sodas anymore because Huck wasn't there to have one with them.

He met her stare with sympathetic eyes. "Huck won't mind if we have a cherry soda, Jenny."

"Why does everybody keep talking about him?" she muttered. "Don't they understand it hurts?"

"They miss him, too," Colt said simply.

"Here's that soda, Colt," Ida Mae said. She eyed him speculatively and asked, "You planning to take care of Huck's girl, now that he's gone?"

The question was loud enough—and volatile enough—to bring conversation in the café to a halt. Colt felt everyone's eyes focus on him except Jenny's. She stared determinedly into her coffee cup. Ida Mae waited expectantly for an answer.

He took a deep breath and let it out. "Jenny and I haven't made any plans beyond a memorial service a week from Friday. We'd like to invite everyone to come, if you'd be kind enough to pass along the word."

"Sure, Colt," Ida Mae said, patting his hand. "I can understand it wouldn't be a good idea to announce any more than that right now."

Colt opened his mouth to tell her she was way off the mark and closed it again. A denial that anything was going on between him and Jenny would likely stir up more gossip than saying nothing.

It was late afternoon by the time they got back to the ranch. Jenny suggested they ride horseback to the stock tank. Apparently the spigot in the stock tank in her south pasture needed to be fixed. She was running on fumes by the time they got there. She dismounted and led her horse over to the aluminium tank for a drink, and Colt followed suit.

"Where's that faulty spigot?" he asked, checking the spigot on the tank, which wasn't leaking as far as he could tell.

"I guess Randy must have fixed it. As long as we're here, we might as well take advantage of the shade."

He eyed her suspiciously. "There never was anything wrong with that spigot, was there?"

"Nope."

There wasn't much grass growing in the shade of the sprawling live oak growing near the tank, but he watched Jenny find a patch of it and sit down. She patted the ground beside her and said, "Join me. It's time for a nap."

Colt sighed. "If we sleep now—"

"Sit down," she ordered, "and shut up."

That brought a snappy salute and a "Yes, ma'am." He dropped onto the ground beside her, suddenly feeling the results of too many haunted nights. He lay stretched out on his side, supporting his head with his palm. "Now what?"

She stretched out, facing him, and laid her cheek on her arm. "Lie down. I can't talk to you when your head's so far above mine."

Reluctantly, he came down off his elbow and laid

his head on his arm, facing her. For a long time they stared at one another without speaking. He reached out to touch her cheek, to brush away a tear. "Don't cry, Jenny. I can't bear it when you cry."

"I can't help it. So many memories are shuffling around in my head."

"Mine, too," he admitted.

"Do you remember the last time we were here?"

He chuckled. "That isn't a day I'm likely to forget."

"I asked you if you'd teach me how to kiss," she said. "Do you remember what you said?"

"'No.' Or more precisely, 'Hell no!'"

Her eyes lit with laughter, and her lips curled up at the corners. "I begged until you relented, because I didn't want my first kiss with Huck to go awry."

"Craziest thing I've ever done in my life," he said. "Teaching my best friend's girl how to kiss."

"I wanted to know where my hands should go and where he'd put his hands."

"All over you," Colt muttered, "if he could get away with it."

He heard Jenny's laugh, a sound like a burbling brook, and realized it had been a very long time since he'd heard anything so pleasing. He smiled at her and let the memory of that long-ago day wash over him.

They'd ridden horseback to the stock tank, because she'd said she had something important to discuss with him in private. While their horses had taken a drink, she'd popped the question. After his refusal, she'd gone to work convincing him.

"You have to help me, Colt," she pleaded. "My first kiss with Huck has to be perfect, because I'll be remembering it the rest of my life. I don't want anything to go wrong."

"That's what makes the first kiss memorable," he argued. "Things go wrong."

She shook her head, her long blond hair shimmering like corn silk in the sunlight. "Please. Do this for me."

He'd been aware of his attraction to Jenny from the first moment he'd looked into her bluer-than-blue eyes, but Huck had been the first one to speak of her. Colt had felt honor-bound to wait and see if things developed between Jenny and Huck before he made his move. To his dismay, Jenny had said yes to Huck's overtures.

More than once Colt had thought of trying to steal Jenny away from Huck. But he knew in his heart that he couldn't live with himself if he betrayed his friend like that. It would taint what he felt for Jenny. So he went along and remained a good friend to both of them.

See how virtue had been rewarded? Jenny wanted him to kiss her first!

More than anything in the world he wanted to hold Jenny Wright in his arms. But he had panicked when she came up with the harebrained notion that he should teach her to kiss. Would she be able to tell from his kiss how much he liked her? What if he got carried away and did something that scared her?

"I'll do this on one condition," he conceded at last.

"Anything," she promptly agreed.

"You never *ever* tell Huck."

"Why not?"

"Believe me, he wouldn't understand."

"Why not?"

"It's a guy thing," he said. "Promise," he insisted.

She crossed her heart with her forefinger. "Cross my heart and hope to die, stick a needle in my eye."

"I guess that'll do," he said.

"Okay, I'm ready," she said.

He rubbed his sweaty palms on the thighs of his jeans. "I'm not. I have no idea where to start."

"Why not put your arms around me?" she suggested.

He reached forward at the same time she reached up, and their arms knocked into each other.

"Oops."

"Sorry."

"See what I mean?" she said, wrinkling her nose. "I guess I'll need to stand still while Huck puts his arms around me. You want to try again?"

"Sure." He slid his left arm around her waist and tugged her toward him. But she didn't move.

She looked up at him in confusion. "What?"

"You need to take a step to get closer," he instructed. He applied pressure to her back again, and this time she responded by closing the distance between them until her breasts were a hairsbreadth from his chest.

"Is this close enough?"

There was no spit left in his mouth, and he croaked, "Yeah. That's probably close enough."

She looked up expectantly. "Now what?"

"Huck will probably put his hand on your head to angle it in the right direction."

"Okay. I'm ready. Go ahead."

He'd only intended to palm her head with his hand, but somehow his fingers got tangled in her hair. "You've got really soft hair," he murmured.

He saw her cheeks pinken. "Thank you. Do you

think Huck will do what you're doing? I mean, slide his fingers through my hair like that?"

"Why do you ask?"

She gave a negligent shrug. "It feels good."

Colt reminded himself he was holding Huck's girl. "He might run his hands through your hair. But don't worry if he doesn't. Every guy is different."

"Okay. Now what?"

"I'm a little taller than Huck, so some of what I'm saying might need to be adjusted for height," he said, trying to remain objective. He reminded himself to keep his hips apart from hers, so she wouldn't discover that his body was reacting as though this game of hers was the real thing. "I can bend down to you, or you can come up on tiptoe to reach me," he explained.

"Or Huck and I could move toward each other—me up, him down." She frowned thoughtfully. "It would be easier if I had my hands on Huck's shoulders. When should I do that?"

"Can you get your arms up between mine?" he asked.

She slowly slid her hands up his chest and around his neck. "How's that?"

His heart felt like a caged bird, racketing around inside his ribs. "That's fine," he managed to rasp. "Now, you slide up on tiptoe, and I'll lower my head."

As she came up on tiptoe she lost her balance. She grabbed him around the neck, and his arm tightened around her, pressing her soft, warm breasts against his chest. He met her startled gaze and said, "Are you all right?"

"I think so. Whew! See why I need the practice? Who knew there were so many pitfalls to a simple kiss?"

He started to push her away, but she clung to his neck and said, "Let's keep going. What is Huck likely to do next?"

Kiss you till he can't see straight, Colt thought. But he said, "Let's see how good you are at hitting a target."

She grinned. "You mean, can I find his lips with mine?"

"Give it a shot."

Her fingertips at his nape urged his head down toward hers. He kept his eyes locked with hers until he couldn't bear the excitement anymore, then closed his eyes and waited for her lips to touch his. When they didn't, he opened his eyes to find her staring at him, her brow furrowed. "What's wrong?" he asked.

"I shouldn't be the one doing the kissing," she said. "Huck will want to be the aggressor."

"The *aggressor?*" Colt said.

"You know, the wolf stalking his prey, the Neanderthal dragging his woman back to his cave."

"Where do women get these ideas?" he said, shaking his head.

"From men," she said with a grin. "Admit it. Men like to make the first move. What would Huck think if *I* kissed *him* first?"

"That you liked him," Colt said flatly.

She looked thoughtful, then shook her head. "I'm an old-fashioned girl. Huck has to be the one to kiss first."

Which meant *he* had to kiss *her* first, Colt realized. "Let's get this over with." He leaned down, but before he could kiss her, she put her fingertips to his lips. "What's wrong now?" he asked in exasperation.

"Huck wouldn't do it like that."

"Like what?"

"In a big hurry."

"He might."

"He'll take his time. He'll make it count. He'll know how important this first kiss is. Do it right," she said.

"Do it right?" he muttered. "I'll do it right. Watch me *do it right*."

He threaded his fingers through her hair again, then used his hold to angle her head back so her lips were aimed up at his. He lowered his head slowly, keeping his eyes on hers, *making it count*. This was the first time he was going to kiss the girl he loved. And he wanted her to know how important this moment was.

He felt a shock as their lips touched, and backed off to stare at her. She looked dazed. He lowered his mouth over hers a second time, feeling the firmness of her lips and then the supple give as she responded to him. He pressed a little harder and felt her hands slide into his hair.

He wanted to taste her, so he teased his tongue along the edge of her lips, waiting for her to open to him.

She broke the kiss abruptly and leaned back to stare at him, her pupils dilated, her lips wet, her body trembling. "What were you doing with your tongue?"

"I was tasting you."

"Will Huck want to do that?"

"I would if I were him," he said simply.

"Why?"

"Because it feels good."

"It makes me feel funny inside." She laughed nervously and said, "Look at me. I'm shaking."

"You want to quit?"

She hesitated, then shook her head. "I'd better practice if I'm going to get it right with Huck. I'm ready now, if you want to try again."

He leaned down and touched her mouth lightly with his once, and then again, teasing kisses that urged her to accept what was coming. He felt her lips become less rigid, felt them ease apart as his tongue slid along the crease, heard her moan as his tongue slid inside her mouth. Her hands clutched his hair as her hips arched instinctively into his.

Then she was jerking herself away and backing up, her hand rubbing at her mouth, her eyes wide, her body trembling. "Ohmigod. What am I doing? What are we doing?"

He stood without moving. He saw her eyes drop to the thick ridge along the zipper of his jeans and knew what had frightened her. But that was going to happen to Huck, too. She might as well know it now, as later.

"It's all right," he said in a matter-of-fact voice. "What happened to you—to us—is normal. It's what happens between a man and a woman when they kiss. I'm sorry if I scared you."

"Will Huck—? Of course he will," she said, thrusting an agitated hand through her hair. "I had no idea it would be like that. So...powerful. You stop thinking, you stop being a rational person, your body just sort of...explodes."

"Yeah," he said, huffing out a breath of air. "That pretty well describes it."

She looked up at him earnestly and said, "Thanks, Colt. I'm going to be forever in your debt. There aren't many friends who'd be willing to help out like this."

"Anytime," he said.

Colt became aware of a horse ripping up grass with

his teeth near his head and opened his eyes, reluctantly letting go of the memory. He leaned up on his elbow and looked down at Jenny. She was sound asleep, her breathing quiet and even. He wondered if her first kiss with Huck had been everything she'd hoped. He'd never asked, and she'd never spoken about it.

"This is for you from Huck," he murmured as he leaned over and gently touched her lips with his. "A kiss good-bye."

Chapter 3

Too late, Jenny realized the trip to the stock tank in the south pasture had been a big mistake. It reminded her of something she'd chosen to forget: Her "first kiss" with Huck had come nowhere close to arousing in her the emotions of her "practice kiss" with Colt.

She had blamed the disturbing difference on the fact a girl could only get her "first kiss" once, and due to her own stupidity, she'd had her first kiss with the wrong man. It was only natural that her "second kiss" wasn't quite so exciting. Of course she'd loved Huck's kisses, because she'd loved Huck. But the spark she'd felt with Colt, that delicious electricity—that total loss of shame and scruples—had never occurred with Huck.

Since lying beside Colt yesterday in the shade of the live oak, those bewitching memories had made their insidious way back into her consciousness. Jenny's mind had begun replaying the moment when Colt's lips first touched hers, when his tongue first traced the seam of her mouth, when she first tasted him.

It was simple curiosity, she told herself, that made her wonder if that electricity had merely been the result of a "first kiss," or whether it would happen if they kissed again. She was ashamed of herself for what she was thinking, but she couldn't get the idea out of her head.

What if Colt could make her feel more than Huck ever had? What if she hadn't been kissed first by the wrong man? What if she'd been engaged to him?

That thought was too painful to face, since it would've meant she'd wasted ten years of her life—and Huck's. If she was going to have second thoughts, she should've had them a long time ago.

When? a voice asked. *After Huck was graduated from the Air Force Academy, he was never around for more than a few days at a time. You were busy with your brothers. You barely had time to make school lunches, let alone worry about your love life. It was convenient for both of you to be "in love." There was no time to stop and think. Until now.*

Jenny supposed everyone went through this sort of soul-searching at the time of such a significant loss. But she wasn't getting the answers she'd expected. She found her thoughts—and her eyes—focused more and more on Colt.

Sunday she went to church and surrounded herself protectively with her brothers. If anyone could keep Colt at a distance, it was Sam and Tyler and James and Randy. The idiot man simply shook each brother's hand as he moved past them into the pew and settled himself right beside her. It was a tight squeeze, because the pews weren't that large, and Sam wouldn't move over at first.

Colt finally speared Sam with a look that sent him scooting. "Hi, Jenny," he said. "I thought you might want company this first Sunday without Huck."

What were her brothers? Sliced baloney? With four brothers at her side, why did Colt think she needed him?

He shared a hymnal with her and sang the familiar refrains in a strong baritone voice that sent shivers down her spine. She found herself wondering how he would sound whispering love words in her ear.

It wasn't until after church, when everyone crowded around, that she conceded she was grateful for Colt's presence. Her brothers hovered, but they were clearly uncomfortable responding to the offers of condolence.

Colt slid an arm around her waist to hold her close enough that their hips occasionally bumped. He shook hands with the men and pulled several blue-haired old ladies close enough to kiss their cheeks. As though he coped with such emergencies every day, he enfolded Randy in a one-armed embrace when her brother unexpectedly broke into tears.

Colt didn't even let go when Sam and Tyler and James came one at a time to bid her good-bye. They were all big, tall men, like their father had been. Sam and Tyler were dark-haired and brown-eyed, while James had green eyes and chestnut hair. They were dressed in suits, but that didn't make them look particularly civilized. They might have been wolves from a free-roaming pack.

They would have intimidated a lesser man. Colt met

them without backing off, staring down Sam when he eyed the way Colt's arm was wrapped around her.

"You look like hell," Sam said to her. "Get some sleep."

"Thanks a lot, Sam," she replied, making a face at him. "I'm trying."

"Try harder," Sam said, chucking her gently under the chin. It wasn't a large gesture of affection, but it was the equivalent of a bear hug from Sam. She met his gaze and saw the worry there and smiled to reassure him. "I'll be fine, Sam."

He turned to Colt and said, "I guess we won't be seeing as much of you, now that Huck's gone."

Jenny held her breath, waiting for Colt to tell Sam that he'd offered to marry her.

Colt shot her a quick look, but all he said was, "I'll be around for a while."

Sam was followed by Tyler, who brushed his knuckles against her cheek and said, "Take care of yourself, sis." He gave Colt a hard look and said, "You be careful now."

Jenny wasn't sure whether it was an admonition to be careful flying jets, or whether Tyler was warning Colt to watch his step around her.

Colt replied, "I'm always careful."

James kissed her brow and whispered, "God works in mysterious ways. We can't know what he has planned for us."

She felt a moment of panic, wondering if James had somehow surmised her unsettling daydreams about Colt. But when she met his gaze, he only looked sad and sympathetic.

"Where's Randy?" Colt asked when her other brothers had all taken their leave.

Jenny looked around the church hall and saw Randy standing in a crowd of teenagers. "He's over there by the Butler twins, Faith and Hope."

"Let's go get him. My mom has invited the two of you to Sunday dinner at Hawk's Pride."

She freed herself at last from Colt's embrace and turned to face him, her hands knotted to keep him from reaching for them. "I can't go, Colt."

"Why not?"

"I couldn't face your parents. Not when I haven't made up my mind yet whether I'm going to marry you."

"They don't know about my proposal," Colt said.

"*I* know about it. I wouldn't feel comfortable. Please, Colt. Give them my regrets."

"I'll tell them now and follow you home. We can pick up something to have for dinner on the way."

Jenny stared after him as he stalked off, wondering how the situation had gotten so completely out of her control. Her attraction for Colt seemed to be growing stronger by the minute—along with her guilt over the rapidity with which she seemed to be transferring her affections from one man to another.

All I have to do is spend a little more time with Colt, and his faults will begin to show, Jenny thought as she waited for Colt to return.

She and Colt and Randy spent the afternoon sitting on the floor around the coffee table in the living room playing a game of Scrabble. She found herself fascinated by Colt's hands. Blue veins were prominent in the backs of his hands, and his knuckles bore tiny tufts of black hair. His nails were clean and cut bluntly, and his fingers were long and thick, with callused pads. She imagined what it might feel like if he slid one inside her. And blushed hotly.

"You look kinda warm, Jenny," Randy said. "You want me to open another window?"

She kept her eyes on the table. "That's a good idea. What's the score?" she asked,

"Colt's beating the pants off you," Randy said.

Jenny closed her eyes and bit her lip to stop the moan from escaping her throat. She'd had a flashing mental image of Colt tearing off her white cotton underwear—she was wearing Tuesday on Sunday. His hand lay on the table right beside hers, large and strong.

"You have such a big, strong...vocabulary," Jenny said, catching herself at the last moment.

"Thanks," Colt said. "I think it's my turn."

"'Xenophile'?" Randy questioned suspiciously as Colt laid down the *x* and *e* before Randy's two-letter word and then the *p-h-i-l-e.* "What's it mean?"

"Someone who's attracted to foreign things."

"Like eels and caviar?" Randy asked.

"Like veiled women," Colt quipped, leering at Jenny.

Jenny picked up a doily that was covering a hole in the arm of the couch upholstery, held it across her nose and mouth and batted her eyelashes. "Take me away, O Sheikh of Araby!" she said melodramatically.

Randy laughed. "I give up. You win, Colt. Game's over."

"Not quite yet," Colt said. He rose and did a bow toward Jenny. "Your wish is my command, O Maiden of the East."

"Is that East *Texas,* suh?" Jenny said with a deep Southern accent, once again batting her lashes.

Colt grabbed a patterned cotton blanket that was

draped across the couch—hiding another worn bit of upholstery—and threw it over Jenny's head as though he were really a sheikh come to kidnap her. While she was laughing uncontrollably, he whisked her up over his shoulder, hauled her into her bedroom and threw her onto the four-poster.

Jenny was still giggling when Colt pulled the blanket off her face. "I don't know when I've had such a good time. Thanks, Colt. I—"

She stopped talking and stared at him. When had he gotten so handsome? Had his cheekbones always been so sharp? His lips so full and wide? She wasn't aware of licking her lips until she heard Colt's sharp intake of air.

She met his gaze and caught a glimpse of something—what?—before his eyes were shuttered.

"Get some rest," he said as he backed his way out of the room. "I'll see you tomorrow."

No faults, she thought with a groan. *Not one damn fault.*

She dreamed of a woman in flowing, see-through silks being carried across the desert by a turbanned sheikh riding a magnificent Arabian stallion. They were running from something, but they couldn't escape because the horse kept getting bogged down in the sand. She looked up and realized a jet was falling out of the sky, about to crash right on top of their heads.

Jenny woke up before the jet hit the ground. She sat up in bed breathing hard and staring at the rising sun, wondering how she could have been laughing and playing such games last night when Huck was never coming back.

On Monday, Colt put new shingles on the leaky

roof. Shirtless. His broad chest was covered in thick, dark curls. She couldn't help making the comparison to sandy-haired Huck, who'd had very little chest hair and not nearly so much muscle. Colt's shoulders bunched and relaxed as the hammer rose and fell.

She stood mesmerized as a single drop of sweat slid down the center of his back until it met his denim jeans. She found herself fascinated by the way the worn blue cloth molded his buttocks.

No faults there, either, she conceded.

Tuesday, Colt dug postholes to repair the rotten gate on the corral. "They used to punish cowboys with this job in the old days," he said, his eyes twinkling.

She found herself entranced by his gaze, unable to look away. His eyes reminded her of sapphires, except they weren't cold, like stone, but warm and welcoming. She noticed the spray of lines at the corners of his eyes where the sun had weathered his skin and realized he wasn't a boy anymore. He was a grown man. A very attractive grown man.

On Wednesday, she sat with Colt on the back porch after supper to drink a chocolate milkshake. She watched his Adam's apple bob as he leaned his head back and swallowed down the thick ice cream. Her body drew up tight as his tongue slipped out to lick the last of the milky chocolate off his upper lip.

"Are you going to drink the rest of that?" he asked, pointing to her half-finished shake.

She held out her frosty glass and said, "Help yourself."

He put his lips on the edge of the glass where hers had been and watched her as he took a sip. Tasting chocolate. Tasting her.

Her mouth went dry with desire.

She leaped up without excusing herself and ran inside, letting the screen door slam behind her, not stopping until she'd reached her bedroom. She closed the door and leaned back against it, aware of her pounding heart and the ache deep inside her.

She wanted him. It was sinful how much she wanted him. And they hadn't even had the memorial service for Huck.

What's wrong with me? How can I be having such thoughts about Colt when it's Huck I love...loved?

Several loud knocks on the door made her skitter away toward the center of the room. "Who's there?"

"It's me, Colt. Are you all right?"

"No, I'm not all right!" she said. *There's something terribly wrong with me. I can't help thinking of you. Wanting you.*

"Open the door, Jenny, and talk to me. I know something's been troubling you these past few days. I'd like to help."

"Go away, Colt." *Don't you understand? You're the problem!*

"Are you upset about that marriage proposal?"

Jenny grabbed at the excuse he'd offered. "It's been on my mind."

"Look, there's no need for you to decide about marriage right away. If you need money for the mortgage payment, I'll provide it, no matter what."

She yanked the door open. "I thought we agreed I can't take your money, Colt."

"It's no big deal, Jenny."

"It is to me."

He reached out and clasped her free hand in his. She

felt the calluses on his fingertips, remembered what she'd been imagining his hands doing and jerked her hand out of his. "This isn't going to work!" she said desperately. "You can't keep coming here every day, Colt."

"Why not?"

"It's indecent!"

"Indecent? What the hell are you talking about?"

"I'm practically a widow—"

"You and Huck were never married. And in case you've forgotten, he was my friend, too."

Jenny stared at him, stricken. It wasn't Colt's fault she was attracted to him. *There's nothing wrong with him. I'm the one who's flawed.*

"I'm sorry," she said.

"If you really don't want me here, I'll stay away," he offered.

"No. Come tomorrow."

On Thursday, Jenny sent Colt out to repair a stall door in the barn while she stripped the beds, did the laundry and mopped the floors. She figured the distance would be good for both of them. If she wasn't forced to look at Colt all day, she was sure she wouldn't find herself thinking about him so much.

By noon she conceded that "absence makes the heart grow fonder." She went hunting for Colt to tell him lunch was ready, because that was the best excuse she'd been able to come up with to go after him.

"Colt? Are you out here?"

"Up here," Colt called down from the loft.

"Lunch is ready," Jenny said.

"Come on up here a minute. There's something I want to show you."

Jenny hesitated, then started up the ladder. When she reached the top, Colt grabbed her under the arms and lifted her the rest of the way up. She felt his touch all the way to her core. She was still standing where he'd left her when he turned and walked toward the corner of the loft.

"Over here," he said, going down on one knee.

Jenny told her feet to move, and they obediently headed in Colt's direction. She knelt beside him to look at what had been hidden in a bed of straw in the corner, then turned to share a smile with him. "They're adorable."

"Their eyes are still closed. They can't be more than a few days old."

"Six of them," Jenny said, counting the nursing kittens. "Jezebel, I didn't even know you'd been courting," she chided the mother cat.

Jezebel purred under Jenny's stroking.

Jenny looked at Colt and realized he was staring at her hand. His eyes locked with hers, his gaze heavy-lidded, his lips full and rigid. She stopped stroking the cat and rose abruptly.

"That stew is going to burn—"

Colt rose and grabbed her arm to keep her from fleeing. "You feel it, too."

She turned to him, her eyes wide with fright. "What are you talking about?"

"Don't bother pretending, Jenny. I've felt your eyes on me all week. I haven't been able to zip my damn jeans in the morning, thinking about you watching me."

She didn't know what to say, so she didn't say anything. A trickle of sweat tickled its way down her back. A fly buzzed, and one of the kittens mewed.

Colt let go of her and shoved his hand through his hair. "I'm afraid I don't know the proper etiquette for this situation. I suppose I should have kept on pretending right along with you, Jenny. But that wouldn't be fair to either of us."

"I can't help it," Jenny said quietly. She searched his face, saw the flare of heat in his eyes and responded to it.

"Neither can I," he replied in a hoarse voice.

"What are we going to do?"

"I could stay away."

"That wouldn't change how I feel," Jenny said. "I wonder if an experiment would help."

"What kind of experiment?" Colt said warily.

"I think maybe you should kiss me."

Colt stared at her. "What will that accomplish?"

She gave a shuddering sigh. "I'm not sure. Maybe nothing."

Colt shook his head and grinned wryly. "I feel like a fifteen-year-old kid again. How do you want to do this?"

She cocked a brow. "You're the expert, as I recall."

"All right. Come here."

As he slipped his arm around her waist, her hands slid up his chest and around his neck. He pulled the rubber band out of her ponytail and threaded his hand into her hair, angling her head for his kiss. She rose a little on tiptoe as his head lowered toward hers. She closed her eyes as his mouth covered hers.

Jenny waited with bated breath as Colt's lips pressed against hers, soft and a little damp. A frisson chased up her spine as his tongue teased the seam of her lips. She opened her mouth eagerly, and his tongue slipped inside. Without any warning, without any urging, her hips rocked into the cradle of his thighs, and she rode the hard ridge that promised so much pleasure.

So much feeling. So much heat. So much more than she had ever felt with Huck.

Jenny sobbed against Colt's mouth.

He put his hands on her shoulders and shoved her away. "Jenny?"

She sobbed again, unable to admit the horrible discovery she'd made. Her eyes blurred with tears until she could no longer see the stark look in his eyes.

He pulled her close, pressing her face against his chest and rubbing her scalp. "I guess your experiment didn't work," he said. "I'm sorry. What happens now?"

There were so many things Colt didn't know. So many things she couldn't tell him. A clock was ticking. She didn't have the luxury of waiting until the guilt was gone. They'd already lost so much time. She didn't want to lose any more. This physical thing between them wasn't love, but she was smart enough to know it was something very special. It didn't happen all the time. It hadn't happened between her and Huck.

Jenny didn't know how long they'd been standing in the loft before she became aware of Colt's heart thudding beneath her ear, of his hand stroking her hair, of his strength wrapped around her frailty. "I have—" She cleared the frog from her throat. "I have a favor to ask."

"Name it," Colt said.

She leaned back and laid her hand on his cheek. "Will you marry me?"

"Are you sure that's what you want?"

"It's the practical thing to do. Considering…everything."

Colt pulled her back into his arms. "It's been awful damned tough on you, hasn't it? All right, we'll do the practical thing and get married."

"In June," she said. "When I would have married Huck."

"Right. I'll just step up to the altar in place of my best friend and say 'I do.' Do you suppose anyone will notice?"

"I will," she said quietly.

Chapter 4

"I'm moving in with Jenny Wright tomorrow," Colt announced to his family at supper that evening.

The astonished faces of his brothers and sisters, the gasp from his mother and the frown on his father's face all demanded an explanation. "We're getting married in June," he said baldly, "on the day Jenny would have married Huck. I'm moving in so I'll be able to finish the repairs that need to be made at the Double D before my leave is over."

"I knew you wanted her for yourself," Jake said in disgust. "But Huck isn't even cold in his grave!"

Colt was out of his seat and reaching for his brother before the last words were out of his mouth. Their father intervened, catching Colt around the chest and holding him back, while Rabb and Avery did the same with Jake.

Colt's hands were fisted at his sides, and his face was flushed with rage. "Take it back, Jake."

"It's the truth," Jake said.

"Did Jenny agree to this?" his mother asked.

Colt tried to answer, but when he couldn't get words past the knot in his throat, just nodded.

"You can't marry Jenny!" Frannie exclaimed. "She's Huck's girl."

Colt felt his stomach roll. They were only saying what everyone else in town would say when they heard what he and Jenny had decided. He'd hoped for more understanding from his family, but he didn't give a damn whether he got it or not. He was going to marry Jenny. "My mind is made up," he said.

"What's the rush?" Avery asked.

"Jenny's going to lose the Double D unless she gets some quick financial help. Marriage is the best security I can offer her."

"I knew she was having trouble making ends meet," his father said. "Are you sure marriage is the best solution to the problem?"

Colt shook himself free. "Huck was my best friend. I owe Jenny whatever help I can give her."

"Everybody sit down, please," his mother said. "Let's discuss this calmly and rationally."

Rabb and Avery let Jake go, and he sat down. Colt was too agitated to rejoin his family at the table. "Look," he said. "There's really nothing to discuss. Jenny and I are getting married, and nothing anybody says is going to stop us."

"We're not trying—"

Colt interrupted his father. "I'm sorry, Dad. I think it'll be more comfortable for everybody if I just move in with Jenny tonight." He turned and headed for his bedroom to pack.

He heard a knock at the door a moment later. He should have known they wouldn't let him go without another lecture. When he opened the door, he found Jenny standing there.

"What are you doing here?"

"I needed to talk to you."

He looked out into the hall, which was surprisingly empty of his parents and siblings, then dragged her inside and closed the door behind her. "What's going on?"

"You tell me," she said. "I sneaked in through the patio door and heard a lot of yelling in the dining room."

His lips flattened. "My family isn't exactly thrilled at my upcoming nuptials."

"Neither is mine," she said. "I called my brothers and told them what we'd decided, and they all came over to try to talk me out of it. Sam was furious. He accused me of carrying on with you all these years. I couldn't believe the things he said. I..." She took a shuddering breath. "It was horrible."

He saw the anguish in her eyes and pulled her into his arms. "I know," he said. "Jake accused me of jumping the gun, too."

"We can't go through with this, Colt."

His heart lurched. He couldn't give her up now. Wouldn't give her up. Even if he was only going to have her for a matter of weeks before he left to return to Egypt.

"Do these second thoughts have anything to do with what happened in the loft? Because—"

She covered his mouth with her hand to silence him. "It's not that. It's the opposition from both our families. I don't want to be at war with my brothers, and I know you love your family as much as I love mine. How can we do this to them?"

"What other choice do we have?"

"I can give up the ranch and move into town."

"You don't want to do that."

She sighed. "No, I don't."

"Our families have been told, and we're both still walking and talking. I'd say the worst is over."

"Is it?" she asked, looking up at him.

"In fifty years, I guarantee you nobody will remember how we ended up married."

She managed a wobbly smile, and Colt felt his heart begin to thump a little harder. He was grateful he no longer had to hide his physical attraction to her, but a larger problem remained. Colt was *in love* with Jenny. It complicated everything; it didn't change anything. The only way to help her was to marry her. Unless she'd take money from him without the connection.

"If you really think marriage is a bad idea, let me make you a loan," he said. "I can work for you at the Double D until my leave is up."

She shook her head. "I couldn't borrow as much money from you as it would take to put the ranch back on sound footing. I'd never be able to pay it all back. And I'm going to need help on the Double D for a very long time. A lifetime."

"Then marry me, Jenny. Huck wouldn't want you to lose the ranch. Huck would kill me if I let you lose the ranch."

The attempt at humor brought a fleeting smile to her

lips. She brushed her fingertips across the front of his shirt, pressing away a wrinkle and causing his body to tense beneath her hand. He held himself perfectly still, loving the touch, wanting it, yet aware of how precarious their relationship was precisely because of their fierce attraction to each other.

Her hand paused near his heart, and he wondered if she could feel it jumping in response to her touch. She looked deep into his eyes, searching, he supposed, for whatever reservations she might find there. There were none. At least none he was willing to let her see.

Finally she said, "All right, Colt. If you're willing to go through with this marriage despite the opposition from our families, I'll go along."

"There is one thing," he said.

"What?" she asked.

"I told my family I was moving in with you tonight."

She shook her head in disbelief. "Colt—"

"I guess I can stay at a hotel in town."

"You can sleep in one of my brothers' rooms."

"Is Randy going to give you any trouble about this?"

"If he does, he can do his own cooking and laundry until he goes off to college." She laid her head on his chest. "I hope we're doing the right thing."

"As long as we're both convinced it's the right thing, then it is," he said with a certainty he wasn't feeling inside. He had plenty of fears.

What if she never learns to love me? What if I can't make her happy?

There were bound to be problems, especially since he would be away in the Air Force. And there was going to be talk. But together they could weather the storm. And Jenny would be his at last.

He'd imagined making love to her a thousand times over the years he'd known her. But that was all he'd ever done. Imagine. He'd never thought his dreams would come true. Soon he'd have the right to hold her naked in his arms. To put himself inside her. He wanted to make love to her. More important, he wanted her love.

There isn't enough time, a voice warned. *You've got less than sixty days before you have to report back for duty in Egypt. Sixty days isn't much time to woo a grieving woman.*

He had to find a way. He had to find the time.

Colt smoothed his hand over Jenny's hair with a sense of wonder. He was going to be sleeping in a room nearby her tonight. In a little more than a month he'd have the right to lie beside her.

I'm sorry, Huck, but she needs me. I know you wouldn't want her to be alone. And I love her.

"How did you get here tonight?" he asked.

"I drove Old Nellie."

Old Nellie was a rusted-out '56 Chevy pickup. "If you'll give me a minute to finish packing, I'll ride back with you," Colt said.

The door opened without anyone knocking, and Colt found himself staring at his brother Jake over Jenny's head. His arms were around her—in comfort—just as her arms held tight to him.

Jake took one look, and his eyes narrowed. "I came here to apologize. Looks like I was right all along."

Colt stared his brother down. He'd done nothing wrong. He'd loved Jenny for years, but he'd never by word or deed done anything to suggest to her how he felt. If Huck had come home and married her, he would have lived his life without her ever knowing he cared. He'd done nothing that required an apology. "Get out, Jake, and leave us alone."

"If alone is what you want, little brother, alone is what you'll get!" Jake backed out, slamming the door behind him.

Colt heaved a gusty sigh. "Damn it all to hell."

"Colt, if this marriage is going to cause problems—"

Colt laid his fingertips against Jenny's lips to silence her and felt himself quiver at that small touch. "Jake only sees things in black and white. He'll get over it—in fifty years or so."

He saw her try to smile…and fail.

"Cheer up," he said, tipping her chin up so he could look into her eyes. "The cavalry is riding to the rescue."

She stepped back, away from his touch. "Thanks, Colt. The least I can do is help you pack. Where do you want to start?"

It didn't take long to pack his things. He hadn't brought much with him from Egypt. He grabbed the small bag and headed down the hall.

His mother was waiting for him there.

"Hello, Jenny," she said, reaching out for Jenny's hand. "I'm very happy for you both."

"Thank you, Mrs. Whitelaw," Jenny replied.

The two women held hands for a moment before his mother turned to him. She didn't say anything, just stared, her heart back in her eyes.

"I'm sorry, Mom," he said at last. "I can't stay here."

She smiled bravely. "I know. I just wish…" She turned quickly back to Jenny and gave her a hug. "I wish you both the best." Then she reached up to touch his cheek. "Take care of yourself, Colt. Don't be a stranger."

She'd made no comment about whether they all planned to attend the wedding next month. He opened his mouth to ask and shut it again. It was better to let sleeping dogs lie.

Jenny slipped behind the wheel of the pickup as he threw his bag into the rusted-out truck bed. He settled onto the torn passenger seat, and she released the clutch and stepped on the gas.

The short drive from his home to hers had never seemed so long. He listened to the noisy rattle in the dash. The *clunk* as the carriage of the truck hit the frame when the worn-out shock absorbers failed. The sound of sand and gravel crunching under the bald tires. And, of course, every breath she took.

Colt searched for some safe subject to discuss. Everything seemed fraught with memories of Huck. Maybe that wasn't so bad. The three of them had been best friends. It was fitting that Huck should be here on this journey with them.

"I miss him already," Colt said into the silence.

"I keep asking myself what he would think about what we're doing," she said.

"He'd understand," Colt said.

"Would he?" she asked, turning to look at him.

"He loved us both. He wouldn't want you to lose the ranch."

Jenny shot him an agonized glance. "I can't believe we're even thinking about—"

"Huck is dead, Jenny. We have to go on living."

"To marry you so soon... It seems... I feel like I'm

betraying Huck. His memory, anyway. I'm attracted to you, Colt, but I don't love you. I loved Huck."

"We both loved him, Jenny. That's why getting married is the right thing to do."

"There's something wrong with the logic in that statement, but I'm too tired to figure it out right now." She pulled up to the kitchen door and shut off the engine. It ran for another couple of seconds before it died. "It looks like Randy's still up."

"Do you want me to talk to him?" Colt asked. "To explain?"

"Randy hasn't said a word against this marriage. I think he understands how bad things are."

And maybe how alone you'd be with Huck never coming back, Colt thought.

Jenny sighed, then pushed the truck door open and stepped down. "Come on in, and I'll show you where to sleep."

Colt grabbed his bag from the truck bed, then followed her up the back steps and into the kitchen. Randy was leaning back against the sink, a can of Pepsi in his hand.

"Hello, Randy. Long time no see," he said, extending his hand to the lanky teenager. Randy's hair was the same blond as Jenny's, but his eyes were hazel instead of blue and looked like they'd seen a great deal more of life than a boy his age should.

Randy hesitated, then took Colt's hand and shook it. "Hi, Colt. What's up?" He flushed as he realized the can of worms such a question might open up. "I mean... I thought you were moving in tomorrow."

"Change of plans," Colt replied. He turned to Jenny, whose face looked drawn. "Where do you want me?"

"Follow me," she said, hurrying from the kitchen.

"You gonna stay in Sam's room?" Randy asked, tagging along behind them.

"I'll stay wherever Jenny puts me."

"Sam's room is next to mine," Randy said. "Down the hall from Jenny's."

"Sounds like a good place to be," Colt said, meeting Jenny's glance over her shoulder. It seemed *down the hall* was as close to his sister as Randy wanted Colt.

Colt didn't know if Sam's old room was where she'd initially wanted to put him, but she took her cue from Randy's suggestion, and he found himself in the doorway to a small, feminine room a moment later.

"This is my sewing room now," she said. "I'll get my things out of here tomorrow."

The small room held a single, brass-railed bed and a bedside table with a delicate porcelain lamp. Her sewing machine sat on a table heaped with clothes that she was either making or mending. In the corner stood a clothing dummy wearing what looked like the beginning of a wedding gown.

The gingham curtains were trimmed in eyelet lace, and the bed was heaped with a bunch of frilly pillows and a pair of rag dolls. It might have been Sam's room once upon a time, but Jenny had made it hers.

This was a side of Jenny he'd rarely seen: the soft, feminine side. She'd done a man's work on the Double D for as long as he could remember, and he'd rarely seen her wearing anything but jeans. Everything in this room was soft, decorated in pastel pink and pale green. The dolls were a surprise. It smelled flowery, like maybe the drawers were filled with some kind of potpourri.

She flushed as he met her gaze. "I'll just take these with me," she said, scooping up the lacy pillows and the dolls, as though she were embarrassed for him to see them. "Randy can get you anything you need," she said as she backed out of the room.

"What bee got into her bonnet?" Randy asked, staring after her.

"I guess she wasn't expecting company tonight," Colt said.

"Why did you come tonight?" Randy asked.

Colt met Randy's troubled gaze and decided to tell the truth. "My family doesn't approve of this marriage any more than your brothers do. I thought it would make everybody more comfortable if I got this move over with."

"If you hurt her, I'll take you out myself."

Colt met the teenager's warning look with a steady gaze. "There isn't a man alive who cares more for your sister than I do, Randy. I only want to help her."

The boy stared at him a moment longer before his shoulders sagged. "Jeez, Colt. We sure can use the help. Things have been pretty tight around here. Jenny hasn't let on to the others how bad things are, but it's a little hard to hide the truth from me, when all we ever have for supper is macaroni and cheese."

Trust a youth to judge the state of things by what he put in his stomach, Colt thought wryly. "Things are going to get better, Randy. I'm here to make sure of it."

"Thanks, Colt. Guess I'll get some sleep. The school bus comes early in the morning."

"Good night, Randy. I'll see you at breakfast."

Colt stripped to his shorts, which was what he'd worn to sleep in for the past ten years, when he might find himself jumping into a flight suit in the middle of the night, and slipped between the covers.

The sheets were printed with roses. The pillow smelled like… Jenny. The springs squeaked and squealed as he turned over, trying to get comfortable. The mattress sagged in the middle, a reminder that everything in the house was old and worn-out and needed to be replaced. He turned out the delicate porcelain lamp and stared into the darkness. He could hear the crickets outside his window and the rustle of the wind through the grass.

It must have been hard to be the one female in a house full of men. With most of them gone, she'd created this feminine haven for herself. When he thought about it a little more, Colt realized it wasn't a woman's room, it was a girl's room. A place, perhaps, to recapture a lost childhood?

Colt remembered a time when he'd come to visit and had helped Jenny feed Randy. The kid loved squashed-up peas. Huck had decided he would rather go play than stay and help, so he'd had Jenny to himself for the whole afternoon—along with her four younger brothers. Her mother had been confined to her bed, watched over by Jenny's aunt.

Colt had enjoyed himself tremendously that day because it was all new to him—feeding Randy, changing Sam's diaper, then making sure Tyler and James took a bath. He'd been able to go home at the end of the day. Jenny had not.

The door opened almost before he heard the knock and was shut again after Jenny slipped inside.

"Colt?" she said.

He sat up and turned on the light. She was wearing an old chenille bathrobe and a pair of fluffy slippers. Her hair was down on her shoulders, and her face looked scrubbed. He felt his body tighten. "What are you doing in here, Jenny?"

"I can't do it, Colt."

He slid his legs over the side of the bed, but kept the sheet over his hips. "Do what?"

"I can't marry you."

He forgot about the sheet as he stood and crossed to take her by the arms. "What's going on, Jenny? I thought this was all settled."

Tears welled in her eyes and one plopped onto her cheek. He brushed it away with his thumb.

"Huck will always be there between us. Don't you see? Someday you're going to want a wife who can love you back, and I—"

"Let me worry about what I need," Colt said, pulling her into his arms. Her body was stiff and unyielding. He leaned back and separated her hands and put them around his waist, then pulled her close.

He was sorry as soon as he did. He could feel the soft warmth of her breasts against his naked chest. Feel her thighs through the wafer-thin robe. He angled his hips away, so she wouldn't become aware of his arousal. *I'm sorry, Huck. I can't help wanting her.*

He took Jenny's head between his hands and tilted her face up to his. "Listen to me, Jenny. I don't expect you to stop loving Huck. His memory will always be with us. I loved him, too, you know." He kissed a tear from her cheek and tasted the salt…and the sweetness of her. "Let me do this for him, for you, for both of you."

"I feel so guilty," she whispered.

"Why?"

"Because I'm glad you're here. Because I'm glad I don't have to face life alone anymore. And you're not even the man who was supposed to come home to me. What's wrong with me, Colt?"

He hugged her tight against him. "Nothing's wrong with you, Jenny. You're just human."

"I'm so tired of trying to hold everything together by myself. You can't imagine what it's been like, Colt. I've been counting the days until Huck got here to take some of the burden off my shoulders. I know it's not fair to lay so much on you. I just can't do it by myself anymore. I can't."

She was weeping in earnest, and Colt lifted her into his arms and sat down on the sagging bed and let her cry. She kept her mouth against his neck to mute the sound, as aware as he was that her brother was in the next room. When the sobs became hiccups, he felt her fingertips move tentatively across his chest. Goose-flesh rose where she touched.

"You're cold," she said.

"It's the breeze from the window," he lied. "I'll close it later."

"I should go to bed. It's late." But she made no move to leave his lap. Her hand stole around his neck, and he quivered as she played with the short hair at his nape. "I'm sorry I fell apart like that."

"You're entitled. I don't know how you've managed to do so much with so little help. Why haven't you said something to Sam and Tyler and James?"

"They've got their own lives. The ranch is my problem."

"And mine now."

"Until your leave is up."

"Yeah," he said, realizing for the first time how little help he was going to be if he left her behind and returned to Egypt.

At last she lifted her head. Her eyes were red-rimmed, and her lower lip was swollen where she'd chewed on it. "I'm so used to carrying all the responsibility on my shoulders, I'm not sure how I'll adjust to having someone around to help."

"I'm sure you'll manage. You always have."

She looked at him strangely. "Yes. I have."

It took Colt a moment to identify what he was feeling, what she'd heard in his voice. He was angry. Furious, really. At his friend. How could Huck have left her alone all these years and gone off to fly jets? Why hadn't Huck stayed home and married Jenny and run the ranch with her? Why hadn't Huck given her babies of her own, instead of leaving her alone to raise her brothers?

He was no better. He'd known for a long time how little time Huck spent with her, how little help Huck had provided, but he hadn't encouraged his friend to marry her. *Because as long as Huck never married Jenny there was always the chance she might be yours someday.*

Colt felt sick inside. It was hard to face such truths. He had a chance now to redress the wrongs of the past. He could be there for Jenny. Love her. Take care of her.

For Huck's sake? Or for your own? a voice asked.

For Jenny's sake, he answered. She deserved a better life, and he was going to make sure she got it.

"You'll feel better after a night's sleep," Colt said as he stood and set Jenny's feet on the floor. He had to unwrap her arms from around his neck. He held her hands for a moment, his thumbs moving across her work-worn knuckles. "I promise I'll always take care of you, Jenny. It's the least I can do for Huck." *And for the woman I love.*

Chapter 5

Jenny rose the next morning feeling—for the first time in a very long time—like anything was possible. She dressed in the same worn jeans, another faded Western shirt, and the same boots with the holes in the soles that were layered with newspaper. But she didn't feel the least forlorn. *Why do I feel so different?* she wondered. Hope. It was as simple as that.

"Good morning."

Jenny was surprised to find Colt in the kitchen ahead of her. His short black hair was still shiny wet from the shower. She must have been more exhausted than she'd thought, to sleep through the groaning water pipes.

He rubbed at the beard darkening his cheeks and chin and said, "Hope you don't mind. Figured I'd wait to shave again till these stitches come out."

Growing up in a houseful of men, she'd seen many

an unshaven face at the breakfast table, but never one she found so appealing. "I'll make us some coffee," she said, suddenly aware that she'd been standing there admiring the way his chest filled out his white T-shirt and the way his jeans molded...everything.

He pointed to the percolator. "Coffee's made." He had a pan on the stove and was laying strips of bacon in it.

"I should be making your breakfast," she said.

He grinned. "Tell you what. You clean up the mess, and we'll call it even."

"Deal," she said, crossing to stand beside him and pour herself a cup of coffee.

The heat of his body reminded her that she was no longer alone. And revived the unwanted attraction that lay between them. She hadn't stopped loving Huck; she'd merely acknowledged this physical *thing* that existed between her and Huck's best friend. She refused to feel guilty for taking the only road open to her.

Jenny took a sip of hot, black coffee, savoring the bitter taste of it, before she swallowed. According to Colt, there had been some delay in returning Huck's body to the States, but the senator had promised to contact Colt regarding the funeral arrangements. "Do you know yet when and where Huck's funeral is being held?" she asked. "I'll need to make arrangements to be there."

"Huck's being buried on the family farm in Virginia, where the senator makes his home when he's in Washington. Family and close friends only. I'm sorry, Jenny. I told the senator you should be there."

"Oh." Huck's father had never accepted her, but it hurt to be excluded from the funeral more than she'd thought it would. Her hands began to tremble, and she carefully set down the coffee cup. Huck wouldn't know she wasn't there. But it was hard to let him go when she'd never gotten the chance to say good-bye. She blinked furiously to fight back the tears. She was done with crying for what couldn't be changed.

Colt's arms closed tightly around her. "Huck will know you wanted to be there. And why you weren't."

"It hurts. Oh, God, I hurt inside."

"Me, too," he admitted hoarsely.

They stood wrapped in a comforting embrace until the smell of burning bacon forced them apart. Colt let go of her, grabbed a fork and turned the blackened bacon. "I hope you like your bacon crisp," he said.

"I like bacon any way I can get it." Jenny flushed as she realized Colt must have made an early morning trip to the convenience store. She and Randy hadn't eaten bacon at breakfast for quite a while, because it didn't fit into their meager budget.

She met Colt's eyes, which urged her not to make a big deal of it. It rankled to accept even this much charity. "Colt, I don't think you should be buying food—"

Randy arrived in the kitchen with his hair askew, teenage whiskers mottling his face, wearing a pair of pajama bottoms and scratching his bare stomach. "I smell bacon."

"Go get dressed," Jenny told him, wanting Randy out of the kitchen so she could finish making her point to Colt. "Breakfast will be ready by the time you are."

"Will you make me a lunch?" Randy asked.

"Sure," Jenny said. "Get moving." Randy was supposed to make his own lunch, but she knew why he hadn't. He hated the monotonous menu of peanut butter and jelly sandwiches, but that was all they could afford. She opened the refrigerator to get out the jelly and gasped. "What did you do? Buy out the store?"

She shot a look at Colt, whose face had taken on a mulish cast. "If I'm going to be eating your food, I figured I ought to provide my share of it," he said.

"Oh, Colt, you shouldn't have done this."

"Don't push me," he said, throwing down the fork he was using to turn the bacon and putting his fisted hands on his hips. "I'm mad as hell about what I've found here. It wouldn't take much to send me over the edge."

"Mad? About what?"

"That you never told me—or Huck, who would've told me—just how bad things are around here. Damn it all, Jenny! Macaroni and cheese? Peanut butter and jelly? Huck was rich, and I've got a trust fund of my own. Why didn't you ask us for help?"

"I didn't want your help."

"Why the hell not?"

Jenny felt her stomach twist into a knot. *Because if I'd asked for help, you'd have found out the secret I've been keeping from both of you.* "Pride," she said, her own fisted hands landing on her hips. "I didn't want to admit how badly I'd failed. There. Are you satisfied?"

Colt huffed out a gust of air, then hooked his thumbs in his back pockets. "I'm sorry. I guess it's easy to criticize when you're not around to see how difficult it is to shoulder the load. But please let me help, now that I'm here."

"All right, Colt." She reached up to get plates from the cupboard and noticed her hands were shaking. Another bullet dodged. She didn't dare tell Colt the truth.

No one knew the truth. Not even Randy, who lived with her.

"Where's breakfast?" Randy asked, setting his book bag on the floor beside the empty table. "The bus'll be here in a couple of minutes!"

Jenny set plates and silverware on the table, then made Randy's lunch while Colt fried a couple of eggs for her brother "over easy," as he'd requested. They were just sitting down with their own eggs, toast and bacon, when Randy stuffed down his third slice of toast and bolted for the door. "See you after school!" he said as the screen door slammed behind him.

"Whew!" Colt said with a grin. "I'd forgotten how hectic school mornings can be."

Jenny managed a smile. "It's hard to believe there's less than a month left before he's done."

Jenny thought of all the years she'd made sure her brothers got off to school. She'd been looking forward to the day when Randy graduated, because it meant she could begin her life with Huck. That wasn't going to happen now. She looked across the table and met Colt's concerned gaze.

"I'm here, Jenny. It's going to be all right."

The comforting words did nothing to ease the tension in her shoulders. "I'm afraid you'll regret this later, Colt." *When you find out the truth about me.*

"Let's take it one day at a time, shall we?"

Jenny released a shuddering breath. "All right. Where do you want to start today?"

"Suppose you tell me."

"If I don't get some fence repaired, what few cattle I have are going to be long gone."

"Fence it is," Colt said as he rose to take his plate to the sink.

The fence was barbed wire stretched between mesquite posts. Some of the posts had rotted, and some of them had been pushed down by cattle rubbing against them. It was hard work digging new postholes and re-stretching the barbed wire. Jenny told herself the lack of supplies had discouraged her from tackling the job. The truth was, it was grueling work that required more brute strength than she had.

As she watched the corded sinews flex in Colt's arms, Jenny conceded there were simply some things a man could do better than a woman. "Thanks, Colt," she said as she stapled the barbed wire into place. "I couldn't have done this without you."

He grabbed the kerchief from his back pocket, lifted his hat and wiped the sweat from his face and neck. He retrieved his T-shirt from the post where he'd left it, hung his Stetson there while he slipped his shirt back on, then resettled the Stetson low enough to shade his eyes. "Digging postholes is a lot harder work than flying jets," he said with a crooked smile.

She pointed at the white contrail left by a jet flying overhead. "So you'd rather be up there than down here?"

He tipped up his Stetson and squinted at the plane overhead. "Flying is all I ever wanted to do." He looked back at her. "But right now, there's no place I'd rather be than here with you."

"Digging postholes?" she said with a teasing grin.

"Better me than you," he said, his voice turning serious.

She turned and headed for the truck, tools in hand. "I don't mind a little hard work."

He caught her by the elbow and swung her around. He held on to her arm while he took the posthole digger and the staple gun out of her hands one at a time and threw them into the rusted-out bed of the pickup. Then he grasped both arms and turned her to face him.

"A little hard work is one thing, Jenny. Running yourself into the ground trying to do too much by yourself is another thing entirely. I've been watching you this past week, and it's plain to me that you're worn-out."

"I can't sleep," she retorted.

"This is more than lost sleep," he said. "You're wrung out. And so skinny a hard wind could blow you over."

She pulled herself free and took a step back. Colt was so much more perceptive than Huck. Huck hadn't noticed how thin she was—and how tired she was—four months ago, when he'd come for the Christmas holidays. Colt was so close to discovering the truth. She wanted to blurt it out to him. But that would send him running for sure.

"I'll admit I'm overworked," she said, feeling her way carefully. "It's been tough doing everything myself. I guarantee you I'll sleep better—and eat better, especially with the way you're shopping—now that you're here."

"I wish you'd said something sooner."

"Would you have stopped flying jets and come home to help me?" she asked in a quiet voice.

He looked stunned at the suggestion. "I… You know I would have…" He shrugged. "I don't honestly know. I like to think I'd have come if you'd said you needed me."

She shook her head. "You're only fooling yourself, Colt. You're just like Huck. All you have to do is sniff jet fuel, and you're off into the wild blue yonder."

He laughed. "I'm not that bad."

"You've asked me to marry you knowing full well you intend to return to Egypt to finish your tour there. What if I said I needed you here? That I wanted you to stay here with me? Would you resign from the Air Force?"

A shuddery breath escaped before Colt said, "Are you asking me to resign?"

Jenny made a face. "I don't know. It hardly seems fair to ask you to stay here when we aren't going to have a real marriage."

"Whoa, there, woman. Who said it wasn't going to be a real marriage?"

She flushed. "I suppose I meant a normal marriage. You know, where the two parties love each other and plan to spend their lives together."

Colt's brow furrowed, and his hands caressed her arms where he'd been tightly gripping her. "I wish I could give you that. I really do, but—"

"We don't love each other, and you plan to spend your life flying jets," she finished for him. She reached up to gently smooth the furrows from his brow with her thumb. "Don't worry, Colt. I'll be fine. I don't blame you for what happened to Huck. Truly I don't."

"I just wish—"

She put her fingertips over his lips. "No regrets. I'm grateful for whatever help you're able to give me during the next few weeks. I'm not going to ask for more."

He pulled her hand down, grasping it in his own. "That's the problem," he said. "You never ask for anything. What is it you want out of life, Jenny? I mean, besides scraping a meager living out of this place?"

"I want—wanted—to wake with my husband beside me and lie in bed listening to the morning sounds. I wanted us to work side by side, making the Double D as wonderful a place to live as it once was. And I wanted children of my own." She sighed wistfully. "It's too late for a family now."

"Why?" Colt asked.

She realized what she'd almost revealed and smiled to distract him. "I'm too old, for one thing. And the man I'm about to marry would rather fly jets." She stepped back and pulled her hand free, breaking all contact between them.

Colt cleared his throat and stuck his thumbs in his back pockets to keep from reaching for her again. "So you're going to spend your life on this godforsaken ranch all alone?"

"I'm sure my brothers will come around on holidays."

"Don't any of them want to live here with you? What's Randy going to do when he finishes college?" Colt asked.

"He wants to go into business for himself and earn lots of money."

"Fine. What about Sam and Tyler and James?"

"Sam's foreman for a nearby ranch," Jenny said. "Tyler's headed to medical school in Houston. And James…"

"What about James?"

She gave him a wondering look. "James is studying to become a minister. So you see, I'm on my own."

Colt saw a great deal. She'd given up her own hopes

and dreams to make sure her brothers realized theirs. Every extra penny must have gone for tuition or books or clothes. That was why the ranch had suffered. She was obviously very proud of them, and their opposition to this marriage was proof of how much they cared for her.

He couldn't just marry her and leave her here to manage on her own. On the other hand, he didn't think he could give up flying, either.

"Have you ever thought about selling the Double D?" he asked.

"I've thought about it," she admitted.

"And?"

Her eyes searched the horizon. He looked along with her and didn't see much, just a few scrub mesquite, some cactus and buffalo grass and bluebonnets, and in the distance, a few craggy bluffs that marked deep canyons similar to those that graced Hawk's Pride.

"I know it doesn't seem like much," she said. "But I love it. I feel connected to everyone who came before me." She turned to look at him. "I want—wanted—my children to grow up here and to love their heritage as much as I do."

Colt imagined Jenny playing with a bunch of kids, tickling them and laughing with them and having fun… without him. Because he'd be off flying jets.

It wouldn't be fair to leave her alone and pregnant.

Is it any more fair to deprive her of the one thing she wants that you can give her?

Colt took two steps toward Jenny and brushed a stray wisp of hair from her brow. His hand lingered on her cheek. "It's not too late for children, if you really want them."

"I can't raise them alone, Colt. Or rather, I won't do that to them. My dad left us and… I just wouldn't do that to any child of mine. Not if I could help it."

"I see." Colt looked deep into Jenny's eyes, wondering how it had come to this—a choice between the woman he had always loved, and the thing he loved doing most.

It didn't make it any easier to know that she didn't love him. That her heart belonged—would always belong—to his best friend.

Chapter 6

Colt studied Jenny in the sleeveless black sheath she'd worn to the memorial service for Huck. She was surrounded by friends who'd come to the Double D to bring mountains of food and offer their condolences. Her hair was gathered in a shiny golden knot at her crown, leaving her neck and shoulders bare, so he could see her body curved in all the right places. But she left a frail shadow on the ground, and her face looked wan. It dawned on him suddenly that she might be sick.

Sick people sometimes die.

Colt forced back the feeling of panic. *Jenny isn't sick. She's just tired.* The fear that she might be ill was like a living thing inside him, clawing at him, tearing at his insides. He knew his feelings were irrational, but his dread was born of firsthand experience.

When he was too young to know better, he'd made

friends of the kids who attended Camp LittleHawk, the camp for kids with cancer started by his mother at Hawk's Pride. He was eight when he met Tom Hartwell. Like many of the kids at camp, Tom had leukemia, but it was in remission. He and Tom had become blood brothers. Tom wanted to fly jets someday. Colt said he'd never thought much about it, but it sounded like fun.

Colt felt his insides squeeze at the memory of the freckle-faced, blue-eyed boy. Tom had worn a baseball cap to cover his head, left bald by chemotherapy. "My hair's really, really red," Tom had said with a grin. "Wait till it grows back in. You won't believe it!"

But the leukemia had come back, and neither Colt's raging nor his prayers—nor the best doctors money could buy—had been able to save his blood brother. Tom had died before Colt ever got a chance to see his red hair.

Jenny's not sick. She's just tired, he repeated to himself.

Nevertheless, he moved hurriedly through the crowd of mourners, briefly greeting neighbors he hadn't seen in years, catching brief snatches of conversation.

"… Remember when Huck and Jenny and Colt…"

"Then Huck and Jenny and Colt went galloping across…"

"—going to take Huck's place at the altar. Can you believe…"

He stood at Jenny's shoulder and knew she was aware of him when she leaned back against him and reached for his hand. He interrupted old Mrs. Carmichael to say, "Jenny and I are going out onto the porch for some air. Please excuse us," and led her away without looking back.

It wasn't easy getting through the kitchen, which was also full of people, including most of his own siblings. He didn't allow anyone to stop them. "Jenny needs some air," he said as he headed inexorably for the back porch.

Even there they found no respite. His mother and father stood on the porch, along with two of Jenny's brothers.

"There they are now," Sam said when he spied them. "I want to talk to you, Colt. I don't think—"

"Not now," Colt said without stopping. "Jenny and I are going for a walk." He put himself between her and everyone else and headed off down the rutted dirt road that led away from the ranch.

Jenny stumbled once in her black pumps, and he put his arm around her waist and kept on walking.

"Where's the fire?" Jenny asked.

Colt stopped abruptly and stared at her. "What?"

"Where are we going in such a hurry?"

Colt realized he'd been blindly running from his fear, which stabbed him anew when he looked down and saw the gauntness beneath her cheekbones and the shadows beneath her eyes. He had to work to keep his voice steady as he asked, "Are you all right?"

She gave him a quizzical look. "My fiancé is dead, and I've agreed to marry another man in a matter of weeks, but otherwise I suppose—"

He shook his head impatiently. "I mean, are you feeling all right? You look so thin, so exhausted. I thought you might be…sick."

She stiffened and looked away. "If I were, I wouldn't expect you to take care of me."

The air soughed slowly from Colt's lungs. Jenny knew better than anyone how assiduously he avoided sick people. When they were kids, he hadn't come near her house for a long time because her mother was dying of cancer, and he couldn't face seeing the ravages of the disease. He put a hand on her shoulder, and she jerked free and turned to face him.

"To answer your question, I'm fine, just very tired and very unhappy," she snapped. "We should go back now."

She'd already started back toward the house when he caught her elbow and turned her around again. "This way," he said, leading her along the twin dirt tracks that had been created by wagon wheels more than a century before.

She went along but asked, "Where are we going?"

"You need to rest."

She laughed. "Rest? You've practically got me jogging in high heels. I'm going to sprain an ankle—"

He scooped her up into his arms, making her cry out in surprise and grab his shoulders. He left the road, heading across country toward a single live oak that created a circle of shade.

She laughed at him uneasily. "Colt, where are you taking me?"

"Somewhere you can take a nap in peace and quiet."

"I've got company at the house."

"All of whom are perfectly capable of entertaining themselves with stories of 'Huck and Jenny and Colt,'" he said.

He set her down on the patchy grass, then sat with

his back against the trunk of the live oak, his legs stretched out in front of him, and pulled her down beside him. "Lay your head on my lap and relax," he said.

"Colt—"

He tugged on her hand. "Humor me, Jenny."

When she was settled with her head on his thigh, she closed her eyes and heaved a great sigh. The wind rustled the leaves of the live oak, and cattle lowed in the distance. A jay complained on a branch above them. They might have been a thousand miles from another human being.

"Thank you, Colt," Jenny murmured. "I didn't realize how much I needed a little peace and quiet."

He reached down and pulled the pins from her hair, then ran his fingers through the silky mass, massaging her scalp where the knot had been.

"That feels wonderful," she said.

Colt wanted to do a lot more, to hold her in his arms, to lie next to her, body to body. Instead he settled his hand on her nape, where he gently massaged the tense muscles.

"I'm not sure I could have heard one more story about Huck and me and you without breaking into tears," Jenny confessed in a quiet voice. "Thanks for rescuing me."

"That's too bad. I've got one I'd like to tell," Colt said.

Jenny's eyes opened, and she started to sit up. "Oh?"

He pressed her back down and said, "Relax. It's a good story, I promise."

"All right. Go ahead."

He could feel the rigidity in her body, the physical wariness. She'd taken so many blows lately, and he wanted to spare her any more pain. But avoiding the subject wasn't the answer. Neither of them was likely to forget the part Huck had played in their lives. They both had to accept his loss and move on.

Colt brushed a stray curl from Jenny's brow and said, "Huck and I were riding camels—"

Jenny's head popped up. "Camels? Really?"

"Lie down and listen," Colt said with a chuckle. When Jenny was settled again with her cheek on his thigh, he continued. "Huck and I were riding camels in Cairo, tourists traveling from one pyramid to the next, when he turned to me and said, 'I wish Jenny were here, because she'd have the nerve to see just how fast this beast can go. We'd be galloping across the desert instead of walking sedately behind some guide.'"

"Did Huck really say that?"

"He did," Colt confirmed. "And he was right. You're an amazing woman, Jenny."

She lifted her head and looked at him. "If I'm so amazing, why didn't he come back sooner? Why did he leave me alone so long?"

Colt hesitated. There was no excuse for Huck's behavior. There was an explanation. "He loved flying."

"More than he loved me," she said bitterly. She sat up abruptly, her back to Colt, her head bowed.

He saw her shoulders heave and knew she was crying again, though she made no sound. He sought words to comfort her. "He missed you terribly, Jenny. He ached for you. He admired you for taking care of your brothers." He had never heard Huck say any of those things out loud, but he had felt them himself, and he couldn't believe Huck hadn't felt them, as well.

"I hate those damned jets!" Jenny said vehemently. "I hate—" A sob cut her off.

Colt could resist no longer. He wrapped his arms tightly around her from behind, pressing his cheek against hers. "Huck's father had a great deal to do with keeping him away, Jenny. The senator didn't think his son should be saddled with the responsibility of raising someone else's family. It didn't help that Huck was rich, and you were poor."

"He thought Huck could do better," Jenny said. "He told me so to my face the one time I met him."

Colt bit back a gasp of disbelief. He'd known how Huck's father felt; he hadn't known Senator Duncan had been so blunt with Jenny. "Huck never let the senator sway him, Jenny. He always loved you."

"Just not enough," Jenny said.

Randy had been watching Faith Butler for almost an hour without going anywhere near her. Faith stuck pretty close to her twin sister, Hope, who'd gathered a crowd of admiring boys around her. Faith stood behind Hope like a shadow of her sister. It had been that way for as long as Randy could remember.

Hope Butler's behavior was *outrageous*. At least, that was the word Jenny used to describe her. Her face was usually slathered with makeup, and she wore her dresses cut low enough to cause problems with the fit of a guy's jeans. She smoked and drank and drove her car like a bat out of hell.

Randy figured she worked so hard to attract attention to herself so nobody would notice Faith. That is, so people would spend more time talking about the difference in their personalities rather than the other, more obvious difference between them.

They were both beautiful, with long, straight black hair they wore parted in the middle, and dark chocolate eyes and smooth, creamy skin. But something had gone wrong when they were in the womb, and Faith's left hand had stopped growing. Her arm ended shortly beyond the wrist, and she wore a plastic prosthetic device with a metal hook that substituted for her missing hand.

Like most of the guys, Randy had been attracted to Hope at first. Some guys said she "put out," and he'd been hoping he'd get lucky and score with her. Somewhere along the line, he'd gotten distracted by Faith.

He watched her now, standing serenely behind her sister, her left hand unobtrusively tucked behind her back. Faith smiled at Hope's anecdotes and seemed not to mind that her sister was the center of attention. Faith never made a big deal about the fact she didn't have a left hand.

Randy wondered if Faith ever minded all the guys paying attention to her sister instead of her, or if she ever felt angry or bitter about being the "imperfect" twin. He wondered what it would be like to date a girl like that. And shuddered involuntarily when he thought of that hook at the end of her arm anywhere near him.

He flushed with shame. It wasn't Faith's fault she was born like that. Remorse moved him in her direction. He walked right up to her and said, "Hi. I noticed your glass is almost empty. Can I get you something else to drink?"

She looked startled and frightened, like a deer he'd come upon suddenly in the brush when he was hunting. He was no more able to hurt her than he'd been able to kill that deer. "I noticed you from across the room," he said.

That only seemed to make her more self-conscious, so he quickly added, "I mean, I was noticing how pretty you look."

Her lashes lowered over her eyes, and two red spots appeared on her cheeks. "Thank you," she said in a barely audible voice.

The more shy she was, the more protective he felt. "I wondered if you might want to go to the movies with me sometime."

Her lashes lifted and she looked up at him and he felt his heart skip a beat. "Are you asking me out?" she asked.

With the full force of her gaze directed at him, he couldn't catch his breath to speak. His mind had turned to mush.

She smiled at his confusion and for the first time her left hand came out from behind her back. "You must have mistaken me for my sister."

He made himself look at the hooked hand she'd brought out to make sure he knew she was the imperfect twin. He shook his head, but was still unable to speak.

She smiled sweetly. "I'll tell Hope—"

"I meant you," he blurted. "I want to take you out on a date."

She looked surprised again. "Why?"

He was startled into a laugh. "That's a stupid question."

She lowered her lashes again. "I meant it seriously. And I'd like an answer."

He wished she would look up, but she didn't, and he didn't have the nerve to reach over and tip her chin up. He noticed they were starting to get attention from some friends of his, and he figured he'd better get this over with before they came over and started giving him a hard time. "I just thought it might be interesting to get to know you," he said.

When she looked up, she caught him glancing at two buddies of his who were whispering behind their hands. "Did someone dare you to go out with me?"

"Are you kidding?" He saw from her face that she wasn't.

"It's happened to me before," she said defensively.

He felt his insides clench and struggled to keep the pity—and anger—from his voice. "All I want to do is take you out on a date."

"So you say."

Frustrated, he'd already turned to leave when she reached out, touching him with the hook. He barely managed to keep himself from jerking away.

"Wait," she said. "If you want to see me, you can come over to my house tomorrow morning."

He raised a brow in question. "What's going on at your house?"

She smiled and his loins tightened. "I'm in charge of making favors for your sister's wedding. You can help. I'll provide lunch."

"All right. I'll see you then."

"Everything all right here?"

Randy was surprised by Hope's interruption. He wouldn't have thought she paid much attention to what her sister did. He caught the militant look in Hope's eyes and realized she was there to protect Faith. "We're done," he said. He opened his mouth to say "See you tomorrow" to Faith, but shut it again when he realized everybody's attention was now turned in their direction.

He walked away without looking back, because he didn't want to see what Faith thought of his hasty retreat. It wasn't that he was embarrassed about their date or anything, but he didn't want to put up with his friends teasing him about it. He knew he wouldn't be able to keep from getting upset, and the more upset he got, the more brutal their teasing would be. Better to keep the whole business to himself.

"Are you all right?" Hope whispered to her sister.

"I'm fine," Faith said.

"He didn't—"

"I'm fine," Faith said with a smile that Hope recognized. Faith used smiles the way a knight used a shield to ward off harmful blows.

Hope would have urged Faith to leave right then, except she hadn't yet found an opportunity to talk with Jake Whitelaw. Not that he wanted to talk to her. Or even knew she was alive. When she'd said hello to him earlier, he'd scowled and replied, "That's the wrong dress for a funeral."

She'd bitten back a sharp retort. Since she'd only worn the dress to get his attention, it had served its purpose. Hope sighed as she looked down at the long legs revealed by the short skirt. Why couldn't Jake have admired her legs instead of criticizing the dress?

Everything she did—smoking, driving fast, even wearing makeup so she'd look older—was calculated to make him notice her. But she might as well be eight years old instead of eighteen. All he saw was a kid. Someday she was going to figure out a way to convince Jake Whitelaw that Hope Butler was the woman of his dreams.

* * *

Colt kept Jenny away from the house as long as he dared, but brought her back in time to say good-bye to everyone. Her family and his were the last to leave, and they stood on the back porch together bidding them farewell.

"We're so glad you're going to be part of the family," his mother said as she hugged Jenny good-bye.

"Colt's a lucky man," his father said as he gave Jenny a kiss on the forehead.

"You'd better take damned good care of her," Jenny's brother Sam warned quietly as he shook Colt's hand.

Colt knew Sam was only worried about his sister, so he simply said, "I will." He wished he could tell Sam that he loved Jenny, but it was too soon after Huck's death to admit to such feelings. Besides, loving her wasn't enough. Huck had loved Jenny, yet he'd left her alone to raise her brothers.

Jake was last in line to say good-bye, and Colt met his elder brother's hard-eyed look without flinching.

"I hope you know what you're doing," Jake said. "I think you're asking for heartache."

"It's my heart," Colt said. "Let me worry about it."

Jake gave a grudging nod. "All right, little brother. Don't say I didn't warn you."

When Colt and Jenny were finally alone, they were completely alone, since Randy had escaped to the movies with some friends. Colt was surprised when he ushered Jenny inside to find the kitchen as clean as a whistle.

"I expected to spend the evening washing casserole dishes," he said. "What are we going to do with all this free time?"

"I've got books that need to be balanced," Jenny said.

Colt shook his head. "Not tonight. You're too tired."

"I'll decide whether I'm too tired," Jenny retorted irritably.

"There. See? You're so tired you're snapping at me."

"I'm not—" Jenny cut herself off and hissed out a breath of air. She gave him a plaintive look. "I don't know how to do nothing, Colt."

"Then we'll do something," he promised as he slid his arm around her waist and headed her into the living room.

"Like what?" she demanded as she plopped down onto the couch.

"Well, there's always necking," he teased as he dropped down beside her. "Let's see if I remember how it's done. I sneak my arm along the back of the couch, like so."

Jenny giggled as she watched his arm move snakelike along the couch behind her.

"Then I take your hand in mine, to kind of distract you from what my other hand is doing." He suited word to deed and threaded the fingers of her left hand with the fingers of his. He waggled his right hand, which now completely encircled her. "Then this hand comes to rest ever so lightly on your shoulder. *Voilà! I yam readee for zee zeduction,*" he said in a terrible French accent.

Jenny laughed. "Being the very good girl that I am, I will, of course, pretend not to notice your hand on my shoulder," she said, joining his game.

"Of course," he agreed, returning her grin with one of his own.

"But secretly," she said, shooting him an impish look, "I'll be enticing you to do more."

His brows waggled. "You will?"

She nodded, grinning broadly.

"How?" he asked, intrigued.

"Oh, in little ways, like making sure that our hands rest on *your* thigh, instead of mine."

Colt looked down and discovered that their joined hands were indeed lying on his thigh instead of hers. He could suddenly feel the heat of her hand through his black suit trousers. A more intense physical response was not long in coming. He hoped to hell she didn't notice. "Then what?" he asked in a raspy voice.

"I'd lean a little closer and bat my eyelashes at you and look demure." She did so in a way that should have been funny, but which merely left him wondering what secrets she was hiding beneath her lowered lids.

He leaned close to her ear and whispered, "Then what?" and felt her body quiver.

"I'd wait to see if you took the bait," she murmured.

"Look at me, Jenny."

She lifted her lids, and their gazes caught and held. He lowered his head toward hers, drawn by her parted lips. He kept his eyes on her mouth, waiting for even the slightest indication that she didn't want this to happen. Sure enough, she backed away.

"I'd resist at first," she said, her eyes lambent but still full of mischief. "But when you least expected it, I'd turn to you and make all your adolescent male dreams come true." She reached out with her free hand, caught his nape and drew his head down to hers, their mouths meshing before she slipped her tongue between his lips to taste him.

An instant later she was on her feet, wiping her

mouth and backing away from him. "Ohmigod. I shouldn't have done that."

He was on his feet and headed toward her, his hands outstretched in supplication. "It was just a game, Jenny."

"You're right. I'm tired. I need to rest. Good night, Colt."

An instant later she was gone.

Colt took a step after her and stopped himself. His body was rock hard with no hope of satisfaction, but he only had himself to blame. "What did you expect, Whitelaw?" he muttered. "When you play with fire, you'd better damn well expect to get burned."

Chapter 7

Jenny woke to the sound of a hammer against wood. The sun was high and a warm breeze billowed the lace curtains at the open window. She hadn't set her alarm because it was Saturday, and she didn't have to make sure Randy got off to school on time. But it was rare that she slept so late.

Then she remembered. *I kissed Colt last night. And not by accident. I wanted it to happen. I helped it to happen. And I could have done a lot more. He wouldn't have stopped me.*

She had fled, afraid of the powerful feelings evoked by that brief meeting of lips. It wasn't like her to run away, but nothing about the past ten days had been the least bit normal. It was time to face facts. Time to stop pretending her life had even the remotest chance of turning out happily ever after.

She couldn't marry Colt. It wouldn't be fair. Not unless she told him the truth about herself. And she knew what would happen if she did that. She had to call the whole thing off. Now. Before it was too late.

Jenny yanked on a pair of jeans and slipped into a chambray shirt. She ran a brush through her hair but didn't even take time to put it up in a ponytail. The noise was coming from the back of the house, and as she hurried through the kitchen she saw the remnants of two blueberry pancake breakfasts in the sink. She stopped at the screen door and stared.

Colt and Randy were working side by side, both stripped to the waist. Colt's shoulder muscles flexed as he supported a portion of the back porch roof while Randy slipped a new post in place under it. Colt's bronzed skin glistened with sweat and beads of perspiration pearled in the dark hair on his chest. His jeans had slid down so she could see his navel and the line of black down leading into his jeans.

Her body tightened viscerally.

Jenny was shocked at how quickly she'd responded to the sight of Colt's half-naked body and clutched at the doorjamb to keep herself from bolting again. She would surely get over this aberrant attraction once Colt was gone. She started to push the screen door open but hesitated when he spoke.

"That's it, boy. Easy does it." Colt let go of the rotting post he'd been holding, and the weight of the roof settled onto the new post.

"Holy cow! We did it!" Randy exclaimed.

"We make a good team," Colt said, laying a hand across Randy's youthful shoulders. Her brother beamed with pride.

Jenny felt her throat swell closed. This was what her brothers had missed. A father to teach them to be men. She'd done her best, but there were some things a mother couldn't provide.

She swallowed down the ache in her throat that arose whenever she acknowledged what had been stolen from her...from all of them...when their father had run away rather than face their mother's illness. She'd been the eldest, the one who remembered him best, so his abandonment had hit her the hardest. She wasn't about to set herself up for that kind of heartache again.

"How long are you going to hang around?" Randy asked.

Jenny saw the startled look on Colt's face. She didn't usually eavesdrop, but she was curious to hear his answer.

Colt picked up a hammer to knock the post farther into place and said, "Long enough to help your sister put this place back together."

"How long is that?" Randy persisted.

"What does it matter to you?" Colt asked. "If I understood your sister right, you're headed off to college in the fall. Bring me one of those rails, will you?"

Randy brought him a porch rail and squatted beside him as he measured and began to saw. "I'm asking because I am going off to college. I hate the thought of leaving Jenny here all alone."

"Yeah," Colt agreed. "That's tough. You want to try nailing this in place?"

"Sure," Randy said.

Jenny watched as Colt showed Randy how to run a plumb line so the porch rail would be straight. She wondered for a moment how he could know so much about carpentry, until she remembered Colt had been trained his whole life to take over Hawk's Pride. There wasn't much he didn't know about running a ranch, and that included the kind of repairs he'd been doing for the past ten days.

Jenny had discovered it was easier to do the repairs herself than take the time to train her brothers. She realized now that she had cheated them of the pride in a job well-done and herself of the pleasure of teaching them that she saw on Colt's face.

"I'm real worried about Jenny living here all alone," Randy admitted as he began nailing the rail in place. "I mean, when you go back to flying jets."

"Maybe I can talk Jenny into selling this place and coming with me."

Randy turned to gape at Colt, and the hammer came down on his thumb. "Yow!" He leaped up and flung his hand around, trying to ease the pain. Eventually the thumb ended up in his mouth.

By then Jenny was out the door and standing on the porch beside her brother, reaching for his hand. "Are you all right?"

Randy yanked his hand away and said angrily, "Why are we bothering to fix this place up, if you're just going to sell it?"

"I never agreed—"

"This is our home," Randy interrupted. "You can't sell it!"

Jenny was furious with Colt for putting such an idea in Randy's head, but equally annoyed with her brother. "You know I'd never sell the Double D if I had a choice." She shot a quick glance at Colt, who looked chagrined. "It appears I may not have a choice."

Randy turned to Colt. "Is that true, Colt? Are you going to force Jenny to sell the Double D?"

Colt's lips pursed, and he shook his head. "I was only suggesting it might be better if she did."

"How would you feel if your parents sold Hawk's Pride?" Randy demanded. "What if it belonged to someone else and you could never go back? You'd hate it, wouldn't you?"

"I guess I would," Colt conceded. "But—"

"No buts," Randy said. "Look, I've got to get out of here. I promised I'd ride over and visit a friend this morning." He grabbed his shirt from the rail where he'd left it and turned to Jenny, his face anguished. "Just don't do anything without thinking it through, all right?"

"Shouldn't you wash up first?" Jenny suggested, knowing as soon as the words were out of her mouth how much Randy would resent them.

"I'll rinse off at the sink in the barn." He practically ran down the porch steps, headed for the barn.

Jenny whirled on Colt, determined to send him away. But the words caught in her throat. She met his gaze and remembered what had happened the previous night. She had to speak quickly, or she'd lose the will to speak at all.

"When did you intend to let me in on this little plan of yours to sell the Double D?" she asked pointedly.

"It's not a bad idea."

"Forget it! If you didn't want to marry me, all you had to do was say so. I can manage on my own. I always have."

"You shouldn't have had to carry the burden by yourself for so long," he retorted. "Huck should have been here."

She looked into Colt's eyes and drew a sharp breath. "Don't you dare pity me! I don't need your sympathy. I don't need anyone. I can manage on my—"

He grabbed her shoulders and shook her. "Damn it, Jenny. Why won't you let me help?"

"I don't want you here. I don't want you touching me or kissing me or…or touching me!"

She fought him, but his arms circled around her, pulling her close so she couldn't strike out at him. He was saying something, but the sound was drowned out by the pulse pounding in her ears. She kicked his shin and heard him yelp, but he held on. One of his hands tangled in her hair, and he yanked her head back. "Look at me, Jenny. Look at me!"

She stared into eyes that were filled with compassion. And regret. And something else she was afraid to name.

"I'm glad you kissed me last night," he said.

Jenny felt her heart begin to race. "It can't happen again, Colt. Huck's only been dead—"

"We're alive. We're going to be husband and wife. It's not as if we're strangers. We've been friends for a long time."

"*Friends.* Nothing more."

"Not yet," he said softly. His lips had a certain fullness and rigidity she recognized, and which made her heart pound all the harder.

"You're a beautiful woman, Jenny. Why are you so surprised that I find you desirable? Or that you might desire me? Why are you fighting so hard not to feel anything?"

She swallowed hard. *Because it can't last. Because it's entirely likely I'm not going to be here on this earth much longer than Huck.*

"You can grieve Huck and still go on living," Colt said in a gentle voice.

She was frightened by how persuasive he sounded. She groped for an explanation that he would accept—besides the truth. "I can't just forget Huck. He was—"

"Never here," Colt said implacably. "How often did you see him over the past ten years?"

"I saw him lots!" Jenny retorted.

"Twelve times," Colt said. "I know because I came with him every time except the last. I was here more than he was, because he spent most of his leave with his father."

"He wrote me—"

"Cards—on birthdays and holidays. I know. I made sure of it."

Jenny's stomach churned. "He loved me, Colt."

His thumb caressed her jaw, but his hold on her hair tightened, forcing her to look up at him. "I know. And you loved him. But be honest, Jenny. If you hadn't been tied to this ranch, hadn't been tied down raising four brothers, would you have kept on loving a man who was never there for you?"

Jenny's eyes misted, and her nose stung with the threat of tears she refused to shed. "You can leave anytime, Colt. Go sniff some jet fuel. Get out!"

"I'm not going to leave you, Jenny. I'm not going to walk away, no matter how hard you push me. Between us, we're going to figure out what to do. There's got to be a solution that'll work for both of us. All we have to do is find it."

"I don't need you! I—"

He kissed her hard, cutting off speech. Then his

mouth softened, and his lips moved over hers, searching for some response.

Jenny's heart skipped a beat before blood surged to her center. She clutched at Colt's bare shoulders, unsure whether she wanted to pull him close or push him away. When she hesitated, his tongue slid into her mouth for a taste, and she was undone. All thought flew out of her head, replaced by sensation.

This is what was always missing with Huck. The need to merge body and soul with another human being. The need to make two halves into one whole. The need—

The kiss ended as abruptly as it had begun. Colt looked dazed. And as distraught as she felt herself. He let her go and took a quick step back. He didn't seem to know what to do with his hands, and he finally stuck his thumbs in his back pockets. "I think maybe we'd better set some ground rules. I want—"

"Holy cow! Holy cow, Jenny! Look what I found!"

Jenny tore her troubled gaze from Colt's face and looked toward the barn. Randy was mounted on his chestnut gelding, but he was pointing at a large animal that was partially hidden from view in the corral behind the barn. "What is it?" Jenny called back to him.

"My wedding gift to you," Colt answered for Randy.

"You got me an animal for a wedding gift?" she said, her brows lowering in confusion as she headed for the corral.

Colt kept pace with her. "Not just any animal," he said. "A Santa Gertrudis bull from the King Ranch."

Jenny halted in her tracks and turned to stare. "Are you kidding? You're *not* kidding," she said as she got a good look at Colt's face. She couldn't catch her breath.

The Santa Gertrudis breed, three-eighths Indian Brahman and five-eighths British Shorthorn, had been developed in the early twentieth century on the King Ranch, which still produced some of the finest Santa Gertrudis cattle to be found anywhere in the world. A bull like the one he described would cost a fortune— and could save the Double D.

Jenny turned and raced for the corral. Randy was off his horse and leaning over the corral, ogling the deep, cherry-red-colored bull when she reached him. "Ohmigod!" she breathed. "It's Rob Roy."

"None other," Colt confirmed with a grin as he put a booted foot up on the corral and leaned over to admire the bull. "Do you like him?"

Jenny couldn't breathe.

Rob Roy had been named grand champion Santa Gertrudis bull at the most recent stock show in Fort Worth. All by himself, this bull could put the Double D in the black.

Randy whooped and said, "Holy cow!"

"Do you like him?" Colt asked softly. "I mean, I thought about getting you something a little more romantic, like a diamond—"

Jenny clutched Colt around the neck and gave him a quick kiss on the mouth. Just as quickly, she let him go and stepped back. It was too tempting to cling to him. "It's a *perfect* gift. No woman could ever have a more perfect gift."

Then she remembered she was planning to call off the wedding.

"I guess there won't be any more talk about selling the Double D," Randy said as he mounted his gelding. "Wait'll I tell everybody about this!"

He kicked his horse into a lope, shrieking like a Comanche on a raid and kicking up a cloud of dust that Jenny waved away.

Jenny turned back to Colt and said, "How could you have teased Randy like that, saying you thought I should sell the Double D, when you'd already bought Rob Roy?"

"I wasn't teasing," he said.

"But with Rob Roy—"

"One bull isn't going to solve all your problems, Jenny. In fact, he's only going to make more work for you. I suppose with the income he'll bring in you could hire a man to help you out, but—"

"I'll still be alone, because you're not going to be around," Jenny finished for him.

"I made my choice a long time ago, Jenny."

Jenny couldn't keep the bitterness from her voice. "I know, Colt. You and Huck both. Like I said, I can take care of myself." She opened her mouth to call off the wedding, but what came out was, "Thanks for the bull. It's the nicest gift anybody's ever given me."

Jenny turned and headed toward the house. She tried to walk, but she was feeling too much, hurting too much, and she started to run. She waited for the sound of Colt's footsteps coming after her.

But she never heard them.

Randy's heart lurched when he caught sight of Faith through the open kitchen window of her house. "Hi, Faith."

"Hi, Randy. Let me finish here at the sink, and I'll let you in."

Randy shifted from foot to foot on the back porch.

Faith's dad was foreman for a neighboring ranch, and Randy noticed their single-story white clapboard house sported a fresh coat of white paint. Pink and purple petunias grew in profusion along the back porch. He had a moment to think how much Jenny would have appreciated the paint and the petunias before Faith unhooked the screen door and held it open for him.

He stared at her, stricken mute, unable to move.

Faith smiled shyly and said, "Won't you come in?"

"Uh. Okay."

The instant he stepped inside, he was assailed with a sense of order and the smell of Pine Sol. It was a far cry from his house, which suffered from too much work and too few people to do it.

"I'm glad you decided to come," Faith said.

"I said I would."

"I know but… I'm glad," she repeated, lowering her lids and hiding her eyes from him.

He recognized it for the defensive gesture it was, and couldn't help resenting it. He wasn't going to hurt her. If she'd just give him half a chance, he'd prove it.

He looked around the kitchen, not surprised to see it was pristine. The Butler girls had always come to school in starched and ironed dresses and with their hair in arrow-straight pigtails. At least, they had until Hope took the bit in her teeth and began to defy her parents. After that, it was only Faith who came to school perfectly dressed.

He took advantage of the fact Faith's eyes were averted to take a long look at her. Her left hand was hidden behind her back, so the image she presented was one of perfection. Her long-sleeved pink oxford-cloth shirt had a crisply starched collar and was belted into jeans that had a stiff crease. Her boots were so shiny he could have seen his reflection in them. Her straight black hair was tucked behind her ears.

He thought of the quick dousing he'd given himself in the barn. He'd rinsed off the worst of the sweat, but he wasn't precisely clean. His shirt wasn't ironed because Jenny had long ago given him the responsibility for doing it, and he'd decided he didn't mind the wrinkles. His boots were too scuffed to hold a shine, if he'd been inclined to give them one, which he wasn't.

Randy suddenly felt self-conscious. He should have taken a little more time to make himself presentable. He looked at the large kitchen table full of wedding paraphernalia and realized things were set up so they'd be sitting next to each other.

And me smelling like a workhorse.

"I…uh… I'm not sure how long I can stay," he said, wondering how he could make a graceful exit before she got a good whiff of him.

"Great! You're here!" Hope said, breezing into the kitchen. "I was afraid you wouldn't come, and I'd get stuck with Faith wrapping all that birdseed in net and tying it with ribbons."

Randy was relieved to see Hope wasn't dressed any better than he was. Her skintight jeans were torn at the knees, and she wore a Western shirt with the sleeves ripped out, strings still dangling, the tails tied in a knot that revealed a great deal of her midriff. Her tangled hair hung over her shoulders in disarray.

He almost smiled at the contrast between the sisters. Looking at them, you might easily get the wrong idea about which was the imperfect twin.

"You're not going to abandon us!" Faith said anxiously to her sister.

"I can help for a little while," Hope said. "But I've got other plans for later on." Hope plopped down into a chair on the opposite side of the rectangular oak table. "Let's get going. The sooner we start, the sooner this'll be done."

"You can sit here, Randy," Faith said, gesturing with her right hand to one of the two seats beside each other across from Hope.

He hesitated, then slid into the chair she'd indicated, because he wanted to sit next to her. After all, it was why he'd come. "What do you want me to do?" he asked.

"You can hold the pieces of net while I measure out the birdseed. Then I'll hold the net while you tie the bow. How does that sound?" Faith asked.

"All right, I guess," Randy replied. It dawned on him that she was going to need two hands. And that she was going to be using that hook on the end of her left arm as one of them. He felt a little jittery at the thought, and steeled himself not to shudder or do anything that would make her uncomfortable.

He glanced up and caught Hope watching him through narrowed eyes. And realized she was there not to help her sister with the wedding favors, but to protect Faith from him. He wanted to reassure Hope, but at the moment he wasn't certain how he was going to react when Faith hauled out that hook and started using it so close to his own hands.

Then he saw Faith's right hand was trembling and realized she was as scared as he was. A lump the size of Texas constricted his throat, and his chest felt like four football linemen had piled onto it.

He reached out and picked up a piece of net and placed it on the table in front of her. "Ready for—" He cleared his throat and said, "Ready for some seed."

He watched her pick up a two-pound plastic bag of birdseed at the top with her real hand, then grasp the bottom with the hook and aim the open corner onto the net. Too much poured out.

"Oh," she said, setting the bag down abruptly. Her eyes darted nervously in his direction, then focused on the mess she'd made.

He felt his heart pounding hard in his chest. If he blew this, he was pretty sure he wasn't going to get a second chance. "It's all right," he said, reaching quickly for another piece of net. "I'll divide this in two." He suited word to deed and poured half the birdseed onto the second piece of net. "Now what?"

"Get a piece of that pink ribbon over there."

The narrow silk ribbon had already been cut into lengths. While he grabbed the ribbon, she gathered the net around the seed with one hand, and held it closed at the top with the hook.

As nonchalantly as if he tied ribbons into bows every day, he surrounded the net below her hook with the ribbon and tied a creditable bow. "How's that?" he said when he was done.

She released the hook from the net and slid it away as she surveyed his work, but he noticed she didn't retreat with it under the table. "Pretty terrible," she announced at last.

He shot her an astonished look and saw she was smiling at him. His heart did a flip-flop. He looked back at the lopsided bow and said in an unsteady voice, "I'll do better on the next one."

"Hey, there! Anybody home?"

Randy looked over his shoulder at the screen door and said, "Hi, Jake."

"Hi, Jake," Faith said.

"I'll see to Jake," Hope said. "You two just keep on with what you're doing."

"I've got that delivery of hay your father ordered," Jake said when Hope pushed open the screen door. "Ask him where he wants me to put it."

"I'll show you," Hope said. "Follow me."

Hope was glad Randy hadn't turned out to be a jerk. Otherwise she wouldn't have been able to leave Faith behind with him. She'd been waiting a long time for the chance to get Jake Whitelaw alone.

This was it.

His shirt was dirty, the sleeves rolled up to reveal strong, sinewy forearms. His Stetson was sweaty around the brim, and shaggy black hair was crushed at his nape. His cheeks were hollow, and he had a sharp nose and wide-set, ice-blue eyes. He was half a foot taller than she was, lean at the hip, but with broad, powerful shoulders. He made her body come alive just looking at him.

"How are you, Jake?" she said, walking with her shoulders back so her breasts jutted and her hips swayed.

He eyed her sideways. "Just dandy," he muttered.

"Daddy wants that hay in the barn," she said, hop-skipping to keep up with his long strides.

"Why didn't you just say so? You don't need to come with me, little girl. I know where it goes."

Little girl. Hope ground her teeth. She'd show him she was no *little girl!* "There's some stuff needs to be moved first," she hedged. "Machinery that's too heavy for me to pick up by myself."

"Why didn't your daddy move it?"

"I told him I could do it. That is, before I realized how heavy it was," she fibbed.

Jake didn't look suspicious, but it wasn't going to take long once they got inside the barn for him to realize she'd lied. The space where the hay was supposed to be stacked had been cleared out that morning. She opened the door and went inside first, then waited for him to enter before she closed the door behind him.

Sunlight streamed through the cracks between the planks of the wooden barn, leaving golden lines on the empty, straw-littered dirt floor.

He turned to confront her. "What the hell is going on, little girl?"

She was backed up against the door to keep Jake from leaving. She put her hand over the light switch when he reached for it, afraid of what she'd see in his eyes in the stark light of the naked overhead bulb. He didn't force the issue, merely stepped back and stood facing her, his legs widespread, his hands on his hips.

"What happens now?" he said. "You want sex? Take off your jeans and panties and lie down over there on that pile of straw on the floor."

Hope's eyes went wide when he started to unbuckle his belt. "Stop! Wait." She was shocked by his brutally frank speech, by the rough sound of his voice, by his plain intention of taking what she seemed to be offering without any pretense of romance. This wasn't how she'd imagined things happening between them.

He had his shirt unbuttoned and was ripping it out of his jeans when he paused and looked her right in the eye. "You chickening out, little girl?"

Maybe if he hadn't made it a dare, she would have

run, which was what she realized he expected her to do. She stared right back at him and began untying the knot at her midriff.

"I'm not going anywhere."

She watched his eyes go wide, then narrow. A muscle jerked in his cheek. He no longer seemed interested in taking his clothes off. He was too busy watching her. Waiting, she suspected, to see how far she would go.

Her mouth was bone-dry, but she wanted him to know why she was doing this. "I… I love you, Jake."

He snorted. "Get to it or get out."

Her cheeks pinkened with mortification, but she refused to run. It wasn't easy undressing in front of him. She kept her eyes lowered, while she fumbled with the knot. He stood watching, waiting like a lone wolf stalking an abandoned calf, certain of the kill.

When the knot came free, her shirt fell open. She let it slide off her shoulders and onto the floor, revealing the pure white demi-cup push-up bra she'd bought with her babysitting money, which revealed just about everything but her nipples.

When she lifted her gaze to his face, she was frightened by what she saw. His eyes had a dangerous, feral look, his jaw was clenched tight, and his hands had balled into fists. He looked distant, unapproachable, but she forced herself to walk up to him, to slide her hands around his neck, to lift up on tiptoe to press her lips against his.

A second later she was shoved up hard against the barn door with Jake's hips grinding against her own. His tongue was in her mouth taking what he wanted, and she was so full of sharp, exciting sensations that she couldn't breathe.

Just as suddenly he backed off, leaving her with Jell-O knees that wanted to buckle, a heart that was threatening to explode and her insides tied up tight, hurting and wanting. "Jake," she said. It was a cry of emotional pain. A plea for surcease from her unrequited need.

"I'm twice your age," he said flatly. "You're too damn young for me, Hope."

"You want me," she said boldly.

It would have been hard to deny. His jeans bulged with abundant evidence of his desire. "I'm a grown man. Old enough to know better," he said with a disgusted sigh. He unbuttoned and unzipped his jeans, but only so he could tuck his shirt back in. He buttoned his shirt, buckled his belt and adjusted his clothes, then leaned down and picked up her shirt. "Put this on," he said.

She did as she was told. She hadn't gotten what she'd expected when she'd come in here with Jake. But she'd gotten what she wanted. Proof that he desired her. Proof that if she pushed long enough and hard enough, she might convince him that she was what he needed.

Her hands were shaking too much for her to tie a knot in the shirttails.

"I'll do it," he said, pushing her hands out of the way.

Her stomach quivered as his knuckles brushed against her flesh. She glanced up and saw the feral look was back in his eyes. He yanked the knot tight and stepped back.

"Now get the hell out of here!" he snarled.

Hope yanked open the barn door and ran.

Chapter 8

"Rise and shine, lazybones," Colt said with a laugh as he pulled the covers off Jenny.

She rolled over, then sat up and stared. He'd done it again. Brought her breakfast in bed. The first time he'd arrived unannounced it had provided a few awkward moments, since all she'd been wearing was one of Randy's old T-shirts, the cotton so thin it provided a revealing display of her suddenly peaked nipples.

That incident had led to the first of a dozen silly gifts Colt had given her over the past two weeks.

"If you're really into men's clothes, I thought you'd appreciate these," he'd said when he presented her with a pair of navy blue men's cotton pajamas.

A set of flower-patterned china cups and saucers had come next. "You need to see something beautiful when you wake up each morning. I've got you," he'd said, making her blush with pleasure, "but I thought you might like these."

One morning she'd stepped outside the kitchen door and discovered the entire back porch was lined with hanging baskets of pink and white impatiens. "I owe you some flowers," he'd said. "For all the times I never brought you any."

What he meant, of course, was for all the times Huck had never brought her any.

While Colt settled the breakfast tray in her lap, Jenny fingered the solitary diamond that hung on a fragile gold chain around her neck. Colt had given her the necklace last night after Randy had gone to bed, when they were alone in the living room.

"I noticed you're still wearing Huck's ring," he'd said. "But I wanted to give you a diamond. I hope this is all right."

After he clasped the necklace around her throat, she'd reached up to touch the dimensions of the stone, to test the fragility of the chain.

An inexplicable feeling of panic had forced her off the couch and across the room to the fireplace. She'd watched the flames lick at the dry wood they'd gathered together that afternoon and fought the urge to cry.

"What's wrong?" he asked, sensing her distress. He didn't follow her. He waited for her to return on her own.

She twisted the diamond ring on her finger, adjusting it, reminding herself of its presence as she had done for ten long years. Huck's ring had been the one visible proof that they were engaged, that he intended to come back to her. Now Colt had laid his claim, slipping a chain—a delicate one to be sure—around her neck, when he had no more intention of staying with her than Huck had.

The hot tears came without warning, filling her eyes and spilling over. Colt crossed to her then, anxious and concerned. He pulled her into his arms, and she felt his lips kissing away the tears as he murmured words of comfort.

"It doesn't mean anything, Jenny. I don't expect you to love me the way you loved Huck," he said. "It's just a gift. Something from me to you. Be happy, Jenny. Please."

That made her cry all the harder, because it would have been very easy to fall in love with Colt. It was hard not to appreciate a man whose every thought was directed toward making your life easier. But, damn it, she didn't want to fall in love with another man who intended to leave her behind while he went off to fly jets. Especially not someone who was only taking care of her as a duty to his dead friend.

A certain ticking clock reminded Jenny that moments like this had to be seized and enjoyed.

She brushed at Colt's sideburns, which were already growing out, then eased her thumb across the scar on his chin where the stitches had been removed, unable to stop herself from touching him. "I'm crying because I'm happy, Colt. That's all."

He looked deep into her eyes, searching for the truth.

It was the truth. At that moment she was happy. She'd learned a long time ago, as the child of a dying mother, to relish every day for the pleasures it brought her. That lesson was standing her in good stead now.

She saw the lingering doubt in Colt's eyes and did

the only thing she thought might convince him she was
pleased with the gift—and with him. She kissed him
gently on the mouth.

She'd had some inkling in advance of how powerful
her response might be. Yet, she was surprised again.
This kiss was different—more devastating—than the
ones that had come before, because there was no guilt
to dampen pleasure. This kiss was a celebration of joy,
of delight in the man who held her in his arms. Passion
rose quickly and flared hot.

Tentatively, her hands went seeking, feeling the
ropey muscles in Colt's shoulders and sliding down
his strong back. His hands weren't idle, and she gasped
as his palm closed on her breast. The sensation was exquisite because it was so unexpected. Huck had touched
her breasts many times before, but it had never felt like
this. Jenny sought for the difference and found it. There
was reverence in Colt's touch, along with the hunger.

He'd already eased her shirt off and was reaching
for the front clasp of her bra when she suddenly came
to her senses and realized what might happen if she
took this next step with him.

"Colt, no."

His mouth nuzzled the curve of her breast above her
bra, and she nearly swooned before she finally grasped
his hand to stop him.

"Not yet," she pleaded. "I'm not ready. Not yet."

She heard his shuddering breath, felt the tautness
in his shoulders as he brought himself back from the
brink. He kissed her gently on the mouth, his tongue
teasing her lips until she relented and let him come
inside.

To soothe, to taste, to caress.

It was the kind of kiss they might have shared as teenagers in the back seat of his Mustang, when he knew they couldn't go all the way. Deep and rich and thorough. It was lovemaking without the sex.

And she appreciated him all the more for it.

She heard a moan from deep in his throat, a grating sound of both satisfaction and the need for more, before he finally broke the kiss. When she met Colt's eyes, she saw that the fire had been banked, but it wouldn't take much to fan it back into flames. He was leaving the choice up to her. She knew she had to back away, because it was clear he wouldn't—or couldn't.

For a moment last night Jenny had thought about trusting Colt with her secret. Fear had held her back. Once he knew, he would leave for sure. She wanted to hold on to him for as long as she could.

"Good night, Colt," she said as she backed away.

He'd reached down and picked up her shirt, and she'd flushed as she realized she'd forgotten completely about it. He'd given her a lopsided smile and said, "Good night, Jenny. I—" He'd cut himself off, swallowed hard and said, "I'll see you in the morning."

And here he was with breakfast on a tray, fresh from the shower, with eyes that crinkled at the corners with laughter…and her heart on his plate.

"You're going to spoil me, Colt," she said as she held the tray steady and scooted back against the headboard.

"You deserve a little coddling." He settled on the edge of the bed by her knees and grabbed a slice of cinnamon raisin toast slathered in butter.

Jenny picked up a flowered china cup, blew on the steaming coffee, then sipped carefully, grateful for the caffeine. She wasn't quite sure how to act after what had happened between them last night and decided to let Colt set the tone.

Colt was trying to act nonchalant, when that was the last thing he was feeling. He'd been buying Jenny little gifts ever since he'd realized how few of them she'd gotten in her life. He'd given her the diamond last night as a symbol of his love and commitment and as a first step toward asking for that same love and commitment from her.

The wary look in Jenny's eyes reminded him not to push too hard or too fast. But he couldn't shake the feeling that time was running out. His leave was more than half over, and their wedding day was rapidly approaching. Then he happened to glance at Jenny's left hand.

"Where's Huck's ring?"

"I took it off," she said, not meeting his gaze.

He watched her reach with her thumb to rub the empty spot where the ring used to be. His chest ached with hope and with fear. Maybe there was a chance for the two of them after all. He opened his mouth to speak, but she spoke first.

"Don't forget Randy's graduation ceremony is tonight," she said. "I promised him we'd go out to dinner first."

"I won't be late."

"Randy asked if he could bring a date to dinner," she said with a smile.

"Anybody I know?" Colt asked.

"Faith Butler."

Colt's jaw dropped. "*Faith* Butler? Not Hope?"

"Faith," Jenny repeated with a grin. "I couldn't believe it myself. Seems they've been seeing a lot of each other lately."

"Good for Randy. You've done a fantastic job raising him, Jenny. A great job raising all of them." He took a deep breath and plunged. "But it's time you started thinking of yourself."

"What does that mean?" Jenny asked, her eyes cautious.

"Just what I said. Why don't you sell this place and come see the world with me?"

"Colt, you promised—"

He grabbed the tray from her lap and threw it onto the dresser hard enough to make the china cup and saucer rattle, then turned to confront her. "I can't leave you here alone, Jenny. I'd worry too much about you."

"Then stay," she said simply.

He shoved both hands through his short hair, leaving it standing on end. "I'm considering that option."

Her eyes went wide. "You are? What's stopping you?"

He wanted to tell her the truth. That he didn't think he could stand waking up every morning to a wife who was in love with another man. He'd grow to hate her and himself. It was easier to go away—to stay away.

He was afraid to read too much into the fact she'd taken off Huck's ring. It might simply be that it evoked too many painful memories for her to wear it.

And that kiss last night?

Mere gratitude for the gift he'd given her. It was getting harder and harder to conceal his true feelings, but he wasn't about to let Jenny know he loved her when he had no hope of having that love returned.

"I'd like to stay Jenny," he said quietly. "But you're Huck's girl. You always have been, and you always will be."

"Huck is dead," she said, her voice cracking.

"I know," he said sadly. "I can't fight a ghost."

Jenny's brow creased. "Why would you need to?"

If she couldn't figure it out, he wasn't going to explain it to her. So he changed the subject. "I figured we'd start scraping down the barn today so we can give it a new coat of paint."

"I've got a few personal errands to run in town," she said, slipping off the bed and crossing to the dresser to run a brush through her hair. "I'll be back by six to shower and change for dinner."

"You're going to be gone all day?" he asked, startled.

She gave him a smile in the mirror as phony as a three-dollar bill. "I've put off a lot of things that can't wait any longer."

"What aren't you telling me?" he said, frowning. "Is there some complication at the bank? Some problem I don't know about?"

She laughed, a brittle sound that sent a chill up his spine. "It's nothing like that." She set down the hairbrush and turned to face him. "If I'd known you were going to get so upset, I wouldn't have told you about it."

"And then what?" he said, crossing to her, putting his hands on her shoulders from behind and looking at their two faces in the mirror. "You just disappear for the day? You don't think that might have given me a few gray hairs?"

"You're making too much of this," she said, shaking off his hands and sliding past him toward the bathroom, where she could shut herself in—and him out.

He caught her arm and whirled her around. "You don't think I'm entitled to an explanation?"

"I don't have to explain myself to you or anyone else," she said sharply.

"I'm your husband."

"Not yet you aren't!" She jerked her arm free. "And maybe not ever, if this is the kind of inquisition I can expect when I want to go somewhere without you tagging along."

"Tagging along—" He was too furious to finish.

She poked a finger in his chest to back him off. "I've survived a very long time without you, Colt. Don't you get it? I don't need you. I don't need any man. Especially one who only wants to marry me out of a sense of guilt."

"A sense of—" he spluttered. "Where is this coming from?"

"You know very well you're only marrying me because you feel obligated as Huck's friend to make sure the widow's taken care of."

"That's not true!" He grabbed her by the arms and shook her. "I love you, damn it! I always have."

Her eyes went wide, and her jaw dropped. She was speechless, leaving a great deal of silence in which to absorb what he'd said.

Colt felt like he was going to throw up. He let her go, and she took a quick step back. "Jenny, I—"

"I don't understand. You were Huck's friend! Or you pretended to be."

"That's unfair, and you know it. Let's sit down and discuss this. Please, Jenny."

"I have an appointm—" She bit her lip. "I've got errands to run. This discussion will have to wait."

She was backing away toward the bathroom, but

he wasn't going to let her escape so easily. "Wait until when?" he demanded.

"Until later."

He reached out and caught her chin with his hand, forcing her to look at him. "When, Jenny?"

"Later. Tonight," she added when his grip tightened. "Let me go, Colt."

He let her go, and an instant later she was gone.

Colt was still scraping down the barn when Randy approached him after school. Colt was hot and tired and irritable, because he knew he had to decide whether to stay in the Air Force or stay here with Jenny, and an entire day of scraping paint hadn't done much to resolve his dilemma.

It was hard to imagine his life without flying jets. It was impossible to imagine it without Jenny. He wanted both. But it was becoming very clear that he couldn't have both.

"Where's Jenny?" Randy asked.

"She's still in town running errands."

"Oh."

Colt slapped at a fly that had landed on his nose, but it buzzed away unharmed. "What does that mean, 'Oh'?"

"Nothing," Randy said quickly. "You want some help?"

Colt had three-quarters of the barn scraped free of old paint. Maybe with Randy's help he could finish today. "Sure. Why not? There's another scraper on the tool rack in the barn."

Randy slipped his book bag off his shoulder and dropped it on the ground. "I'll be right back," he said.

Colt swatted at the fly again, which was now buzzing his ear. He'd already done all the work that needed to be done on a ladder, so he and Randy worked side by side scraping the lower half of the barn.

"When did you know what you wanted to do with your life?" Randy asked.

Colt shot him a sideways look. "From the time I was a kid. Why?"

"I thought I knew what I wanted, but lately I've been less certain of what I should do."

"I see," Colt said, neither encouraging nor discouraging further discussion of the subject.

"I planned to study business because I figured that's where the money is," Randy said, keeping his eyes focused on the work he was doing. "But earning money doesn't appeal as much to me now as something else does."

"What's changed your mind?" Colt asked.

"I met someone."

Colt smiled. "A woman has a way of making you think twice about a lot of things."

Randy stopped scraping and stared at him. "How'd you know it was a girl?"

"Lucky guess."

"Anyway," Randy continued, "ever since I started seeing this girl, Faith Butler, I've been thinking maybe I'd like to study something else entirely."

Colt resisted the urge to ask what and said, "Mmm-hmm."

"Funny thing is, I don't even know what kind of courses I'd need to take to learn about it."

Colt wanted to know what "it" was, but there was an unwritten code, going all the way back to the days when people came west to escape their checkered pasts, that said a man didn't ask for information that wasn't volunteered. Instead he said, "The university could probably tell you what you need to study."

"I suppose. I guess I'd better find out whether Texas Tech teaches anything about orthotics. Maybe I'll need to go somewhere else."

"I give up," Colt said. "What's orthotics?"

Randy grinned. "Making mechanical limbs for people who need them. Faith says there's a new silicone hand that looks a lot more real than a latex one, but nothing works as well as an old-fashioned hook. I want to invent a mechanical hand that works like a real one—you know, like in the *Terminator* movies."

Colt eyed him speculatively. "What does Faith have to say about all this?"

"We haven't discussed it." Randy began to scrape vigorously on the barn wall. Colt figured that meant he didn't want to discuss the subject with him, either, so he let it drop.

A moment later Randy's hands dropped to his sides, his chin fell to his chest and he heaved a great sigh. "How do you know when you're in love?"

Colt stopped scraping and turned to face the teenager. His first instinct was to tell Randy he was too young to fall in love, that he had a lot of living to do before he settled on one woman, and the best thing to do was ignore the feeling and it would go away. But Randy was four years older than he'd been when he'd fallen for Jenny. And that love had lasted a lifetime.

"Have you asked your sister that question?" he hedged.

Randy's face was suddenly suffused with blood, which could have been the heat, but was more likely embarrassment. "I never needed to before now. And now… I couldn't talk to her now about being in love. I mean, not with Huck dying like that, and you guys getting married in some kind of business arrangement."

"Is that what Jenny told you?" Colt said, his stomach clenching. "That our marriage is a business arrangement?"

"Well, it is, isn't it? I mean, you guys aren't in love or anything. And you're planning to leave and go back to flying jets, so what else could it be? Not that I blame Jenny for marrying you. I mean, how else can she get the money to keep the ranch?"

Colt spoke through his teeth because his jaw was clamped so tight. "Let's get one thing straight, Randy. Our marriage may have some financial benefits for your sister, but it's going to be real in every way." Colt barely kept himself from shouting that he loved Jenny. That would require an explanation that he wanted to make to Jenny first.

Randy's flush heightened. "I'm not criticizing you and Jenny. I just… I always thought people got married because they loved each other and wanted to spend their lives together. I know how hard it was for Jenny all those years with Huck gone. I hate to think of her alone when you're gone, too.

"I'd offer to come back to the ranch after I finish college," Randy said, "but I know that wouldn't really solve the problem. I think I've found the woman I'm going to marry someday, and having me and my wife living here at the Double D would just point out to Jenny how alone she is. I mean, I think I love Faith."

Which brought them back to Randy's original question. "I don't know how to tell you whether this girl is the right one for you," Colt said. "I can only tell you my own experience. When you love someone, your every thought begins and ends with her. What is she feeling? Is she happy? What can you do to make her life easier? And you want her physically. Fiercely, completely. That's part of it. Mostly, love is always considering her needs before your own. Is that how you feel?"

Colt could almost see the tension easing from Randy's shoulders. "Yeah," he said. "That's *exactly* how I feel."

Colt gave him a cuff on the shoulder. "Sounds like you're in love, pal."

"Thanks for listening, Colt."

Colt stood back and surveyed the work they'd done and realized the job was finished. "Why don't you go on in and get cleaned up? There's going to be a lot of demand for that shower if we're all going to get gussied up in time for your graduation ceremony tonight. I'll put away the tools." He reached for Randy's scraper, and the boy handed it to him, then picked up his book bag and trotted toward the house.

Colt stared after Randy, realizing that in talking to the boy he'd found his own answers. His days as a jet pilot were numbered. But to his surprise, he didn't feel resigned or sad or desperate. Because when it came to a choice between having Jenny or living life without her—there really was no choice. If he truly loved Jenny, it meant putting her needs before his own. It meant staying here to be a husband to her instead of running off to fly jets.

And it meant finding a way to handle the pain, if she could never love him back.

Chapter 9

"You look so grown-up," Jenny said as she straightened Randy's tie. She reached up to brush back the lock of golden hair that always fell onto his forehead, and he ducked away.

"Give me a break, Jenny," he said, thrusting his hand into his hair, leaving it mussed. "It's just graduation."

"Just graduation," Jenny repeated past the painful lump in her throat. The tears came without warning.

"Aw, Jenny." Randy's arms closed awkwardly around her, and she laid her head against his shoulder.

"I can't believe you're all grown-up," she said, her voice cracking. She made herself step back, quickly wiped away the tears and once against straightened his tie, while he shifted impatiently from foot to foot.

"Can I leave now? I need to pick up Faith."

"We'll meet you at Buck's Steakhouse. Drive carefully."

He rolled his eyes and said sarcastically, "Yes, Mother." He stopped abruptly, the screen door half open, and turned to face her. "Jenny, I'm sorry. It just slipped out."

"Never mind. Go. You're going to be late."

He disappeared, the screen door slamming behind him.

Jenny had been a mother to her brothers, but she'd warned them against labeling her that way. Because they knew it bothered her, they addressed her as "Mother" whenever they were angry or upset, knowing it would get a rise out of her.

Right now, she felt very much like a mother hen whose nest had just been emptied of its last chick. A huge hole gaped inside her that once had been filled up with the responsibility for her brothers. She didn't feel free. She felt empty. This didn't feel like the beginning of a new life. It felt like the end.

"Hey. Give me a break."

Jenny turned to find Colt wearing a white button-down shirt, khaki slacks and a conservative regimental-striped tie. He leaned against the doorway to the kitchen, a navy suit coat slung over his shoulder, his hip cocked.

"I suppose you witnessed that scene," she said.

"I did."

"I'm going to miss him."

"I know."

A tear slipped down her cheek, and she quickly rubbed it away. "I don't understand where all these tears are coming from," she said with a shaky laugh.

"Don't you?" Colt asked, crossing toward her. He laid his suit coat across one of the ladder-back chairs at the kitchen table and opened his arms. "Come here, Jenny."

She didn't resist his offer of comfort. She took the few steps that put her within his embrace, and his arms closed around her. "I've been waiting and wishing for this day for so long, but now that it's here, I just feel sad," she admitted.

She felt his hand smooth across her hair. Felt his lips at her temple and on her closed eyes.

"I feel like my life is over," she whispered.

"I promise you, Jenny, it's just beginning. Have you been thinking about what I said to you this morning?"

Jenny had thought of little else during the day besides Colt's confession. *I love you. I always have.* "I remember."

"I've decided to resign from the Air Force, Jenny. I want to stay here and marry you and raise babies with you. If that's want you want, too."

Jenny felt her heart squeeze with joy and with pain. "Oh, Colt."

Tell him now, Jenny. If he really loves you, it won't matter.

She leaned back and looked up into his face, surprised at what she found. He was afraid, she realized. Of what? Suddenly Jenny knew. Afraid that she could never love him. That she would always—only—love Huck.

"I told you I've been thinking a lot today, and I have," she said. "About me and Huck. About me and you."

Colt cleared his throat, but he didn't speak. Which was a good thing, because if he'd interrupted her, she might not have been able to say what she knew had to be said.

"There was a time when I loved Huck body and soul. I wanted to make a life with him. I wanted to have his babies. I wanted to grow old with him." Jenny sighed and looked away. "I'm not sure when the loving stopped."

Colt inhaled a sharp breath of air.

She forced herself to look at him. "It wasn't until you said you loved me this morning that I made myself take a brutally honest look at my relationship with Huck. I realized that all these years I haven't been in love with Huck. I've been in love with a dream of what life could be like with him—if he ever settled down."

She lowered her gaze to Colt's throat and watched his Adam's apple bob as he swallowed hard. Her voice was barely audible as she admitted, "The last couple of times Huck came home, we didn't even make love."

"Jenny, I—"

She put her fingertips over his lips. "I'm not finished." She looked at him and said, "I never suspected how you felt. How you feel," she corrected when she felt his mouth open to protest. "I do know I've always been grateful for your friendship. You were there so many times when Huck wasn't."

She felt his lips flatten under her hand and removed it. "I'll admit I'm tempted by what you seem to be offering. But I'm afraid of making the same mistake twice. Maybe we can never be more than friends. You've caught me at a vulnerable time and—"

"Can I get a word in here?"

She gave a jerky nod.

"All I'm asking is that you give us a chance, Jenny. Can you do that?"

"Colt, there are things you don't know. Things—"

He shook his head to cut her off. "The past is the past. We start fresh from here."

Tell him, Jenny.

Jenny opened her mouth, but the words wouldn't come out. It could wait. Maybe there would be no need to tell him anything. Maybe they would mutually decide they didn't belong together any more than she and Huck had. If the buds of feeling she had for Colt began to blossom, that would be soon enough to confess her secret.

"What do you say, Jenny? Will you let me court you?"

"Court me?" she said, her lips curving. "Is that really necessary? I've already promised to marry you."

He smiled for the first time since their discussion had begun. "It's the time-honored way a cowboy wins his lady's love. How about it?"

Jenny gave him a shy look from beneath lowered lashes. "If you insist."

"I do. Are you ready to face the world as a couple?"

"As ready as I'll ever be," Jenny said with a determined smile. "Let's go."

"Do you realize this is our first date?" Colt said as he opened the passenger door to the classic red Ford Mustang convertible he'd been storing at his parents' ranch while he was overseas.

Jenny smiled up at him as she slid into the black leather bucket seat. "This is certainly the right car for it. How about putting the top down?"

"You wouldn't mind?"

"I'd love it," Jenny said. And she did. The night was warm, and the sky was filled with a million stars. She found herself laughing as her hair whipped around her face, making it impossible to see. "I should have brought a scarf," she said.

"Look in the glove compartment," Colt said.

She opened the glove compartment and found a small turquoise silk scarf. "This is mine!"

He shot her a sheepish grin. "I found it in the car after Huck borrowed it."

"I remember when I lost this," she said as she tied back her hair at her nape. "Huck said it must have blown off. But I was sure I'd taken it off when we—" Jenny stopped herself.

"Yeah. That's what I figured, too," Colt said. He shot her a quick look. "You have no idea how much agony I suffered thinking about the two of you in the back seat of this car."

Jenny was grateful for the darkness that prevented Colt from seeing her blush. "Maybe I can make it up to you," she said.

Colt turned to stare at her. "Are you saying what I think you're saying?" His eyes looked hungry, and she felt both frightened and exhilarated at the prospect of joining Colt in the back seat of his Mustang.

A blaring horn brought them both to their senses.

"Watch out!" she cried.

Colt yanked the wheel to avoid the car coming from the opposite direction, overcompensated and went off the road. He hit the brakes, and the Mustang skidded to a halt on the dirt and gravel shoulder.

"Are you all right?" Colt asked.

Jenny was trembling, the result of too much adrenaline. "That was close," she said with a small laugh.

"Yeah. Too close. We could've been killed. And I would've missed getting to kiss you in the back seat of this car." Colt opened his door, trotted around the front of the car, then opened her door. "Out," he ordered.

"Colt, it's the middle of nowhere. What are you doing?"

"We're taking a little trip down memory lane." Once she was out of the seat, he pushed it forward, making a space for her to slip into the back seat. "Get in."

Jenny slid into the back seat and scooted over to make room for Colt, who stepped in behind her. Before she had a chance to think, Colt slid one arm around her shoulder and pulled her close. With his eyes on hers, with their lips only an inch apart, he slowly tugged the scarf from her hair and sieved his fingers into her hair.

"I love you, Jenny. I want to hold you and kiss you and make love to you until I can't see straight."

"Oh, Colt."

Huck had never said such things, even though Jenny had always wished he would. Maybe it was because they'd become sweethearts at such a young age. Maybe it was because Huck hadn't known how much she needed to hear them said.

She couldn't honestly tell Colt she loved him, or even that she was ready yet to make love to him. But she returned the favor of asking out loud for what she wanted.

"I want to kiss you, too," she said. She put her hand at his nape and urged his mouth down to hers, feeling the desire shoot through her as his mouth captured hers.

"I want to touch you," he murmured against her lips.

She suddenly felt shy, like an innocent who'd never been touched. She reached for his hand and brought it to her breast. She moaned in her throat as his hand closed around her breast and his forefinger and thumb rolled her nipple. "Ohmigod," she gasped.

How could she feel so much? How could she need so much? There was something more she wanted. "I want to touch you," she murmured.

Colt made a guttural sound in his throat as his hand left her breast and reached for her hand, guiding it toward his mouth. He kissed her palm, then pressed it against his cheek.

His skin felt soft and smooth after his shave and smelled of piney woods. She found the scar on his chin with her fingertips first, then with her lips. Her hand slid down Colt's throat to his chest, where she felt his heart thudding under her hand.

He held his breath as her hand moved lower, past his belt until she reached the hardness and heat between his legs. He stilled as she tentatively touched, tracing the shape of him, learning the feel of him. He groaned, then grabbed her wrist to stop her exploration.

"I love the way you kiss and touch," he said. "But the first time we make love, I want enough privacy to know we're not going to be disturbed for a good long while. We're already ten minutes late for supper at Buck's Steakhouse."

Jenny managed a crooked smile. "At least I know I have a great deal to look forward to."

Colt laughed. "Come on. Let me help you out of here."

"Wait."

Colt paused halfway out of the back seat. "What's the matter?"

She grinned. "You're going to have to help me find my scarf."

Colt laughed, kissed her quickly on the mouth, then pulled the scarf from his jeans pocket and gave it back to her.

It took them only five minutes after they were on the road to reach Buck's Steakhouse. To Jenny's surprise, Colt curved his arm possessively around her waist as he led her inside. She knew he didn't give a damn what people thought. He never had. But she'd lived here for more than fifteen years as Huck's girl. She couldn't help feeling a little trepidation as they stepped inside the restaurant.

She hadn't overestimated the effect their appearance arm-in-arm would have on their friends and neighbors. Curious eyes focused on them as she and Colt followed the waitress to their table. Jenny shivered. It felt like a caterpillar was crawling on her skin.

"Ignore them," Colt whispered in her ear. "They'll get used to it."

Jenny wasn't so sure. They might get used to seeing her with Colt, but people in small Texas towns had very long memories. When she and Colt were old and gray, her name would still be linked with Huck's when it came up in conversation.

Assuming you live that long.

It had been dishonest not to tell Colt all the facts before he began his courtship. But it was entirely likely that once he knew the truth, he'd hightail it in the other direction. Jenny wanted to be wooed. She wanted to fall in love with Colt, perhaps even make love with him someday. Was that so wrong?

"You're beautiful, Jenny," Colt murmured. "I'm the envy of every man here."

She flushed with pleasure and turned to look at him. The admiration was plain in his eyes, along with something else.

Love.

That was how she justified keeping her secret. Colt already loved her. He had nothing to lose by trying to win her love. She was the one risking everything. She was the one planning to fall in love with a man who might very well leave her in the end—as her father had left her mother—not because he didn't care, but because he cared too much.

She was glad Randy and Faith were sitting at the table, because otherwise she might have been tempted to confess everything. She was surprised to see that Hope had come along.

"Hello, girls," Jenny said. "You're both looking very pretty tonight."

"Thank you, Miss Wright," they replied in unison.

The twins did look remarkably pretty, Jenny thought, but for identical twins, they also looked remarkably different. Hope wore a sophisticated strapless black sheath that was cut low enough to reveal a great deal of cleavage. Faith was dressed in a simple, V-necked powder blue dress with capped sleeves.

Hope's hair was swept up in an elegant French twist, and she wore earrings that dangled, drawing male attention to her slender throat and bare shoulders. Faith wore her straight black hair tucked behind her ears, which held tiny diamond studs.

Faith looked like the fresh-faced teenager she was, with only a hint of pink lipstick to emphasize her natural beauty. Her dark eyes glowed from within.

Hope's face was expertly made up, but she looked like a picture in a book, not a real person, and beyond the thick mascara on her lashes, Jenny saw a hint of desperation in the girl's dark eyes.

"Hope didn't have any other plans, so Faith asked if she could come along," Randy said. "I said it'd be fine. It's okay, isn't it?"

"Sure. I'm glad you could both join us," Jenny said as Colt seated her. She knew Randy well enough to sense he was annoyed at Hope's presence, but she was proud of him for being gracious. "Looks like there's plenty of room at the table," she said.

"Jake asked if he could join us," Colt said. "So I asked Buck to make sure we had a big table."

Jenny eyed Colt speculatively, but he didn't explain why Jake had invited himself along for a celebration to which he could have only a tenuous connection.

Then Jenny looked across the table at Hope, all dressed up with no date at her side, and remembered how Hope had cornered Jake on her back porch during Huck's wake. Hope had flirted openly, but Jake hadn't seemed interested. Had Hope known Jake would be coming tonight? Was that why she'd invited herself along?

Jenny prayed the young woman hadn't developed a crush on Jake. Since his divorce five years ago, he'd been hell on women. Hope's youth might provide some protection from Jake's crude behavior, but if she pushed, Jake was likely to shove right back.

Jenny had an unsettling thought. What if Jake had arranged for Hope to be here so he could meet with her?

Once Jenny had ordered iced tea, she hid behind the menu and leaned over to ask Colt, "Did Jake say why he wanted to join us?"

Colt shrugged. "He always has a steak at Buck's on Friday night. When he realized we were coming, he asked if he could join us. Do you mind?"

"Of course not," Jenny said. "I always liked Jake." She'd liked him a lot better before he'd been married to Lucy Palance, a girl he'd met when they were in college. Their ten-year marriage hadn't seemed to bring much happiness to either of them. She'd often seen Jake with women over the past five years, but they weren't the kind of female a hardworking rancher married.

So Jenny was amazed when Jake showed up with a schoolteacher on his arm. Miss Amanda Carter was not only a proper lady, she was also fun-loving and pretty. She was twenty-nine and still unmarried, though she'd been pursued by all the most eligible bachelors in town. She wore a tailored cream-colored silk suit that accented her female curves. Amanda was exactly the sort of woman Jenny would have chosen as a second wife for Jake. She just wasn't the sort of woman she'd expected to find at Jake's side. Was Jake turning over a new leaf?

Jenny glanced at Hope and saw from the girl's stunned expression that she might very well have known Jake was coming tonight but hadn't expected him to show up with a date. The blood leached from her face until her eyes were like two burned spots on a sheet of parchment.

Judging from Faith's equally stricken expression, she was aware of her sister's distress. Faith had seated herself so her good hand was next to Randy, so it was necessary to reach out to Hope with her prosthesis.

Jenny watched in surprise as Hope tightly gripped the metal hook for comfort, as though it were a flesh-and-blood hand.

Hope's eyes never left Jake's face. She seemed to be waiting for something. *For Jake to acknowledge her,* Jenny realized.

Jake avoided speaking directly to Hope, or even looking at her, by saying to Amanda, "You know the Butler twins."

"I do," Amanda said with a smile. "You both look very pretty tonight."

"Thank you, Miss Carter," Faith replied.

Hope said nothing. Her gaze dropped to her lap, and color—an entire rose garden of color—suddenly grew on her pale cheeks. Her jaw was clamped, and she was blinking furiously.

Jenny gave Jake a surreptitious glance to see whether he was affected by Hope's despair and caught him stealing a look at Hope from the corner of his eye. It dawned on her that Jake was very much aware of Hope, that his indifference was a calculated act. He apparently cared for Hope a great deal more than he wanted her to know. And just as apparently had decided she was too young for him.

What was it about the Whitelaw men that made them fall in love with unavailable women? Jenny wondered. She only had Colt to judge by, but if Jake was crazy enough to go through such an elaborate charade to discourage Hope, he wasn't going to be happy with a substitute bride, even one as appropriate as Miss Amanda Carter.

Jake ordered a beer for himself and Amanda, then asked if she wanted to dance to the live country and western band that played at Buck's on Friday and Saturday nights. A moment later Jake pulled Amanda into his arms and began two-stepping around the wooden dance floor. Jake was a good dancer, and Jenny was forced to admit the couple looked very much like they belonged together.

A glance at Hope revealed tight lips and narrowed eyes.

Hope had obviously gotten the message Jake had sent by bringing along Miss Carter tonight. It wasn't the gentlest setdown Jenny had ever seen a man give a woman. But it was certainly effective.

She felt sorry for Hope. And angry at Jake. This was Hope's graduation night, one of the most important nights in her life. What Jake had done was cruel, even if he'd believed it was necessary.

Colt leaned over to speak in her ear. "What's got you frowning?"

"Your brother is an idiot," she whispered back.

"I've always thought so," Colt agreed with a grin. "What has Jake done this time?"

"Coming here with Amanda was—"

Before she could finish, the music stopped and Jake and Amanda headed back toward the table. Jake seated Amanda next to Hope, then sat across from her.

"Thanks, Jake," Amanda said. "That was fun."

"You're a good dancer, Amanda," Jake replied.

Jenny watched as Jake stole another glance at Hope. The teenager's chin had dropped to her chest, and she was twisting her paper napkin into a knot. It was small comfort to see the flash of pain in Jake's eyes.

As soon as Amanda was settled and had taken a sip

of her beer, she turned to the twins and asked, "Have you girls decided yet where you're going to college?"

Jenny had expected Faith to answer, but to her amazement, it was Hope who spoke. She lifted her head until her chin jutted and her shoulders were squared. Her eyes gleamed with unshed tears, but her voice belied her agitation as she replied, "Faith and I have both been accepted at Baylor, Miss Carter."

"Have you decided on a major yet?" Amanda inquired.

Hope's chin lifted another notch. "Animal husbandry."

Jake choked on his beer.

"I want to learn how to put the right mare with the right stud," Hope said, staring right at Jake. "That's so important when you want to end up with good stock, don't you agree, Mr. Whitelaw?"

Jake's eyes narrowed. "Absolutely."

Jenny figured any second now things were going to get ugly. She opened her mouth to intervene, but Jake spoke first.

"That's why I proposed to Miss Carter tonight."

Hope inhaled sharply.

"I didn't know you two had been seeing each other," Jenny said to Amanda.

"I've had my eye on Jake for a long time. He's been a hard man to pin down," Amanda said with a smile. "But he was worth the wait," she said, leaning over to kiss Jake on the mouth.

"Congratulations," Colt said, grinning and slapping Jake on the back. He stood up enough to lean over and kiss Amanda on the cheek. "I can always use another sister. I wish you both the very best."

Jenny turned to see how Hope was handling this latest announcement and discovered her chair was empty. The shredded napkin lay on the empty plate where she had been.

Jenny's gaze shot to Randy, who shrugged helplessly. To Jenny's surprise, it was Faith who saved the day.

"Hope hasn't been feeling well today," Faith said as she stood. "I think we'll wait and eat at the senior picnic later tonight. Will you excuse us, please?"

"Be careful on the—"

"I know," Randy said, cutting Jenny off as he rose to go with Faith. "I'll drive slow. See you at the ceremony, sis. Bye, Colt. Bye, Miss Carter. Congratulations, Jake."

Once the teenagers were gone, the empty seats at the table loomed large. Jenny searched for something to say, but could think of nothing. Jake's face looked pale, and Jenny noticed he had let go of Amanda's hand.

"You're not the only one with news, Jake," Colt said with a smile to his older brother. "You can wish me happy, too. I've decided to resign from the Air Force and stay at the Double D with Jenny."

Jake's lips curled in a bleak smile. "Well, little brother, looks like we're both going to settle down and live happily ever after."

Jenny shivered as a chill of foreboding ran down her spine.

Chapter 10

"Why are you so fidgety?" Faith whispered.

Randy shot a glance at Faith, who was sitting next to him on the front seat of Old Nellie, then at Hope, who was sitting to Faith's right, and then back to the winding dirt road. "Guess I'm just excited about graduating."

After what had happened at supper, he should've known Faith wouldn't go to the senior picnic without Hope. Randy was beginning to wonder if he'd ever get Faith alone.

Everyone had brought along jeans and T-shirts to change into at the rest rooms at school, because the picnic consisted of a midnight hot dog and marshmallow roast around a bonfire at the Whitelaw ranch. The Whitelaw Brats had started the tradition, and long after their youngest had graduated, Zach and Rebecca Whitelaw continued to make the site at Camp Little-Hawk available for the party.

Drinking alcohol was forbidden, and couples were discouraged from wandering off into the dark. Randy figured one couple wouldn't be missed in all the excitement, and he'd made special plans for himself and Faith—if he could manage to separate her from her sister.

This year Jenny had volunteered to be one of the chaperons, along with Colt and his brother Jake. Randy supposed that meant Miss Carter would be present, too.

Too bad for Hope.

Faith had told Randy about Hope's crush on Jake. He felt sorry for her after what had happened tonight, Jake getting engaged and all, and he understood Faith didn't want to leave her twin alone at a time like this. But he was determined to have some time alone with her.

"We're here," he announced as he pulled Old Nellie in line with two dozen other vehicles. "I've got a blanket in the bed of the pickup we can sit on," he said to Faith.

"I'll get it," Hope volunteered, hopping out of the truck.

Within minutes, Randy was sitting next to Faith on a blanket beside the fire—with Hope perched on Faith's left side. He racked his brain to think of a way to distract Hope. Once he found it, he had to wait almost an hour before he found a moment when Jenny was busy enough that he and Faith could escape the party without their absence being immediately detected.

"Say, Hope," he said at last. "Why don't you see if Jake wants to roast some marshmallows? He's been standing over there all by himself with his arms crossed, just staring into the fire, ever since Miss Carter left to take care of her mother."

He watched Hope hesitate, then rise. "All right," she said. "I will."

Randy waited barely long enough to see the back of Hope before he turned to Faith and said, "Would you like to take a walk with me?"

She laid her right hand in his and said, "Sure."

He helped her to her feet and edged out of the light of the fire and into the shadows beyond. They weren't the only ones who'd decided to "take a walk." They passed several couples standing in the dark kissing. Most lingered just outside the light from the fire. For what he had in mind, Randy wanted more distance.

"Where are we going?" Faith asked as he led her farther into the moonlit darkness.

"Just a little farther," he said.

"It's awfully dark out here."

Randy stopped and looked up. "There's got to be a zillion or so stars up there, and the moon's pretty full. Trust me, Faith," he said, squeezing her hand.

She squeezed his hand back and followed without more argument. He saw the concern on her face when a glow appeared in the distance. They slid down an incline and into a gully, where he had previously set out a Coleman lantern, a blanket, and a picnic basket.

"We're here," he announced.

"What's all this?" Faith asked, turning to look at him.

Her eyes were wide and wary, and Randy knew he was about to find out whether she really did trust him. "I wanted us to have our own party," he said. "Do you mind?"

Her smile was slow in coming, but when it finally arrived, the muscles in his stomach unclenched. "I think it's a wonderful idea," she said. "Won't your sister wonder what's happened to us?"

He settled onto a ring-patterned quilt that had been made by his mother and pulled Faith down beside him. "We're no farther away than a shout, if anybody really wants to find us. I just thought... I wanted some time alone with you tonight."

"Why?"

He was gripping her right hand tightly, trying to get up the courage to say what he was feeling. "You know I like you an awful lot," he managed.

"I like you, too, Randy."

"I want you to be my girl," he blurted. He could feel the heat in his face where the blood had rushed. He was tempted to look away, but he made himself face her while he waited for her answer.

"You know we're going to different colleges in the fall," Faith said tentatively. "I'm headed for Baylor in Waco, and you'll be at Texas Tech in Lubbock. They're hours and hours apart."

"We could each drive halfway on the weekends," he said.

"We've never even kissed," Faith said with a gentle smile, "and you want me to drive halfway across Texas—"

Randy leaned over and touched her lips with his. The shock was electric. He broke the kiss and stared, stunned, into her eyes. She looked equally shaken.

Faith's right hand came up to touch her lips as she searched his face. "I've never been kissed before. Is it always like that?"

"It's never been like that for me," he said.

"It was good?"

"Better than good. Terrific," he replied. "You want to try it again?"

"Oh, yes," she whispered.

He moved slower this time, pressing his lips more firmly against hers, but feeling the same delicious, unbelievable shock to his senses. His heart catapulted in his chest, and his body turned rock hard. His mouth slanted over hers, seeking more, and his tongue went searching.

She was breathing as hard as he was, and he felt her body quiver as the kiss grew into something greater than the thing it was. Their bodies remained separate, but their souls merged.

He wanted to hold her in his arms, to touch her. He reached out to encircle her waist and drew her close so he could feel her soft breasts against his chest. He was aware of her right arm around him, holding him, but she kept her left arm down and her body on that side angled away.

"Put your arms around me, sweetheart," he whispered.

"But—"

"Please, Faith." She had to trust him not to hurt her. He only hoped he was worthy of that trust.

Slowly, hesitantly, her arm with the prosthesis attached encircled his waist. He could feel the plastic against his back, the nudge of the metal hook at its end against his flesh. She looked up at him, searching for repugnance, for revulsion or disgust.

Randy kept his expression neutral, knowing how important it was that he accept this part of her that was no part of her. "It's okay," he said. "I can handle it."

She gave a shaky laugh. "I'm not sure I can."

"It's no big deal. Just a bunch of plastic and metal you need because you don't have a hand."

She stared at him wonderingly. "You don't mind?"

He separated their bodies, though it was the last thing he wanted to do, and slid his hands down her arms. He made himself take her hook in his right hand, while his left hand held hers. He didn't wince, though her fingernails dug into him, because he didn't want her to think he minded holding that hook.

"You've never really told me how this works," he said, staring at the hook that lay in his open palm.

"It's myoelectric."

In response to his confused look, she explained. "Impulses from the brain are received in receptors in the elbow of the device."

"So you *think* this hook open and closed?"

"That's about it," she said with a smile.

"Neat," he said. "Now, will you put your arms around me, please, and give me another kiss."

She grinned. "With pleasure."

Her enthusiasm was such, that very shortly they were lying side by side on the quilt, their bodies aligned, their mouths merged. Randy was having a hard time breathing, let alone thinking, but he knew they had to stop. Faith trusted him. He had to be worthy of that trust.

He broke the kiss and pressed his face against her neck. "We have to stop, Faith."

Her hand tangled in the hair at his nape, and he shivered at the exquisite sensations her touch provoked. She kissed his temple and whispered, "If you want, I'll be your girl."

"Oh, God, Faith." That provoked another deep kiss, to express his gratitude and his love. When her tongue traced the seam of his lips, he opened his mouth and let her in. And felt her become a part of him. Four years wasn't so long to wait. *Four years*. "I can't wait, Faith," he groaned against her neck.

"I want you, too," she confessed breathlessly.

He'd meant he couldn't wait four years to marry her, but as he looked into Faith's lambent eyes, he realized she'd mistaken his meaning. Well, he'd wanted her trust. She'd given it to him in spades. He brushed her hair back from her face with a trembling hand. "I meant—"

"There you are!" an accusing voice cried.

Randy sat bolt upright, bringing Faith with him. They found themselves staring into four disapproving faces.

Hope was wearing jeans, a cut-off T-shirt and cowboy boots, but as she marched the twenty or so feet that separated her from Jake Whitelaw, she felt naked, as though he could see through all the trappings to the vulnerable female inside.

Jake's eyes never left hers, but his grim look warned her away. She ignored it and walked up to him, carrying the unbent hanger she was using to roast marshmallows. "How about a roasted marshmallow?" she asked.

He hesitated, then said, "Sure. Why not?"

He followed her to a table that had been set up with bags of marshmallows and waited while she stuck a couple on the end of the wire hanger. "How do you like yours?" she asked as she crossed with him back to the fire.

"Hot on the outside, soft and sweet on the inside."

"That's me," she said softly. "Hot and soft and sweet."
She looked at him and saw the glowing embers flare.

"I warned you before to stay away," he said. "I don't
play games with little girls."

She held the hanger over the fire, making sure the
marshmallows stayed well out of the flames. "I'm not
playing, Jake. And I'm not a little girl. I know exactly
what I want. I want you."

"I'm engaged to be married."

"You don't love her. You love me. You want to touch
me, to kiss me, to put yourself inside me."

He stood behind her, close enough that she could
feel the heat of him, but he didn't touch her. She felt his
moist breath against her ear. "I thought you'd learned
your lesson in the barn."

Hope felt the heat on her face and was grateful she
could blame it on the fire. "It seemed to me that you
liked what you saw," she said brazenly.

"Too damn much," he muttered.

She angled her head to meet his gaze, and the heat
in his eyes melted her bones. She stiffened her knees
to keep them from buckling. "Don't marry her, Jake.
Marry me."

He swore under his breath, but he never took his
eyes off hers.

"I'll make you a good wife. I can—"

"Shut up. Shut the hell up," he said in a guttural voice.

"Hey there, Hope!" Colt yelled from the other side
of the fire. "Your marshmallows are on fire."

Hope jerked around and discovered the two marshmallows had been swallowed in flames. She yanked
them out of the fire and blew hard to put them out, but

it was too late. They were both charred beyond recognition.

"Let that be a warning," Jake murmured in her ear. "You keep playing with fire, little girl, you're going to get burned. Go away, Hope. Get as far from me as you can."

He moved away and left her standing alone. It was then Hope noticed that Faith and Randy were missing.

Colt told himself he must have misconstrued the look that passed between Hope Butler and his brother Jake before her marshmallows caught fire. He considered whether he ought to confront Jake but decided it wasn't necessary. His brother knew better than to get involved with a girl half his age, especially when he was engaged to another woman.

But he had to admit that an evening campfire in the middle of the prairie had a way of encouraging romance. Colt had fond memories of a night he and Huck and Jenny had roasted marshmallows with friends and family around a similar campfire. Mac Macready, who'd later married his eldest sister, Jewel, had sat around the campfire vying for Jewel's attentions with Gavin Talbot, who'd ended up marrying his sister Rolleen.

"What's put that smile on your face?" Jenny asked.

"I was remembering a time when we were fourteen and we did this."

"The night Mac Macready warned off Gavin Talbot from Jewel?" Jenny inquired.

"You remember that, too?"

She laughed. "The way sparks were flying between

Mac and Jewel, we didn't need a fire to roast marsh-mallows."

"They're an old married couple now with three kids. Gavin and Rolleen have four between them. Where has the time gone? I can't wait till we've got a brood of our own."

Jenny's face blanched.

"Jenny? What's wrong?" Colt asked.

"I never realized you wanted a big family."

"I guess I never thought about it before, because I never wanted to marry anyone but you. I assumed you'd still want kids. Are you saying you don't?"

"I've already raised one family, Colt. I'd like a little time for myself. I'll understand if that changes your mind about marrying me."

Colt felt like he'd been kicked in the stomach. But Jenny and kids went together like peanut butter and jelly. She'd always loved kids. Apparently, raising four boys by herself had taken its toll. "I suppose I can live without having kids," he said slowly.

"Don't do me any favors," Jenny snapped.

He caught her arm before she could escape. "Hold it right there! I've told you it's okay."

"You don't mean it," she said. "I saw the look in your eyes, Colt. You're shocked and disappointed."

"So what if I am? It's not the end of the world. I'll get over it."

"Will you?"

"When it comes to a choice between you and kids," he said, "there's no question which I'd choose. I've waited too long for you, Jenny. I love you too much to give you up for any reason."

"You say that now," she said. "What about later?

What about a year from now or five years from now? What if you change your mind?"

"All I can do is tell you how I feel right now," Colt said. "Nothing could make me leave you, Jenny."

She looked stricken. She opened her mouth to speak, but they were interrupted by Hope Butler.

"Miss Wright, my sister is missing and so is your brother Randy."

"They've probably gone for a walk," Colt said.

"I've looked around, but I can't find them," Hope said. "I'm worried."

Colt exchanged a glance with Jenny. They both knew why the couple had probably disappeared. If it was up to him, Colt would have waited for them to return. He was in a position to know Randy's feelings about Faith, and knowing Jenny, he was sure she'd raised her brother to respect a woman's feelings. Randy wouldn't be doing anything Faith didn't want.

But the fear in Hope's eyes was real and couldn't be ignored.

"What's up?" Jake asked as he joined them.

Colt watched as Jake exchanged an inquiring look with Hope.

"Faith and Randy are missing," Hope said.

"I'll go take a look for them," Jake said.

"I'm coming with you," Hope said.

Jake halted in his tracks.

It was plain Jake didn't want her along, and equally clear Hope wasn't going to be left behind. Colt remembered the look he'd seen pass between the two of them at the campfire. "Why don't we all go?" he said. "It shouldn't take us long to find them."

Jake shot him a look of appreciation, then headed into the shadows with Hope a step behind him.

"She's in love with him," Jenny murmured as they followed after them.

Colt frowned. "I hope you're wrong."

"I don't believe I am."

"She's only eighteen."

"I fell in love with Huck when I was fourteen," she reminded him.

"Poor Hope," Colt said, shaking his head.

"Poor Jake," Jenny countered.

"What do you mean?"

"Have you seen the way he looks at her?"

Colt remembered the look he'd seen Jake and Hope exchange. "He can't be thinking of doing anything about it," he said half to himself.

"Oh, he won't do anything about it," Jenny said. "The idiot."

"What are you saying? That he should go after her? He just got engaged!"

"He's a fool to ignore his feelings. He should admit he loves her, and let her love him back."

"I suppose you think I should have told you I loved you, even when it was hopeless."

Jenny stopped and turned to face him. "Maybe if you'd said something fifteen years ago we would've been together when there was still a chance—" She cut herself off and hurried to catch up to Jake and Hope.

Colt's mind was reeling. Jenny had always—only—loved Huck. Hadn't she? As soon as he caught up to her he demanded, "Are you saying you had feelings for *me* fifteen years ago?"

"It doesn't matter now," she said. "We can't look

back, Colt. We can't focus on what might have been.
We have to live in the here and now. I shouldn't have
said anything."

Colt should have felt ebullient at Jenny's revelation.
It took him a moment to figure out what was bothering him.

*Maybe if you'd said something fifteen years ago
we would have been together when there was still a
chance—* A chance for what? Colt wondered. For true
love? For a family? What was it she'd been about to
confess?

In the far-off glow of a lantern, Colt spied Randy
and Faith lying on a quilt. Jake and Hope reached them
first.

"There you are!" Hope said in an accusing voice.
"What are you doing to my sister?"

"I'm fine, Hope," Faith said, quickly rising to her
feet and self-consciously rearranging her blouse.

Hope turned on Randy. "What's the big idea sneak-
ing off into the dark with my sister?"

"Hope, that's enough," Faith said. "I came with
Randy willingly. We were just talking."

Hope snorted. "Talking. Right. That's why your lips
are all puffy and—"

"That's enough," Jake said.

"Can't you see—"

"Leave them alone," Jake said. "Your sister's entitled to make her own choices."

"But—"

"Randy, why don't you take Faith back to the fire,"
Jenny said. "Colt and I will gather up these things for
you."

"Thanks, sis," Randy said. "Come on, Faith."

"I'll walk you back," Hope said, reaching a hand toward her sister.

"I'm going with Randy," Faith said, meeting her sister's gaze, but not moving toward her.

Colt saw the shock and pain on Hope's face as Faith took the hand Randy held out to her and began walking back to the fire, leaving Hope behind.

Colt would have stepped into the breach, but Jake beat him to it.

"I'll walk you back," he said to Hope.

"I don't need an escort," she retorted, turning and marching back toward the fire.

"I'll make sure she gets back okay," Jake said as he left Colt and Jenny alone.

Instead of picking up the blanket, Jenny sat down on it. "Join me?"

"We're supposed to be chaperoning kids."

"They'll manage without us for a few minutes," she said, patting the blanket beside her. "Join me."

Colt wasn't going to turn down the chance to be alone with Jenny under a moonlit sky. He sat down cross-legged on the blanket. "Now what?" he said.

"If I have to ask, you aren't the man I think you are," she said teasingly.

Colt leaned over and kissed her on the mouth. The sound of satisfaction in her throat made him ache. He reached out to palm her breast and heard a moan of pleasure that sent his blood thrumming through his veins. He lowered Jenny onto the blanket until they were fitted together from breast to belly. "We missed doing this as kids, didn't we?" he said.

"Uh-huh."

"I'll make it all up to you, Jenny," he promised.

"I only wish you could," she murmured against his neck.

"What does that mean?"

"Only that some moments are lost forever, Colt. That's all."

The sadness in her voice made him want to weep. "Just promise you'll let me try, Jenny."

She leaned over and gave him the softest of kisses. "All right, Colt," she said as she met his gaze in the moonlight. "I promise to let you try."

Chapter 11

"You look good enough to eat," Colt said.

Jenny blushed as she stepped farther into the living room. "Thank you, Colt."

He held out his arms, and she walked into his embrace, letting her body settle against his. "This feels good," she said.

"No argument from me," he said. "I can hardly wait till you're my wife. How's that wedding gown coming along?"

"It's not finished yet."

Their wedding was one week away, but Jenny hadn't finished making her wedding dress. There was a good reason for the delay. She still wasn't sure there was going to be a wedding, for the simple reason she hadn't yet told Colt her secret.

He'd become so dear to her that she couldn't bear the thought of losing him. The temptation was overwhelming not to tell him at all. But how could she take vows "to love and honor and cherish" in the midst of such a deception?

Trust him, Jenny. He loves you. It won't matter.

Colt's arms tightened around her. "Is it my imagination, or are you losing weight?"

Jenny stiffened. "It's this dress," she said.

He held her out at arm's length and critically surveyed the short black satin sheath held up by narrow rhinestone straps. It was cut low enough in front to reveal her modest cleavage and short enough to reveal her long, slender legs.

He whistled, long and low. "You're one gorgeous lady, Miss Wright. But once you're mine, I think we're going to put a few pounds back on those beautiful bones."

She didn't dare meet his gaze, afraid he would find something in her eyes that would give her away. Worry had caused her to lose her appetite. But explaining even that much would require her to reveal the source of her anxiety—the secret she was keeping from him. "We'd better get going. Your mother and father will be wondering where we are."

"I'm not sure I want to share you with anybody else just yet."

"Randy will—"

"Randy left fifteen minutes ago to pick up Faith."

"Your parents—"

"My parents won't mind if we're a little late to our own engagement party."

"Colt, I don't think—"

"Don't think," he murmured as he pulled her back into his arms. "Just let me hold you. I can't believe this is real. For so many years I dreamed of moments like this, and now I want to enjoy every one of them."

She hid her face against his neck and clutched at his shoulders. "I love you, Colt."

She heard his sharp intake of air before he separated them so he could look into her eyes. "I've been waiting a long time to hear you say that."

"There's just one thing—"

His mouth captured hers in a kiss of claiming, preventing the words that might have torn them apart.

A frisson of pleasure shot through her. How could Colt make her feel so much, so fast? It had never been like this with Huck. Never. Her nipples peaked with the brush of his hand across the satin. He kissed her throat, then suckled, causing her insides to draw up tight. She moaned, a sound of desire and despair.

Her heart beat against her ribs like a butterfly caught in a jar, as he reached for the zipper at the back of her dress. It slid down easily, and the straps fell off her shoulders along with the top of the sheath. Beneath it she wore a black merry widow. The avid look in his eyes made her body quiver with anticipation. He reached behind her to unhook the bra, and she panicked.

"Colt, no!"

His hands paused, but his eyes quickly sought hers for an explanation. "What's wrong?"

"I…" Her hands gripped his arms, as though to shove him away. *Tell him. Tell him. Tell him.*

"This isn't the right time," she said breathlessly. She saw the disappointment in his eyes, but, thank God, no suspicion. "We're supposed to be at your parents' home in twenty minutes."

His lips curled in a lopsided grin. "I'm sure I'd enjoy making love to you however little time we took." He held up a hand to stay her protest. "But I'm willing to wait, if that's what you what."

"It's what I want."

He lifted the straps back onto her shoulders and reached around her to zip up the dress. All the while, his hips were pressed against hers, so she could feel his arousal. She ached for him, yearned for him. And feared his discovery of the truth.

"It's all right, Jenny," he murmured in her ear. "I understand why you're afraid."

"You do?" she said, her voice catching in her throat.

He nodded solemnly as he brushed her hair back behind her shoulders. "You're afraid it won't be the same with me—" He swallowed hard and corrected himself. "As *good* with me, as it was with Huck. Just remember that I love you. If you want me to do something differently, all you have to do is ask."

She wanted to tell him he was wrong, that he made her feel so much more than Huck ever had. But she bit back the words. It wasn't Huck's fault he hadn't made her feel more. It wasn't Huck's fault she hadn't been in love with him. She hadn't known what a difference love would make. Until Colt had come along and shown her.

Jenny leaned forward and kissed Colt gently on the lips, feeling the need that arose whenever she touched him. "I love the way you touch me, Colt. I love the way you kiss me. I want to make love to you. But I need a little more time."

"We're getting married in a week," he reminded her. "Do you want to wait until our wedding night? Is that what you're telling me?"

She couldn't wait that long. Colt had to know the truth before they stood in front of a preacher and said vows that bound them for a lifetime. *A lifetime. Who are you kidding, Jenny?* She couldn't mislead Colt any longer. It seemed time had run out.

Jenny swallowed past the lump in her throat. "Tonight," she said. "After the party."

"I'm going to hold you to that promise," Colt said, leaning down to kiss her tenderly on the mouth.

As she stepped out onto the back porch, Jenny stopped abruptly. Parked at the door was a brand-new forest-green Jeep with a gigantic yellow bow on the hood. She turned to Colt, who was grinning.

"Do you like it?"

"Oh, Colt. It's too much." *Especially when you may not want anything to do with me after tonight.*

"I'd hand the world to you on a platter, if I could."

"I don't know what to say."

"Say you like it."

Jenny smiled. "I like it." She stepped off the back porch and walked completely around the Jeep, peering inside.

Colt pulled the ribbon away from the vehicle, then reached into his trouser pocket to retrieve the key. "You want to drive?"

"Oh, yes, please."

Jenny didn't say much on the trip to Hawk's Pride because her heart was lodged in her throat. This was all a dream, and she was afraid to wake up. Colt was everything Huck had never been—generous, thoughtful, helpful—and he made her body hum whenever he touched her.

But he wasn't perfect. He had one fatal flaw. He

couldn't bear to be around sick people. She'd gotten the measles when she was sixteen, and Colt hadn't come to visit her once until she was well again.

When she'd questioned him later, he'd admitted, "Something happens inside me when I see somebody I know who's sick in bed." He had put a hand to his belly. "My insides sort of squeeze up tight, and I can't breathe."

She'd laughed at him and asked, "What do you do when you get a cold?"

"Oh, I don't have any problems when *I'm* sick. Only when somebody else gets ill."

"What do you do when one of your brothers or sisters gets sick?" she asked.

"I stay away until they're well."

"You can't mean that," she said.

"I most certainly do."

"You don't even bring them magazines or something to drink?"

Colt shook his head.

"That's awful!"

"I didn't say I was proud of the way I act," he said. "And believe me, I've tried to get over it. I visited Avery's bedroom when he got the mumps, but it was a disaster. I was with him maybe a minute when my hands started trembling, and I broke out in a sweat. I barely got out of there before I lost my lunch!"

"Why do you suppose that happens?" she asked.

"I think I'm afraid," he confessed in a low voice.

"That you'll get sick, too?"

"That someone I care about will die."

"People don't die of a cold, Colt, and not very often anymore from measles or mumps," she chided.

He grimaced. "I know that! I didn't say what I feel makes sense. It's just what I feel. I can't help it. So don't give me a hard time about it. Okay?"

In all the years she'd known Colt, she hadn't once seen him visit anyone in the hospital. When her mother was sick, he only came by when he was sure he wasn't going to catch a glimpse of her in bed. Another time, when he discovered Tyler and James had chicken pox, though he'd already had the disease himself, instead of coming inside, he offered to help with the chores in the barn.

Jenny wished she had told Colt the truth from the beginning. It was going to be much harder to give him up now than it would have been before he'd come to mean so much to her.

"For a lady on her way to a party, you don't look very happy," Colt observed.

Jenny made herself smile. She was determined to enjoy their engagement party, especially since it might be their last night together. "I was thinking how strange life is. If Huck hadn't been killed... I would have missed so much."

"I feel the same way. I miss him a lot, but if he were here, I wouldn't have you."

Jenny reached a hand across the seat to Colt, and he gripped it tightly. "I'm glad we found each other," she said.

"Me, too."

Jenny brought the Jeep to a stop at the back door to the Whitelaws's ranch house. The whitewashed adobe house, with its barrel-tile roof, had been built in a square around a gigantic moss-laden live oak, and the party had spilled into the grassy central courtyard.

Jenny felt Colt's arm slide possessively around her waist as he escorted her into the fray.

"Hey, there, Slim," he said, shaking hands with an old high school friend. "Buck, Frank," he said, shaking more hands.

"Congratulations, Colt," Buck said. He dipped his head, touched the brim of his Stetson and said to Jenny, "We all wish you the best, Miss Wright."

"Thanks, Buck," she said.

There was something lovely about being surrounded by friends who'd known you since the days when you'd all played ring-around-the-rosie together. At the same time, it was unsettling to see the speculation in their eyes as they tried to gauge whether she and Colt might have been lovers when she was still Huck's girl.

A huge beef was being barbecued on a spit, and there was a keg of beer, along with iced tea and soft drinks. A group of women, Amanda Carter among them, were setting up a buffet table with side dishes everyone had brought. Jenny's brother Tyler was pounding on one leg of the sawhorse table with a hammer, while Colt's brother Rabb held it up.

She looked for Jake and found him standing in a circle of ranchers and their foremen, including Zach Whitelaw, her brother Sam, Wiley Butler—and his daughter, Hope. She located Randy and Faith talking with a bunch of teenagers beneath an arbor of bougainvillea.

She looked at Colt and realized he was making a similar survey to locate his siblings and his myriad aunts, uncles and cousins. "You've sure got a big family," Jenny murmured.

"Yeah," Colt said. "And a close one. It was great growing up as one of the Whitelaw Brats."

Jenny turned her eyes away. If Colt married her, he wasn't going to be adding any branches to this awesome family tree. He'd said he didn't mind, that she was enough for him. But seeing all these Whitelaws with their children and grandchildren made her realize how much Colt would be giving up if he married her.

It would be easier to push him away now than to endure the regret in his eyes for however much time they had together.

Stop it, Jenny. Stop looking for reasons to break up with Colt. Oh, you can come up with a few. He'd be happier flying jets than living with you. He'd be happier marrying someone who could give him kids. He'd be happier if he didn't have to hang around and maybe watch you die. But isn't the choice really up to him? Are you going to give him a chance to choose you?

That was the crux of the matter. Jenny wasn't sure she had the strength to survive Colt's rejection. It was easier to avoid that possibility by rejecting him first. She could drive him away. He wouldn't stay where he wasn't wanted.

But one of the lessons the past two precarious years had taught her was to reach out for happiness. Loving Colt made her happy. Making love with Colt would bring her joy. After that… Life was uncertain. No one got any guarantees.

Jenny turned to Colt and let him see the need she felt, the yearning to be held and loved. "How soon do you think we can leave without our absence being noticed?"

Colt's eyes lit with a fire that warmed her insides.

"My father wants to say a few words and make a toast. After that, I think we could slip away."

"Why don't you see if he wants to do that now?" Jenny said.

"Come with me," he said. "We'll ask."

Colt's parents were surprised that he wanted them to make their speeches so early in the evening, but they were more than willing to accommodate their youngest child.

"May I have your attention, please," Zach said, arranging Jenny and Colt between himself and Colt's mother, Rebecca. "Before we carve up that beef, I'd like to say a few words to my son and future daughter-in-law."

The noise died down, but it didn't get completely quiet. Babies still cried and children still played. But the adults gathered around them, drinks in hand, ready to offer toasts to their future happiness.

"First I want to thank Jenny for loving my son. And my son for being smart enough to settle down and marry her."

There was general laughter, shouts of "Hear! Hear!" and clinking beer glasses.

"I want to tell my son how proud I am of him. How much we feel blessed for having been given the chance to make him a part of our family. I only hope he and Jenny find as much joy in raising their Whitelaw Brats, as we did in raising ours."

There was more laughter, more clinking glasses.

Jenny felt her face turn to stone. She was afraid to look at Colt, afraid to look at anyone. She prayed that Colt would let the statement pass, that he wouldn't feel the need to tell his parents, "My future wife doesn't want children."

From the corner of her eye, Jenny saw that Colt's face was frozen in a smile. A muscle in his jaw jerked, and she realized his teeth must be clenched.

Then it was Rebecca's turn to speak. Colt's mother put her arm around Jenny and said, "We know you and Colt could live on love alone, but we've decided a little bread wouldn't hurt. We hope you'll let us pay off the mortgage on the Double D as a wedding present."

There was a gasp and then applause.

Jenny's heart was stuck in her throat. There was no way she could speak. She could barely breathe, she was so overwhelmed with joy and with pain. This good family had raised a wonderful son, and all she had offered him—all of them—was deceit.

"I'm sorry," she blurted. "I can't accept your gift. Because I can't marry your son."

Colt didn't know when he'd been so angry with anyone in his life. "Don't you dare run away from me," he snarled, grabbing Jenny's arm as she reached for the door to the Jeep. "What the hell's going on, Jenny?"

She was panting, and her eyes look frightened. "You heard me. I can't marry you."

"What is it you're so scared of?" he demanded.

She looked like a deer caught in a set of headlights. "This—the two of us—would never work."

Colt realized they'd acquired an audience. Not surprising, considering the bombshell Jenny had dropped. He was still reeling himself. "Get in," he said. "We're going home."

"You are home, Colt."

"Get in the damned car, Jenny." When she didn't move, he swept her up in his arms, carried her around the hood of the Jeep and deposited her in the passenger's seat. "Don't get any smart ideas," he warned.

He half expected her to leap out of the Jeep and run. She was good at running from trouble, his Jenny. But the running was going to stop. Here. Tonight.

Colt started the engine and spun the wheels, kicking up dirt and stones as he backed out of the driveway. "Buckle up," he said. "It's liable to be a bumpy ride."

He didn't say another word until he cut the Jeep's engine at Jenny's back door. "Come inside. We're going to talk."

"I have nothing more to say," Jenny said as she shoved open her door and hurried up the back steps. "Go home, Colt. Leave me alone. I don't want to see you again."

"That isn't going to cut it, Jenny. I told you I wasn't going to leave you. And I meant it."

Jenny reached the porch first and whirled on him. "What if I don't love you?"

Colt froze with his boot on the bottom step. "What?"

Jenny turned her back on him and thrust both hands through her hair. "I lied when I said I loved you."

"I don't believe you," Colt said, his voice soft but furious. "Turn around and look at me. Say it to my face, goddamn you!"

Jenny dropped her hands to her sides. She turned slowly until she was facing him. Her eyes brimmed with tears, and her mouth was curled down at the corners. "I thought I could go through with this. To save the ranch. But I can't."

Colt hissed in a breath. It sounded like the truth. "Oh, God, Jenny."

"Go home, Colt."

"I can't," he said, the words torn from his throat. "You're home for me, Jenny. I still want you. I still need you."

"I won't marry you, Colt. That would be a living hell for both of us."

"You made a promise to me earlier this evening. I expect you to keep it," he said implacably.

He saw her confusion, the moment when she realized what he meant. Her nostrils flared, and her lips thinned. "It wouldn't be lovemaking, Colt. It would be sex."

"Sex is fine with me," he said, moving up the steps toward her.

Jenny took a step back. "Don't come any closer."

"I intend to get a hell of a lot closer before the night is over," he said, backing her up against the frame of the house. He shoved his knee between her legs and pinned her body against the wall with his hips. His hands thrust into her hair, angling her head back at a painful angle. "You're mine, Jenny. You've always been mine. You just didn't know it."

"Colt, I—"

His mouth covered hers, angry and afraid, searching for answers that always seemed a step beyond his reach. A spark of electricity leaped between them, shocking his senses. His body hungered as much as his soul, and he felt a sense of desperation that was impossible to deny. There was nothing gentle about his kisses. He forced her lips open for his intrusion, biting them, sucking on them, demanding a response.

Her body betrayed her. And he knew he had her soul.

He lifted his head and stared down into her panicked eyes. "You lied, Jenny. I don't know why. But before we're through, I'm going to find out the truth."

"You can't handle the truth," she cried. "Why do you think I've been lying!"

"We can discuss this later," he said as he thrust his hips against hers. "After we've made love."

"Colt, you can't—"

"Watch me." He picked her up and carried her into the house.

Colt snapped on the tiny lamp that sat on Jenny's chest of drawers, then threw her onto the four-poster. He began stripping himself while she watched in stunned disbelief. He took off his shirt, then yanked off his boots and socks. He pulled down jeans and Jockey shorts together and stood before her completely naked.

He heard her gasp, saw her eyes go wide.

"That's something else Huck and I *didn't* have in common," he said. "Move over, Jenny. Make some room for me."

She scuttled across the bed and landed on the floor in the shadows on the opposite side. He stalked around the foot of the bed and dragged her to her feet. "Need a little help getting undressed?"

Before she could protest, he had her zipper down and the black sheath stripped off her shoulders. His arms imprisoned her as he unsnapped the black merry widow. He felt her tense as he pulled it free and threw it onto the floor. Her eyes slid closed as he looked at her naked breasts for the first time. He leaned over and kissed the tips, one at a time, and heard her harsh, indrawn breath.

Then he slipped one nipple into his mouth and suckled.

She cried out and her hands reached for him, grabbing handfuls of his hair to hold him where he was. "Oh, Colt. It feels…it feels…"

She didn't finish the sentence. But she didn't have to. He could see the ecstasy on her face.

He shoved the sheath the rest of the way down, only to discover she was wearing a garter belt and black nylons. "This is the kind of gift a woman plans for her lover, Jenny."

She didn't deny it.

"I thank you," he said as he looked his fill.

He took off her black silk panties but left the nylons and garter belt, since they weren't in his way. He pulled her close, reveling in the feel of the soft fabric and her even softer flesh against his own. He kissed her eyes, her nose, her cheeks, her lips. He caressed her arms, her back, her stomach. Any part of her he could find. But he came back often to her breasts, because she seemed to have so much sensation there.

To his surprise and pleasure, she touched him in return. Her hands marveling, seeking, scratching, squeezing, making his body pulse and tighten and yearn.

It had been too long since he'd had a woman. He was afraid if she kept touching him, he would spill himself too soon. So he laid her on the bed and caught her hands and pinned them against the pillows and made himself go slow.

"Colt, I can't wait," she begged.

"Another kiss here," he said, his lips against her belly. "And here," he said, moving his mouth lower.

Her body writhed beneath his caresses and then became taut. "Please," she gasped.

He took his time. And he brought her joy.

She was like no other woman he had ever known.
Softer. Sleeker. More responsive.

He kept his weight on his arms as he spread her
legs with his knees and positioned himself between
her thighs. "I'll be as gentle as I can, Jenny. Let me
know if I hurt you."

He was so big. And she was so small. Suddenly he
was afraid. He looked into her eyes and saw that she
was not.

Then she reached for him, pulling him toward her,
and he pushed slowly into the warmth and wetness of
her. She angled her hips, gasping as he sank to the hilt.

"You fit," she said, surprise evident in her voice.

He couldn't help smiling. "Did you think I wouldn't?"

"I wondered," she said, her hands brushing the hair
from his forehead. "But I'm glad you do."

"Me, too," he said with a smile.

He took his time, moving slowly, kissing her face
and her throat, his hands moving over her, feeling,
touching her perfect body—except for one spot on her
breast. He felt her stiffen as his fingers traced the blemish. A dimple in her flesh. And some kind of scar.

His body didn't allow him time to consider what
he'd found. It demanded culmination. He lifted her
legs and wrapped them around his waist and drove
them both toward satisfaction. He waited for her. And
it wasn't easy. But he was many times rewarded, because her climax came so close in time with his own,
that both of them were lifted higher. He threw his head

back and gritted his teeth against the almost unbearable pleasure, as he spilled his seed in her womb.

Afterward, he pulled her close, kissing her again.

"I love you, Jenny. I love you," he said between panting breaths.

"And I love you, Colt," she admitted in a quiet voice.

He didn't have the strength to ask all the questions that were tumbling around in his head. So long as she loved him, they could work everything out. He still had no idea what had made her so frightened. But he felt certain that whatever it was, they could handle it together.

As he held her close, his fingertips grazed the blemish on the side of her breast, almost beneath her arm. He lifted his head to look, but he could barely make out the dimpled flaw in the shadowy light. "What is that?" he asked.

"A scar," she said.

"I didn't know you were hurt. How did it happen?"

"I wasn't hurt. I have cancer. Had cancer. May still have cancer," she said breathlessly.

Colt sat up and stared down at her. He swallowed hard. Sweat beaded on his brow. His body began to tremble. He bolted from the bed and ran for the bathroom, his hand over his mouth. He barely made it in time.

Chapter 12

It took Colt a moment to realize where he was when he woke up. Not in Sam's bedroom at the Double D, but in his own at Hawk's Pride. He felt the sweat break out on his forehead at the mere thought of *Jenny* and *cancer* together in the same sentence.

Oh, God. What had he done?

Memory returned like a hideous nightmare, and he saw himself, eyes wide with horror, stomach churning, and then his ungainly race for the bathroom. He recalled the foul taste of vomit, and the hot wash of shame.

Colt groaned in agony and pressed the heels of his hands against his grainy eyelids.

He'd failed her. She'd shared her trouble with him, trusted him, given him a chance to prove his love. And he'd failed her…and himself.

Oh, God. Why cancer? Of all the maladies in the world, why give my Jenny cancer?

Then he remembered more. Jenny had come into the bathroom, dampened a cloth and gently wiped the sweat from his brow and the spittle from his mouth. He'd kept his eyes closed, afraid of what he'd see in her eyes if he looked at her. Then her touch was gone.

"Go home, Colt," she'd said in a flat voice. "Go home."

When he'd come out of the bathroom, he'd found his clothes laid out on the bed and Jenny nowhere in sight. He'd had an urgent need to see her. To make excuses for himself. To explain what had happened.

But he didn't need to explain. Jenny understood his irrational fear of illness better than anyone.

Sick people sometimes die.

No. Not my Jenny. Not so young. Not when she's barely had a chance to live!

Colt struggled to remember her exact words. *I have cancer. Had cancer. May still have cancer.*

The terror of what she'd said had kept him from asking for more information. He speculated with what little knowledge he had.

The dimpled scar meant she'd had some sort of surgery. A lump removed? And then what? Radiation? Chemotherapy? How had that been possible without anyone noticing the effects of such treatment? The vomiting. The hair loss.

Of course. It had been easy to conceal her illness when she was so very much alone. She'd only have to hide it from him and from Huck for a few days at most while they were home on leave. For the past two years she'd been alone on the Double D except for Randy, who was probably in on the secret. It was likely Randy knew everything and had been sworn to silence. He had to talk with Randy. Randy would be able to tell him the details he hadn't gotten from Jenny.

Colt leaped out of bed and dragged on some clothes. He shoved his feet into a pair of boots, grabbed his battered Stetson and left the house as quietly as he'd returned late the previous evening.

As he approached the Double D ranch house, Colt felt the bile rise in his throat. He swallowed it down. His skin felt clammy as he quietly shut the door of his Mustang and moved up onto the back porch. The back door was unlocked. Even in these dangerous days, Westerners left their doors open as a gesture of range hospitality. Strangers were welcome.

A man who betrayed his woman's faith and her trust likely was not. So he entered as silently as he could and made his way down the hall to Randy's bedroom. Colt knocked once, then opened the door and stepped inside, closing it behind him.

Randy was still sound asleep, the covers thrown off, so Colt could see the boy wore only a pair of cotton pajama bottoms. Colt sat on the edge of the bed, gave Randy's shoulder a shove and whispered, "Wake up."

Randy rolled over, scraping at the sand in his eyes and yawning. "Oh. Hi, Colt." He shoved himself upright and scratched at his belly. "Sorry I was so late getting in last night. I saw Jenny's door was closed and your bed was empty and I figured… Well, I didn't want to bother the two of you, so I just—"

"This visit isn't about how late you came in last night," Colt interrupted. "It's about—" His throat constricted, making speech difficult, but he forced the words out. "About Jenny's cancer."

Colt saw the flicker of pain on Randy's face before it was replaced by guilt. "She finally told you, huh?"

"Yeah," Colt said, releasing a gust of air.

Randy looked anxiously over Colt's shoulder toward the door. "Is she coming here to tell me about it?"

Colt was confused. "You mean she hasn't said anything to you before now?"

Randy swallowed hard and shook his head. "I—" His voice broke, and he cleared his throat. "I figured it out for myself. There were days she'd be sick. And she lost weight. And once I heard her crying. Then I found a bill from the doctor, and I knew."

"You never confronted her and asked for the truth?" Colt asked, incredulous.

Randy shook his head. "If she'd wanted me to know, she'd have told me."

"Did you at least share what you knew with your brothers?"

Randy's chin dropped to his chest, and he shook his head.

"It never occurred to you to write to Huck. Or to me? To tell someone who could give her some help?" Colt said, his rage as palpable as his voice was quiet.

Colt saw a tear drop onto the sheet.

"I was scared," Randy said in a voice hoarse with tears he was trying not to shed. "I kept hoping it would go away. Jenny's always been so strong. I figured if she really needed help, she'd ask for it. But she never did."

Colt pulled the tearful boy into his arms, and felt Randy's arms close tightly around him. How awful it must have been for him to know. How terrified he must have been of losing his sister. Colt offered comfort and received it in return. In a little while he asked, "When did you first notice Jenny was ill?"

"Two years ago," Randy answered.

Two years, Colt thought. And she hadn't yet succumbed to the disease. But she looked so frail. And she'd lost weight even since he'd come home. Didn't she have to see the doctor sometime?

Then he remembered the day she'd spent in town, the day she hadn't invited him along. *She must have seen a doctor then.* Maybe he could find out who it was and ask— No. A doctor wouldn't tell him Jenny's secrets. And he shouldn't be asking. If he wanted to know anything, he should get it from her.

He patted Randy's back and said, "Don't worry, boy. I know now, and I'm going to take care of her."

Randy sat back and scrubbed at his eyes with his hands. "You don't know what a relief it is to hear you say that."

Colt tousled Randy's hair. "Go back to sleep." He rose and headed down the hall toward Jenny's room, stiffening his buckling knees and determinedly swallowing down the nausea that rose as he approached her door. He felt the sweat bead on his forehead and fought back a wave of dizziness as he reached out to knock on her door.

"Jenny, it's Colt. Let me in."

There was no response. He wouldn't have blamed her if she never wanted to see him again. But he wasn't going to leave this time—or ever again. Even if he spent the rest of his life hanging over the toilet bowl every morning, he was here to stay.

He knocked again. "At least say something," he said. "Let me know you're all right."

Silence.

"I'm coming in," Colt said. "We need to talk." He turned the doorknob, but it was locked.

He laid his cheek against the smooth wood. She'd locked him out, and herself inside. "Please, Jenny. Give me another chance."

He waited, his ear pressed against the door, for any sign that she might relent. And then he heard her reply.

"Good-bye, Colt."

He's gone.

Jenny stared, dry-eyed, at a water mark in the ceiling where the rain had leaked before Colt fixed the roof. There was no repairing such a stain. It could be painted over, but in her experience, it had a way of seeping back through. It was better just to tear down the ruined part and get rid of it.

Better to send Colt away, than to let him try to make amends. She would never—could never—forget his reaction last night. Or forgive it. It was hard enough facing her illness, without seeing her own terror reflected back in his eyes.

What did you expect? a voice asked. *That he would be miraculously cured? That his abhorrence of illness would magically disappear because you were the one who was sick? Did you think he'd pull you into his arms and tell you everything would be all right, that he was there for you, always and forever, "in sickness and in health"?*

Foolish woman. Did your father stay to help your

mother? Whom have you ever been able to rely on be-sides yourself?

Jenny felt cold and empty inside, as though a block of ice had frozen around her, insulating her from the world, from its pain and its joys. She wanted to spend the day in bed with the covers pulled up over her head. But there were animals to be fed, chores to be done and a life—however brief—to be lived.

She left the bed and walked across the room to stare at her naked body in the mirror. The slight defect in her breast didn't even show from the front. She had to turn sideways and lift her arm to see it. There was only a slight indentation in her skin and a thin scar where the cancerous tissue had been removed.

She turned away and headed for the shower. She made the spray as hot as she could stand it and stood there as long as she dared, wishing the warmth would seep into her bones and melt the ice that held her feelings frozen inside. If only she could cry, she might feel better. But all she could muster was an awful sense of desolation.

She dressed in the most comfortable jeans she owned and her favorite shirt. She made herself smile into the mirror as she dried her hair, hoping that would make her feel better. Her grin had the look of a corpse in rictus.

That did make her smile. The curl of her lips was fleeting, a single instant of relief from the oppressive sorrow she felt. But it gave her hope that she could survive this second, even more devastating loss of a loved one.

She smelled coffee as she headed toward the kitchen. She was grateful there would be something hot and strong to drink, but she wasn't looking forward to seeing Randy. The two of them were going to have some hard times together—considering it was no longer possible to save the Double D.

She stopped dead on the threshold to the kitchen. Colt stood with his back to the sink, his hips resting against the counter, his hands gripping it on either side.

"What are you doing here?" she said cuttingly.

"I thought you might need some coffee," Colt replied.

She watched him swallowing furiously. Any second, he was going to have to bolt for the bathroom.

"Oh, for heaven's sake! Eat a cracker," she snapped.

"Will that help?" he said, his face tinged with green.

"It works for pregnant women with nausea. It ought to work for you." She crossed to the cabinet and pulled out a box of soda crackers, ripped open the bag and stuck a cracker in front of his mouth. "Open up." He opened his mouth, and she stuck it inside.

He bit off a bite, chewed carefully and swallowed. He took another small bite, and another, until the cracker was gone. "Thank you," he said at last.

His color still wasn't too good, and sweat dotted his forehead, but at least he didn't look in imminent danger of puking. "Sit down," she ordered. "Have you tried drinking any of that coffee you made?"

"Not yet," he admitted.

"Something carbonated might be better for your stomach." She crossed to the ancient refrigerator, pulled out a can of ginger ale and popped the top. "Drink this."

He looked wary. "My stomach—"

"Drink it," she ordered, shoving the can into his hand.

He took a sip, then looked down at her. "Satisfied?"

"I'll be satisfied when you're gone from this house."

"I'm not leaving," he said.

"I make you sick, Colt. Physically ill. You look worse than a calf with the slobbers."

He grimaced. "That bad? Then you shouldn't be shoving me out the door. Sick as you make me out to be, I'm likely to ruin the upholstery in my Mustang. Now *that* would make me truly ill."

Jenny felt a rising hope shoving its way upward from inside, trying to get out. But there was no way it could get past the ice that was frozen around her heart.

"Why are you here, Colt?"

"I need some answers, Jenny. I want to know about your cancer."

She was shocked to hear him say the word aloud. She watched to see if he was going to be sick, saw him swallow hard and reach for another saltine.

He's trying, Jenny. Give him a chance.

She'd given him a chance. And he'd broken her heart. It had taken all night to put the pieces back together. Why should she let herself be hurt again?

"All I want to do is talk," he said, anticipating her refusal. "Have a cup of coffee and talk with me, Jenny. You owe me that much."

She stiffened. "I don't owe you anything. Not after last night."

She watched all the blood leave his face. She pulled a kitchen chair out from the table, grabbed him by the arm and shoved him into it. "Put your head down before you faint," she said, shoving his head between his knees.

Too late, she realized she should never have touched

him. His hair felt soft beneath her fingertips, and the warmth of the skin at his nape heated her skin. Melting the ice. Thawing her heart.

She jerked her hand away and backed up. She turned and crossed to the percolator and poured herself a cup of coffee. He started to lift his head, and she snapped, "Keep your head down!"

She placed a handful of saltines and the can of ginger ale on the table in front of him, then retrieved her cup of coffee—a mug, not one of the delicate china cups he'd given her—and sat down on the opposite side of the table from him. "All right. Take your time and come up slow."

He looked pale, but at least he was no longer white as a ghost.

"Ask your questions. Then get out."

"Why didn't you tell Huck? Or me? Why did you keep it a secret?"

"I was afraid if I told Huck it would be the excuse he needed never to come back," she said. "And we both know how you feel about sick people."

"You didn't give us a chance."

"You were both thousands of miles away. In Germany, I think. Or was it somewhere in Southeast Asia? Huck had a dozen chances to quit flying and come home and marry me. He never took one. Why should I think my being sick would make a difference?"

She saw the pain and regret on Colt's face, but he didn't contradict her.

"How far along was the cancer before you discovered it?" he asked.

"Because of my family history, my gynecologist suggested I get a baseline mammogram when I turned thirty, a healthy mammogram for comparison purposes, to make it easier to identify anything abnormal if it showed up in the future. Since my mother got breast cancer when she was thirty-four, I figured it might be a good idea.

"Except, that first mammogram revealed a tiny spot, not much bigger than a pencil tip, but there, just the same." She shivered and took a sip of hot coffee to warm the cold inside.

"It was a shattering moment," she admitted, meeting Colt's gaze with difficulty. "There was something hard and foreign inside me, attacking me, trying to kill me."

She watched Colt swallow hard and reach for a saltine.

"I couldn't even feel a lump," she continued inexorably, mercilessly detailing the facts he'd demanded. "But it was there. Without the mammogram, I might not have known until it was too late."

"So you had surgery to remove the cancer?" Colt asked.

"My doctor performed a lumpectomy."

She saw Colt cringe and remembered how she'd felt the first time she imagined a knife slicing through the soft flesh of her breast. "My doctor told me she thought she'd gotten all the cancerous tissue. But there was no way to know whether the disease would come back. I had radiation."

"How?" he asked, his brow furrowing. "I mean, without anyone but Randy finding out."

"Randy knows?" she said, her eyes darting toward the doorway that led to his room. She started to rise, to go to her brother, to assuage his fear.

Colt grasped her wrist from across the table and held her in place. "Randy's fine. I want to hear the rest of it."

She sank back into her chair, staring at his hand until he released her. Her eyes locked with his. "The rest of it. You mean the fury and resentment I felt? The fear of losing a part of me to the surgeon's knife? And of all things, a breast—the part of a woman that most symbolizes her femininity, the one truly sensual gift she can give to her husband and lover, the means of nursing her children.

"I ranted at fate. I was quite melodramatic. I frightened the horses in the barn. Better them than Randy or any of my brothers."

"You should have told them."

"Don't tell me what I should have done! Do you think I don't know they would have dropped everything to come running? Do you think I don't know how much they care? But I love them just as much as they love me. What could they do, really, to change anything? The cancer is either going to kill me, or it's not. Nothing they do or say is going to change that.

"In the meantime, their lives would have been turned upside down. They would have been miserable worrying about me. It was better my way."

"How do you think they're going to feel when they find out the truth?" Colt asked.

"If the lumpectomy had worked, they would never have needed to know."

She saw Colt go still. Saw the growing awareness in his eyes of what she'd just revealed.

"It's back?" he asked, his voice grating like a rusty gate.

She threaded her hands together in front of her, gripping them so hard her knuckles turned white. "I had a follow-up mammogram the day I went into town by myself. The doctor called last week. She wants me to come in for a needle biopsy. She's afraid she made a mistake not doing more radical surgery the first time."

Jenny saw Colt was swallowing furiously. He closed his eyes and gritted his teeth so hard she saw a muscle jerk in his cheek as he fought off the nausea. When he opened his eyes, the terror was barely hidden behind a facade of composure. "Is that why you never finished the wedding dress?" he asked.

She nodded.

"When is the biopsy scheduled?" he asked.

"I was going to spend the day in town tomorrow 'running errands,' for the wedding," she confessed. "I have to be at the doctor's office at eight-thirty. I planned to have the surgery, recuperate at her office, and be home in the afternoon."

"I'll go with you," he said.

"You don't need—"

"How the hell do you know what I need?" he said in a voice filled with barely controlled rage. "I need to live my life with you. I need to go to sleep with you in my arms and wake up with you in the morning. If all we're going to have is a few months or years together, I want every minute I can get."

"I have *cancer,*" she said, emphasizing the word.

"And it makes me sick—literally—to know that," he retorted. "I'm as angry and frightened as you are, Jenny. Maybe more so, because I've wanted you all my life, and now, when I thought we'd have a lifetime together, you tell me you may already be dying. I don't know how to cope with the anger I feel. Or the fear."

They stared at each other for a long moment, both aware of the crossroad they had reached. Jenny could go on alone, or she could ask Colt to join her.

"You could hold on to me," Jenny said at last, reaching a hand across the table.

Colt grasped her hand like a lifeline. Their fingers entwined, but soon that wasn't enough for either of them. As though led by some unseen hand, they both rose and moved around the table toward each other. Colt's arms closed around Jenny, and she knew she was where she belonged.

"Give me another chance, Jenny," Colt whispered.

The ice cracked around her heart, leaving the pulsing organ exposed and vulnerable, capable of feeling… everything. "Oh, Colt."

"Don't deny me, sweetheart. Let me love you. Let me be a part of your life for however long we have left together on this earth."

What woman could refuse an offer like that? "All right, Colt. For as long as we have together, I'm yours."

Chapter 13

The hardest thing Colt had ever done was sit in the doctor's office, surrounded by sick people, and wait for Jenny while she underwent a needle biopsy on her breast. Jenny had explained Colt's problem to her doctor, who had prescribed something to control his nausea.

But no pill could relieve his dread that Jenny might die from cancer. The disease was arbitrary; it killed with equal disregard for age or gender, race or creed. And Jenny was right; there was nothing he could do about it.

Except live life with her to the fullest every day.

The instant they left the doctor's office after the outpatient surgery was completed he said, "Marry me, Jenny. On Saturday, as we planned."

"We won't have the results from the biopsy by then," she countered as he helped her into his Mustang.

"I don't care."

"There's no time to finish my wedding gown."

"I dropped it off with my mother this morning. She's taking care of it," he said as he settled into the driver's seat. "Any more excuses?"

She eyed him solemnly. "I don't think it's fair to you. I may not have very long to live."

"I'll take whatever time I can get."

"You seem determined to do this."

"I am."

"What will people say?"

He shot her a triumphant grin. "I know I've won when that's the only argument you can come up with. You know I don't give a damn what other people say. If it feels right to you and me, that's all that matters. Will you marry me on Saturday?"

She chewed on her lip for a moment, then seemed to make up her mind. He held his breath until she said, "All right. Okay. You win. I'll marry you on Saturday."

He hit the brakes and swerved the convertible to the side of the road, skidding to a stop on the shoulder.

"What's wrong?" Jenny cried.

"Nothing's wrong," he said. "I simply felt an irresistible urge to kiss you silly, that's all."

Impossibly, unpredictably, she laughed. "You're crazy, Colt!"

"Crazy in love with you," he said, leaning over to touch his lips to hers.

She moaned, and he deepened the kiss, slipping his tongue inside her mouth and tasting her. His heart beat wildly in his chest, with joy and with fear. She was so very precious. How would he bear it—Colt forced himself to focus on the delicious sensations caused by her tongue sliding between his lips, touching the roof of his mouth, then withdrawing to be followed by his tongue, tasting her.

He would find a way to make her understand that, even if more radical surgery became necessary, it wouldn't matter to him. The only thing that mattered was keeping her alive. He broke the kiss at last, but pressed his cheek against hers. "I love you, Jenny."

"And I love you," she whispered.

"We'd better get going," he said, forcing himself back to his own side of the car. "We've got lots of company waiting at home."

"Oh, Colt. What have you done?"

"What you should have done two years ago. I called your brothers, had them meet me at Hawk's Pride, and told them about the cancer."

"You had no right!" Jenny said, her hands clenching into fists.

"I have every right," he retorted. "I love you. That means I'll do everything within my power to make your life easier and happier. Even if it means making your brothers' lives a little unhappier."

"What did they say?" she asked anxiously. "How are they taking the news?"

"How do you think they took it? They were angry and hurt." He rubbed his jaw and said, "Sam took a swing at me. He thought I'd known all along and had kept it from them."

"I'm sorry. Sam always was a little hotheaded."

"Once I explained, he apologized. But now that they know, they want to be there for you, Jenny. It was all I could do to keep them from coming to the doctor's office this morning. They compromised by agreeing to see you after the surgery at the Double D."

"How can I face them?" she said.

"Just remember they love you."

When they arrived at the house, they found all four of her brothers putting a coat of fresh, white paint on the house. But they weren't the only ones at work. All of Colt's brothers and sisters had joined in to make various improvements on the property.

The shutters on all of the windows, as well as the front door, had been painted a deep green that matched Jenny's new Jeep. Flowers and shrubs had been planted around the front porch, and an entire lawn had been laid in thick patches of green.

"Ohmigod, Colt! Look what they're doing," Jenny said.

"It's a wedding gift, Jenny. From my family and from yours. They're helping to make our house a home."

Colt saw the sheen of tears in Jenny's eyes and felt his own throat swell with emotion. "You don't mind, do you? James and Tyler suggested it, and I said it sounded like a good idea. When Mom and Dad and Jake heard what your brothers planned to do, they wanted to be a part of it. And when my brothers and sisters—"

She cut him off with a kiss. "I love them for it," she said simply. "All of them." She let herself out of the car before he could get the door for her and headed around to the front of the house to survey their work.

Colt had to walk fast to keep up with her. "Jenny, are you sure you're up to this?"

She smiled at him over her shoulder. "I want to thank them, Colt. I want to tell them all how wonderful I think everything looks."

And she did, even going so far as to drop onto her knees and tuck a little extra earth around the red geraniums his mother was planting beside the front steps.

Jenny had guts, all right. And stamina. He kept a wary eye on her, wanting to make sure she didn't do too much. The surgery had been done with a local anesthetic, and Jenny swore she was okay. But Colt had seen enough of Jenny to know that if someone she loved asked her to pick up a house, she would give it try.

When the painting was finished, Jenny watched over the cleanup, and more than one brother said, "Yes, Mother," as she issued instructions on how it should be done. As the afternoon wore on, her too-bright eyes and her too-fast speech told him she had reached the limits of her endurance.

He announced it was quitting time, and everyone should gather on the back porch for a glass of iced tea and fresh-baked, hot-from-the-oven chocolate chip cookies his sister Cherry had made. Jenny sat in one of the two wooden rockers on the back porch—a gift from his parents—while his mother occupied the other. His father stood behind his mother, in much the same protective way Colt stood behind Jenny. Some of his siblings sat in chairs that had been brought outside from the kitchen.

Sam and Tyler leaned on the porch rail, while Randy sat cross-legged at Jenny's feet, with Faith by his side. His brother Jake leaned against the house, his eyes focused on Faith's sister Hope, who was sitting with Colt's sister Frannie on the wooden swing Jake had hung by ropes from the porch rafters that afternoon.

There was a lot of laughter and joking, everyone careful to keep the mood light. No one had spoken the "C" word all afternoon. No one had mentioned the desperate disease that had brought them together.

"I can't thank you all enough," Jenny said for the umpteenth time. "This was a wonderful surprise."

"You should have told us sooner," Sam said curtly.

Jenny stopped rocking. It got so quiet Colt could hear the single fly buzzing around the last chocolate chip cookie on the plate. He put a hand on Jenny's shoulder and squeezed.

I'm here, love. You're not alone.

She smiled gratefully at him over her shoulder, then met Sam's embittered gaze. "I thought I could spare you this pain," she said. "I was wrong. Please forgive me."

"We can't get back the two years you stole from us," Sam said.

Jenny arched a brow. "I've been right here, Sam."

"But I didn't know—I would have come—" Sam lifted his hat, forked his fingers through his hair, then resettled the Stetson low on his brow. "What are we supposed to do now?"

"What you've always done," Jenny said. "Be there when I need you."

Once the subject had been opened, it seemed there were others who needed to speak.

"When will you get the results of the biopsy?" Tyler asked.

"On Monday."

"What about the wedding? Is that on or off?" James asked.

Jenny reached up and laid her hand over Colt's, which still rested on her shoulder. She smiled and said, "The wedding is on."

"On Saturday? Before you know the results?" Sam asked, staring hard at Colt.

"On Saturday," Colt confirmed.

"Which reminds me, I have a wedding dress to finish," Colt's mother said, rising from her rocker.

"I've got some errands to run," Jake said. "Can I give anybody a lift anywhere?"

"I need a ride into town," Hope said, jumping up from the swing.

"If you're driving Hope into town, can you take me and Faith, too?" Randy said, rising and then helping Faith to stand.

"Why not?" Jake said. "Anybody else? I've got one of the vans."

Everyone else had their own transportation. In a matter of minutes, the porch was empty except for Colt and Jenny. "Come sit with me on the swing," he said, taking her hand and helping her out of the rocker.

As Colt sat down on the hanging swing and lifted Jenny into his lap, she slid her arms around his neck and laid her head in the crook of his shoulder. He could feel her warm breath against his throat.

He set the swing in motion with the toe of his boot, and they sat without speaking and watched the sunset. The sky was streaked with bright yellows and rosy pinks, and the sun looked like an orange ball as it began its descent beyond the horizon.

"All we need to make this picture-perfect is a dog at your feet," Jenny murmured.

"That can be arranged," Colt said as his lips curved in a smile.

A jet broke the sound barrier, and Colt looked up,

knowing he wouldn't be able to see it, but searching the sky, anyway.

"Will you miss it very much?" Jenny said quietly.

"Flying? Sure. I'd be lying if I said I wouldn't. But life is about choices, Jenny. Being with you is the right choice for me."

"What if—"

"You want to play that game? All right. What if I get bucked off my horse tomorrow and break my neck? What if we get abducted by aliens? What if—"

Jenny giggled. "Abducted by aliens?"

"What if the cancer does come back?" he said seriously. "It won't change anything. I plan to treasure every moment I have with you—however many there are."

He felt her kiss his throat, then his chin, then the side of his mouth. He turned his head and blindly found her mouth with his. He felt her moist breath against his flesh as she whispered, "I have the irresistible urge to kiss you silly. Will you please take me to bed?"

Living life to the fullest, Colt mused as he lifted Jenny and carried her into the house, definitely had its compensations.

As Randy helped Faith into the back seat of the van, Hope jumped into the front with Jake. Randy shot a glance at Faith to see whether she thought he ought to try to do something to get Hope to sit in back with them. She gave a slight shake of her head, and he slid into the back seat with her.

As they headed toward town, the silence in the front seat was palpable.

"How about some music?" Hope said finally, turning on the radio.

Jake glanced at her, then aimed his eyes back at the road without speaking.

Randy was grateful for the noise, because it meant he could talk to Faith in the back seat without being overheard. "Does Hope really have something to do in town? Or is she just trying to get Jake alone?"

"Do you really have an errand?" Faith countered. "Or do you just want to get me alone?"

Randy grinned and slid his hand along her jeans from her knee upward along her inner thigh until she reached over to clamp a hand over his to stop him. "I definitely want to get you alone," he said. "But I actually have an errand in town. I promised I'd pick up some white ribbon for Jenny. Now, answer my question."

Faith removed his hand and set it on his own thigh, then laid her hand on the inside of his thigh close enough to his zipper to cause serious repercussions. She shot him a mischievous sideways look from beneath lowered lashes. "My suggestion is that you mind your own business. I plan to keep you so well occupied that you won't have time to worry about what's going on between Hope and Jake."

Randy made a strangled sound in his throat as Faith's hand brushed tantalizingly across his erection and disappeared back onto her own side of the seat. "That sounds fair," he said.

For the rest of the ride into town, Randy wasn't aware of anything except Faith's teasing touches, her impish glances, the intimate promises she was making that he hoped she planned to keep. He responded with caresses of his own and heated glances and a whispered question. "When?"

He saw her cheeks pinken, and knew she'd heard him. "We can slip away during your sister's wedding reception. My parents won't miss me for a few hours during all the celebration."

"Will you let me see your other hand? I mean, without the prosthesis?"

Her mouth flattened into an unhappy line. "You may not like what you see. Is it really necessary?"

He took her hand in his, caressing the normal fingers. His mind had conjured up an image of deformity beneath her prosthesis that he was sure couldn't be worse than the real thing. "You take it off at night, when you go to bed, don't you?" he asked.

She nodded.

"If we're going to spend our lives together, I figure I better get used to how you look without it."

"Maybe you won't want to be with me anymore after you see me without it."

He was surprised that Faith was able to state her fear so clearly and succinctly. If he could accept the hook and the plastic arm, he didn't think real flesh and bone—no matter how malformed—could make him reject her. But he knew words alone weren't likely to assuage her fear. "You'll just have to take that chance," he said at last. "Unless you want to break up right now."

He watched myriad emotions—doubt, fear, hope— flicker across her face as she evaluated the risk, and balanced the possible reward. *Like Colt did with Jenny,* he realized. *Balancing the risk of losing her against the joy of loving her.* As Faith must balance the risk of trusting him against the joy of being fully loved.

"All right," she said at last. "I'll let you see my hand. But only if you promise—"

He squeezed her trembling hand to cut her off and said, "It'll be all right, Faith. Believe me. It won't make a difference."

He only hoped he was right.

Jake was angry. Hope recognized the signs. The vertical lines on either side of his mouth became more pronounced because his jaw was clamped, and his eyes narrowed to slits. There was an overall look of tautness to his body—shoulders, hands, hips—that suggested a tiger ready to leap.

She knew she shouldn't have invited herself along. She knew Jake didn't want her around. She also knew he didn't want her around because he was tempted by her presence, like a beast in rut responding to the relentless call of nature.

Hope let her gaze roam over Jake and saw his nostrils flare as her eyes touched what her hands could not. She wondered whether she ought to push him into something irrevocable. Like taking her virginity.

He would marry her then. She was sure of it. But would he love her? She didn't want him without his love. She knew that much. But she was running out of time. Why, oh, why, had he gotten engaged to Miss Carter? She wouldn't feel this desperation if he hadn't forced her hand. She knew in her bones that they belonged together, and she didn't intend to lose him to another woman.

When they arrived in town, Hope was surprised that Jake volunteered to drop off Randy and Faith first after setting a time to pick them up again. She offered a reassuring smile in response to Faith's anxious look as she and Jake drove away.

"You haven't asked where I want to be let off," she said when Jake had driven half the length of the main street in town without stopping.

He shot her a look filled with scorn. "Don't insult my intelligence. You haven't got any errands to run. But I do. So sit there like a good little girl and be still."

It was the *little girl* that did it. It was a flash point with her and always would be, because it diminished who she was, which was more than the sum of her age. She began to unbutton her blouse right there, driving down Main Street.

Jake glanced in her direction and nearly had an accident. "What do you think you're doing?"

"Taking my clothes off?"

"Do you want to get me arrested?"

"I'm not a minor, Jake. We're two consenting adults."

"I'm engaged. I'm promised to another woman."

"Not once word of this gets around," she said, glancing at the passersby who gawked in through the window as she pulled her shirt off her shoulders, leaving her wearing only a peach-colored bra.

Jake swore under his breath and gunned the engine, heading for the old, abandoned railroad depot on the outskirts of town. He braked to a halt in front of the depot and turned to glare at her. She saw the flicker of heat as he glimpsed the fullness of her breasts above her bra.

"What the hell do you think you're doing?"

"I'm not a little girl, Jake. I don't know what I have to do to prove it to you."

"I'm not going to marry you, Hope. You're not what I want. I want someone who can share my memories of the world, someone who's lived a little."

"I can catch up," she said desperately.

He shook his head. "No, little girl. You can't."

Hope felt her chin quivering and gritted her teeth to try to keep it still. "So you're going to marry Miss Carter?"

"Yes, I'm going to marry her. Put your blouse back on, Hope."

She grabbed her shirt and tried to get it on, but the long sleeves were inside out, and her hands were shaking too badly to straighten it.

She heard Jake swear before he scooted across the bench seat, pulled the shirt from her hands and began to pull the sleeves right-side out. He held the shirt for her while she slipped her arms into it. Her cheek brushed against his as she was straightening. She turned her head and discovered his mouth only a breath from her own. Their eyes caught and held.

She wasn't sure who moved first, but an instant later their mouths were meshed, and his tongue was inside searching, teasing, tasting. He was rough and reckless, his hands cupping her breasts as a guttural groan was wrenched from his very marrow. His mouth ravaged hers as his hands demanded a response.

She couldn't catch up. He was moving too fast.

And then he was gone. Out the opposite door. She scrambled after him, pausing in the driver's seat when she spied him leaning against the van, his palms flat against the metal, his head down, his chest heaving.

He stood and faced her. "That was my fault," he said. "I…" His eyes were full of pain and regret.

"You're formidable, Hope. I'll grant you that. Somewhere out there is a very lucky young man."

"I want *you*," she cried.

"I belong to someone else."

"You're only marrying Miss Carter because you don't think you can have me. But you can," Hope insisted. "There's nothing stopping us from being together except your own stubborn bias against my age."

"Your youth," he corrected.

She snorted. "Eighteen years isn't that much. Lots of men marry younger women."

"You need to go to college. You need to find out what you want to do with your life. Maybe you'll decide you want more out of life than simply being some rancher's wife. If I were to marry you now, the day might come when you decided marriage to me wasn't fulfilling enough, that you needed to go find yourself."

"Is that what happened with your first wife?" Hope asked, her eyes wide.

"I've seen it happen," Jake said without answering her question directly. "You're too young to know what you'd be giving up, Hope. Go to school. Get an education. Find out what you want to do with your life."

"If I do that, if I go to college, will you wait for me?"

She saw the struggle before he answered, "In four years I'll be forty. I—"

"Wait for me," she said, stepping out of the van. "Don't marry Miss Carter. Promise you'll wait for me."

"I can't promise anything, Hope. There's another person in this equation you're not considering. I've proposed to another woman, and she's said yes. Unless Amanda breaks the engagement, I'm honor-bound to marry her."

"Even if you don't love her?"

"Who says I don't?"

The shock of his words held Hope speechless. "How could you love her and want me like you do?"

He shoved a frustrated hand through his hair. "I respect and admire her. And she loves me. We can have a good life together."

"You *don't* love her," Hope said accusingly.

"I don't know what I feel anymore," he retorted. "You've got me so damned confused—"

"Wait for me," Hope said. "There are such things as long engagements."

"That wouldn't be fair to Amanda," Jake said stubbornly.

"It is if you don't love her. Don't you think she'll notice? Don't you think she'll miss being loved?"

Jake stared at the ground, then back at her. "I'll go this far," he said. "I won't press her to get married. But I'm not going to walk away if she sets a date."

"Thank you, Jake. At least that gives me a chance."

Jake shook his head. "I'll say this much. Life with you would never be boring."

Hope laughed. "I hope I get a chance to prove that to you someday."

Chapter 14

"Stand still, Jenny, or I'll never get all these buttons done up," Rebecca said.

Jenny looked at herself in the oval standing mirror in the corner of her bedroom, hardly able to believe that she was the beautiful woman reflected there. She looked like Cinderella, ready for the ball, except her dress was white, instead of pink. She'd pieced the dress together herself, but Colt's mother had finished it, adding lace and ribbons and seed pearls like one of Cinderella's mice.

The satin gown had a wide boat neck, open almost to her shoulders, with long sleeves that tapered to the wrist. The bodice was fitted to the waist with a wide skirt belling out below. A narrow train decorated with tiny seed pearls began where the last cloth buttons ended in back and trailed several feet behind her.

Jenny reached up to adjust the net veil, held in place by a circlet of fresh white daisies, and brushed at a stray wisp of hair at her temple that had escaped the knot of golden curls at her crown. "Are you done yet?" she asked.

"Not yet," Rebecca said.

"Whatever made you decide to put thirty-two buttons down the back instead of using a zipper?"

Rebecca smiled. "I was thinking of my son."

Jenny's brows lowered in confusion. "I don't understand. A zipper would make it easier for him to get me out of this dress in a hurry."

Rebecca's smile became a grin. "I know. But think how much his anticipation will have built by the time he gets the last button undone."

"If his patience lasts that long," Jenny said with a laugh.

Rebecca joined her laughter. "There. All done." She put her hands on Jenny's shoulders and looked at their side-by-side faces reflected in the mirror. "My son loves you, Jenny. I'm only beginning to understand how much. I wish you both all the joy that love can bring. I'm sorry your mother isn't here to see you today. I know she'd be very proud of all you've accomplished."

Jenny felt the sting in her nose and the tickle at the back of her throat. "Thank you, Mrs. Whitelaw."

"I wish you'd call me Rebecca. Or Mom, if you wouldn't mind."

Jenny turned and hugged Colt's mother. "I've missed having a mom. It'll be good to have one again."

Rebecca levered Jenny to arm's length and looked

her over. "You're beautiful, Jenny, inside and out. I wish you much happiness with my son."

Jenny looked at Colt's mother through misted eyes. "Thank you, Mom."

Rebecca grabbed a Kleenex from the box on the dresser and dabbed at the edges of her eyes. "We'd better get moving if you don't want to be late to your own wedding." She reached down to pick up the dragging train, brought it around and layered it carefully over Jenny's arm. "There. Are you all set?"

"Ready as I'll ever be," Jenny said.

"Are you sure there's nothing else you need?" Rebecca asked.

"Let's see. Something old—my mother's pearl necklace. Something new—this beautiful gown. Something borrowed—the Whitelaw family Bible you gave me to carry. Something blue—my wedding bouquet of bachelor's buttons. I have everything I need."

"Except a groom," Rebecca said with a laugh. "I'll see you at the church."

Once Rebecca was gone, Jenny didn't linger long in her bedroom. She knew her four brothers were waiting in the living room to escort her to church. As she came down the hall she heard Randy say, "Holy cow!"

The moment she stepped into the living room, her brothers, who'd been lounging on the furniture, all stood up. Sam spoke first.

"I'll be damned. You're gorgeous, Jenny."

Jenny smiled. "Thank you, Sam."

"Stunning," Tyler said.

"The prettiest bride I've ever seen," James added.

"Holy cow!" Randy repeated.

Jenny laughed. "I'd love to stand here and listen

to more of your compliments, but I think it's time we left for church."

The four brothers exchanged looks before Randy stepped forward. "We got together and decided to give you something special as a wedding gift."

Randy looked into the inside pocket of the navy blue suit jacket he was wearing but didn't find what he was looking for. He looked in the other side of the coat and pulled out some papers. He stepped forward and handed them to Jenny. "For you."

"What's this?" she asked.

"A honeymoon," Sam said.

"At the Grand Canyon," James added.

"We figured you deserved a *monumentally* good time," Randy said with a grin.

"We'll take care of the ranch while you're gone," Tyler said, cutting off the objection on the tip of her tongue.

Jenny was astonished. "I don't know what to say."

"'Thank you' might be nice," Sam said.

Tears filled Jenny's eyes, and she tried to sniff them back.

"Don't you like it?" Randy asked, confused by her tears.

"I'm overwhelmed," Jenny said. "Thank you all." She held her arms wide, and her brothers moved to hug her all at once. She gave them each a kiss wherever she could reach.

Randy wiped the kiss from his cheek and said, "We don't have time for any more of this mushy stuff right now. We're gonna be late if we don't get outta here."

"Right, brat," Sam said, tousling Randy's hair. "So get moving."

Jenny laughed, banishing her tears, and followed her brothers out of the house.

Her wedding day had dawned sunny, but the ceremony was scheduled for eleven-thirty to avoid the heat of the day. The reception was being held in the courtyard at Hawk's Pride, beneath the cool shade of the moss-draped live oak.

Jenny's stomach was full of butterflies, which she suspected was normal for a bride on her wedding day, but she had put her fears on hold. Today was about joy and love.

Once they arrived at church, she waited by herself in a small room off the vestibule, while her brothers helped to seat guests. In a departure from the norm, Jenny had neither bridesmaids nor a maid of honor. She didn't have any close girlfriends, and she didn't know any of Colt's sisters well enough yet to feel comfortable asking them to stand in such a role. She had asked her four brothers to stand up with her instead.

"If you're going to be unconventional, I don't see why I can't do the same thing," Colt had said.

"Meaning what?" Jenny asked.

"How about a Best Lady instead of a Best Man?"

"Who did you have in mind?"

"My sister Jewel," Colt said. "She was like a second mother to me, and we've always been close. If you don't mind, I think she could hang on to the rings as well as one of my brothers. And Frannie will kill me if Jewel gets to dress up and she doesn't. So I guess I'd better include her.

"Actually, it might balance things better if I use all my sisters for 'groomsmen,'" Colt mused. "That way, with Rolleen and Cherry, we'll have an even number of girls and guys coming down the aisle. What do you think?"

"It sounds like a wonderful idea!" Jenny said.

"Who's going to give away the bride?" Colt asked.

"I don't know. I forgot all about that."

"It's usually a parent or an older relative," Colt said.

"I don't have any of those. Any suggestions?"

"As long as we're being unorthodox, how about my parents? They've adopted eight of us kids. I don't see why you can't adopt them."

Jenny smiled. "Done."

"Then it's all settled," Colt said.

"What will people think?" Jenny wondered.

"This is our wedding," Colt said. "We can do as we damn well please."

Colt was wishing they'd eloped. He was standing in his father's bedroom, dressed in a black dinner jacket, studded white dress shirt, cummerbund and black trousers, fidgeting nervously as his father tried for the third time to tie his bow tie. His brothers watched the comedy of errors from vantage points around the room.

"Hold still," Zach said as he adjusted the black silk, "and give me a fighting chance to get this straight."

"It's too tight," Colt said, slipping his finger between the bow tie and his throat.

"That's the marital noose you feel tightening around your neck," Jake said.

"Just because your marriage didn't work out—" Rabb began.

"The bride's got cancer," Jake said.

"*Had* cancer," Avery corrected.

"May still have cancer," Colt said quietly. "And if

she does, we'll deal with it. I love her. Be happy for me, Jake." He met his brother's remote, ice-blue eyes and felt as though they were miles apart.

Jake shrugged. "It's your funeral."

Avery hissed in a breath.

"Bad choice of words," Jake said repentently. "I don't know what's wrong with me today. I hope you and Jenny have a long and happy life together, Colt. I really do. I'll see you after the ceremony," he said, backing his way out of the room.

It was clear, at least to Colt, that Jake considered marriage on a par with walking through a minefield barefoot. Which made Colt wonder why his brother had gotten himself engaged to Amanda Carter. And whether Jake would follow through and take a second trip down the aisle. Only time would tell.

"I'd better get going," Rabb said. "I promised Mom I'd help greet people at the church."

"Me, too," Avery said as he followed Rabb out the door.

Colt's father stepped back to admire his handiwork. "That ought to do it," he said.

"Any last words of advice?" Colt said.

"Be happy," Zach said.

Colt saw the tears in his father's eyes and felt his throat swell with emotion. "Thanks, Dad."

He took the step that put him within his father's reach and felt his father's arms surround him. As a child, he'd found support and succor, even surcease from pain, within these strong arms. Zach Whitelaw had taken a child that was not his own flesh and blood and made of him a devoted son.

"I love you, Dad," he said.

His father gave him a quick hug, then pushed him away. "We'd better get going. Your mother will kill me if I don't get you to the church on time."

"Sure. Then she'll kiss you all over till you're well again."

"Maybe being late isn't such a bad idea," Zach said with a laugh.

They made the trip to the church in Colt's Mustang convertible with the top down. The wind ruffled Colt's hair and left his bow tie once more askew.

"Let me fix that tie," Zach said.

Colt waved at friends and neighbors as his father arranged his bow tie, then watched his father head for the front of the church. He headed for a door at the rear, where the choir usually assembled, and which was used during weddings for the groom and his "groomsmen."

The room was filled with his sisters, arranging their hair and putting on makeup and getting dressed. Colt grinned as he observed the cacophony and confusion. It felt like old times. Cherry was walking around in a bra and half slip; Jewel's hair was still in hot curlers; Frannie was buttoning up Rolleen's dress, while Rolleen talked on a cell phone.

"Hi," Colt said.

"Finish buttoning Rolleen for me," Frannie said. "While I pin some flowers in my hair."

Colt crossed to Rolleen and began buttoning up her dress. "Who's that on the phone?" he asked.

"Gavin's grandmother," she whispered back. "The baby's teething and has a little fever."

"When you finish with Rolleen, can you do me?" Cherry said, pulling her dress on over her head.

Colt crossed to the sister who'd been most like him

in temperament, the other rebel in the family. Cherry had come to the Whitelaw family as a mutinous four-teen-year-old juvenile delinquent and ended up—in Colt's humble opinion—as a damned good wife and mother. "How're the twins—both sets—and what's-his-name?" he asked.

"The girls are in the high school pep squad, and the boys are into G.I. Joe. What's-his-name hit a home run in his Little League game this morning. Why do you think I'm running so late?"

"Tell Brett I said congratulations," Colt said.

"You can tell him yourself at the reception. He'll be there, along with forty-three dozen other scream-ing Whitelaw brats."

Colt groaned. "Surely you jest!"

"I'm not off by much," Cherry warned.

"Colt, will you come hold this mirror so I can see the back of my hair?" Jewel said.

"Duty calls," Colt said as he buttoned the last but-ton on Cherry's dress. "Hey there, Jewel," he said as he took the mirror from his eldest sister and held it up for her. "How's it going?"

"There's a lump in my hair," she said. "Right…" She reached up, trying to locate it backward in the mirror.

"There?" he said, poking at a cowlick at the back of her head.

"That's it. Stubborn little cuss." She took the mirror from his hand and threw it onto the table in front of her. "Why do I bother? Plain brown eyes, plain brown hair, plain old face. You'd think I'd get used to it."

Colt tipped her chin up and surveyed her face, which still bore remnants of the faint, crisscrossing scars she'd acquired in the car accident that had originally left her orphaned. "You look pretty good to me," he announced.

She brushed his hand away and wrinkled her nose. "You have to say that. You're my brother."

The organ began to play and Jewel looked at her wristwatch. "Oh, Lord. Five minutes. Is everybody ready?"

Colt looked around. The chaos had ceased. Before him stood his four sisters looking remarkably lovely in pale rose full-length gowns. Every dress was cut in a different style that had been especially designed by Rolleen to make the most of each sister's assets.

"You all look...wonderful," Colt said, his voice catching in his throat.

"You look pretty wonderful yourself," Jewel said, crossing to link her arm with his. "Come on, Colt. It's time we made our appearance in church."

They walked out to stand in front of the altar and wait for Jenny to appear. Her brothers had already taken their places on the opposite side of the altar. Colt found his parents sitting in the front pew, waiting for the appropriate moment to give away the bride, and smiled at them. His mother dabbed at her eyes with his father's hanky and smiled back.

Their choice of attendants might have been unusual, but Jenny had selected Lohengrin's "Wedding March" as the processional. At the sound of the familiar opening chords, the congregation stood, and Colt searched the back of the church, waiting for his first look at the bride.

Jenny walked down the aisle alone, as she had lived most of her life. Colt felt his throat constrict as he caught sight of her. She looked ethereal. He could see her face through her veil, and her joyous smile made his heart swell with love.

His parents met her and said the words that gave her into his care. He reached out and took her hand, then turned with her to face the preacher.

"Dearly Beloved," the minister began. "We are gathered here…"

The vows were familiar, but they seemed to have a great deal more meaning, Colt discovered, when you were the one taking them.

"Do you, Jennifer Elizabeth Wright, take this man to be your lawful wedded husband, to have and to hold… to love and to cherish…all the days of your life?"

"I do," Jenny said.

Then it was his turn.

"Do you, Colt David Whitelaw, take this woman to be your lawful wedded wife, to love and to honor…in sickness and in health…as long as you both shall live?"

Colt's throat was so swollen with emotion, he couldn't speak. He nodded, but the minister was waiting for the words. He felt Jenny squeeze his hand. "I do," he rasped.

Putting the simple gold band on Jenny's third finger somehow linked them together. When she placed a gold band on his finger in return, it felt as though the two of them had been made into one.

Then the minister was saying, "By the power vested in me, I now pronounce you husband and wife. You may kiss the bride."

Colt's hands were trembling as he lifted the veil and looked into his wife's shining eyes. He lowered his head slowly, touched her lips gently, then gathered

Jenny in his arms and gave her a kiss that expressed all the tumultuous emotions he felt inside.

The congregation began to applaud.

Colt lifted his head, grinned sheepishly, then slipped Jenny's arm through his and, to the swell of organ music, marched with his bride back down the aisle.

The newlyweds were spending one night at the Double D before they left for their honeymoon at the Grand Canyon the following morning, so Randy was supposed to spend the night in Colt's room at Hawk's Pride to give his sister and her new husband some privacy.

It had been difficult for Randy to keep his mind on the wedding ceremony, when he knew he had a test of moral courage coming up in a matter of hours. Once the wedding reception was in full swing, he planned to sneak into Colt's bedroom with Faith—and see what she'd been hiding beneath her prosthesis.

He hadn't seen Faith before the ceremony began, and in all the excitement afterward, they'd ended up going to Hawk's Pride in separate cars. He searched for her in the courtyard and spied her near the punch bowl. He hurried in her direction, but stopped ten feet away and gawked.

She wasn't wearing the prosthetic device.

She had on a pair of white cotton gloves that ended at the wrist, exposing her arms. The left glove had something inside it to fill out the fingers, but apparently the gloved hand wasn't functional, because Faith didn't use it when she helped herself to a cup of punch. Her left arm, including the wrist, which was usually covered by the prosthetic device, looked perfectly normal.

It was the rest of her hand—or rather lack of it—he needed to see.

But suddenly he was in no hurry to see it. He stayed by Faith's side all afternoon. He laughed with her as Jenny cut the wedding cake and stuffed a big piece into Colt's laughing mouth. He shared a shy glance with her as Colt retrieved the garter from Jenny's leg, and he cheered with her as Colt's brother Rabb caught it. He stood by her side as Hope leaped high and grabbed Jenny's bridal bouquet.

He even took her with him when he helped decorate Colt's Mustang convertible. The guys ended up spraying as much shaving cream on each other as on the car, and made water balloons and threw them, too, before finally tying a bunch of old cowboy boots to the back bumper and declaring they were done.

Shadows were growing on the lawn before Randy finally acknowledged that putting off this reckoning wasn't going to make it any easier. He took Faith's right hand in his and said, "Will you come with me?"

"Where are we going?"

"Colt's room."

He saw the flash of fear in her dark eyes before she gripped his hand and said, "All right."

The house was built in a square, and it should've been easy to find Colt's room, since he'd been there once before, but he went down the wrong hallway, and they ended up going down three more hallways, full of wandering wedding guests, before he found the one he wanted.

He knocked on the door, in case anyone was in the room, then looked both ways to make sure no one was watching, and stepped inside. Once he and Faith were both inside, he closed the door and locked it. When he turned back around, Faith was sitting at the foot of the bed staring back at him. He crossed and sat down beside her…on her left side.

"I've never seen you wear gloves before," Randy said, unsure how to begin.

"I've had this special glove for quite some time. My doctor designed it especially for me. I just never had a reason to wear it." She held out her hands for him to see. "I look pretty normal," she conceded. "But it's more aesthetically pleasing than functional. In an emergency I can use the heel of my hand." She waggled her left hand to show the flexibility allowed by the bit of palm she had. "But I miss the versatility I get with a hook."

She was chattering, Randy realized, because she was frightened. And he was listening, because he was afraid to speak. They made a fine pair, he thought wryly.

"Take off the glove," he said. "Or would you rather I do it?"

"I'll do it," she said quickly.

He had situated himself on her left side purposely, to make sure there'd be no hiding anything—neither her hand, nor his reaction. He steeled himself for what he would see, tensing his muscles, gritting his teeth to hold back any sound of disgust or dismay that might come out.

She kept her eyes lowered. The glove was attached around her wrist with a Velcro strap, and there was a tearing sound as she pulled it free. She laid the glove on the bed beside her and dropped her left hand into her lap.

Randy kept his own eyes lowered as he examined what she'd revealed. The skin was pale, because it never saw the sun. There was a bit of a wrist and five tiny nubbins that had never grown into fingers. He reached over and slid his hand under hers, feeling her tremble as he did so.

"It's okay, Faith. Your hand just stopped growing. That's all."

She laid her head on his shoulder and closed her eyes. A tear dropped off her lash and onto his palm where he cradled her hand. He leaned over and licked up the tear. And kissed her hand.

He felt her right hand on his head, and then her kiss on his hair.

"I love you, Randy," she said.

He sat up, then lifted her left hand and drew it toward his cheek. "I love you, too, Faith."

He knew the courage it had taken for her to trust him. He willed her to believe in him and felt his heart thump hard in his chest when she lifted her left hand and caressed his cheek. He covered her hand with his own, then leaned over to kiss her lips.

A hard knock on the door broke them apart.

"Who is it?" Randy called, jumping to his feet.

"Who do you think?" Hope said. "Have you got my sister in there?"

"I'm here," Faith answered, crossing to open the door for her sister. "What's wrong?" she asked.

Randy watched as Hope looked down at her sister's uncovered hand, then up at his face. A smile curved her lips. "Why, nothing's wrong," she said with a grin. "Nothing at all."

At that moment Sam came walking past the door,

noticed Randy and Faith and said, "Jenny and Colt are getting ready to leave the reception. You might want to come and see them off."

"Just let me get my glove," Faith said, turning back to the bed. "And I'll be ready to go."

"I'll see you two out back," Hope said, heading for the courtyard.

Randy and Faith weren't far behind her.

Randy had stuck at least a dozen pieces of net filled with birdseed into his coat pockets, so he'd have plenty of birdseed to shower on Jenny and Colt.

"Untie those ribbons," Faith instructed. "And pour the birdseed into your hand, so it'll be ready to throw."

"Oh."

"Will you untie mine, too?"

"Sure," Randy said, realizing that she was essentially one-handed without her hook. "I'm gonna invent something, Faith."

"What?"

"A hand—like in the *Terminator* movies—that you can really use."

"Oh, Randy. I hope you do."

Randy heard cries of "Here they come! Get ready!"

He turned to find his sister, Colt's arm wrapped tightly around her waist, her eyes bright, her smile wide, making her way through the crowd.

The reception was half over before Jenny realized the significance of the wedding gift her brothers had given her. She searched frantically for Colt and found him drinking champagne and laughing with his brothers. She dragged him away to the arbor, chasing away

at least a dozen shrieking children to have even a mod-
icum of privacy.

"My brothers gave me a wedding gift," she said. "A
honeymoon trip to the Grand Canyon."

"I know all about it," he said, alternately tickling
his sister Cherry's five-year-old twin boys, Chip and
Charlie. "We leave tomorrow morning, 7:00 a.m. flight
out of Amarillo."

"The doctor's office doesn't open till eight."

"So what?" Colt said, hefting Rolleen's ten-year-
old son, Kenny, up over his shoulder and letting him
drop until he was dangling by his heels. Kenny howled
with glee.

"Don't you see? We won't have the test results before we leave," Jenny said.

"We're going to have a honeymoon whether you
have cancer or not," Colt replied. "The news will wait
till we get back." He leaned over and kissed her on the
nose, struggling to stay upright with Chip and Charlie
each entwined around one of his legs like vines around
an oak. "Anything else bothering you?" he asked.

She lifted a brow and said, "Well, if we're going
to get up so early in the morning, isn't about time we
took our leave?"

Colt's eyes went wide, and then he smiled. "Mrs.
Whitelaw, that's the best suggestion I've heard all day,"
he said, prying the twins off his legs.

"Thank you. I love getting compliments from my
husband."

Colt's gaze locked hers. "Husband. That has a
nice sound." He slipped his arm around her waist and
headed for the car. "Let's go, wife."

Jenny went with Colt to tell his parents they were leaving, and the word spread quickly.

"Hurry up if you want to get a last look at the bride and groom before they take off!"

"Does everybody have some birdseed?"

Jenny ducked and laughed as birdseed caught in her hair and her eyelashes and slid down the front of her dress.

Colt laughed and ducked right along with her. "Hurry up, wife, or we're going to turn into two bird feeders!"

Colt didn't even open the door to the convertible, just dropped her in over the top, then came running around and jumped in behind the wheel.

As they drove away, Jenny reached across the seat and took Colt's hand. He smiled at her, and she smiled back. This was the beginning of a new life. A new love. And happily ever after.

Epilogue

Benign. Jenny had never heard a sweeter word. She still had three more years before she'd feel satisfied that the cancer was truly gone. But she'd been given a respite, a time in which to live life to the fullest. And a husband who was determined to help her do it.

Jenny snuggled closer to Colt, spooning her body against his. She heard him make a sound of pleasure in his throat and whispered, "Are you awake?"

"I am now."

She pulled his arms tighter around her, and he cupped her breasts and held her close. It was always like this after they made love, holding each other, re-affirming their joy with each other.

"I visited my doctor today," Jenny said.

She felt Colt stiffen. "Oh?" he murmured cautiously.

"I wanted to ask her what she thought about me getting pregnant."

"I see," Colt said. "And what did she say?"

Jenny turned over in Colt's arms, so she could see his face. "She said it was up to me."

"There's no risk to you?" Colt asked.

"I didn't say that. But I think what we have to gain is worth what risk there is. I want us to have children, Colt. Is that too much to ask?"

"I already feel like I've dodged a bullet," Colt confessed. "I want kids, but not at the risk of losing you."

Jenny pressed her face against Colt's throat and felt his arms close around her. "If we have a boy, we can name him Huck."

She heard him chuckle. "Huckleberry Whitelaw. Now there's a name to give a kid nightmares."

Jenny smiled. "Growing up in a houseful of boys, I always wanted a little girl."

"We could name her Becky," Colt said.

Jenny laughed. "And the next boy Tom."

"Three kids," Colt said. "That's a houseful."

"Not like the eight your parents raised," she pointed out.

"Three's plenty for me," he said, lifting his head and finding her mouth with his.

They kissed slowly, letting the passion rise, feeling the hope and ignoring the fear. They would find a way to be happy, living each day and loving each night. For all the rest of their lives.

* * * * *

"I appreciate you coming," he said.

"You said it was important."

Paul nodded as he gestured for her to take a seat.
Sitting down, Simone stole another quick glance toward
the bar. The two strangers were both staring blatantly, not
bothering to hide their interest in the two of them.

Simone rested an elbow on the tabletop, turning
flirtatiously toward her friend. "Do you know Tom and
Jerry over there at the bar?" she asked softly. She reached
a hand out, trailing her fingers against his arm.

Her touch was just distracting enough that Paul didn't
turn abruptly to stare back, drawing even more attention
in their direction. His focus shifted slowly from her
toward the duo at the bar. He eyed them briefly before

turning his attention back to Simone. He shook his head. "Should I?"

"It might be nothing, but they seem very interested in you."

Paul's gaze danced back in their direction and he took a swift inhale of air. One of the men was on a cell phone and both were still eyeing him intently.

"We need to leave," he said, suddenly anxious. He began to gather his papers.

"What's going on, Paul?"

"I don't think we're safe, Simone."

"What do you mean we're not safe?" she snapped, her teeth clenched tightly. "Why are we not safe?"

"I'll explain, but I think we really need to leave."

Simone took a deep breath and held it, watching as he repacked his belongings into his briefcase.

"We're not going anywhere until you explain," she started, and then a commotion at the door pulled at her attention.

Don't miss
Reunited by the Badge *by Deborah Fletcher Mello*
available October 2019 wherever
Harlequin® Romantic Suspense
books and ebooks are sold.

www.Harlequin.com

Need an adrenaline rush from nail-biting tales
(and irresistible males)?

Check out **Harlequin Intrigue®**,
Harlequin® Romantic Suspense and
Love Inspired® Suspense books!

New books available every month!

***

CONNECT WITH US AT:

Facebook.com/groups/HarlequinConnection

 Facebook.com/HarlequinBooks

 Twitter.com/HarlequinBooks

 Instagram.com/HarlequinBooks

 Pinterest.com/HarlequinBooks

ReaderService.com

**ROMANCE WHEN
YOU NEED IT**

SGENRE2018R

CHAPTER ONE

She struggled to surface from the black hole trying to suck
her back down. Her head hurt and she could barely open her
eyes. Every part of her body ached so badly she began to
think death would be a relief. But her heart, buried behind
bruised and broken ribs, beat strong, pushing blood through
her veins. And with the blood, the desire to live.

Willing her eyes to open, she blinked and gazed through
narrow slits at the dirty mud-and-stick wall in front of her.
Why couldn't she open her eyes more? She raised her hand
to her face and felt the puffy, blood-crusted skin around
her eyes and mouth. When she tried to move her lips, they
cracked and warm liquid oozed out on her chin.

Her fingernails were split, some ripped down to the quick,
and the backs of her knuckles looked like pounded hamburger

meat. Bruises, scratches and cuts covered her arms.

She felt along her torso, wincing when she touched a bruised rib. As she shifted her search lower, her hands shook and she held her breath, feeling for bruises, wondering if she'd been assaulted in other ways. When she felt no tenderness between her legs, she let go of the breath she'd held in a rush of relief.

She pushed into a sitting position and winced at the pain knifing through her head. Running her hand over her scalp, she felt a couple of goose egg–sized lumps. One behind her left ear, the other at the base of her skull.

A glance around the small cell-like room gave her little information about where she was. The floor was hard-packed dirt and smelled of urine and feces. She wore a torn shirt and the dark pants women wore beneath their burkas.

Voices outside the rough wooden door made her tense and her body cringe.

She wasn't sure why she was there, but those voices inspired an automatic response of drawing deep within, preparing for additional beatings and torture.

What she had done to deserve it, she couldn't remember. Everything about her life was a gaping, useless void.

The door jerked open. A man wearing the camouflage uniform of a Syrian fighter and a black hood covering his head and face stood in the doorway with a Russian AK-47 slung over his shoulder and a steel pipe in his hand.

Don't miss
Driving Force *by Elle James,*
available October 2019 wherever
Harlequin® books and ebooks are sold.

www.Harlequin.com